Heaven Sent

An anthology of angel stories
edited by Peter Crowther

A SIGNET BOOK

SIGNET

Published by the Penguin Group
Penguin Books Ltd, 27 Wrights Lane, London w8 5tz, England
Penguin Books USA Inc., 375 Hudson Street, New York, New York 10014, USA
Penguin Books Australia Ltd, Ringwood, Victoria, Australia
Penguin Books Canada Ltd, 10 Alcorn Avenue, Toronto, Ontario,
Canada m4v 3b2
Penguin Books (NZ) Ltd, 182–190 Wairau Road, Auckland 10, New Zealand

Penguin Books Ltd, Registered Offices: Harmondsworth, Middlesex, England

First published 1995
1 3 5 7 9 10 8 6 4 2

Published by arrangement with DAW Books, Inc.

Printed in England by Clays Ltd, St Ives plc
Set in 10½/12½ pt Bembo Monophoto

Contents

Foreword

PETER CROWTHER

I think the idea for this book has been sitting around inside my head for years, just waiting for something to come along and blow the dust off it.

That catalyst could so easily have been the wings-seeking Clarence in *It's a Wonderful Life*, or Cary Grant ice-skating in *The Bishop's Wife*, or the eternally dapper David Niven wandering up that impossibly long staircase in *A Matter of Life and Death*. It could have been, but it wasn't.

It could have been any one of the stories that regularly featured in the old ACG comic books of the 1950s and 1960s, notably *Forbidden Worlds* and *Adventures Into the Unknown*, in which wives and husbands died or got killed and then came back when their loved ones were in some kind of difficulty. In these stories, I remember, ACG would always show Heaven as an idyllic Elysian Fields-style environment, where the dead just kind of lounge around, reading books or playing ball with the 'staff', occasionally looking down through the mists to see what's happening back on Earth. But it wasn't that either.

It could have been Patrick McGrath's chilling tale of divine imprisonment, 'The Angel', or Edgar Pangborn's 'Angel's Egg', or Henry Kuttner's 'The Misguided Halo', or even any of Thorne Smith's *Topper* books . . . I'm sure there are many more I can't remember. But it wasn't even any of those.

No, the genesis of this book was a *Quantum Leap* episode in which Sam 'leaps' into the body of a yellow-cab driver and promptly drives his car over an old woman. The woman simply stands up and dusts herself down. She's an angel.

So, that's how it started: but why actually *produce* a book of angel stories? The answer is simple. By their very nature, they centre on the two things that move the entire world: hope and retribution, goals to strive for and prices to pay.

But are the characters that drift through the following pages really angels, or are they simply ghosts? And what's the difference anyway?

Of the eighteen storytellers in this collection, only two have taken the classical view of angels as messengers (*angelos* being Greek for 'messenger'). As Peter Lamborn Wilson points out in his excellent *The Little Book of Angels* (Element, 1993), there is no such thing as an abstract idea in the traditional science of angelology. All ideas are spiritual forces, and all spiritual forces are persons. Thus even a book may be an angel, a living personification of the Heavenly Word.

After all, there are angelic alphabets: the English magus and alchemist John Dee received angelic transmissions in the Enochian alphabet, and Jewish magicians used angelic letters in their amulets and kabbalistic meditations. Eleggua (or Legba), the *orisha* from the African religion of the Yoruba who presides over all borders, thresholds and beginnings, is regarded as language itself, ambiguous, two-faced, treacherous and occult.

There are many more – and you'll read about them in Storm Constantine's introduction – but surely Dante's double-act of Virgil and Beatrice is the most apposite (and, with the possible exception of Gabriel, the best-known), the one being the writer Dante most admires, the other being the woman he loves.

Words and feelings. That's what it all comes down to in the end. It's nice to think that, although they have to die, people stick around somewhere near, providing strength and encouragement and maybe even throwing up a helpful mitted hand to catch a couple of the spit-balls that curl out of left field every now and then and bean you when you least expect it.

I must say, I'd like to think of my father relaxing at a table in some eternally sun-drenched pub – inevitably named 'The Heavenly Arms' – where a ruddy-cheeked, Falstaffian landlord pours him generous measures of brandy-and-orange while he keeps one watchful eye on the racing form and the other on protecting my back.

And so this book is for my dad, simply because I figure he's closer to the truth than anyone else I care about. It's also for all those people who believe in something – though they don't exactly know what it is – and for those who still possess just a little of that sense of wonder we all had once upon a time.

Introduction

STORM CONSTANTINE

Was it coincidence that the day the manuscript for *Heaven Sent* arrived on my doorstep was also the day I met writer Andrew Collins for the first time? Well, it could have been but for the subject matter of the manuscript and the current project of Mr Collins – namely, angels. Both Andrew and Pete Crowther had contacted me because they knew of my interest in these winged beings (of the leathery and feathery variety) and that I had written about them extensively in my own work. I have always been fascinated by angels – not the fluffy, twee denizens of cheap Christmas cards but the darker, shadowy presences of occult literature and religious mythology – which, I suspect, prompted Pete to ask me to write an introduction to this collection.

'Angel' is a broad term that covers an enticing selection of entities. In one of its most benign aspects, the angel is cast as an invisible guardian, a spirit guide, watching over its appointed charge in life and guiding the departing spirit into the unknown realm beyond death. Other legends speak of more aggressive protectors, monstrous creatures invoked in magical rites (for good or ill), wielding various forms of occult weaponry: whirling, fiery swords, winds, vipers, thunderbolts, etc. Elsewhere we find the holy avengers, culling damned souls, such as the seven Angels of Punishment, who include among their ranks such humourless entities as Kushiel, the 'Rigid One of God', and Makatiel, the

'Plague of God'. There is a brand of occultism devoted solely to the invocation of angelic forms – Enochian Magic – which utilizes the language of angels, said to have been transcribed by the Elizabethan occultist John Dee. Angels are the intermediaries between the divine and the not-divine, messengers of the Deity, dog's bodies of the heavenly spheres. They can bring Glad Tidings of Great Joy or point the Finger of Doom.

Andrew Collins is currently researching a book about the Nephilim, a breed of angel in which I've always had a deep interest and about which I intend to write a novel in the near future. The stories surrounding these sinister beings are ripe for plundering by writers, and, synchronicity being what it is, there are no doubt at least a dozen authors working on synopses similar to my own at this very moment. According to lesser-known contemporaries of Old Testament books, the Nephilim were disreputable hybrids, spawned when a band of angels, known as the Watchers, went rogue, disobeyed heavenly law and took human women as lovers. The progeny of their union were monstrous babies, who had to be delivered by what amounts to Caesarean section and who grew up to be cannibalistic giants. Andrew has an encyclopaedia for a brain (no, possibly an advanced supercomputer), and the number of stories, fables and historical facts and fictions he can recall at lightning speed is phenomenal. I spent a day in his company attempting to absorb the torrent of information he had to impart, in the hope it would serve as a backbone for my proposed novel (in the event, I think I gleaned enough for at least a trilogy). The fallen Watchers were dark and terrible, possessed of superior knowledge that they bestowed upon humanity against the ruling of their god, an act for which they suffered the most ghastly punishments, described in gleeful detail in the ancient Books of Enoch. It is doubtful that these spirits would ever find employment posing for Christmas cards. Such was the intensity, the pervading atmosphere of dark power, surrounding these stories, that I was extremely nervous about turning the light off when I went to bed that night. For an agonizing moment I thought I saw an unnaturally tall, shadowy form with glowing red eyes in the corner of my room, then realized, after a heart-stopping moment, that I was looking at the reflection of my clock-radio in the mirror. This would never do! Nightmares eagerly awaited me once consciousness was surrendered. On went the light, out came the manuscript to *Heaven Sent*. I hoped to find more benign spirits within its pages, and the first two stories I read that night mercifully calmed my nerves and, once I felt able to face the dark again, accompanied me into a demon-free slumber. (Fortunately, I had decided to read them in order, and I'm talking particularly to *you*, Ms Ptacek!)

I first began researching angelology in the (very) early stages of devising my Wraeththu trilogy around 1977. Luckily, I came across a very wonderful out-of-print book in the library where I worked: Gustav Davidson's *Dictionary of Angels*. Recently the book has been reprinted, and I recommend it to anyone interested in angelology. Davidson's book is a must for every lover of trivia, stuffed as it is with a multitude of angelic lists, forgotten myths and infernal hierarchies gleaned from a variety of religious traditions, including Judaism, Cabbala, Christianity, Islam and Zoroastrianism. I had never realized angels were so legion, literally, or so *specialized*. Not only are there several angels for each season, planet and weather condition, there are hundreds of others responsible for precise duties, such as Ram-Khvastra, the Angel of Rarefied Air; the Angels of Quaking (unnamed!); Zahun, the Angel of Scandal; Tubiel, the Angel Over Small Birds; and Rahab, the Angel of Insolence. Naturally, there are angelic officers for the relatively commonplace, exemplified by the Angels of War, Lust, Love, Death, Salvation, etc. For pregnant women, who have the time and the breath, there are seventy amulet angels which can be invoked at the time of childbirth (reciting them may be one way to take your mind off the discomfort, I suppose). Many of the listed spirits seem to have been troublesome creatures, forever at odds with their presiding deity and plotting to overthrow heavenly rule. The angels of ancient legend are rarely sugary creatures, adorned with only two big, feathery wings and garbed in white frocks. Originally, for example, the cherubim were monstrous creatures, not adorable little babies with chubby faces and diminutive wings. One definition cites them as being a blue or golden-yellow colour, having the form of a winged man but with a fourfold head: that of an eagle, lion, man and ox. They also stand on wheels and carry flaming swords. (See Garry Kilworth's story in this collection for a *Dictionnaire Infernal* rendition of a cherub.) Kerubiel, the leader of the cherubim, is described as being 'full of burning coals'. The seraphim (another traditionally cute throng) are described as fiery serpents, having four faces and six wings, who roar like lions. Perhaps unfortunately, they are also fond of singing.

If you happen to be at the mercy of the demon of disease, Sphendonael, call for the assistance of the angel Sabrael — he's the only one who can help. Should you attempt to invoke Hauras (once a celestial power, now fallen on bad times), make sure you don't do it in Hell, because he's a leopard there and will adopt a man-like shape only when conjured up by an exorcist on Earth. Feeling uncontrollable jealousy? The angel Balthial will help you thwart the machinations of the evil genius responsible. Let's hope the angel Sebhael never sells his story to the tabloids; he's in charge of the books in which the good and evil actions of man (*sic*) are recorded. Should a love affair be going badly, a man can invoke the services of Miniel, who is able to 'induce love in an otherwise cold and reluctant maid; but for the best results, the invocant must be sure he is facing south'. Take heed. Oh, should you need a magic carpet, Miniel can oblige in that department too. There is a patron angel for writers as well, although I've been unable to remember his name or look him up, which means, I think, he can't appreciate the way I'm describing his peers and must be deliberately preventing me from misrepresenting him. Perhaps I should be careful: that's one guardian spirit I certainly don't want to lose as a friend!

But all the above are angels from the past. In this book you will be reading about angels of the present, the newly fledged denizens of the winged imaginations of their creators. The stories in this collection reflect what the term 'angel' means to each contributor. Several stories are concerned with the 'Guide into the Afterlife' aspect, such as Charles de Lint's 'The Big Sky', with its dextrously evoked shadow city where the lost dead walk, shrinking from the Light; Christopher Evans's 'House Call' (with its distinctly sinister undertone); and, with its venomous humour, Jane M. Lindskold's short but acid-drop sweet 'Relief'. Other stories tell of guardian angels, departed spirits, who return with messages for the living, such as Ken Wisman's 'Letting Go', which shows that the dead can continue to learn from life; Kathy Ptacek's 'The Visit', in which the ethereal vision of an angel reveals itself, at close quarters, to be something unpleasantly different from what it seems from a distance; Nina Kiriki Hoffman's 'Part-singing', in which a living girl finds inspiration and courage from the dead; and Stephen Laws's touching 'Gordy's A-OK' (which, even upon a second reading, made me feel a bit lumpy-throated and misty-eyed). Other writers have totally reinvented the angel, such as Ian McDonald in his story 'Steam', set on his personal wild and colourful terra-formed Mars (featured in his novel *Desolation Road*), Judith Moffett in 'The Realms of Glory', with its mysterious dénouement (I'm still puzzling, Judith: was it the real thing at the end or wasn't it?), and Ed Gorman in 'Synandra', in which the Angel of Death takes on new flesh as she traverses time and space in her journey of destruction. If you want a real whiff of the inferno, put nose to page in John Brunner's exquisitely gruesome tale 'Real Messengers'. In 'Spirit Guides' Kristine K. Rusch's protagonist has a special relationship with the angels of destruction, but his enlightenment involves learning the exact nature of that relationship. In 'Wings', a post-modernist fable, James Lovegrove takes us into an angel city where the heavenly hosts inhabit what seems to be a para-American town, and a young boy-angel learns how to cope with a crippling *difference* that has made him an outsider. Garry Kilworth, in 'Cherub', tells a cautionary tale of what can happen if you should invoke an angel in self-defence, and in Bruce D. Arthurs's 'Angel Blood', the phrase 'fallen angel' takes on a distinctly alternative meaning. Gary A. Braunbeck's 'After the Elephant Ballet' is a surreal emotional journey (another misty lumpiness when I read this – thanks, Gary!), and the final story in the collection, the masterly 'In Gethsemane' by Stephen Gallagher, invokes the angel of conscience.

There is one other story, Michael Bishop's 'Spiritual Dysfunction', that I've left mentioning until last because the angels that manifest themselves within it are probably the closest relations to those who rustle through the pages of Davidson's *Dictionary*. (The Angelspeak they use is certainly more tolerable than Enochian; I like to think angels have a sense of humour and a sharp turn of phrase!) The author draws upon one of my own favourite sections of Milton's *Paradise Lost*, concerning whether or not angels have sex and, if they do, how. The characters are 'real' angels in that Hashmal was traditionally the chief of the order of Hashmallim, the 'fire-speaking angel', who 'surrounds the throne of God', Raphael is one of the archangels and Sariela is (presumably) taken from Sariel, one of the fallen angels described in the books of Enoch who was responsible for teaching humanity the forbidden knowledge of the 'courses of the moon'. As this could be interpreted as including a woman's monthly cycle, it's pertinent that Michael chose Sariel to be a female angel, for more than one reason. Angels, on the whole, are represented as male, although they are supposed to be sexless. There are very few instances of female angels in the old legends, which undoubtedly reflects the patriarchal views of the period when the stories were first created. Refreshingly, there are at least seven female angels in these stories, which shows that the modern form is helping to redress the balance.

I have always found Pete Crowther to be a sympathetic and creative editor, with a sensitivity for the feel of a story and respect for the author's aspirations. The achievements of the individual writers aside, I'm sure he's been just as responsible for producing such a highly readable, thought-provoking and well-crafted collection. Don't just take my word for it. Read on. Mysteries await you, and journeys, and quite a few scares. But if by any chance one of the creepier offerings is the last one you read before turning off the light, just remember these stories are *Heaven Sent*.

And it's probably just your clock-radio you can see glowing in the corner.

Letting Go

KEN WISMAN

Alex Layton floated in the far corner of the tiny New England church where he had come each Sunday for most of his adult life.

His wife Lois, his daughter Jen, his son Billy and his son Eric sat in the first pew, just below the podium by the altar. Billy and Jen looked grim. Lois kept dabbing at her eyes with a white handkerchief. But little Eric just stared up at his father floating in the far corner where the sun threw shadows, his father who sparkled like streaks of sunlight on the bottom of a pond.

Hello, Eric, Alex Layton said.

'Hello, daddy,' Eric whispered.

A crowd of people sat behind the family. Relatives Alex Layton hadn't seen for years. And old friends.

To the left of the altar, at the podium, the minister stood and spoke in solemn tones: 'How do you measure a man? By how tall he stood? By how strong he was? By how much money he earned? Or do you measure a man by how much he loved?'

Alex had loved the old minister. Alex was glad he was delivering the eulogy. It would be straight from the heart. Not like what was usually said at such affairs:

'So sorry he passed on . . .'

'It's so terrible knowing he's gone . . .'

The pastor continued, his voice quavering with emotion: 'If love is the measure, then Alex Layton stood tall, the richest of men and the strongest.'

Sweet man, Alex thought. The minister could very easily have been delivering the eulogy for himself.

Alex floated down and hovered just above the coffin. Without emotion he looked through the closed case. *Passed on? Gone?* To everyone there – save one.

Little Eric smiled at Alex.

Alex smiled back.

'Don't leave, daddy,' Eric whispered.

Not on your life.

A few short days before, Alex Layton had felt the tightness in his chest like a huge mailed fist closing around his heart. A moment of pain and fear and he was floating free, watching his wife and two sons and daughter being consoled by the doctor.

And then he was floating away and outside the hospital. It was like dropping down a long, dark tunnel. A light waited on the other side.

The light showed him things. It showed him his life like one long thread from end to end. And though there was no judgement in the light it dwelled on moments of love and happiness and times shared.

Then the light showed him another light like an ocean. And Alex was asked to join the light that seemed to sing to him with a music that wasn't like any earthly music but that sang through everything. And Alex felt an overwhelming urge to go into the light and beyond it to see what was there and the meaning of death.

But Alex was sad and there was something that held him. And when he looked back he saw a thin connecting thread that stretched all the way back through the tunnel to the earth that was like a speck in the universe . . .

Three days after the funeral, Alex Layton hovered above

the headpost on Eric's bed. Lois and Jen and Billy sat on the edge. Eric, being the youngest, was in his pajamas and ready for sleep.

Lois spoke to the children in soft tones: 'It's been a few days now, kids. And I know it's hard, but we've got to put some of it behind us and get on with our own lives. I'll be going back to my job tomorrow. I want you all to return to school.'

Billy put on a brave face. 'Okay, mom.' It wasn't hard to see that he, the oldest, felt he was the man of the house now. How old was he? Eleven.

Jen, nine and the most emotional of the three kids, felt no restrictions about holding back her feelings. 'I miss dad,' she said, her voice cracking.

Lois put her arm around her, and Jen sobbed. Then Billy leaned his head on to his mother's shoulder and buried his face. He cried silently, ashamed of his tears.

Eric crawled out from under the covers and hugged his family affectionately. But he shed no tears.

Later, when Jen and Billy were asleep, Lois returned to the room and, seeing Eric awake, sat on the side of his bed.

'Sweetheart,' she whispered, 'it's okay to cry.'

Eric stared at her with his huge, brown eyes. But he said nothing.

'What I mean is it's all right to mourn for your father,' she said.

And Alex knew that Eric was on the verge of telling Lois the truth. *Don't tell her, son. It would only upset her more*, Alex said.

Later, when Lois went away, little Eric spoke to where his father glowed in a corner of the ceiling. 'Daddy, are you like the angels mom used to tell me about? Are you my guardian angel?'

You bet.

'G'night, daddy.'

'Night, son.

But Alex no longer needed sleep. Instead he played the whole scene back and thought about his family.

His wife Lois. Sensitive. But on the inside quite strong and drawing on that innate strength now to pull her family together.

His daughter Jen. She most likely taking the longest time to forget the pain. But in the end as strong as, if not stronger than, her mother.

His son Billy. He would weather it best perhaps.

The truth was that, once the pain was forgotten, each would find his or her niche in life. For Jen he had had great expectations. A doctor perhaps with her compassion. Billy, a leader. Lois – with necessity motivating her – rising to a high position at her job.

And Eric? Little Eric. There was the rub.

. . . and poised between life and death Alex Layton had hesitated. Then Alex asked the light to repeat certain scenes from his life, and the light complied.

And suddenly Alex was there in the delivery room with his wife looking down at the tiny, frail infant. Alex knew without the doctor telling him that something was wrong. And Alex wasn't at all surprised later when the doctor told him about the complications and the heart murmur and how the boy would need extra care until he was old enough to be operated on and the problems could be corrected . . .

Alex followed Eric to school. When Eric got to the schoolyard, most of the other kids ignored him. Alex, who could see much clearer into people now, saw that it wasn't unkindness that kept the other kids away. No, they were a little afraid of Eric. He was the kid with the father who died and death was a mystery they were all just learning about.

Eric didn't seem to mind the isolation. He smiled and whispered: 'Are you still there, daddy?' And Alex, who was invisible to his son in daylight, said back: *Still here*.

Then the bell rang and Alex followed his son inside.

Eric's teacher, Mr Hodkins, was a tall, thin man with a sour face. And the very first thing he announced was a spelling bee.

'We'll use the words we've been studying the past two weeks,' the teacher said. 'Let's split up into two groups.'

It was, of course, unfair, since Eric had missed a week. And especially unfair since Eric was quite good at spelling, and this bee counted as a test.

But the spelling bee progressed well for Eric. He went through the first five rounds with ease, whereas everyone else was eliminated save one boy in his group and a boy and a girl in the other.

'Mountain,' Mr Hodkins said, pronouncing the word distinctly. He gave it to Rachel Childress, who was on the other side. Rachel missed the word and Mr Hodkins gave it to Jimmy O'Neill, who was on Eric's side. Jimmy missed and the word bounced over to Judy Nelson.

She any good? Alex asked.

'No one's ever beaten her,' Eric whispered.

'Mountain,' Judy said. 'M-O-U-N-T-A-I-N.' She smiled with supreme confidence at Eric. Obviously Judy Nelson wasn't above flaunting her superiority and taking advantage of being Mr Hodkins's favorite.

'Excellent,' Mr Hodkins said.

Alex could see that Eric was nervous. In the last two rounds they had entered unknown territory and Eric had stayed alive by blind luck.

Then Alex saw something he didn't like. He could see down into the soul of people and knew things about them and what they were thinking.

Mr Hodkins was eager to get the bee over with. It was a foregone conclusion that Judy Nelson would win it, and they were already fifteen minutes into the history lesson. Mr Hodkins did not look at the list when he chose the next word.

'Eric, spell – uh – chrysanthemum,' Mr Hodkins said offhandedly.

There was a slight murmur in the class. Those who had studied knew it wasn't a word on their homework list.

Your teacher isn't playing fair, son, Alex said. He was surprised that he could still feel so much anger. *Let's even up the sides.*

'I don't understand, daddy,' Eric whispered.

'What was that?' Mr Hodkins said, smiling and glancing at the clock.

Repeat after me, said Eric's father.

'C-H-R-Y-S-A-N-T-H-E-M-U-M,' Eric repeated.

The class gasped. A few clapped.

Mr Hodkins looked puzzled. He recovered and gave Judy Nelson an easy word which she spelled but not with her usual bravado.

Mr Hodkins thought a moment. 'Pterodactyl,' he said.

The class groaned. An impossible word. A word beyond the ability of a mortal man to spell.

And yet Eric called out unfalteringly: 'P-T-E-R-O-D-A-C-T-Y-L.'

The whole class clapped and cheered. They were totally behind Eric now.

'Uh–bounty.' Mr Hodkins addressed Judy Nelson.

The class laughed. A few booed and jeered.

Judy's face burned with shame. 'I don't know that one, Mr Hodkins,' she said.

'Try,' Mr Hodkins said with unnecessary sternness.

Judy broke into tears. 'I don't know it,' she said. She sat in her seat and buried her head in her arms.

The class held its breath.

'B-O-U-N-T-Y,' Eric called out.

And half the class rose to crowd around him and pat him on the back.

. . . and after Alex had asked the light to play back the scene of Eric's birth, Alex asked to see the nights that followed. The nights Alex lay in his bed listening for the monitor alarm, hating the sound of it yet listening with all his being because it was the only way to know that Eric's breathing had stopped. And Alex watched those nights when he ran with all his might into the room to snatch his son up to breathe life back into his chest.

And something passed between Alex and his son then. Something like love but deeper than love . . .

Alex followed his son home after school. Eric had no friends. He was shy and felt his difference – the years on the monitor, the illnesses, living on the edge of death, all had made him an introverted child. And every attempt on Alex's part to break him out of that mold had failed.

Alex was enjoying the spring afternoon through his son, who walked at a slow pace. Eric laughed a lot and talked in subdued tones to his father. Many people passed, but Eric was young enough that talking to himself wasn't such an oddity, and the people only smiled.

Then Eric came to the middle of a block where large oaks with low branches grew. He threw his books down, turned and waited.

What's up? Alex asked.

'You'll see,' said Eric.

Soon a small figure came around the corner. And Eric ran to a branch on the oak and hung upside-down. The figure came to the spot, stopped and looked at Eric.

Pretty, Alex said. He chuckled to himself. Kids grew so quickly. He himself didn't show interest in a girl till he was twice Eric's age.

'Hi,' Eric called to the girl.

'Hrrmp,' the girl said, turning away.

Doesn't seem to be impressed, Alex said to Eric. *Not surprised. Hanging from a tree isn't exactly an original idea.*

The girl yawned and appeared on the point of making a quick departure.

Let's show her something really good, Alex said. *You game?*

Eric giggled and nodded. And suddenly he was doing slow loops around the branch. The loops increased in speed and suddenly Eric was hurtling up to the bough above.

Eric whirled around the bough, changed direction and whirled around again.

Get ready, now, Alex said. *Here comes the grand finale.*

Eric laughed and closed his eyes and hurtled into space, turned three impossible somersaults and stood on the branch of an oak twenty feet away. Eric tightroped the thin branch, reached the end, jumped up, somersaulted and landed on his feet on the ground – right next to the girl.

Ask her if you can carry her books, Alex said.

'Can I carry your books?' Eric asked shyly.

The girl, her mouth agape and eyes glassy, handed over her books without a word.

. . . and Alex had asked the light for one more set of scenes. Of the time when Eric was old enough for his operation.

And Alex was watching there in the hospital with his son in an oxygen tent, still unconscious, but wanting to be there when his son woke up.

'Don't leave me, daddy.'

'Not on your life.'

And how Alex got special permission to stay in the hospital to be near to his son. And how Alex took a leave of absence from work to be home with Eric until he recovered.

'I'm afraid, daddy.'

'I'm here, son. I won't leave.'

And it was to show the light that Alex called for these memories and to ask the favor . . .

On a particularly bright and sunny morning Alex followed his son out of the house and into the garage where Eric mounted his bike. And Alex followed his son like a kite attached, as the boy cut through the breeze of the fine morning that smelled like clean sheets and fresh milk and grass grown richly green.

Feet up, Alex said to his son.

Eric giggled and raised his feet and his father pushed the bike along at a fast clip so that the wind cut cool and exhilarating around his face. Then Eric came to the park where a group of boys were gathered, some from his class, some from a grade or two higher.

'We can't play,' one of the boys was saying. 'You need eighteen and we still only have seventeen.'

This elicited a series of suggestions that were each voted down. Then one of the boys noticed Eric watching from a distance. 'How 'bout that kid?'

'Naw,' said a boy named Bingo Honneger. He stood a head taller than everyone else and was one of the team's captains. 'He stinks. Besides he's too short.'

But Eric seemed the only solution at hand, and some of the other boys disagreed.

'He never plays anyhow.' Bingo Honneger looked contemptuously at Eric.

Eric was about ready to remount his bike, but Alex said, *Tell them you'll play.*

'I'll play,' said Eric.

'Not on our side you won't,' Bingo Honneger said.

The other captain conferred with his players. 'Look. We put the shrimp out in right where he can't do much harm. And we let him bat last.'

There was reluctance. 'You got a better idea?' the captain said. And the game began.

Eric's team took the field first. Eric borrowed a mitt from someone on the other side and ran out to right field.

Alex hovered above his son. *How'd that big kid get that nickname?* Alex asked.

'Fighting,' Eric whispered. 'He always tries to pop the other guy in the nose. When he does, the kids standing around yell, "Bingo!"'

I knew kids like that when I was a boy, Alex said. *I always wished there was someone around to take them down a peg or two.*

The first batter got up and hit a grounder right at the first baseman and was out. The second kid struck out and, after a lengthy altercation, sat down. Then the third batter hit a grounder between the shortstop and the third baseman, who collided. And before things could be sorted out, the kid was on second base.

Fourth up, batting cleanup, was Bingo Honneger.

If anything's hit your way put your glove out, Alex said. Then he floated in and above Bingo Honneger and home plate. The boy was eyeing Eric out in right and taking his practice swings pointed in that direction. He knew where to hit it.

Bingo connected with the first pitch. The ball arched up, but for Alex it was all in slow motion. He grabbed the ball and steered it, and from his bird's-eye view he watched his son below.

Eric ran, his head up, his glove out. He ran, his legs striving and straining. He closed his eyes, knowing he'd miss but trying with all his might none the less. Then he heard the *thwack* in his glove and, looking down, he saw the ball resting like an egg in its nest.

'You little turd,' Bingo Honneger said to Eric as he ran in. 'Real lucky catch.' And he tripped Eric by sticking out his leg.

Eric picked himself up and dusted himself off. A couple of the other kids on the other side laughed as they took the field.

Don't worry, son, Alex said. *We'll nail this guy*.

But the first inning didn't produce much for Eric's side. Just two quick singles and three quick outs.

The game proceeded apace. The fielding got a little shakier, the arguments louder. Eric, who was at the bottom of the order, got up two times but had no opportunity to hit the ball. Bingo Honneger, who pitched for the other side, claimed sudden lapses in control and threw the softball at Eric. Bingo hit Eric once in the shoulder and once in the leg.

Then it was the bottom of the ninth. Bingo Honneger's side was winning 9 to 6. The middle of the order was up for Eric's side. But the first batter grounded to the first baseman and the second batter struck out.

Then the third kid hit a clean shot over the shortstop's head. The fourth batter was hit by the ball. The fifth was on on an error. And Eric was up.

If ever there was a set-up for a grand-slam homerun, this was it.

Bingo Honneger was too crafty to hit Eric a third time and force a run in and pitch to the lead off man. No, he would pitch to the kid and go home the hero.

Bingo lobbed one in and Eric swung. It was a weak swing, but it connected. And the softball flew across the ground as slowly as a butterfly flies on an August afternoon.

Bingo Honneger felt like a hawk feels when it sees a mouse in the grass and yards away from its hole. He flew from the mound and pounced on the ball. But the ball seemed to take a bad bounce and arched over his head.

Bingo had good reflexes, and he turned and lunged at the ball where it had come to rest ten feet behind him. He covered the ball with his mitt, scooped it up and reached in with his right hand to throw to first – except the ball wasn't there.

'Behind you,' the shortstop called.

Bingo looked around, spotted the ball, dove for it and threw it to first. The ball sailed six feet over the first baseman's head. The first baseman rushed to retrieve it. Meanwhile, Eric ran around first and was on his way to second and one run was home.

The first baseman threw the ball to second base. But

Bingo Honneger was on the run to back up the second baseman, and Bingo somehow lost his footing and collided with the second baseman. The ball sailed past third base. Meanwhile, Eric ran around second and was on his way to third and two runs were home.

By the time the third baseman got to the ball, three runs were home, and Eric was rounding third. The third baseman threw toward home and hit the cut-off man, Bingo Honneger. Bingo caught the ball easily enough but it dropped out of his mitt. Bingo dove for the ball, but wherever he put his hand, the ball just wasn't – it seemed to have a mind of its own.

Finally, the captain of Eric's team went out to Bingo Honneger on the field. He bent, picked up the ball and looked at Bingo Honneger as though he were crazy.

'Game's over,' the captain said, and he dropped the softball into Bingo's mitt.

. . . and when the last scene had been shown, Alex explained to the light why he couldn't leave the earth yet. There were things still left undone. Troubles he had not helped Eric to weather and work through, things he had never told his son.

And the light had let Alex follow the thread back . . .

After the game Alex followed Eric to his bike, and they pedaled through the neighborhood. Around supper time, Alex had his son head for home.

Eric was walking his bike by the lot with the oak trees, when Bingo Honneger pushed his way out of the bushes.

'Been waitin' to talk to you, turd,' Bingo said. He knocked over Eric's bike.

Eric, a head and a half shorter, stood his ground.

'I don't know how you done it,' Bingo said. 'But what you done was real stupid.'

He pushed Eric down.

'I'm gonna smash your face in if you even dare to stand,' Bingo said.

I want you to stand slowly, Alex told his son. *And I want you to repeat everything I say. Let me do the rest.*

Eric stood, and Bingo Honneger lunged at him. But Eric sidestepped, stuck out his leg and the bigger boy went sprawling. Bingo rose in a rage, his arms swinging. Eric's arms blocked each punch deftly, now left, now right.

Then Eric slipped his right hand under Bingo's belt – and lifted Bingo two feet off the ground.

'Bullies come in all sizes, in all ages,' Eric said. 'Every once in a while they pick on the wrong person. I'm the wrong person. Don't do it again.'

Bingo was terrified. His legs and arms paddled like a turtle's. Eric let him drop to the ground. Bingo stood and ran and never looked back.

. . . and the light had followed Alex to the earth. Alex could sense the light waiting just at the entrance to the tunnel. He could sense it watching, observing, but never interfering with what Alex did . . .

On Monday, Alex followed his son back to the schoolyard. Bingo Honneger was there with some of his cronies. Bingo talked loudly within earshot of Eric. But when Eric came close to the group, Bingo broke from the circle and ran a little way off.

The other kids laughed. Some gathered near Eric, who was encouraged by their laughter. He walked toward Bingo. Bingo backed away. Eric ran ten steps. Bingo ran twenty.

That's enough, son, Alex said.

'He deserves it,' Eric whispered. 'He deserves it good.'

Eric stomped his feet and Bingo Honneger turned and ran down the road to the jeers and taunts of everyone on the playground.

The bell rang. Once the class was inside, Mr Hodkins took them through the reading assignment. Then he announced a surprise quiz in arithmetic.

Eric wrote his name on the top of the paper passed to him and paused.

What's wrong? Alex asked.

'I didn't do my assignment,' Eric whispered.

Why not? Alex asked.

'Help me, daddy,' Eric said.

I can't, Alex said.

'You did before,' Eric said.

That was different, Alex said.

'If you don't, I'll flunk.'

Alex sighed and helped and swore it would be the last time.

Later, at lunch, the boys in the class chose sides for three-inning softball. Eric's reputation had preceded him, and he was one of the first ones picked. He was put at shortstop, a position of status.

Eric's side was up first, and he was third man in the line-up. The first batter was on on an error. The second batter hit a clean double up the middle. When it came to Eric's turn, he just stood at the plate and let the first ball whiff by without a swing.

'Help me,' Eric said under his breath.

You can hit it without my help, Alex said. *Eye on the ball. Level swing.*

Eric took a swing and missed. Strike two.

All right, but this is the last, Alex said.

And the next ball Eric hit cleanly through the second baseman's legs and reached safety at first.

In the field, Eric whispered, 'Help me with the grounders, daddy. I'm real bad with grounders.'

Not this time, Alex said. *You're on your own.* He moved off and away from his son.

Eric, who couldn't see his father in daylight, closed his eyes and put down his mitt.

The first boy up whacked a vicious grounder straight at Eric. The ball hit a stone, bounced and struck Eric in the forehead. He fell unconscious to the ground.

. . . and now in the second week on earth the light drew toward Alex where he hovered in Eric's room near the unconscious boy's bed.

It wasn't supposed to happen like this, *Alex said to the light.* You saw him. He was turning into a bully. And a cheat.

The light said nothing. Instead, it showed Alex scenes from his life.

In the first scene, Alex was holding Eric's hand as the boy walked along. And suddenly Alex let go and Eric took his first few steps on his own. And before falling down, Eric smiled with such a look of triumph and accomplishment that it brought tears to Alex's eyes . . .

In the second scene, Alex was following behind and holding the back fender of Eric's first two-wheeler bike. Eric fought to stabilize the handlebars, and when he looked back Alex let go. Eric went down the block and back again and the same look of triumph was in his eyes . . .

In the third scene, Alex held his son's hand as Eric boarded the bus for the first time for kindergarten. There was no look of triumph this time as he let go. But when the boy returned that day the smile was there and the sense of accomplishment . . .

I understand, *Alex said to the light.* I understand.

While the boy was unconscious, Alex entered his dreams. He appeared to Eric as he had appeared in his prime – tall, strong, handsome. The boy went to him and hugged him. Then Alex held the boy at arm's length.

'Listen to me, Eric,' Alex said. 'Some of what I tell you now might not make sense right away. But later, when you're older, it will.'

'You're going to leave me, aren't you?' the boy said and hugged his father.

'I can't take every test for you, Eric. I can't hit every ball. If I rob you of your chance to lose, then I rob you of your chance to win. I can't go through your lifetime giving you what you've got to earn for yourself.'

'I'll do my homework next time,' Eric said. 'I promise, daddy. I promise.'

'I know you will,' Alex said.

'Don't leave, daddy.'

'I'd only be cheating you out of your own life if I stayed,' Alex said. 'Remember, Eric. Remember. Sometimes loving is letting go.'

Alex faded in the dream. Eric grabbed at the air and suddenly he was awake.

Lois smiled at him. 'You got quite a bump on the head.'

'He's gone, mom,' Eric said.

She looked puzzled.

'Dad is gone,' Eric said. He burst into sobs.

She smiled through her own tears, happy that Eric

was at last able to let go, sad for his pain. 'Your father loved you so much,' she said. '*That* you will always have, Eric. But he's gone now. And sometimes, even though you love someone, you've got to let go.'

Eric nodded. 'That's what he said, mom.'

'Then you know it must be true.' And Lois drew him to her and surrounded him with her arms.

Wings

JAMES LOVEGROVE

The bell rang, and suddenly the corridors and shafts of the school were filled with moving bodies, and the classrooms, libraries, laboratories and gymnasia were left hollow and empty and echoing, dust and loose leaves of paper settling even as the teachers were still shaping their lips around the words 'Class dismissed'. Through the building the children flew with a great racketing roar, celebrating with their screams and whoops and yells the death of another school day. Out into the yard they spilled, there to clasp hands and share jokes and exchange grins and promise to meet up again later that afternoon, or tomorrow, or whenever. Then, dividing into pairs and knots of three or four and the odd solemn single, off they went along the windy streets of Cloudcap City, satchels in hand, skirts and shirt-tails fluttering, whirling like thistledown to all six corners of the compass.

Amid all this fever to escape, Az plodded along in his usual ungainly way. A few classmates patted him on the shoulder and said, 'See you,' as they sped past, but Az's slow progress meant that no one was going to stay beside him for long. It just wasn't possible. It took him over a minute to traverse a corridor or to clamber up or down a shaft, using the metal rungs specially fitted into the walls for him, whereas it took the rest of them a handful of seconds. They swooped like swifts, like swallows, while Az was a struggling, lumbering beetle.

The last few children were taking off from the yard as Az finally emerged, blinking, into the sunshine. He watched them rise into the sky, wave to one another and flit off in different directions. He waved too, in the hope that at least one of them might glance back and see him and return the gesture, but their eyes were fixed on the horizon, home and freedom. Alone, and sunk in his own thoughts, Az crossed the yard.

Usually he would have caught the airbus and travelled home with the old people and the fledglings and all the other lame ducks, but when he came through the school gates he found Michael waiting for him on the landing platform in his Corbeau. Michael was returning the admiring glances of a pair of girls who were wafting by on the other side of the street, but catching sight of Az, he forgot about them, raised a hand and cried out, 'Hey, little brother! Hop aboard!'

Az climbed into the passenger seat beside Michael, dumping his satchel between his feet. Michael hit a switch on the Corbeau's dashboard, and the blades began to rotate above their heads.

Over the rising whine of the engine and the *vip-vip-vip* of chopped air, Michael shouted, 'Good day at school?'

Az shrugged. 'So-so.'

Michael looked carefully at the little guy and saw the gloom in his face, smeared there like a cumulo-nimbus in a blue sky. He didn't ask what the matter was. He merely said, 'Hey, I've got an idea. Why don't we stop by the Ice Castle on the way home? I bet you anything there's a sundae waiting there with your name on it.'

'Thanks. No,' said Az, buckling on his safety belt.

'OK, why don't we pop over to the Aerobowl, then?

I've got free passes. Come on. The Thunderhead Eagles
are playing the Stratoville Shrikes.'

'Oh.'

'"Oh"? What does that mean – "Oh"? The *Shrikes*,
Az. You *love* the Shrikes. They're your all-time balloonball heroes.'

'No. 'S all right, really. Thanks. I just want to go
home.'

Michael frowned. 'Well, OK. If you say so. If you're
sure.' He glanced out of the cockpit to check the street
was clear, then pushed forward on the joystick. The
autogyro sprang from the landing platform, soaring up
into the sparkling air.

The Corbeau, the latest model in the Airdyne 3-Series,
was *the* status-symbol two-seater of the moment – sleek,
tapered, a giant's teardrop cast in bronze, every inch of
the surface of its fuselage smooth and gleaming, from
the nose-cone with its ring of rivets to the scallop-
grooved tail-fins – and Michael flew it with the requisite
recklessness, slipping and side-sliding through the air
channels, descending suddenly, just as suddenly climbing, overtaking, undertaking, the aircraft responding to
the tiniest nudges on the joystick and pedals as though it
were an extension of its pilot, a mechanized extrapola-
tion of Michael's own abilities. And had Az been in any
kind of a good mood, he would have been laughing
uproariously as they nipped around the other traffic and
whizzed past his schoolfellows at breakneck speed, leaving them standing just as they had left him standing
earlier. But today not even a fast ride in a classy piece of
aero-engineering could lift his depression. If anything, it
served to deepen it.

They zoomed down Sunswept Avenue, great cubes
of apartment block blurring by on either side, took a

right on to Cirrus Street, then an up on to Jayhawk, and shortly the Corbeau was settling down on the landing-platform that poked out like a rectangular tongue from their parents' front porch. Az leapt out and was about to make his way up to the front door when Michael grabbed him by the arm and turned him around with a gentle but forceful strength, bringing them face to face.

'Listen, little brother,' he said softly.

Az averted his gaze.

'I know it's not easy for you,' Michael continued, 'and I know that sometimes it must feel like the whole world's against you because of what you don't have or what you *think* you don't have. Just remember this — it doesn't matter. You're still our Az, and one lousy pair of wings isn't going to change that. If I thought it would, I'd cut mine off and give them to you right now. You understand that, don't you?'

Az nodded dumbly, not looking up.

'Good. Well, take it easy on yourself. And maybe we'll go down to the 'bowl at the weekend. How about that? Would you like that?'

Az nodded again, and Michael let him go.

The whine of the autogyro rose behind him as he wandered slowly up to the porch. Michael's 'Catch you later!' was cut short by the slamming of the front door.

'Dear?' His mother's voice, from the kitchen. 'Azrael?' She came out into the hallway, drying her hands on a dishtowel. 'Was that Michael I heard just now? Isn't he going to stay for dinner?'

Az shook his head. 'I don't know.'

'Some girl, I bet,' said his mother indulgently, the wrinkles around her eyes multiplying.

'Maybe,' said Az. Then: 'I'm going up to my room.'

To get to the upper storey of the house Az had to use

a contraption his father had built for him, a space-con-
suming succession of cantilevered wooden steps that
rose diagonally through the ceiling and creaked loudly
underfoot. His parents used the steps too whenever he
was around. As a rule, they made sure to walk as much
as possible when he was in the house, out of respect for
his feelings.

His room was like any other twelve-year-old's room,
save that the door went down all the way to the floor
(another of his father's DIY adaptations). The carpet
was strewn with clothing, books, pieces of a long-aban-
doned jigsaw, some small die-cast biplanes and a larger-
scale model of a Corbeau which Michael had given him
for his birthday, saying it would do until Az was old
enough to earn his pilot's licence, at which point Michael
would buy him the real thing. He dropped his satchel in
the middle of all this debris and stretched out on his
bed, flat on his back. Lying on his back, Az reflected,
was the one thing he could do that no one else could.
Some compensation. Yeah, right. What a talent. The
kids at school were *constantly* asking him to show them
how well he could lie on his *back* . . .

He stared up at the ceiling for a long time, trying to
think of nothing. At some point, during the slow fade
of the afternoon, he fell asleep.

And he dreamed.

*One morning Az wakes up to find he has grown a
fully-fledged pair of wings. He doesn't know how they
got there, he doesn't dare ask why. He simply accepts.*

*His parents are happy and amazed. His mother cries,
his father thumbs some grit from his eye. They forgive
Az. For what, they do not say, but it is enough for Az
to be forgiven. He kisses them both, and prepares to fly*

*off to school under his own steam for the first time
ever.*

*Flying, he finds, is not so difficult. He has the instinct
for it, and now he has the means. A little practice, a bit
of plummeting and frantic fluttering, and he's on his
way.*

*Heads turn and mouths gape in the school yard.
Cries go up. 'Look!' 'Look at that!' 'Did you ever . . .?'
'Who'd have thought . . .?'*

*Az alights in the middle of the yard, and his peers
cluster round him, jabbering excitedly. They fire off a
million questions at him. They ask him if they can
touch his wings. He tells them they can. They touch
them with reverential awe and care. It tickles.*

*Word gets around, and before he knows it Az is a
celebrity in school. He is clapped and cheered wherever
he goes. When he glides down a shaft with his wings
outstretched, every feather intricately splayed to catch
the air, he descends into a hail of hurrahs. When he kites
along a corridor, keeping pace with the rest of his class
as they hurry from one lesson to the next, they grin and
encourage him every flap of the way. During break
time Az is asked to join half a dozen impromptu games
of balloonball, and though he has never played before,
has only ever watched from the sidelines, he soon gets
the hang of it and even scores a Horizontal Slide. The
final seal is put on his popularity when Mrs Ragual
interrupts her PE lesson to ask Az for a demonstration.
The class goes outside and Az soars and barrel-rolls and
loops-the-loop for their benefit. Mrs Ragual tells him
he is not just a good flyer, he is a great flyer. Then the
rest of them join him in the air, and together, under
Mrs Ragual's approving eye, they pass a happy, truant
half-hour simply doing what they like to do best, wheel-*

ing and whirling and squealing and squalling like a flock of mad seagulls. All the time Az is the centre of attention, the focus of everybody's admiration. After all, anyone who can make one of Mrs Ragual's torture sessions fun has to be some kind of a hero . . .

He woke up. He dared to touch his back.

Still wingless.

He rolled disconsolately over on to his side to look out of the window at Cloudcap City, laid out in neat rows and columns and files, up, down, left, right, reaching as high as the stratosphere and as low as the cloudtop and as far as the horizon, each block suspended by means of six-way electromagnetic positional stabilizers to form a three-dimensional latticework of buildings, between and through and around which tiny figures and aircraft of all shapes and sizes were threading their way. Most of the buildings were cubic in shape, but there were oddities. The cylinder of the Freefall Dance Palace was one, the annular Aerobowl another, the spike-spired mace-ball fantasy of the Cathedral of the Significant God a notable third.

The air being clear and his eyes sharp, Az could make out the bird-trawlers a mile down on the cloudtop, casting their nets into the wilderness of white. He could also make out the sky-mines that ringed the city, forming a circle of stability on which the whole meniscus of floating buildings depended. The sky-mines looked like tulips balancing on lofty, delicately slender stems which pierced the cloudtop and went all the way down to the Ground, from where they sucked up the juices that kept the city running.

He lay there watching the view for he didn't know how long. It seemed like no time and all time had passed when his mother called up from below, summoning him down for dinner.

Az clumped down to the kitchen, from which emanated smells that even his gloom-ridden brain recognized as mouth-watering.

'Go and call your father,' said his mother. 'Then you can lay the table.'

Az went out into the hallway again, walked along a little way and stopped at the large trapdoor that led down to his father's workshop. He listened hard, and heard from below faint sounds of banging and tocking, clonking and clanging.

Construction.

While a working man, his father had spent much of his spare time dabbling in home improvements, which were usually for Az's benefit, like the steps and all the doorways in the house. When his forty-year career as a maker and mender of clocks had finally wound down, however, he had turned his hand to invention and had begun building a series of thises, thats and the others – gadgets that he hoped one day to patent and sell by the million, devices intended to make everyone's lives that little bit easier. So far not a single one had proved patent-feasible. A portable trouser press had made its mark in all the wrong ways. A clockwork toothbrush had been a gum-mangling disaster. But he went on making these things none the less, toiling away by the uncertain light of a gas lantern, in the strictest of privacy, hope springing eternal with the completion of every new invention until that invention blew a gasket or slipped a cog or collapsed in a heap or simply failed to start. Then it was 'Oh, well, back to the drawing board' with a sigh that contained neither defeat nor despair. It was almost as if Az's father wasn't really looking forward to the day when one of his devices worked and was a success and made his fortune and meant that he never had to make anything else again. The old man was happy just to be in his workshop, out of harm's way, tinkering, occupying his hands and his time.

Az called down, and the sounds of construction ceased and his father's muffled voice came up.

'Yes?'

'Dinner.'

'Coming.'

A moment later his father bustled into the kitchen. 'Give me a hand here, won't you, son?' He turned his back, and Az helped him unzip and wrestle out of the plastic slip-covers he wore over his wings to protect them from dust and stray sparks. His father's plumage had greyed at the edges, was rough in patches like a fledgling's and had gaps where pinfeathers had fallen out and would never grow back. But they were fine, proud wings all the same, and in excellent condition for a man his age.

'Outside, please,' said Az's mother, referring to the dusty wing-covers. Her husband obediently popped them out through the door on to the back porch. 'I shudder to think of the state of that workshop,' she went on. 'Knee-deep in shavings and scrapings and woodchips and what-have-you.'

Az's father clasped a fist to his chest and said, 'I would rather die than have you clean in there.'

'I wasn't offering,' she replied. 'I was merely remarking.'

While Az finished laying the table, his father washed his hands in the sink. Drying them on a towel, he said, quietly, as if it was no matter at all, 'Do you know, I really think I'm on to something this time.'

Az's mother, who had heard this statement, or statements pretty much like it, a hundred times before, said, without looking up from the stove, 'That's good, dear.'

Az said nothing.

But when his father sat down at the table, there was a gleam in his eyes Az could not remember seeing there before, a light of excitement brightening the well-yellowed whites. 'No, I mean it,' he said. 'I've been working on this particular project for some weeks now, and I think I'm close to cracking it.'

'Eat,' said Az's mother, placing laden plates in front of them.

They ate. His parents, reckoning Az was not in a communicative mood, left him alone and chatted between themselves, chewing over trivialities and inconsequentialities the way old married couples do when the weighty subjects have been thoroughly discussed and all that remains is the nitty-gritty and the fine-tuning and the splitting of hairs.

Finally Az could bear it no longer, and said, 'What?'

'*What* what?' said his father.

'What is it? The something that you're on to? What?'

The gleam re-entered the old man's eyes. 'Never you mind, Az. Wait and see.'

By this time his mother was intrigued too. 'Go on, Gabe,' she said. 'Give us a clue.'

'What, and ruin the suspense?'

'Is it going to make us rich?' Az asked.

His father made a great show of considering the question. 'Well, in one sense, yes. In another sense, no.' He grinned enigmatically. 'Wait and see.'

Az waited several days and still did not see. Every afternoon when he came home from school he would stop quietly by the trapdoor and listen to the tink and bonk and clatter and whack-whack-whack of industry and the tuneless humming with which his father often counterpointed the rhythm of his labours. The sounds seemed no different from the sounds his father usually made down there. They were infuriatingly ordinary.

His attempts to extract from his father even the tiniest hint as to what was taking shape in the workshop were met with gleeful stonewalling. Endless questions could be asked over the dinner table, only to be answered with a 'Maybe' or a 'Could be' or a simple 'Not saying'. Once, recalling that his father had recently bought in several sheets of copper, Az asked whether these had some bearing on the mystery, but his father pointed out, rightly, that he was constantly buying in sheets of copper. It was, he said, the most tractable and obliging metal to work with.

One evening, while flicking through a magazine, Az held up each page of advertising in turn and showed it to his father, asking, 'Is it like that?' To which, in every instance, his father replied, 'Something like that. Only completely different.' Eventually Az became so aggravated that he threw the magazine down and left the room, hearing his father chuckle merrily behind him.

There was no question of secretly investigating the workshop, violating the privacy of his father's *sanctum sanctorum*, so in the end there was nothing for it but to wait and wonder.

One good thing, though, came of this continuing mystery. Az was so busy thinking about what might be in the workshop that he forgot to dwell on his own problems. Teachers marked the disappearance of his depressive fits and were quietly pleased, although a tendency to daydream in class was noted in the normally diligent pupil. His classmates were for the most part indifferent to the change in his temperament, although a few of them did notice that Az no longer scowled so hard when he walked. His mind seemed to be elsewhere, on something outside himself. The more sensitive among them recognized this to be a healthy sign.

Eighteen days after his first announcement, Az's father made a second, more impressive, announcement.

It came one dinnertime. Michael had dropped by on his way to pick up a girl called Raphaella and take her to a harp recital at the Cathedral of the Significant God. The family was halfway through the main course when Az's father tapped his wine glass with his fork, cleared his throat and said, 'A short speech.'

Everyone groaned.

'A *very* short speech. Just to say that this Saturday will see the unveiling of a device that is going to make us the happiest family alive. I want you to be there, Michael, if you can make it.'

'This isn't another of your exploding specials, is it, dad?' said Michael. 'Like the self-heating coffee cup?'

'It's something,' said the old man, with an extravagant display of self-restraint, 'that is going to make us the happiest family alive.'

Michael turned to Az. 'We're going to be million-aires,' he said with a confident wink.

That night Az hardly slept at all. It was ridiculous, he knew, to get all excited over a dumb invention of his father's that might not even work. But there it was. His father's enthusiasm was infectious. And so Az lay awake, trying to imagine what form the device would take, what use it could be put to, how big it would be, how practical, and he ached for Saturday to come so that he could see which, if any, of his suppositions turned out to be true.

The day of the unveiling arrived, and Az and his mother watched Michael and the old man haul the device up from the workshop and carry it out on to the landing-platform. The device was covered by a tarpaulin, so that all anyone could say about it was that it was twelve feet long, thin at either end, bulky in the middle, and angular all over. Az thought of the dinosaur skeleton in the Museum of Ancient Artefacts.

'Well?' said Az's mother, giftwrapping her impatience in a laugh.

'One moment,' said his father. 'First, a short speech.'

As before, the family groaned, as they were supposed to.

Pretending not to notice, Az's father ruffled his wings and grasped his lapel like a politician. 'Once,' he began, 'long ago, we were not Airborn but Groundling, and we lived an earthbound life, circumscribed on all sides by natural boundaries – mountains, rivers, seas. Since then, the race has moved onwards and upwards, and now we live lives as close to perfection as it is possible to get. We are paragons, living embodiments of all that the Groundlings aspired to. This is our heritage and our privilege. A privilege that should not be denied to anyone. Least of all, to the flesh of my flesh.' Here, he looked straight at Az, and suddenly everyone – except Az – had a pretty good idea what lay hidden beneath the tarpaulin.

There might have been more to the speech, but Az's father sensed that the game was up and, like any good showman, he knew he should not let the audience get ahead of him, so with a grand flourish he swept back the tarpaulin, revealing his creation to the world.

Four faces were reflected in a relief mosaic of burnished copper. Three of them gawped, wide-eyed. The fourth grinned with pride.

Finally, someone spoke. It was Az's mother.

'Wings,' she exclaimed, the word tailing up into a question.

'Wings,' her husband confirmed, bringing the word back in to land.

And wings they were. Larger than lifesize, correct in every detail, lovingly crafted in beaten copper. A pair of metal, mechanical wings.

Every feather was there, perfect down to the fine comb-teeth of its filaments and pinned into place with a free-floating bolt; every joint, too, from the ball-and-sockets at the base of the armatures to the hinges at the elbows; and a complex system of pulleys and wires connected the ensemble to a leather harness which was just the right shape and just the right size for the ribcage of a young boy of twelve.

'Come on then,' said Az's father, taking Az by the shoulder. 'Let's try them on, shall we?'

Michael stepped forward to help, and together he and the old man loaded the wings on to Az's back and tightened the straps of the harness around his chest.

Az submitted passively to the fitting, not knowing what to think, not really thinking anything. The wings were very heavy, and when his father and Michael let go, he teetered and would have overbalanced if Michael had not caught and steadied him.

Az barely listened as his father explained how the wings worked. 'You see, they're designed to take the action of the muscles in your shoulders and translate it into wingbeats, so you'll simply be employing the natural abilities God gave you. You may have some trouble adjusting to them at first, but that's only to be expected. There's no reason why instinct shouldn't take over almost straight away. Trust me, Az. You'll be up and soaring in no time.'

Bookended by Michael and his father, Az staggered to the edge of the landing-platform, the wings making a soft, shimmering clatter with each step as hundreds of copper feathers shook against one another. He peered down. The rippled surface of the cloudtop was awfully far below. The bird-trawlers plying their trade down there looked as tiny as gnats.

He glanced back over his shoulder. At first he could see nothing but copper wing, but he dropped his shoulder slightly and the wing flattened out, and then he could see his mother. There were tears in her eyes. 'Go on,' she said to him, smiling bravely. 'Don't be scared. You'll be fine.'

But he wasn't scared. He was embarrassed. The clench of his jaw wasn't one of determination but one of humiliation. He felt clumsier than ever, burdened by these huge metal prostheses. He felt neither Airborn nor Groundling but a horrid amalgamation of the two. A joke, a parody. What would they think of him at school if he turned up on Monday morning strapped into this ugly, clattering copper contraption?

'I don't think I can go through with this,' he said.

'Nonsense,' said his father, mistaking the tremor in Az's voice for fear. 'Michael and I will make sure you're all right, won't we, Michael? Whatever happens, you won't come to any harm. Trust us.'

'Will you at least hold on to me?' Az implored.

'The only way to learn is the way I learned,' said Michael. 'The way we all learn.'

'What way is that?' said Az dubiously.

'The hard way,' said Michael, and with a grin that was devoid of malice and yet still wicked, he grabbed Az's arm. Az's father on the other side did the same, and together, chanting, 'One, two, three,' they heaved Az out over the edge and into space.

And let go.

There was a moment of sheer disbelief, followed by a moment of sheer terror. Then all that was lost in the sickening up-rush of falling. The weight of the wings yanked Az head over heels on to his back, and down he went in a wind-shivered clatter of metal. Down he plummeted, making no attempt to right himself or flap the wings, unable even to entertain the notion of saving himself. Down in a state of dreamlike apathy, with no thought except that he was going to die. Hypnotically down, past building after building, past windows and doorways, past light aircraft and happy citizens out for a Saturday morning glide. Down, down, down, with no hope of rescue, and no desire for it either. Down without a gasp or a scream, for an elastic stretch of seconds, the platform above receding, the house and all the houses around it shrinking, the sky growing smaller and filling up with more and more city. Down towards the cloudtop and the Ground from where the Airborn race once sprang and which now lay forever hidden.

There was a tentative knock at the door.

'Can I come in?'

'Sure, dad.'

Az glanced up from the book he was reading, an adventure story about sky pirates, as his father entered the room. The old man's head was contritely bowed, and his wings drooped so low their tips were almost touching the floor. The look of shame that hung on the old man's face was so comical, Az could hardly fail to smile.

His father gestured to the edge of the bed. 'May I?'

Az nodded.

The old man sat down. There was a long silence while he deliberated over his next move, then he reached out and laid one hand on Az's leg. He patted the leg, the action affectionate yet mechanical. It was clear that he had several things to say but no idea in what order to say them.

Az helped him out. 'I'm sorry if I hurt your feelings.'

'My feelings?'

'By not trying.'

'Oh. Well, I wouldn't say my feelings were *hurt*, exactly. I was a little ... disappointed? No, not even that. I did hope ... Well, it doesn't matter now. How *I* feel doesn't matter. It's how *you* feel that matters.'

'I feel fine. Honestly.'

'The doctor said there may be some delayed shock.'

'I feel absolutely fine, dad. Guilty, though.'

'Guilty?'

'For letting you down.'

'You didn't let me down, Az,' said his father with an exasperated laugh. 'How can I get that into your thick skull? I don't mind. Really I don't. It's enough for me that you're alive and well.'

'Well, I think I did. I mean, the wings would have worked. Almost certainly. Definitely. If I'd tried. I just didn't try. I didn't want to try.'

'Oh,' said his father. For the sake of his own conscience, it was what he had been hoping to hear. 'Well, anyway, you'll be pleased to learn that I've taken the damned things along to the scrapyard. Never again.'

'But you are going to carry on with your inventions?'

Az's father frowned. 'Perhaps. The fun's sort of gone out of it.'

'But what about making your million?'

'It's just a dream.'

'Dreams are important.'

'Az,' said his father, then paused. 'When your mother was pregnant with you, the doctors suggested she . . . she shouldn't have you. Health reasons. She wasn't so young any more. But she was prepared to take the risk. Quite determined, as a matter of fact. And because she was, I was too. We both wanted you more than we'd ever wanted anything, no question about it. And when you came, we couldn't have been happier. We loved you the instant we set eyes on you. You were different, but that only made you special.' His father looked deep inside himself. 'Even so, it hasn't always been easy. You understand. For any of us. The looks we sometimes get, that mixture of compassion and disappointment, like we've somehow let the whole race down. Sometimes . . . Anyway, what I'm saying is, I was wrong to try to make you the same as everyone else. I'd convinced myself I was doing it for you, but of course I was just doing it for myself. And now I can't help thinking what would have happened if Michael hadn't been so quick off the mark, if he hadn't caught you when he did . . .'

'But he did, and I'm fine. It just wasn't meant to be, dad. That's all there is to it.'

'Please believe me when I say that I had your best interests at heart. It just never occurred to me . . . I just assumed that to fly must be your dream, your greatest, wildest dream.'

'Oh, but it is, dad, it is. I dream about having wings

all the time. The thing is, I've got so used to the fact that it's never going to happen, it doesn't bother me so much any more. Sometimes it's better to have a dream and not have it fulfilled than make do with something that's like your dream but not quite as good.'

'Say I'm forgiven anyway.'

'You're forgiven anyway.'

'Thank you.' The old man thought about tousling his son's hair but checked himself. That was something you did to little children. To boys. Instead he patted Az's leg one more time, and left the room.

Az shut his book and turned over to look out of the window.

Cloudcap City, his home, lay suspended in the bright afternoon sunshine, shadowless and huge, its interstices busy with traffic, thriving with life. It pleased Az to think that, even if only for a handful of seconds, he had plunged through that city unaided, unsupported; that he had had a taste of flight, however brief and unwelcome. It filled him with a weird kind of serenity.

In this world he would always be a floor-bound, wing-less freak. There was no changing that. But in his dreams . . .

In his dreams, he would always be able to fly.

Spirit Guides

KRISTINE KATHRYN RUSCH

Los Angeles. City of the Angels.

Kincaid walked down Hollywood Boulevard, his feet stepping on gum-coated stars. Cars whooshed past him, horns honking, tourists gawking. The line outside Graumann's Chinese clutched purses against their sides, held windbreakers tightly over their arms. A hooker leaned against the barred display window of the corner drug store, her make-up so thick it looked like a mask in the hot sun.

The shooting had left him shaken. The crazy had opened up inside a nearby burger joint, slaughtering four customers and three teenaged kids behind the counter before three men, passing on the street, rushed inside and grabbed him. Half a dozen shots had gone wild, leaving fist-sized holes in the drywall, shattering picture frames and making one perfect circle in the center of a cardboard model of a bacon-double cheeseburger.

He'd arrived two minutes too late, hearing the call on his police scanner on his way home, but unable to maneuver in traffic. Christ, some of those people who wouldn't let him pass might have had relatives in that burger joint. Still and all, he had arrived first to find the killer trussed up in a chair, the men hovering around him, women clutching sobbing children, blood and bodies mixing with french fries on the unswept floor.

A little girl, no more than three, had grabbed his sleeve and pointed at one of the bodies, long, slender, male and young, wearing a '49ers T-shirt, ripped jeans and Adidas, his face a bloody mass of tissue, and said, 'Make him better,' in a whisper that broke Kincaid's heart. He cuffed the suspect, roped off the area, took names of witnesses before the back-up arrived. Three squads, fresh-faced uniformed officers, followed by the swat team, nearly five minutes too late, the forensic team and the ambulances not far behind.

Kincaid had lit a cigarette with shaking fingers and said, 'All yours,' before taking off into the sun-drenched, crowded streets.

He stopped outside the Roosevelt and peered into the plate glass. His own tennis shoes were stained red, and a long brown streak of drying blood marked his Levis. The cigarette had burned to a coal between his nicotine-stained fingers, and he tossed it, stamping it out on the star of a celebrity whose name he didn't recognize.

Inside stood potted palms and faded glamour. Pictures of motion-picture stars long dead lined the second-floor balcony. Within the last ten years, the hotel's management had restored the Roosevelt to its 1920s glory, when it had been the site for the first-ever Academy Award celebration. When he first came to LA, he spent a lot of time in the hotel, imagining the low-cut dresses, the clink of champagne flutes, the scattered applause as the nominees were announced. Searching for a kind of beauty that existed only in celluloid, a product of light and shadows and nothing more.

El Pueblo de Nuestra Señora la Reina de los Angeles de Porciuncula.

The City of Our Lady, Queen of the Angels of Porciuncula.

He knew nothing of the Angels of Porciuncula, did not know why Felipe de Neve in 1781 named the city after them. He suspected it was some kind of prophecy, but he didn't know.

They had been fallen angels.

Of that he was sure.

He sighed, wiped the sweat from his forehead with a grimy hand, then returned to his car, knowing that home and sleep would elude him for one more night.

Lean and spare, Kincaid survived on cigarettes, coffee, chocolate and bourbon. Some time in the last five years he had allowed the LAPD to hire him, although he had no formal training. After a few odd run-ins and one overnight jail stay before it became clear that Kincaid wasn't anywhere near the crime scene, Kincaid had met Davis, his boss. Davis had the flat gaze of a man who had seen too much, and he knew, from the records and the evidence before him, that Kincaid was too precious to lose. He made Kincaid a plain-clothes detective and never assigned him a partner.

Kincaid never told anyone what he did. Most of the cops he worked with never knew. All they cared about was that when Kincaid was on the job, suspects were found, cases were closed and files were sealed. He worked quietly, and he got results.

They didn't need him on this one. The perp was caught at the scene. All he had to do was write his report, then go home, toss the tennies in the trash, soak the Levis and wait for another day.

But it wasn't that easy. He sat in his car, an olive-green 1968 Olds with a fading, pine-shaped air-freshener hanging from the rear-view mirror, long after his colleagues had left. His hands were still shaking, his nostrils still coated with the scent of blood and burgers, his ears clogged with the faint sobs of a pimply faced boy rocking over the body of a fallen co-worker. The images would stick, along with all of the others. His brain was reaching overload. Had been for a long time. But that little girl's voice, the plea in her tone, had been more than he could bear.

For twenty years he had tried to escape, always ending up in a new town, with new problems. Shootings in Oklahoma parking lots, bombings in upstate New York, murders in restaurants and shopping malls and suburban family pick-ups. The violence surrounded him, and he was trapped.

Surely this time they would let him get away.

A hooker knocked on the window of his car. He thought he could smell the sweat and perfume through the rolled-up glass. Her cleavage was mottled, her cheap elastic top revealing the top edge of brown nipple.

He shook his head, then turned the ignition and grabbed the gear shift on the column to take the car out of park. The Olds roared to life, and with it came the adrenalin rush, hormones tinged with panic. He pulled out of the parking space, past the hooker, down Holly-wood Boulevard toward the first freeway intersection he could find.

Kincaid would disappear from the LAPD as mysteriously as he had arrived. He stopped long enough to pick up his clothes, his credit cards and a hand-painted coffee mug a teenaged girl in Galveston had given him twenty years before when she mistakenly thought he had saved her life.

He merged into the continuous LA rush-hour traffic for the last time, radio off, clutching the wheel in white-knuckled tightness. He would go to Big Bear, up in the mountains, where there were no people, no crimes, nothing except himself and the wilderness.

He drove away from the angels.

Or so he hoped.

Kincaid drove until he realized he was on the road to Las Vegas. He pulled the Olds over, put on his hazards and bowed his head, unwilling to go any farther. But he knew, even if he didn't drive there, he would wake up in Vegas, his car in the lot outside. It had happened before.

He didn't remember taking the wrong turn, but he wasn't supposed to remember. They were just telling him that his work wasn't done, the work they had forced him to do ever since he was a young boy.

With a quick, vicious movement, he got out of the Olds and shook his fist at the star-filled desert sky. 'I can't take it any more, do you hear me?'

But no shape flew across the moon, no angel wings brushed his cheek, no reply filled his heart. He could turn around, but the roads he drove would only lead him back to Los Angeles, back to people, back to murders in which little girls stood in pools of blood. He knew what Los Angeles was like. Maybe they would allow him a few days' rest in Vegas.

Las Vegas, the fertile plains, originally founded in the late 1700s like LA, only the settlement didn't become permanent until 1905, when the first lots were sold (and nearly flooded out five years later). He thought maybe the city's youth and brashness would be a tonic, but even as he drove into town, he felt the blood beneath the surface. Despair and hopelessness had come to every place in America. Only here it mingled with the *cajing-jing* of slot machines and the smell of money.

He wanted to stay in the MGM Grand, but the Olds wouldn't drive through the lot. He settled on a cheap, tumble-down hotel on the far side of the Strip, complete with chenille bedspreads and rattling window air-conditioners that dripped water on to the thin brown indoor-outdoor carpet. There he slept in the protective dark of the black-out curtains, and dreamed.

Angels floated above him, their wings so long that the tips brushed his face. As he watched, they tucked their wings around themselves and plummeted, eagle-like, to the ground below, banking when the concrete of a major superhighway rose in front of them. He was on the bed, watching, helpless, knowing that each time the long white tail feathers touched the earth, violence erupted somewhere it had never been before.

He started awake, coughing the deep, racking cough of a three-pack-a-day man. His tongue was thick and tasted of bad coffee and nicotine. He reached for the end table, clicking on the brown glass bubble lamp, then grabbed his lighter and a cigarette from the pack resting on top of the cut-glass ashtray. His hands were still shaking, and the room was quiet except for his labored breathing. Only in the silence did he realize that his dream had been accompanied by the sound of the pimply faced boy, sobbing.

It happened just before dawn. A woman's scream, outside, cut off in mid-thrum, followed by a sickening thud and footsteps. He had known it would, the minute the car had refused to enter the Grand's parking lot. And he had to respond, whether it was his choice or not.

Kincaid paused long enough to pull on his pants, checking to make sure his wallet was in the back pocket. Then he grabbed his key and let himself out of the room.

His window overlooked the pool, a liver-shaped thing

built in the late fifties of blue tile. The management left the terrace lights on all night, and Kincaid used those to guide him across the interior courtyard. In the half-light he saw another shape running toward the pool, a pear-shaped man dressed in the too-tight uniform of a national rent-a-cop service. The air smelled of chlorine, and the desert heat was still heavy despite the early morning hour. Leaves and dead bugs floated in the water, and the surrounding patio furniture was so dirty it took a moment for Kincaid to realize it was supposed to be white.

The rent-a-cop had already arrived on the scene, his pasty skin turning green as he looked down. Kincaid came up behind him, stopped and stared.

The body was crumpled behind the removable diving board. One look at her blood-stained face, her swollen and bruised neck, her chipped and broken fingernails and he knew.

All of it.

'I'd better call this in,' the rent-a-cop said, and Kincaid shook his head, knowing that if he were alone with the body, he would end up spending the next few days in a Las Vegas lock-up.

'No, let me.' He went back to his room, packed his meager possessions and set them by the door. Then he called 911 and reported the murder, slipping on a shirt before going back outside.

The rent-a-cop was wiping his mouth with the back of his hand. The air smelled of vomit. Kincaid said nothing. Together they waited for the Nevada authorities to show: a skinny plain-clothes detective, whose eyes were red-rimmed from lack of sleep, and his female partner, busty and official in regulation blue.

While the partner radioed in, the rent-a-cop told his

version: that he had been making his rounds and heard a couple arguing poolside. He was watching from the window when the man back-handed the woman and then took off through the casino. The woman didn't get up, and the cop decided to check on her instead of chasing the guy. Kincaid had shown up a minute or two later from his room in the hotel.

The plain-clothes man turned his flat gaze on Kincaid. Kincaid flashed his LAPD badge, then told the plain-clothes man that the killer's name was Luther Hardy, that he'd killed her because her anger was the last straw in a day that had seen him lose most of their $10,000 savings on the Mirage's roulette table. Even as the men spoke, Hardy was sitting at the only open craps table in Circus Circus, betting $25 chips on the come line.

Then Kincaid waited for the disbelief, but the plain-clothesman nodded, thanked him, rounded up the female partner and headed toward Circus Circus, leaving Kincaid, not the rent-a-cop, to guard the scene. Kincaid rubbed his nose with his thumb and forefinger, trying to stop a building headache, feeling the rent-a-cop's scrutiny. Kincaid could always pick them, the ones who had seen everything, the ones who had learned through hard experience and crazy knocks to check any lead that came their way. Like Davis. Only Kincaid was new to this plain-clothes man, so there would be a hundred questions when they returned.

Questions Kincaid was too tired to answer.

He told the rent-a-cop his room number, then staggered back, picked up his things and checked out, figuring he would be halfway to Phoenix before they discovered he was gone for good. They would call LAPD, and Davis would realize that Kincaid had finally left and would probably light a candle for him later that evening because he would know that Kincaid's singular talent was still controlling his life.

Like a hick tourist, Kincaid stopped on the Hoover Dam. At eight a.m. he stood on the miraculous concrete structure, staring at the raging blue of the Colorado below. An angel fluttered past him, then wrapped its wings around its torso and dove like a gull after prey. It disappeared in the glare of the sunlight against the water, and he strained, hoping and fearing he'd catch a glimpse as the angel rose, dripping, from the water.

The glimpses had haunted him since he was thirteen. He'd been in St Patrick's Cathedral with his mother, and one of the stained-glass angels had left her window, floated through the air and kissed him before alighting on the pulpit to tickle the visiting priest during mass. The priest hadn't noticed the feathers brush his face and neck, but he had died the next day in a mugging outside the subway station at 63rd and Lexington.

Kincaid hadn't seen the mugging, but his train had arrived only a few seconds after the priest died.

Years later, Kincaid finally thought to wonder why he hadn't died from the angel's kiss. And, although he still didn't have the answer, he knew that his second sight came from that morning. All he needed to do was look at a body to know who had driven the spirit from it and why. The snapshots remained in his mind in all their horror, surrounded by faces frozen in agony, each shot a sharp moment of pain that pierced a hole in his increasingly fragile soul.

As a young man he believed he could stop the pain, that he had been given the gift so that he could end the horrors. He would ride out, like St George, and defeat the dragon that had terrified the village. But these terrors were as old as time itself, and instead of stopping them, Kincaid could only observe them and report what his inner eye had seen. He had thought, as he grew older, that using his skills to imprison the perpetrators would help, but the deaths continued, more each year, and the little girl in the burger joint had provided the final straw.

Make him better.

Kincaid didn't have that kind of magic.

The angel flew out of the wide crevice, past the canyon walls, its tail feathers dripping just as Kincaid had feared. Somewhere within a two-hundred mile radius, someone would die violently because an angel had brushed the earth. Kincaid hunched himself against the bright morning, then turned and walked along the rock-strewn highway to his car. When he got inside, he kept the radio off so that the news of the atrocity would not hit him when it happened.

But the silence wouldn't keep him ignorant for ever. He would turn on the TV in a hotel, or pass a row of newspapers outside a restaurant, and the information would present itself to him as clearly and brightly as it always had, as if it were his responsibility, subject to his control.

The car led him into Phoenix. From the freeway the city was a row of concrete lanes, marred by machine-painted lines. From the sidestreets it had well-manicured lawns and tidy houses, too many strip restaurants and the ubiquitous mall. He was having a chimichanga in a neighborhood Garcia's as he watched the local news and realized that he might not hear of an atrocity after all. He finished the meal and left before the national news aired.

He was still in Phoenix at midnight and had not yet found a hotel. He didn't want to sleep, didn't want to be led to the next place where someone would die. He was sitting alone at a small table in a high-class strip joint, sipping bourbon that actually had a smooth bite instead of the cheap stuff he normally got. The strippers were legion, all young, with tits high and firm and asses to match. Some had long, lean legs and others were all torso. But none approached him, as if a sign were flashing above him, warning the women away. He drank until he could feel it – he didn't know how many drinks that was any more – and was startled that no one noticed him getting tight.

Even drunk, he couldn't relax, couldn't laugh. Enjoyment had leached out of him decades ago.

When the angel appeared in front of him, he thought it was another stripper, taller than most, wrapped in gossamer wings. Then it unfolded the wings and extended them, gently, as if it were doing a slow-motion fan dance, and he realized that its face had no features, and its body was fat and nippleless like a butterfly's.

He raised his glass to it. 'You gonna kiss me again?' His thoughts had seemed clear, but the words came out slurred.

The angel said nothing – it probably couldn't speak since it had no mouth. It merely took the drink from him and set the glass on the table. Then it grabbed his hand, pulled him to his feet and led him from the room like a recalcitrant child. He wondered vaguely how he looked, stumbling alone through the maze of people, his right arm outstretched.

When the fresh air hit him, the bourbon backed up in

his throat like bile. He staggered away from the beefy valets behind the potted cactus and threw up, the angel standing beside him, still as a statue. After a moment, he stood up and wiped his mouth with the crumpled handkerchief he kept folded in his back pocket. He still felt drunk but not as bloated.

Then the angel scooped him in its arms. Its body was soft and cold as if it contained no life at all. It cradled him like a baby, and they flew up until the city became a blaze of lights.

The wind ruffled his hair and woke him even more. He felt strangely calm, and he attributed that to the alcohol. Just as he was getting used to the oddness, the angel wrapped its wings around them and plummeted toward the ground.

They were moving so fast, he could feel the force of the air like a slap in his face. He was screaming – he could feel it, ripping at his throat – but he could hear nothing. They hurtled over the interstate. The cars were the size of ants before the angel extended its wings to ease their landing.

The angel tilted them upright, and they touched down in an empty, glass-strewn parking lot that led to an insurance office whose door was surrounded by yellow police tape. He recognized the site from the local newscast he had caught in Garcia's: ever since eight that morning, the insurance office had been the location of a hostage situation. A husband had decided to terrorize his wife who worked inside and, although shots had been fired, no one had been injured.

He stared at the building, felt the terror radiate from its walls as if it were a furnace. The insurance company was an old one: the gold lettering on the hand-painted window was chipped, and inside he could barely make out the shape of an overturned chair. He turned to ask the angel why it had brought him there, when he realized it was gone.

Kincaid stood in the parking lot for a moment, one hand wrapped around his stomach, the other holding his throbbing head. They had flown for miles. He still had his wallet but had no idea where he was or how he would find a pay phone.

And he didn't know what the angel had wanted from him.

He sighed and walked across the parking lot. The broken glass crunched beneath his shoes. His mouth was dry. The police tape looked too yellow in the glare of the street light. He stood on the stoop and peered inside, half hearing the voices from earlier in the day, the shouts from the police bullhorn, the low, tense voice of the wife, the terse, clipped tones of her husband. About noon he had gone outside to smoke a cigarette – his wife hated smoke – and had shot a stray dog to ward off the policeman who had been sneaking up behind him.

Kincaid could smell death. He followed his nose to the side of the building. There, among the gravel and the spindly, flower-less rose bushes, lay the dog on its side. It was scrawny, and its coat was mottled. Its tongue protruded just a bit from its open mouth. Its glassy eyes seemed to follow Kincaid, and he wondered how the news had missed this, the sympathy story amidst all the horror.

The stations in LA would have covered it.

Poor dog. A stray in life, unremembered in death. Just standing over it, he could see the last moments – the enticing smell of food from the police cars suddenly mingled with the scent of human fear, the glittery eyes of the male human and then pain, sharp, deep, and complete.

Kincaid crouched beside it. In all his years he had never touched a dead thing, never felt the cold, lifeless body, never totally understood how a body could live and then not live within the same instant. In the past he had left the dead for someone else to clean up, but here no one would. The dog would rot in this site of trauma and near-human tragedy, and no one would take the care to bury the dead.

Perhaps that was why the angel brought him, to show him that there had been carnage after all.

He didn't know how to bury it. All he had were his hands. But he touched the soft soil of the rose garden, his wrist brushing the dog's tail as he did so.

The dog coughed and struggled to sit up.

Kincaid backed away so quickly he nearly fell. The dog choked, then coughed again, spraying blood all over the bushes, the gravel and the concrete. It looked at him with a mixture of fear and pain.

'Jesus,' Kincaid muttered.

He pushed himself forward, then grabbed the dog's shoulders. Its labored breathing eased and its tail thumped slightly against the ground. Something clattered against the pavement, and he saw the bullet, rolling away. The dog stood, whimpered, licked his hand and then trotted off to fill its empty stomach.

Kincaid sat down in the glass and gravel, staring at his blood-covered hands.

Phoenix.

A creature of myth that rose from its own ashes to live again.

He had been such a fool.

All those years. All those lives.

Such a fool.

He looked up at the star-filled desert sky. The angel that had brought him hovered over him like a teacher waiting to see if the student understood the lecture. He couldn't relive his life, but maybe, just maybe, he could help one little girl who had spoken with the voice of angels.

Make him better.

'Take me back to Los Angeles,' he said to the angel. 'To the people who died yesterday.'

And, in a heartbeat, he was back in the burger joint. The killer, an overweight, acne-scarred man with empty eyes, was tied to a chair near the window, a group of men milling nervously around him, the gun leaning against the wall behind them. All the children were crying, their parents pressing the tiny faces against shoulders, trying to block the sight. The air smelled of burgers and fresh blood.

A little girl, no more than three, grabbed Kincaid's sleeve and pointed at one of the bodies, long, slender, male and young, wearing a '49ers T-shirt, ripped jeans and Adidas, his face a bloody mass of tissue, and said, 'Make him better,' in a whisper that broke Kincaid's heart.

Kincaid crouched, hands shaking, wishing desperately for a cigarette, and grabbed the body by the arm. Air whistled from the lungs, and the blood bubbled in the remains of the face. As Kincaid watched, the face returned, the blood disappeared and a young man was staring at him with fear-filled eyes.

'You all right, friend?' Kincaid asked.

The man nodded, and the little girl flung herself in his arms.

'Jesus,' someone said behind him.

Kincaid shook his head. 'It's amazing how bad injuries can look when someone's covered with blood.'

He didn't wait for the response, just went to the next body, and the next, his need for a cigarette decreasing with touch, the blood drying as if it had never been. When he got behind the counter, he gently pushed aside the pimply faced boy sobbing over the dead co-worker, and then he paused.

If he reversed this one, they would have nothing to indict the killer on.

The boy's breath hitched as he watched Kincaid. Kincaid turned and looked over his shoulder at the killer tied to the chair near the entrance. Holes the size of fists marred the drywall and made one perfect circle in the centre of a cardboard model of a bacon-double cheese-burger. It would be enough.

He grabbed the body's shoulders, feeling the grease of the uniform beneath his fingers. The spirit slid back in as if it had never left, and the wounds sealed themselves as they would on a video tape run backwards.

All those years. All those wasted years.

'How did you do that?' the pimply faced boy asked, his face shiny with tears.

'He was only stunned,' Kincaid said.

When he was done, he went outside to find the back-up team interviewing witnesses, the ambulances just arriving, five minutes too late.

He lit a cigarette and said, 'All yours,' before taking off into the sun-drenched, crowded streets.

Now he had to keep moving. No jobs with police departments, no comfortable apartments. He had to stay one step ahead of a victim's shock, one step ahead of the press who would some day catch wind of his ability. He couldn't let them corner him because the power was not his to control.

He was still trapped.

He stopped outside the Roosevelt and peered into the plate glass. His own tennis shoes were stained red, and a long brown streak of drying blood marked his Levis. The cigarette had burned to a coal between his nicotine-stained fingers before he had a chance to take a drag, and he tossed it, stamping it out on the star of a celebrity whose name he didn't recognize.

All those years and he never knew. The kiss made some kind of cosmic sense. Even Satan, the head of the fallen angels, was once beloved of God. Even Satan must have felt remorse at the pain he caused. He would never be accepted back into the fold, but he might use his powers to repair some of the pain he caused. Only he wouldn't be able to do it alone, for each time he touched the earth he would cause another death. What better to do, then, but to give healing power to a child, who would learn and grow into the role?

Kincaid's hands were still shaking. The blood had crusted beneath his fingernails.

'I never asked for this!' he shouted, and people didn't even turn as they passed on the street. Shouting crazies were common in Hollywood. He held his hands to the sky. 'I never asked for this!'

Above him angels flew like eagles, soaring and dipping and diving, never coming close enough to endanger the Earth. Their featureless faces radiated a kind of joy. And, although he would never admit it, he felt that joy too.

Although he would not slay the dragon, he wouldn't have to live with its carnage either. Finally, at last, he could make some kind of difference. He let his hands fall to his sides and wondered if the Roosevelt would shirk at letting him wash the blood off inside. He was about to ask when a stray dog pushed its muzzle against his thigh.

'Ah, hell,' he said, looking down and recognizing the mottled fur, the wary yet trusting eyes. He glanced up, saw one angel hovering. A gift, then, for finally understanding. He touched the dog on the back of its neck and led it to the Olds. The dog jumped inside as if it knew the car. Kincaid sat for a moment, resting his shaking hands against the steering column.

A hooker knocked on the window. He thought he could smell the sweat and perfume through the rolled-up glass. Her cleavage was mottled, her cheap elastic top revealing the top edge of brown nipple.

He shook his head, then turned the ignition and grabbed the gear shift on the column to take the car out of park. The dog barked once, and he grinned at it before driving home to get his things. This time he wouldn't try Big Bear. This time he would go wherever the spirit led him.

House Call

CHRISTOPHER EVANS

The minicab drew up at the kerb, and Alan climbed out. He fumbled in his pockets, found a note and passed it through the window to the driver. Rain fell from the night sky as he stood there blearily, waiting for his change and wondering whether he'd given the man a fiver or a tenner. The clock on the dashboard said 11:25. It was New Year's Eve.

'Keep the change,' he said to the driver in a sudden access of seasonal spirit. 'Keep it.'

He lurched away towards his front gate. A gust of wind loosed a spray of droplets from the telephone wire above, and they cascaded down on him. Alan didn't care. It was a filthy night, the old year going out with a fury. The minicab pulled off and diminished into the night.

Up the path to his front door. His keys – where were his keys? Eventually he located them in the inside pocket of his overcoat. With the sedulous application of someone who knows himself to be drunk, he fitted the Chubb into the lock and turned it. Then the Yale. It was a palaver, but they'd been burgled three times in the last two years.

They. Him and Louise.

The hallway was cold and dark. The whole house felt unlived-in. Always did these days. Without switching on the light he went through into the kitchen. He took the bread knife from the drawer. Laid it across his bare wrist.

'Please don't do that,' a voice said conversationally.

He jumped, nicking himself and dropping the knife. The voice – a woman's – had come from the front room, through the open door.

Cautiously he moved to the doorway. The room was lit only by the sodium street lamp outside. He put a hand around the doorjamb, found the switch, flicked it on.

She was sitting in the armchair by the window, smart and businesslike in a navy-blue skirt with a matching jacket over a white blouse. About the same age as himself, thirty-fivish, with cropped fair hair and a purposeful look. Legs crossed, arms folded in her lap.

'Good evening,' she said with a smile.

'Who are you?'

'There's no need to be alarmed, Mr Prentice.'

'What are you doing in my house? How did you get in here?'

She rose slowly, still smiling, tights swishing as she uncrossed her legs. Alan involuntarily took a step back.

'Please don't worry. I didn't break any windows or force any locks. Why don't you take your coat off? It's a terrible night, and you must be soaked.'

He held his ground in the doorway. 'Stay where you are. I want to know how you got in here.'

'Can I first confirm that I'm in the right place? This is 143 Woodward Avenue, and you are Alan Paul Prentice?'

She was holding an electronic organizer like the one his boss carried at the office.

'What is this? Are you selling something?'

'Hardly. It's New Year's Eve. I'm here to help you. By the way, you're bleeding.'

There was the tiniest of cuts on his wrist. He grabbed the kitchen towel roll, tore off a strip and put it to the nick on his wrist, all without taking his eyes off her. He wondered if she had any accomplices lurking elsewhere. She looked perfectly composed, more like an executive than an intruder. There was no obvious sign of anyone else, but then he wasn't exactly at the peak of alertness. He'd drunk too much too quickly at Tom's and Erica's party.

'What's going on?' he said. 'How did you get in here?'

She closed her organizer and smiled at him. 'I think perhaps you should sit down. You look rather unsteady on your feet.'

He advanced into the room. 'If you don't tell me who you are and how you got in here, I'm going to phone the police.'

She didn't look perturbed. 'There's no need for that. I'm your Spiritual Actualizer.'

'What?'

She repeated it.

'Is this some kind of joke? Did Tom and Erica put you up to it?'

'This is no joke, Mr Prentice, no joke at all. Do you mind if I smoke?' She produced a silver cigarette case. 'I've been sent here to help you with your problems, to make your wishes come true. You get three, by the way. There are certain provisos and restrictions, but otherwise you can have whatever you want. Just ask and I'll deliver.'

She sounded quite serious, looked quite sane. She put a gold lighter to her cigarette.

'I'm phoning the police,' he said, snatching the receiver from its cradle.

'Your phone won't work, Mr Prentice. See? Don't worry. It's not broken, just temporarily incapacitated.'

The line was totally dead, as if the wires had been cut. He slammed it down.

'What the hell is this? Who are you?'

'I've told you who I am. I'm your Spiritual Actualizer.'

'Stay there.'

He darted into the living room, checked the hallway again, peering up the stairs.

'There's no one else in the house, Mr Prentice,' he heard her say.

'You think I'm going to take your word for that?'

She came into the hall, still looking quite unruffled.

He took her by the wrist. 'Better still, you come with me.'

She did not struggle as he led her up the stairs. Even her protests were weary: 'This really is a waste of time, you know. Please let go of my wrist. If I didn't want you to find me here, would I have sat there in the middle of your lounge? Don't forget to check the bathroom and the wardrobes.'

There was nothing in either of the two bedrooms, nothing under the beds. The bathroom was empty. The wardrobes held only clothes.

'Do you have an ashtray somewhere?' she asked.

'This isn't a joke.'

'I'm perfectly well aware of that, Mr Prentice. Do you mind if I call you Alan?'

They were on the landing. Alan was at a loss. He released his grip on her wrist. She smelt of expensive perfume – far too expensive for a burglar or a con-artist.

'Shall we go back downstairs?' she suggested. Now it was she who took his wrist.

'I could make a citizen's arrest, you know. You're trespassing.'

He let her lead him down the stairs. 'You're a little drunk for that, don't you think? Oops. Now look what I've done. Ash on your stair carpet.'

She brushed it in with the toe of her shoe. Alan paused to take off his overcoat and hang it up. Then he followed her through into the lounge.

'There's an ashtray on the mantelpiece,' he told her. 'The one that looks like a lump of coal.'

He flopped on the sofa while she crushed out the cigarette. The cut on his wrist had already stopped bleeding. In fact, he couldn't even see it any more.

'Now,' she said, 'shall we proceed immediately to a demonstration?'

'A demonstration?'

'Make a wish. Any wish. I'll tell you if it's allowed by our codes of practice. If it is, then I'll make it come true. As if by magic.'

'Do you think I'm a fool?'

'Not at all. If my information is correct, you have a degree in biochemistry and are presently working on developing a better kind of mouthwash.'

'Who sent you here? Was it someone from Personnel?'

'I have nothing to do with your employers, Alan. I am, as I've said three times already, your Spiritual Actualizer.'

'You can grant wishes.'

'That's correct.'

'Like an angel. A fairy godmother.'

A small frown creased her elegant features. 'We don't use that term any more because of its storybook connotations. But my function is the same. I can do what you

60

would think of as magic. I can make your deepest desires real. Of course I don't expect you to believe me. But I would ask you to suspend your disbelief for a few moments and make a wish.'

She sounded so patient, so reasonable.

He sighed. 'This is ridiculous.'

'Humour me. You've nothing to lose.'

'Is this one of those *Candid Camera*-type set-ups?'

'There are no hidden cameras, Alan, just you and me. I really would appreciate it if you'd allow me to demonstrate my capabilities. My time here is limited. Think of something you really want, something you would be truly amazed to find you suddenly have.'

'And you'll arrange it?'

She nodded. 'I'll make it happen.'

'I want a Rolls-Royce parked outside my front gate.'

'Very well. Would you like to go over to the window and look out?'

She hadn't moved; she was still standing in front of the fireplace. For the hell of it, Alan heaved himself off the sofa and went over to the window.

The Rolls was white, rain beading its pristine paintwork under the street lamp beyond the privet hedge.

'It's a Corniche,' she was saying. 'Brand-new, of course. I chose a white one so it would be easier to see in the dark.'

He looked at her, then back at the car, then back at her again. She was smiling, not smugly but with the smile of the vindicated.

'I know what you're thinking,' she told him. 'Perhaps I have an accomplice near by who's just driven up in the car. It could be an incredible coincidence, or there could be some other rational explanation. Perhaps you're dreaming, perhaps you mentioned your fantasy to a friend and forgot about it, perhaps you talked in your sleep and someone overheard, perhaps you're drunker than you think.'

'Louise told you I've always dreamed of having one.'

'I've never met your wife, Alan, though I don't expect you to believe me. Why don't you go outside and examine the car? You'll find the doors open and the keys in the ignition. It has a full tank of petrol and zero mileage on the clock. No? You surprise me.'

There was no one in the car as far as he could see. He hadn't heard it drive up.

'It has to be a trick.'

'Yes, well. I think it would be wiser if we went on immediately to your second wish. To convince yourself it wasn't a fluke.'

He was ready for her. 'I want a million pounds. In cash. Right here in front of me.'

And there it was. No flashing lights or puffs of smoke. Just an open attaché case, crammed full of notes.

'I've thrown in the case for free,' she said as he fell to his knees in front of it. 'It's more traditional that way, I think, don't you?'

He took out a bundle. They were all £100 notes. He held one up to the light. It looked genuine, watermark and all.

'Christ Almighty.'

'I did advise you to sit down earlier. Would you like a drink?'

He was flicking through the bundle. 'I'll have a vodka and tonic.'

'Coffee would be more advisable, don't you think? You over-indulged at the party. There, it's on the table beside you.'

And it was. Hot and black, in his favourite green china cup. He could smell it.

'Two sugars, I believe,' she said. She couldn't resist a certain smugness to her tone now. 'It's free, by the way, in case you were wondering. We always provide refreshment when necessary.'

She sat down in the armchair again and lit another cigarette, balancing the ashtray on the arm of the chair.

'Let me assure you you're not going mad,' she told him. 'I know you've been under strain lately and that the party was particularly traumatic. But this is real. I'm here to help you.'

'All this money. I'm rich.'

'But it doesn't make you happy, does it? Sometimes clichés are woefully accurate.'

He got up, still holding a bundle of notes. 'What's the catch?'

'The catch? Do you mean, what do you have to give me in return? Nothing. There are absolutely no strings attached. Again, I don't expect you to believe me. But it's true. Your three wishes are *gifts*. They don't have to be paid for.'

He sniffed the wad, sat down, laying it on his lap, putting both hands over it. She was waiting for him to say something.

'I don't believe any of this.'

She waited.

'Why me? Why me of all the people in the world?'

'Quite simply, you were chosen at random.'

'What do you mean?'

'As you can imagine, millions of people all over the world need our help, and there are only a limited number of us. Our selection method is weighted towards the poor and victims of disaster, which is only fair, I think you'd agree. But we do try to help people with severe problems of all kinds, be they physical or emotional. You desperately need help, don't you, Alan?'

Her words prompted a sudden urge to cry. He quashed it. 'What are you talking about?'

'Denial is a typical response, perfectly natural in the circumstances. Six months ago your wife, Louise, walked out on you. There was no third party involved, despite your suspicions – she simply didn't want to live with you any longer. You'd been together for nearly ten years, and you were devastated. You've been coping, doing your job as usual and muddling through, and just lately you thought you were coming to terms with the fact that the separation was permanent. You even decided to go to Tom's and Erica's New Year's Eve party tonight – the first time you've socialized with mutual friends since the separation. You arrived early, began drinking, chatting, and you started to enjoy yourself. Then Louise walked in – with another man. All the hurt, the betrayal, the desolation, came back in full force, and you couldn't bear to look at them talking and laughing together. You saw red, didn't you?'

Tears were running down his cheeks. He nodded.

'So you lurched across the room and hit him, the other man.'

'It was more of a push.'

'You knocked over a whole table of drinks. There was a fuss. You stormed out. You walked through the rain until you found a cab.'

Louise's new man was apparently called Bill. That was all he knew about him, apart from the fact that he looked handsome and sturdy, the outdoors type. That alone had made Alan want to punch his face in.

'The bastard.'

'Louise only met him a fortnight ago, if that's any consolation. No, I don't suppose it is. There's no need to be embarrassed – I've seen men cry before. You came home feeling suicidal, didn't you? Love is a terrifying thing, Alan. Here, have a tissue.'

She had come over, perched herself on the arm of the chair and put an arm around his shoulder. Now she was offering him a box of tissues. Pink tissues. He pulled a few out and blew his nose.

'The question is – what are we going to do about it? I'm offering you a once-in-a-lifetime opportunity to transform your life totally, to change everything for the better.'

He looked up. 'I want her back.'

'I'm sure you do. And in the past that could have been arranged, in the twinkling of an eye. Louise completely in love with you, to the end of her days. Happily ever after. But unfortunately it's no longer possible. We now frown on directly manipulating the lives of third parties in order to satisfy our clients' wishes.'

'What are you saying? You can't do it?'

'Not *can't* but rather *won't*. We've never been allowed to kill, and now we're also required to respect the integrity of the individual and do nothing to infringe their freedom of choice and right to self-fulfilment provided they harm no one else. It's a reflection of the times.'

Alan turned the words over in his head. She sounded as if she was reciting from a manual. He found it hard to think clearly; he was still fuddled with drink.

'Just who are these "we"? Is it an organization? An Angels' Union? The Sisters of Mercy? The Fraternity of Fairy Godmothers?'

She was not amused.

'I'd prefer it if you used our modern title. I'm afraid that answering those questions would constitute your third wish, which would be a complete waste, don't you think? Suffice it to say that we're relatively few in number and quite overworked. As you're doubtless aware, the world is not a happy place.'

He went over to the window again. The Rolls was still there, solid and superior under the dismal suburban night. He was still clutching the bundle of notes, and the rest was still in the case on the floor. All his.

'I still don't believe this.'

She lit another cigarette. 'You do now. Deep down, you're convinced. The car and the money are quite real, aren't they? That's why we have three wishes, incidentally – the first as demonstration, the second as affirmation and the third as gratification. Three hierarchies of credulity, if you like. That's the theory, at least. Of course, many of our clients continue to make a hash of it. Wealth, power, sex – that's what most want. Or think they want. By the way, don't ask me to solve all the world's problems at a stroke. I don't have enough "magic", as it were, for that. None of us does. We can only deal with individuals.'

'You shouldn't smoke. It's bad for you.'

'Not for me it isn't. I don't want to rush you, but I really would appreciate a decision on your third wish. I have several more calls to make tonight, and already I'm late. In the old days, people took our appearance pretty much for granted and got their wishes over in a trice. Now we have to spend a lot of time on preliminaries, on actually convincing people we can do the job.'

He was doing his sluggish best to consider the implications of what she was, what she could do.

'It doesn't make sense,' he said.

'What doesn't?'

'If you're going around making people suddenly rich or famous or whatever, then others would get suspicious. Or the people themselves would talk. Word would get around.'

She blew a perfect smoke ring.

'I really shouldn't be telling you this, but they can't. We do allow them to remember what's happened, but they're painlessly rendered incapable of communicating about it. As for the rest of the world, it simply adjusts itself around the changes without knowing they've happened. That's another aspect of our "magic".'

'Wait a minute. How does that fit in with respecting other people's integrity? I mean, you must make them forget things.'

'We try to minimize enforced changes, but some are inevitable. No system is perfect where human beings are concerned. It was much worse in the old days, of course, when people could have practically anything they wanted. They could take over other people's lives or swap existences with them. For example, Queen Victoria was actually Letty Devine, a "photographer's model" from Stepney. They swapped places in 1840 after one of my visits.'

'You're kidding? Wait a minute, photography wasn't invented then, was it?'

'In olden times the changes were even more radical. Until the fifteenth century Atlantis really existed. Several colleagues of mine were forced to move the entire population to Ibiza because a Sicilian trader bore a grudge. The Golden Horde was the whim of a disgruntled Russian peasant, and America was the creation of a Welsh clerk named ap Meryk who wanted a continent named after himself. That was our biggest job. Vampires used to be commonplace before a saintly Transylvanian nun had them turned into vegetarians three hundred years ago. And those are just a few examples close to home.'

'You're having me on.'

'Why would I want to do that? But please don't ask me to tell you any more. I've already said too much.' She stubbed out the half-smoked cigarette. 'Have you decided on your final wish? If you want my advice, settle for happiness or contentment. By definition, they never fail to satisfy.'

'No.'

'Why not?'

'Don't you see? If you *made* me happy, it would be like having a lobotomy. Like surrendering control of my life.'

She looked incredulous. 'Do you think I'd turn you into some sort of grinning cabbage? I'd simply be facilitating what *you* want.' She sighed. 'People these days have some strange ideas about free will.'

'If I can't have Louise back, there's nothing I want.'

'I don't believe you really mean that.'

'Yes, I do. I wish I was dead.'

She opened her mouth to say something, then seemed to reconsider. 'I assume you're speaking rhetorically.'

'No. I mean it.'

'I've already explained that our code of practice doesn't permit murder. Or even a kind of suicide by proxy.'

Did he mean it? Or was he just currying sympathy? No. He had the money, he had the car, but it all seemed worthless without Louise. At that moment he hated her for being so important to him, for ruining his life.

'You don't have to kill me,' he said. 'Just arrange it so I've never existed.'

She shook her head. 'It would amount to the same thing. It's out of the question. You do realize you're depressed, not thinking clearly?'

He realized he was slouching against the window, cheek pressed to the glass. He raised himself upright and tried to muster a little dignity.

'I think I'm the best judge of that,' he said loftily.

'Think of it in strict biochemical terms, if you prefer. Your brain is generating neurochemicals that are making you look on the black side. They're warping your powers of judgement.'

'That's a moot point, isn't it? On the same basis, even if I wasn't depressed, my perceptions would still be the product of a different assortment of neurochemicals.'

'Exactly. And you talk to me about free will! It's the thorniest subject you can think of, especially in my line of work.'

He really was in no fit condition to debate the meaning of existence with her. He allowed a less elevated feeling of self-pity to swamp him.

'Nothing in life matters to me any more,' he said, knowing even as he spoke that he was mouthing a cliché, that his life had finally descended to the level of a bad scene in a soap opera. And, like a character in a soap opera, he was trapped in the role: 'I'd be happy to end it now.'

She shook her head brusquely. 'You're an intelligent man, Alan, and you mustn't waste this opportunity on something as negative as suicide. In any case, it isn't an option, as I've already explained.' Her tone was almost curt, but now it softened: 'If you won't help yourself, then what about helping others?'

'How do you mean?'

'Well, I hesitate to mention it, but you have the right sort of qualifications, and I think you'd show a healthy interest in our work . . .'

'What are you saying?'

'Well, we're always looking for new helpers. New Actualizers. Don't look so shocked. I had an important job in Renaissance Rome when I got my chance, though you wouldn't think it to look at me now. At the time I thought Satan himself had come to take me to Hell. It would be much easier for you, I can assure you. If you'd like to join us, it could be arranged in an instant. Simply make it your final wish. You'd feel no different to begin with, but you'd gain access to all our professional secrets and powers.'

Rain lashed the window pane. Outside, a bedraggled dog was cocking its leg against the rear wheel of the Rolls.

'Are you serious?'

'Perfectly. You'd be my helper for a while, travelling around with me on my calls, learning the ropes, as it were. I cover Western Europe, with a Polynesian inter-lude every January for variety. I'm due there next. It's tremendously rewarding. We save a lot of people who are absolutely desperate. Every visit makes the world a happier place in some small way.'

Or take the money. A million pounds and the Rolls. Enough to last him the rest of his life. However long that might be.

'Assuming I went with you. What would happen? About my life here?'

'We could arrange it whatever way you wished. Leave your body here, lying on the carpet. No, don't be alarmed. You'd still be alive, with me, in the same physical form as before. Think of the advantages. You'd be immortal, for a start. You'd be able to understand and speak any language or dialect in the world. You'd be able to travel anywhere in an instant and do "magic".'

He thought about it. 'I'm not sure.'

'You could leave a suicide note behind if you liked.'

This appealed to him. A suicide note to make Louise feel guilty.

'Would I remember my life here?'

'Of course. A proper sense of identity is crucial. You'll remember everything, even your bitterness about Louise. But that will fade eventually. Our work is the perfect antidote, in the long term, for all personal problems. It broadens your perspectives beyond all imagining.'

'Could you arrange for her to find the body?'

'Louise?'

'She just waltzed out and left me heartbroken. I owe her one.'

She frowned. 'It isn't . . . Well, I suppose I could bend the rules just this once, as a personal favour to you. There, how about that?'

The case of money was gone from the carpet, and in its place lay a body. His body. Both wrists had been slashed, one arm draped artistically across the chest, the other stretched out, clutching a scrap of paper. There was blood everywhere. The face was deathly white, frozen in a final expression of dignified despair.

'God,' Alan said admiringly, 'that's gross. I look terrible.'

'See the note clutched in the right hand? It says: *Louise, I did it for you.*'

'Oh, that's good. Is it in my hand-writing?'

'Of course. I wouldn't neglect a significant detail like that. The pen's on the coffee table. It's the Sheaffer she gave you for your thirtieth birthday.'

He was impressed, even though the sight of himself made him feel queasy. Then he had second thoughts.

'Wouldn't it make her feel terribly guilty?'

'I'm pleased you thought of that. I've arranged it so it will only last twenty-four hours. Then she, and everyone else, will forget the note.'

It seemed a sensible compromise, though perhaps twenty-four hours was a little short. A year might have been better. But he didn't want to quibble.

'You're good at this, aren't you?'

'I've had centuries of practice. Louise is already on her way over, in case you're interested.'

He was, indeed he was.

'Can we stay and watch?' he said eagerly.

'That would be rather ghoulish, don't you think?'

He didn't like to admit that he wanted to see and hear her scream.

'She might just throw up, you know, or rush straight back out again. Or she might be very composed and businesslike. You rarely get the reaction you expect, especially with a grisly death.'

Obviously she was experienced at this sort of thing. He wondered if perhaps he was too mean-spirited for it.

'You said you had an important job in Rome.'

She was checking her organizer, her next appointment. Alan thought he glimpsed the word Tahiti on the screen.

'Yes, I was a man then, and in those days all Actualizers had to be female, so I made the change.'

'A man?'

'Actually, I was the Pope. It took quite a while to

adjust, I can tell you. But we're equal-opportunity employers now – you'd stay the same sex. Unless, of course, you wanted a change.'

'You're having me on.'

Her eyes twinkled in the dim green light from the screen. 'There's only one way to find out. What do you say?'

Really, she was quite attractive. That would be another bonus.

'All right, I'll do it.'

'Wonderful. Just take hold of my hands.'

Her hands felt cool in his. His palms were sweating.

'I'm scared.'

'There's no need to be. In the blink of an eye, we'll be somewhere else and you'll have the same powers as me. Just let me do all the talking. You'll soon see how it's done.'

'No flashing lights or puffs of smoke?'

She gave him a wink. 'We're more subtle than that these days.'

The clock on the mantelpiece started chiming.

'Happy New Year,' he said.

'Out with the old and in with the new. Close your eyes.'

He did so. 'I don't even know your name.'

'I'll answer to anything. But you can call me Lucy.'

He felt a rush of hot air and wondered if it was Tahiti. Then they were gone, and there was only his corpse on the floor. It seemed to be grinning.

The Big Sky

CHARLES DE LINT

> We need Death to be a friend. It is best to
> have a friend as a traveling companion when
> you have so far to go together.
>
> *Attributed to Jean Cocteau*

I

She was sitting in John's living room when he got home
from the recording studio that night, comfortably en-
sconced on the sofa, legs stretched out, ankles crossed, a
book propped open on her lap which she was pretending
to read. The fact that all the lights in the house had been
off until he turned them on didn't seem to faze her in
the least. She continued her pretense, as though she
could see equally well in the light or dark and it made
no difference to her whether the lights were on or off.
At least she had the book turned right-side up, John
noted.

'How did you get in?' he asked her.

She didn't seem to present any sort of a threat —
beyond having gotten into his locked house, of course —
so he was more concerned with how she'd been able to
enter than with his own personal safety. At the sound of
his voice, she looked up in surprise. She laid the book
down on her lap, finger inserted between the pages to
hold her place.

'You can see me?' she said.

'Jesus.'

John shook his head. She certainly wasn't shy. He set his fiddlecase down by the door. Dropping his jacket down on top of it, he went into the living room and sat down in the chair across the coffee table from her.

'What do you think?' he went on. 'Of course I can see you.'

'But you're not supposed to be able to see me – unless it's time, and that doesn't seem right. I mean, really. I'd know, if anybody, whether or not it was time.'

She frowned, gaze fixed on him, but she didn't really appear to be studying him. It was more as though she was looking into some unimaginably far and unseen distance. Her eyes focused suddenly and he shifted uncomfortably under the weight of her attention.

'Oh, I see what happened,' she said. 'I'm so sorry.'

John leaned forward, resting his hands on his knees. 'Let's try this again. Who are you?'

'I'm your watcher. Everybody has one.'

'My watcher.'

She nodded. 'We watch over you until your time has come, then if you can't find your own way, we take you on. They call us the little deaths, but I've never much cared for the sound of that, do you?'

John sighed. He settled back in his chair to study his unwanted guest. She was no one he knew, though she could easily have fit in with his crowd. He put her at about twenty-something, a slender five-two, pixie features made more fey by the crop of short blonde hair that stuck up from her head with all the unruliness of a badly mowed lawn. She wore black combat boots; khaki trousers, baggy, with two or three pockets running up either leg; a white T-shirt that hugged her thin chest like a second skin. She had little in the way of jewelry – a small silver ring in her left nostril and another in the lobe of her left ear – and no make-up.

'Do you have a name?' he tried.

'Everybody's got a name.'

John waited a few heartbeats. 'And yours is?' he asked when no reply was forthcoming.

'I don't think I should tell you.'

'Why not?'

'Well, once you give someone your name, it's like opening the door to all sorts of possibilities, isn't it? Any sort of relationship could develop from that, and it's just not a good idea for us to have an intimate relationship with our charges.'

'I can assure you,' John told her, 'we're in no danger of having a relationship – intimate or otherwise.'

'Oh,' she said. She didn't look disappointed so much as annoyed. 'Dakota,' she added.

'I'm sorry?'

'You wanted to know my name.'

John nodded. 'That's right. I – oh, I get it. Your name's Dakota?'

'Bingo.'

'And you've been . . . watching me?'

'Well, not just you. Except for when we're starting out, we look out after any number of people.'

'I see,' John said. 'And how many people do you watch?'

She shrugged. 'Oh, dozens.'

That figured, John thought. It was the story of his life. He couldn't even get the undivided attention of a loonie.

She swung her boots to the floor and set the book she was holding on the coffee table between them.

'Well, I guess we should get going,' she said.

She stood up and gave him an expectant look, but John remained where he was sitting.

'It's a long way to the gates,' she told him.

He didn't have a clue as to what she was talking about, but he was sure of one thing.

'I'm not going anywhere with you,' he said.

'But you have to.'

'Says who?'

She frowned at him. 'You just do. It's obvious that you won't be able to find your way by yourself, and if you stay here, you're just going to start feeling more and more alienated and confused.'

'Let me worry about that,' John said.

'Look,' she said. 'We've gotten off on the wrong foot – my fault, I'm sure. I had no idea it was time for you to go already. I'd just come by to check on you before heading off to another appointment.'

'Somebody else that you're *watching*?'

'Exactly,' she replied, missing or, more probably, ignoring the sarcastic tone of his voice. 'There's no way around this, you know. You need my help to get to the gates.'

'What gates?'

She sighed. 'You're really in denial about all of this, aren't you?'

'You were right about one thing,' John told her. 'I am feeling confused – but it's only about what you're doing here and how you got in.'

'I don't have time for this.'

'Me neither. So maybe you should go.'

That earned him another frown.

'Fine,' she said. 'But don't wait too long to call me. If you change too much, I won't be able to find you and nobody else can help you.'

'Because you're my personal watcher.'

'No wonder you don't have many friends,' she said. 'You're really not a very nice person, are you?'

'I'm only like this with people who break into my house.'

'But I didn't – oh, never mind. Just remember my name and don't wait too long to call me.'

'Not that I'd want to,' John said, 'but I don't even have your number.'

'Just call my name and I'll come,' she said. 'If it's not too late. Like I said, I might not be able to recognize you if you wait too long.'

Though he was trying to take this all in his stride, John couldn't help but start to feel a little creeped out at the way she was going on. He'd never realized that crazy people could seem so normal – except for what they were saying, of course.

'Goodbye,' he said.

She bit back whatever it was that she was going to say and gave him a brusque nod. For one moment, he half-expected her to walk through a wall – the evening had taken that strange a turn – but she merely crossed the living room and let herself out of the front door. John waited for a few moments, then rose and set the deadbolt. He walked through the house, checking the windows and back door before finally going upstairs to his bedroom.

He thought he might have trouble getting to sleep – the woman's presence had raised far more questions than it had answered – but he was so tired from twelve straight hours in the studio that it was more a question of could he get all his clothes off and crawl under the blankets before he faded right out? He had one strange moment: when he turned off the light, he made the mistake of looking directly at the bulb. His uninvited guest's features hung in the darkness along with a hundred dancing spots of light before he was able to blink them away. But the moment didn't last long and he was soon asleep.

2

He didn't realize that he'd forgotten to set his alarm last night until he woke up and gave the clock a bleary look. Eleven fifteen. Christ, he was late.

He got up, shaved and took a quick shower. You'd think someone would have called him from the studio, he thought as he started to get dressed. He was doing session work on Darlene Flatt's first album, and the recording had turned into a race to get the album finished before her money ran out. He had two solos up first thing this morning, and he couldn't understand why no one had called to see where he was.

There was no time for breakfast — he didn't have much of an appetite at the moment anyway. He'd grab a coffee and a bagel at the deli around the corner from the studio. Tugging on his jeans, he carried his boots out into the living room and phoned the studio while he put them on. All he got was ringing at the other end.

'Come on,' he muttered. 'Somebody pick it up.'

How could there be nobody there to answer?

It was as he was cradling the receiver that he saw the book lying on the coffee table, reminding him of last night's strange encounter. He picked the book up and looked at it, turning it over in his hands. There was something different about it this morning. Something wrong. And then he realized what it was. The coloured

dust wrapper had gone monochrome. The book and . . .
His gaze settled on his hand and he dropped the book in
shock. He stared at his hand, turning it front to back,
then looked wildly around the living room.

Oh, Jesus. Everything was black and white.

He'd been so bleary when he woke up that he hadn't
noticed that the world had gone monochrome on him
overnight. He'd had a vague impression of gloominess
when he got up, but he hadn't really thought about it.
He'd simply put it down to it being a particularly
overcast day. But this . . . this . . .

It was impossible.

His gaze was drawn to the window. The light coming
in was devoid of colour where it touched his furniture
and walls, but outside . . . He walked slowly to the
window and stared at his lawn, the street beyond it, the
houses across the way. Everything was the way it was
supposed to be. The day was cloudless, the colours so
vivid, the sunlight so bright it hurt his eyes. The richness
of all that colour and light burned his retinas.

He stood there until tears formed in his eyes and he
had to turn away. He covered his eyes with his hands
until the pain faded. When he took his palms away, his
hands were still leached of colour. The living room was
a thousand monochrome shades of black and white.
Numbly, he walked to his front door and flung it open.
The blast of colour overloaded the sensory membranes
of his eyes. He knelt down where he'd tossed his jacket
last night and scrabbled about in its pockets until he
found a pair of shades.

The sunglasses helped when he turned back to the
open door. It still hurt to look at all that colour, but the
pain was much less than it had been. He shuffled out on
to his porch, down the steps. He looked at what he

could see of himself. Hands and arms. His legs. All monochrome. He was like a black and white cut-out that someone had stuck on to a coloured background.

I'm dreaming, he thought.

He could feel the start of a panic attack. It was like the slight nervousness that sometimes came when he stepped on stage – the kind that came when he was backing up someone he'd never played with before, only increased a hundredfold. Sweat beaded on his temples and under his arms. It made his shirt clammy and stick to his back. His hands began to shake so much that he had to hug himself to make them stop.

He was dreaming, or he'd gone insane.

Movement caught his eye down the street, and he recognized one of his neighbours. He stumbled in the man's direction.

'Bob!' he called. 'Bob, you've got to help me.'

The man never even looked in his direction. John stepped directly in front of him on the sidewalk and Bob walked right into him, knocking him down. But Bob hadn't felt a thing, John realized. Hadn't seen him, hadn't felt the impact, was just walking on down the street as if John had simply ceased to exist for him.

John fled back into the house. He slammed the door, locked it. He pulled the curtains in the living room and started to pace, from the fireplace to the hallway, back again, back and forth, back and forth. At one point he caught sight of the book he'd dropped earlier. Slowly, he walked over to where it lay and picked it up. He remembered last night's visitor again. Her voice returned to him.

If you change too much . . .

This was all her fault, he thought.

He threw the book down and shouted her name.

'Yes?'

Her voice came from directly behind him and he started violently.

'Jesus,' he said. 'You could've given me a heart attack.'

'It's a little late for that.'

She was wearing the same clothes she'd worn last night except today there was a leather bomber's jacket on over her T-shirt and she wore a hat that was something like a derby except the brim was wider. There was one other difference. Like himself, like the rest of his house, she'd been leached of all colour.

'What did you do to me?' he demanded.

She reached out and took his hand to lead him over to the sofa. He tried to pull free from her grip, but she was stronger than she looked.

'Sit down,' she said. 'And I'll try to explain.'

Her voice was soothing and calm, the way one would talk to an upset child – or a madman. John was feeling a little bit like both at the moment, helpless as a child and out of his mind. But the lulling quality of her voice and the gentle manner of her touch helped still the wild drumming of his pulse.

'Look,' he said, 'I don't know what you've done to me – I don't know how you've done this to me or why – but I just want to get back to normal, OK? If I made you mad last night, I'm sorry, but you've got to understand. It was pretty weird to find you in my house the way I did.'

'I know,' she said. 'I didn't realize you could see me, or I would have handled it differently myself. But you took me by surprise.'

'I took *you* by surprise?'

'What do you remember of last night?' she asked.

'I came home and found you in my living room.'

'No, before that.'

'I was at High Lonesome Sounds – working on Darlene's album.'

She nodded. 'And what happened between when you left the studio and came home?'

'I . . . I don't remember.'

'You were hit by a car,' she said. 'A drunk driver.'

'No way,' John said, shaking his head. 'I'd remember something like that.'

She took his hand. 'You died instantly, John Narraway.'

'I . . . I . . .'

He didn't want to believe her, but her words settled inside him with a finality that could only be the truth.

'It's not something that anyone could have foreseen,' she went on. 'You were supposed to live a lot longer – that's why I was so surprised that you could see me. It's never happened to me like that before.'

John had stopped listening to her after she'd said, 'You were supposed to live a lot longer.' He clung to that phrase, hope rushing through him.

'So it was a mistake,' he said.

Dakota nodded.

'So what happens now?' he asked.

'I'll take you to the gates.'

'No, wait a minute. You just said it was a mistake. Can't you go back to whoever's in charge and explain that?'

'If there's anyone in charge,' she said, 'I've never met or heard of them.'

'But –'

'I understand your confusion and your fear. Really I

do. It comes from the suddenness of your death and my not being there to help you adjust. That's the whole reason I exist – to help people like you who are unwilling or too confused to go on by themselves. I wasn't ready to go myself when my time came.'

'Well, I'm not ready either.'

Dakota shook her head. 'It's not the same thing. I wasn't ready to go because when I saw how much some people need help to reach the gates, I knew I had to stay and help them. It was like a calling. You just aren't willing to accept what happened to you.'

'Well, Christ. Who would?'

'Most people. I've seen how their faces light up when they step through the gates. You can't imagine the joy in their eyes.'

'Have you been through yourself?' John asked.

'No. But I've had glimpses of what lies beyond. You know how sometimes the sky just seems to be so big it goes on for ever?'

John nodded.

'You stand there and look up,' she went on, 'and the stars seem so close you feel as though you could just reach up and touch them, but at the same time the sky itself is enormous and has no end. It's like that, except that you can feel your heart swelling inside you, big enough to fill the whole of that sky.'

'If what's waiting beyond these gates is so wonderful,' John wanted to know, 'why haven't you gone through?'

'One day I will. I think about it more and more all the time. But what I'm doing now is important and I'm needed. There are never enough of us.'

'Maybe I'll become a watcher instead – like you.'

'It's not something one takes on lightly,' Dakota said.

'You can't just stop when you get tired of doing it. You have to see through all of your responsibilities first, make sure that all of your charges have gone on, that none are left behind to fend for themselves. You share the joys of your charges, but you share their sorrows, too. And the whole time you know them, you're aware of their death. You watch them plan, you watch their lives and the tangle of their relationships grow more complex as they grow older, but the whole time you're aware of their end.'

'I could do that,' John said.

Dakota shook her head. 'You have always been sparing with your kindnesses. It's why your circle of friends is so small. You're not a bad person, John Narraway, but I don't think you have the generosity of spirit it requires to be a watcher.'

The calm certainty with which she delivered her judgement irritated John.

'How would you know?' he said.

She gave him a sad smile. 'Because I've been watching you ever since you were born.'

'What? Every second of my life?'

'No. That comes only at first. It takes time to read a soul, to unravel the tangle of possibilities and learn when the time of death is due. After that it's a matter of checking in from time to time to make sure that the assessment one made still holds true.'

John thought about the minutiae that made up the greater portion of everyone's life and slowly shook his head. And what if you picked a person who was really dull? Everybody had slow periods in their lives, but some people's whole lives were one numbed shuffle from birth to death. And since you knew the whole time when the person was going to die . . . God, it'd be like spending your whole life in a doctor's waiting room. Boring and depressing.

'You don't get tired of it?' he asked.

'Not tired. A little sad sometimes.'

'Because everybody's got to die.'

She shook her head. 'No, because I see so much unhappiness and there's nothing I can do about it. Most of my charges never see me – they make their own way to the gates and beyond. I'm just there as a kind of insurance for those who can't do it by themselves and I'm only with them for such a little while. I miss talking to people on a regular basis. Sometimes I see some of the other watchers, but we're all so busy.'

'It sounds horrible.'

She shrugged. 'I never think of it that way. I just think of those who need help and the looks on their faces when they step through the gates.' She fell silent for a moment, then gave him a smile. 'We should go now. I've got other commitments.'

'What if I refuse to go? What happens then?'

'No one can force you, if that's what you mean.'

John held up his hand. He looked around himself. OK, it was weird, but he could live with it, couldn't he? Anything'd be better than to be dead – even a half-life.

'I know what you're thinking,' she said. 'And, no, it's not because I'm reading your mind, because I can't.'

'So what's going to happen to me?'

'I take it you're already experiencing some discomfort?'

John nodded. 'I see everything in black and white – but only in the house. Outside, nothing's changed.'

'That will grow more pronounced,' she told him. 'Eventually you won't be able to see colour at all. You might lose the clarity of your vision as well so that everything will seem to be a blur. Your other senses will become less effective as well.'

'But —'

'And you won't be able to interact with the world you've left behind. In time, the only people you'll be able to see are others like yourself — those too wilful or disturbed to have gone on. They don't exactly make the best of companions, John Narraway, but then, by that point, you'll be so much like them, I don't suppose it will matter.'

'But what about all the stories of ghosts and hauntings and the like?'

'Do you have a particularly strong bond with a certain place or person?' she asked. 'Someone or something you couldn't possibly live without?'

John had to admit that he didn't, but he could tell that she already knew that.

'But I'll still be alive,' he said, knowing even as he said the words that they made no real sense.

'If you want to call it that.'

'Don't you miss life?'

Dakota shook her head. 'I only miss happiness. Or maybe I should say, I miss the idea of happiness because I never had it when I was alive.'

'What happened to you?' John wanted to know.

She gave him a long sad look. 'I'm sorry, John Narraway, but I have to go. I will listen for you. Call me when you change your mind. Just don't wait too long —'

'Or you won't be able to recognize me. I know. You already told me that.'

'Yes,' she said. 'I did.'

This time she didn't use the door. One moment she

was sitting with him on the sofa and the next she faded away like Carroll's Cheshire Cat except with her it was her eyes that lingered the longest, those sad dark eyes that told him he was making a mistake, those eyes to which he refused to listen.

3

He didn't move from the sofa after Dakota left. While the sunlight drifted across the living room, turning his surroundings into a series of shifting chiaroscuro images, he simply sat there, his mind empty more often than it was chasing thoughts. He was sure he hadn't been immobile for more than a few hours, but when he finally stood up and walked to the window, it was early morning, the sun just rising. He'd lost a whole night and a day. Maybe more. He still had no appetite, but now he doubted that he ever would again. He didn't seem to need sleep, either. But it scared him that he could lose such a big chunk of time like that.

He turned back to the living room and switched on the television set to make sure that he'd lost only the one day. All he got on the screen was snow. White noise hissed from the speaker grill. Fine, he thought, remembering how he'd been unable to put a call through to the recording studio yesterday morning. So now the TV wouldn't work for him. So he couldn't interact with the everyday mechanics of the world any more. Well, there were other ways to find out what he needed to know.

He picked up his fiddlecase out of habit, put on his jacket and left the house. He didn't need his shades once he got outside, but that was only because his whole street was now delineated in shades of black and white. He could see the colour start up at the far ends of the block on either side. The sky was overcast above him, but it blued the further away from his house it got.

This sucked, he thought. But not so much that he was ready to call Dakota back.

He started downtown, putting on his sunglasses once he left the monochromic zone immediately surrounding his house. Walking proved to be more of a chore than he'd anticipated. He couldn't relax his attention for a moment or someone would walk into him. He always felt the impact while they continued on their way, as unaware of the encounter as his neighbour Bob had been.

He stopped at the first newsstand he came upon and found the day's date. Wednesday, he read on the masthead of the *Newford Star*. November tenth. He'd only lost a day. A day of what, though? He could remember nothing of the experience. Maybe that was what sleep would be like for him in this state – simply turning himself off the way fiction described vampires at their rest. He had to laugh at the thought. The undead. *He* was one of the undead now, though he certainly had no craving for blood.

He stopped laughing abruptly, suddenly aware of the hysterical quality that had crept into the sound. It wasn't that funny. He pressed up close against a building to keep out of the way of passing pedestrians and tried to quell the panic he could feel welling up inside his chest. Christ, it wasn't funny at all.

After a while he felt calm enough to go on. He had no particular destination in mind, but when he realized he was in the general vicinity of High Lonesome Sounds, he decided to stop by the studio. He kept waiting for some shock of recognition at every corner he came to, something that would whisper, this is where you died. This is where the one part of your life ended and the new part began. But the street corners all looked the same and he arrived at the recording studio without sensing that one had ever had more importance in his life than the next.

He had no difficulty gaining entrance to the studio. At least doors still worked for him. He wondered what his use of them looked like to others, doors opening and closing, seemingly of their own accord. He climbed the stairs to the second-floor loft where the recording studio was situated and slipped into the control booth, where he found Darlene and Tom Norton listening to a rough mix of one of the cuts from Darlene's album. Norton owned the studio and often served as both producer and sound engineer to the artists using his facilities. He turned as John quietly closed the door behind him but he looked right through John.

'It still needs a lead break,' Norton said, returning his attention to Darlene.

'I know it does. But I don't want another fiddle. I want to leave John's backing tracks just as they are. It doesn't seem right to have somebody else play his break.'

Thank you, Darlene, John thought.

He'd known Darlene Flatt for years, played back-up with her on and off through the past decade and a half as she sang out her heart in far too many honky-tonks and bars. Her real name was Darlene Johnston, but by this point in her career everyone knew her by her stage name. Dolly Parton had always been her idol, and when Darlene stepped on stage with her platinum wig and over-the-top rhinestone outfits, the resemblance between the two was uncanny. But Darlene had a deeper voice, and now that she'd finally lost the wigs and stage gear, John thought she had a better shot at the big time. There was a long tradition of covering other people's material in country music, but nothing got tired more quickly than a tribute act so far as John was concerned.

She didn't look great today. There was a gaunt look about her features, hollows under her eyes. Someone mourned him, John realized.

'Why don't we have Greg play the break on his dobro?' Darlene said. She sounded so tired, as though all she wanted to do was get through this.

'That could work,' Norton said.

John stopped listening to them, his attention taken by the rough mix that was still playing in the control booth. It was terrible. All the instruments sounded tinny and flat, there was no bass to speak of, and Darlene's voice seemed to be mixed so far back you felt you had to lean forward to be able to hear it. He winced, listening to his own fiddle playing.

'You've got a lot more problems here than what instrument to use on the break,' he said.

But of course they couldn't hear him. So far as he could tell, they liked what they were hearing, which seemed particularly odd considering how long they'd both been in the business. What did they hear that he couldn't? But then he remembered what his mysterious visitor had told him. How his sight would continue to deteriorate. How . . .

Your other senses will become less effective as well.

John thought back to the walk from his house to the studio. He hadn't really been thinking of it at the time, but now that he did he realized that the normal sounds of the city had been muted. Everything. The traffic, the voices of passers-by, the construction site he'd passed a couple of blocks away from the studio. When he concentrated on Darlene's and Norton's conversation again, listening to the tonal quality of their voices rather than what they were saying, he heard a hollow echo that hadn't registered before.

He backed away from them and fumbled his way out into the sitting room on the other side of the door. There he took his fiddle out of his case. Tuning the instrument was horrible. Playing it was worse. There was nothing there any more. No resonance. No depth. Only the same hollow, echoing quality that he'd heard in Darlene's and Norton's voices.

Slowly he laid his fiddle back into its case, loosened the frog on his bow and set it down on top of the instrument. When he finally made his way back down the stairs and out into the street, he left the fiddle behind. Outside, the street seemed overcast, its colours not yet leached away but definitely faded. He looked up into a cloudless sky. He crossed the street and plucked a pretzel from the cart of a street vendor, took a bite even though he had no appetite. It tasted like sawdust and ashes. A bus pulled up at the kerb where he was standing, let out a clutch of passengers, then pulled away again, leaving behind a cloud of noxious fumes. He could barely smell them.

It's just a phase, he told himself. He was simply adjusting to his new existence. All he had to do was get through it and things would get back to normal. They couldn't stay like this.

He kept telling himself that as he made his way back home, but he wasn't sure he believed it. He was dead, after all – that was the part of the equation that was impossible to ignore. Dakota had warned him that this was going to happen. But he wasn't ready to believe her either. He just couldn't accept that the way things were for him now would be permanent.

4

He was right. Things didn't stay the same. They got worse. His senses continued to deteriorate. The familiar world faded away from around him until he found himself in a grey-toned city that he didn't always recognize. He stepped out of his house one day and couldn't find his way back. The air was oppressive, the sky seemed to press down on him. And there were no people. No living people. Only the other undead. They huddled in doorways and alleys, drifted through the empty buildings. They wouldn't look at him and he found himself turning his face away as well. They had nothing they could share with each other, only their despair, and of that they each had enough of their own.

He took to wandering aimlessly through the deserted streets, the high points of his day coming when he recognized the corner of a building, a stretch of street, that gargoyle peering down from an utterly unfamiliar building. He wasn't sure if he was in a different city, or if he was losing his memory of the one he knew. After a while it didn't seem to matter.

The blank periods came more and more often. Like the other undead, he would suddenly open his eyes to find himself curled up in a nest of newspapers and trash in some doorway or huddled in the rotting bulk of a sofa in an abandoned building. And finally he couldn't take it any more.

He stood in the middle of an empty street and lifted

his face to grey skies that only seemed to be kept aloft by the roofs of the buildings.

'Dakota!' he cried. 'Dakota!'

But he was far too late and she didn't come.

Don't wait too long to call me, she'd told him. *If you change too much, I won't be able to find you and nobody else can help you.*

He had no one to blame but himself. It was like she'd said. He'd changed too much and now, even if she could hear him, she wouldn't recognize him. He wasn't sure he'd even recognize himself. Still he called her name again, called for her until the hollow echo that was his voice grew raw and weak. Finally he slumped there in the middle of the road, shoulders sagged, chin on his chest, and stared at the pavement.

'The name you were calling,' a voice said, 'did it belong to one of those watchers?'

John looked up at the man who'd approached him so silently. He was a nondescript individual, the kind of man he'd have passed by on the street when he was alive and never looked at twice. Medium height, medium build. His only really distinguishing feature was the fervent glitter in his eyes.

'A watcher,' John repeated, nodding in response to the man's question. 'That's what she called herself.'

'Damn 'em all to hell, I say,' the man told him. He spat on the pavement. ''Cept that'd put 'em on these same streets and Franklin T. Clark don't ever want to look into one of their stinkin' faces again – not unless I've got my hands around one of their necks. I'd teach 'em what it's like to be dead.'

'I think they're dead too,' John said.

'That's what they'd like you to believe. But tell me this: if they're dead, how come they're not here like us?

How come they get to hold on to a piece of life like we can't?'

'Because . . . because they're helping people.'

Clark spat again. 'Interferin's more like it.' The dark light in his eyes seemed to deepen as he fixed his gaze on John. 'Why were you calling her name?'

'I can't take this any more.'

'An' you think it's gonna be better where they want to take us?'

'How can it be worse?'

'They can take away who you are,' Clark said. 'They can *try*, but they'll never get Franklin T. Clark, I'll tell you that. They can kill me, they can dump me in this stinkin' place, but I'd rather rot here in hell than let 'em change me.'

'Change you how?' John wanted to know.

'You go through those gates of theirs an' you end up part of a stew. Everythin' that makes you who you are, it gets stole away, mixed up with everybody else. You become a kind of fuel, that's all. Just fuel.'

'Fuel for what?'

'For 'em to make more of us. There's no goddamn sense to it. It's just what they do.'

'How do you know this?' John asked.

Clark shook his head. 'You got to ask, you're not worth the time I'm wastin' on you.'

He gave John a withering look, as though John was something he'd stepped on that got stuck to the bottom of his shoe. And then he walked away.

John tracked the man's progress as he shuffled off down the street. When Clark was finally out of sight, he lifted his head again to stare up into the oppressive sky that hung so close to his face.

'Dakota,' he whispered.

But she still didn't come.

5

The day he found the infant wailing in a heap of trash behind what had once been a restaurant made John wonder if there wasn't some merit in Clark's anger towards the watchers. The baby was a girl and she was no more than a few days old. She couldn't possibly have made the decision that had left her in this place – not by any stretch of the imagination. A swelling echo of Clark's rage rose up in him as he lifted the infant from the trash. He swaddled her in rags and cradled the tiny form in his arms.

'What am I going to do with you?' he asked.

The baby stopped crying, but she made no reply. How could she? She was so small, so helpless. Looking down at her, John knew what he had to do. Maybe Clark was right and the watchers were monsters, although he found that hard to reconcile with his memories of Dakota's empathy and sadness. But Clark was wrong about what lay beyond the gates. He had to be. It couldn't be worse than this place.

He set off. Now he had a destination in mind, now he had something to look for. He wasn't doing it for himself, though he knew he'd step through those gates when they stood in front of him. He was doing it for the baby.

'I'm going to call you Dolly,' he told the infant. 'Darlene would've liked that. What do you think?'

He chucked the infant under her chin. Her only response was to stare up at him.

John figured he had it easier than most people who suddenly had an infant come into their lives. Dolly didn't need to eat and she didn't cry unless he set her down. She was only happy in his arms. She didn't soil the rags he'd wrapped her in. Sometimes she slept, but there was nothing restful about it. She'd be lying in his arms one minute, the next it was as though someone had thrown a switch and she'd been turned off. He'd been frantic the first time it happened, panicking until he realized that she was only experiencing what passed for sleep in this place.

He didn't let himself enter that blank state. The idea had crept into his mind as he wandered the streets with Dolly that to do so, to let himself turn off the way he and all the other undead did, would make it all that much more difficult for him to complete his task. The longer he denied it of himself, the more seductive the lure of that strange sleep became, but he stuck to his resolve. After a time, he was rewarded for maintaining his purposefulness. His vision sharpened; the world still appeared monochromatic, but at least it was all back in focus. He grew more clear-headed. He began to recognize more and more parts of the city. But the gates remained as elusive as Dakota had proved to be since the last time he'd seen her.

One day he came upon Clark again. He wasn't sure how long it had been since the last time he'd seen the man – a few weeks? A few months? It was difficult to tell time in the city because the light never changed. There was no day, no night, no comforting progression from one into the other. There was only the city, held in eternal twilight.

Clark was furious when he saw the infant in John's arms. He ranted and swore at John, threatened to beat him for interfering in what he saw as the child's right of choice. John stood his ground, holding Dolly.

'What are you so afraid of?' he asked when Clark paused to take a breath.

Clark stared at him, a look of growing horror spreading across his features until he turned and fled without replying. He hadn't needed to reply. John knew what Clark was afraid of. It was the same fear that kept them all in this desolate city: death. Dying. They were all afraid. They were all trapped here by that fear. Except for John. He was still trapped like the others; the difference was that he was no longer afraid.

But if a fear of death was no longer to be found in his personal lexicon, despair remained. Time passed. Weeks, months. But he was no closer to finding those fabled gates than he'd been when he first found Dolly and took up the search. He walked through a city that grew more and more familiar. He recognized his own borough, his own street, his own house. He walked slowly up his walk and looked in through the window, but he didn't go in. He was too afraid of succumbing to the growing need to sit somewhere and close his eyes. It would be so easy to go inside, to stretch out on the couch, to let himself fall into the welcoming dark.

Instead he turned away, his path now leading towards the building that housed High Lonesome Sounds. He found it without any trouble, walked up its eerily silent stairwell, boots echoing with a hollow sound, a sound full of dust and broken hopes. At the top of the stairs, he turned to his right and stepped into the recording studio's lounge. The room was empty, except for an open fiddlecase in the middle of the floor, an instrument lying in it, a bow lying across the fiddle, horsehairs loose.

He shifted Dolly from the one arm to the crook of the other. Kneeling down, he slipped the bow into its holder in the lid of the case and shut the lid. He stared at the closed case for a long moment. He had no words to describe how much he'd missed it, how incomplete he'd felt without it. Sitting more comfortably on the floor, he fashioned a sling out of his jacket so that he could carry Dolly snuggled up against his chest and leave his arms free.

When he left the studio, he carried the fiddlecase with him. He went down the stairs, out on to the street. There were no cars, no pedestrians. Nothing had changed. He was still trapped in that reflection of the city he'd known when he was alive, the deserted streets and abandoned buildings peopled only by the undead. But something felt different. It wasn't just that he seemed more himself, more the way he'd been when he was still alive, carrying his fiddle once more. It was as though retrieving the instrument had put a sense of expectation in the air. The grey dismal streets, overhung by a brooding sky, were suddenly pregnant with possibilities.

He heard the footsteps before he saw the man: a tall, rangy individual, arriving from a side street at a brisk walk. Faded blue jeans, black sweatshirt with matching baseball cap. Flat-heeled cowboy boots. What set him apart from the undead was the purposeful set to his features. His gaze was turned outward, rather than inward.

'Hello!' John called after the stranger as the man began to cross the street. 'Have you got a minute?'

The stranger paused in mid-step. He regarded John

with surprise, but waited for John to cross the street and join him. John introduced himself and put out his hand. The man hesitated for a moment, then took John's hand.

'Bernard Gair,' the man said in response. 'Pleased, I'm sure.' His look of surprise had shifted into one of vague puzzlement. 'Have we met before?'

John shook his head. 'No, but I do know one of your colleagues. She calls herself Dakota.'

'The name doesn't ring a bell. But then there are so many of us – though never enough to do the job.'

'That's what she told me. Look, I know how busy you must be, so I won't keep you any longer. I just wanted to ask you if you could direct me to . . .'

John's voice trailed off as he realized he wasn't being listened to. Gair peered more closely at him.

'You're one of the lost, aren't you?' Gair said. 'I'm surprised I can even see you. You're usually so . . . insubstantial. But there's something different about you.'

'I'm looking for the gates,' John told him.

'The gates.'

Something in the way he repeated the words made John afraid that Gair wouldn't help him.

'It's not for me,' he said quickly. 'It's for her.'

He drew back a fold of the sling's cloth to show Gair the sleeping infant nestled against his chest.

'I see,' Gair said. 'But does she want to go on?'

'I think she's a little young to be making that kind of decision for herself.'

Gair shook his head. 'Age makes no difference to a spirit's ability to decide such a thing. Infants can cling as tenaciously to life as do the elderly – often more so, since they have had so little time to experience it.'

'I'm not asking you to make a judgement,' John said. 'I'm just asking for some directions. Let the kid decide for herself once she's at the gates and can look through.'

Gair needed time to consider that before he finally gave a slow nod.

'That could be arranged,' he allowed.

'If you could just give me directions,' John said.

Gair pulled up the left sleeve of his sweatshirt so that he could check the time on his wristwatch.

'Let me take you instead,' he said.

7

Even with directions, John couldn't have found the gates on his own. 'The journey,' Gair explained, 'doesn't entail distance so much as a state of mind.' That was as good a description as any, John realized, as he fell in step with his new companion, for it took them no time at all to circumvent familiar territory and step out on to a long boulevard. John felt a tugging in that part of his chest where his heart had once beaten as he looked down to the far end of the avenue. An immense archway stood there. Between its pillars the air shimmered like a heat mirage and called to him.

When Gair paused, John came to a reluctant halt beside him. Gair looked at his watch again.

'I'm sorry,' he said, 'but I have to leave you now. I have another appointment.'

John found it hard to look at the man. His gaze kept being drawn back to the shimmering air inside the arch.

'I think I can find my way from here,' he said.

Gair smiled. 'I should think you could.' He shook John's hand. 'Godspeed,' he murmured, then he faded away just as Dakota had faded from his living room what seemed like a thousand lifetimes ago.

Dolly stirred against John's chest as he continued on towards the gates. He rearranged her in the sling so that she, too, could look at the approaching gates, but she turned her face away and for the first time his holding her wasn't enough. She began to wail at the sight of the gates, her distress growing in volume the closer they got.

John slowed his pace, uncertain now. He thought of Clark's cursing at him, of Gair telling him that Dolly, for all her infancy, was old enough to make this decision on her own. He realized that they were both right. He couldn't force her to go through, to travel on. But what would he do if she refused? He couldn't simply leave her behind either.

The archway of the gates loomed over him now. The heat shimmer had changed into a warm, golden light that washed out from between the pillars, dispelling all the shadows that had ever taken root in John's soul. But the infant in his arms wept more pitifully, howled until he covered her head with part of the cloth and let her burrow her face against his chest. She whimpered softly there until John thought his heart would break. With each step he took, the sounds she made grew more piteous.

He stood directly before the archway, bathed in its golden light. Through the pulsing glow, he could see the big sky Dakota had described. It went on for ever. He could feel his heart swell to fill it. All he wanted to do was step through, to be done with the lies of the flesh, the lies that had told him this one life was all, the lies that had tricked him into being trapped in the city of the undead.

But there was the infant to consider and he couldn't abandon her. Couldn't abandon her, but he couldn't explain to her that there was nothing to fear, that it was only light and an enormous sky. And peace. There were no words to capture the wonder that pulsed through his veins, that blossomed in his heart, swelled until his chest was full and he knew the light must be pouring out of his eyes and mouth.

Now he understood Dakota's sorrow. It would be heartbreaking to know what waited for those who turned their backs on this glory. It had nothing to do with gods or religions. There was no hierarchy of belief. No one was denied admittance. It was simply the place one stepped through so that the journey could continue.

John cradled the sobbing infant, jigging her gently against his chest. He stared into the light. He stared into the endless sky.

'Dakota,' he called softly.

'Hello, John Narraway.'

He turned to find her standing beside him, her own solemn gaze drinking in the light that pulsed in the big sky between the gates and flowed over them. She smiled at him.

'I didn't think I'd see you again,' she said. 'And certainly not in this place. You did well to find it.'

'I had help. One of your colleagues showed me the way.'

'There's nothing wrong with accepting help sometimes.'

'I know that now,' John said. 'I also understand how hard it is to offer help and have it refused.'

Dakota stepped closer and drew the infant from the sling at John's chest.

'It is hard,' she agreed, cradling Dolly. Her eyes still

held the reflected light that came from between the gates, but they were sad once more as she studied the weeping infant. She sighed, adding, 'But it's not something that can be forced.'

John nodded. There was something about Dakota's voice, about the way she looked that distracted him, but he couldn't quite put his finger on it.

'I will take care of the little one,' Dakota said. 'There's no need for you to remain here.'

'What will you do with her?'

'Whatever she wants.'

'But she's so young.'

The sadness deepened in Dakota's eyes. 'I know.'

There was so much empathy in her voice, in the way she held the infant, in her gaze. And then John realized what was different about her. Her voice wasn't hollow; it held resonance. She wasn't monochrome, but touched with colour. There was only a hint, at first, like an old tinted photograph, but it was like looking at a rainbow for John. As it grew stronger he drank in the wonder of it. He wished she would speak again, just so that he could cherish the texture of her voice, but she remained silent, her solemn gaze held by the infant in her arms.

'I find it hardest when they're so young,' she finally said, looking up at him. 'They don't communicate in words, so it's impossible to ease their fears.'

But words weren't the only way to communicate, John thought. He crouched down to lay his fiddlecase on the ground, took out his bow and tightened the hair. He ran his thumb across the fiddle's strings to check the tuning, marveling anew at the richness of sound. He thought perhaps he'd missed that the most.

'What are you doing?' Dakota asked him.

John shook his head. It wasn't that he didn't want to

explain it to her, but that he couldn't. Instead he slipped the fiddle under his chin, drew the bow across the strings, and used music to express what words couldn't. He turned to the gates, drank in the light and the immense wonder of the sky and distilled it into a simple melody, an air of grace and beauty. Warm, generous notes spilled from the sound holes of his instrument, grew stronger and more resonant in the light of the gates, gained such presence that they could almost be seen, touched and held with more than the ear.

The infant in Dakota's arms fell silent and listened. She turned innocent eyes towards the gates and reached out for them. John slowly brought the melody to an end. He laid down his fiddle and bow and took the infant from Dakota, walked with her towards the light. When he was directly under the arch, the light seemed to flare and suddenly the weight was gone from his arms. He heard a joyous cry, but could see nothing for the light. He felt a beating in his chest as though he was alive once more, pulse drumming. He wanted to follow Dolly into the light more than he'd ever wanted anything before in his life, but he slowly turned his back on the light and stepped back on to the boulevard.

'John Narraway,' Dakota said. 'What are you doing?'

'I can't go through,' he said. 'Not yet. I have to help the others – like you do.'

'But –'

'It's not because I don't want to go through any more,' John said. 'It's . . .'

He didn't know how to explain it and not even fiddle music would help him now. All he could think of was the despair that had clung to him in the city of the undead, the same despair that possessed all those lost souls he'd left there, wandering for ever through its deserted streets, huddling in its abandoned buildings, denying themselves the light. He knew that, like Dakota and Gair, he had to try to prevent others from making the same mistake. He knew it wouldn't be easy, he knew there would be times when it would be heartbreaking, but he could see no other course.

'I just want to help,' he said. 'I have to help. You told me before that there aren't enough of you, and the fellow that brought me here said the same thing.'

Dakota gave him a long, considering look before she finally smiled. 'You know,' she said, 'I think you do have the generosity of heart now.'

John put away his fiddle. When he stood up, Dakota took his hand and they began to walk back down the boulevard, away from the gates.

'I'm going to miss that light,' John said.

Dakota squeezed his hand. 'Don't be silly,' she said. 'The light has always been inside us.'

John glanced back. From this distance, the light was like a heat mirage again, shimmering between the pillars of the gates, but he could still feel its glow, see the flare of its wonder and the sky beyond it that went on for ever. Something of it echoed in his chest and he knew Dakota was right.

'We carry it with us wherever we go,' he said.

'Learn to play that on your fiddle, John Narraway,' she said.

John returned her smile. 'I will,' he promised. 'I surely will.'

Relief

JANE M. LINDSKOLD

In desperate moments, there is a spot in the center of the forehead that begs for the solid caress of a bullet. With a shuddering breath, Connie pressed the gun to that very spot.

'Don't,' said a voice, dulcet and commanding.

The word stopped Connie's finger from tightening around the trigger. She peeked out between her lashes, certain that the room had been empty when she had locked the door and windows. Yet, miraculously, a slender figure was sitting across the worn kitchen table from her.

'I'm drunk,' she muttered. She should be if the empty Jim Beam bottle was any testimony. The problem was, she had never felt more sober.

She forced her eyes open and stared at the man (woman?) across from her: blond cornsilk hair, translucent blue eyes, skin of pearl kissed with rose. He (she?) wore a simple, elegant white gown with a gently scooped neckline and matching downy feathered wings that towered to brush the ceiling.

'I'm really drunk,' she repeated, wishing that she believed herself, 'and you're an angel.'

'Yes, I am,' the angel replied. 'Your distress cried out to me. I paused in my contemplation of eternity to stop you from stepping into mortal sin.'

'Mortal sin?'

'Suicide. Despair. Belief that your problems are

greater than God's ability to grant relief.'

'Hah,' Connie barked a bitter laugh. 'Mortal sin doesn't scare me. I'm living in hell now; at least death and damnation would eliminate stupid hope that things could improve.'

'Tell me what has driven you to this impasse,' the angel suggested. 'There must be a way to help.'

'Fine,' she started ticking off points on her fingers. 'My husband is a hopeless ne'er-do-well. My job is about to be cut. I have bleeding ulcers, migraines, corns, and my louse of a husband gave me genital warts. My blood test came back HIV positive – and I've never even placed myself at risk. My house is slowly deteriorating around me, and my cat just died. I'm tired of trying to hold everything together. I just want to end it.'

She stared defiantly at the angel, who studied her with placid, blue eyes.

'So, angel, what do you think?'

'Hand me the gun,' the angel said. 'There is always a solution.'

Connie smiled, suddenly grateful, and pushed the gun across the table. 'Take it. What should I do?'

'Bow your head,' the angel said, 'and close your eyes.'

Connie obeyed, never seeing the angel raise the gun, level it steadily at her temple and pull the trigger. Her head exploded into blood and splatters of brain and bone.

The angel addressed the listening air.

'That wasn't suicide, Father. That was murder.'

Wings spread, the angel paused before leaping into the waiting vacancy between here and now.

'And mercy.'

Spiritual Dysfunction and Counterangelic Longings,
or
Sariela: a Case Study in One Act

MICHAEL BISHOP

Night. The interior of the Cat's Eye Bar, Grill, & Pinball Parlor on the outskirts of Ackley, Georgia, USA. To the right (from the audience's pov), a pair of high-finned, cut-down 1957 Chevy convertibles (one hot-pink, one turquoise) wedged together, bumper to bumper, on blocks: the bar.

Nine stools in front of it: upended airplane turbines with revolving leather seats. A mirror behind the bar reflects liquor bottles and glasses; it wears a swag of fishing net and is plastered with beer ads, travel stickers and soiled pieces of US and Latin American highway maps.

Left of the double-car bar, and up a half-step, extends a sawdust-sprinkled drinking area, jukebox room and dance floor. Rickety tables and cane-back chairs. A bank of lit-up Li'l Abner, Snuffy Smith, and Grandpa Clampett pinball machines shares rear-wall space with a jukebox, a Roller Derby video game and an Art Deco thermoplastic Drew Barrymore umbrella and fly-reel stand.

A few shadowy human figures slump at the back tables, nursing their booze and/or piecing together jigsaw puzzles of the Little Grand Canyon, log-like alligators in the Okefeeno-kee Swamp or the Waving Girl statue on Savannah's River

Street. A downstage table to the far left sits vacant, with a battered dessert cart behind it and an overgrown bonsai apple tree in a glazed Ming pot to one side in front of it — as a pretentious mythological symbol.

It is a chilly, damp Friday, the 7th of January, anno Domini *1994 (as ostensibly civilized Western Earthlings reckon, subdivide and pigeon-hole time). But in the Cat's Eye — except for the video game and the Lucite umbrella stand — it could be 1963 (before JFK's assassination), 1972 (shortly after the break-up of the Beatles), 1985 (near the premier of* A Lie of the Mind *at the Promenade Theater) or 1991 (on the evening the Minneapolis Twins took the World Series from the Atlanta Braves in a domed stadium draped, it appeared, with Hefty trash bags).*

The BARTENDER, *a handsome twenty-six-year-old farm-boy type with a long jaw and mismatched ears (one could belong to Meg Ryan, one to Evander Holyfield) sets a rosy cherub (raspberry ginger ale and Albigensian bitters) before his four-year-old son,* AUBREY, *and squints ceilingward.* AUBREY *floats a worm-eaten pecan in his rosy cherub and repeatedly kicks the rear door of the turquoise Chevy with his Payless penny loafers. The other five patrons at the car bar ignore the boy's toe drumming.*

BARTENDER: Raphael? (*Squints, cocks his head, listens*) Hey, Raffy. Your table's ready.

RAPHAEL *materializes at the table by the dessert cart and the symbolic bonsai. His head nearly touches the ceiling. He wears tight black leather pants, a beaded Choctaw vest over his otherwise unclad torso and a white terrycloth headband on which the Magic Marker motto BEGOTTEN TO RAZE HELL is fuzzily emblazoned. He has huge wings: a single pair only.*

Sitting, he props one wing, the left, on the dessert cart and holds the other aloft so that it casts an oxymoronically luminous shadow over the entire dance floor, even to the near edge of the double-Chevy bar. He glances at his naked wrist, shakes his head disgustedly, then looks about the Cat's Eye as if for a waitress or a tardy drinking chum.

RAPHAEL: Hashmal, we have an appointment. Appear at your earliest convenience. Please.

HASHMAL *manifests at the bar, between* AUBREY *and a hungover patron who doesn't even notice the chief of the angelic order known as dominions.* HASHMAL — *like* RAPHAEL, *a daunting seven feet or more tall* — *wears a brocaded jerkin, plum-colored tights with a sewn-in codpiece and matching calf-high, slipper-soled, suede boots.*

He pays for a draft Michelob Dark and turns to carry it up the half-step and across the floor to RAPHAEL's *table. His pivot causes havoc:* HASHMAL's *wings trail him like a pair of feathery drag chutes, sweeping a Coors Silver Bullet, a highball glass of watered Wild Turkey, the ignition key to a Dodge Dakota pick-up and a woman's tortoise-shell compact on to the butt- and sawdust-strewn floor.*

AUBREY *looks after* HASHMAL *wide-eyed, but no one else at the bar reacts, either to mumble, 'Watch it, buddy,' or to snatch a wisp of down from one of his pillaging wings.*

HASHMAL *sits across from* RAPHAEL, *toasts him, grimaces when the jukebox starts to shake the joint with the raucous Garth Brooks anthem 'Friends in Low Places'.*

RAPHAEL: You're inappropriately dressed.

HASHMAL: Beelzebub calling Moloch vile.

RAPHAEL: I mean for the era.

HASHMAL: I manifested. Never mind my attire. Just tell me what urgency requires my presence . . . *here.*

RAPHAEL: Sariela, of whom I have charge as captain of all guardian spirits. You, as captain of the order regulating angelic duties, need to hear how Sariela has proved negligent, just as I need your advice and counsel about what to do to help this unhappy spirit.

HASHMAL: Sariela? Sariela? The name has a slippery sort of familiarity.

RAPHAEL: May I tell you the story?

HASHMAL: You *do* outrank me. Always have. Always will.

RAPHAEL: (*Refolding his wings, leaning forward*) We posted Sariela, a guardian of deliberately feminine aspect, to protect a newlywed couple from this very town, Ackley, Georgia, USA, Earth, Sol Planetary System, Milky Way Galaxy, Local Cluster Number –

HASHMAL: I *know* where we are.

RAPHAEL: (*Sotto voce*) If not when. (*To* HASHMAL) The couple to whom we posted Sariela go by the names Philip and Angel Marie Hembree. We sent her –

HASHMAL: *Angel* Marie? The woman's name is *Angel* Marie? How odd. Such ironic synchronicity.

RAPHAEL: A simple coincidence. It's only a name. In any event, we posted Sariela to the Hembrees on their wedding day, August 15, *anno Domini* 1993, the thirty-second anniversary of Philip's birth. Angel Marie had insisted that they marry on this day as a precaution against Philip's ever forgetting their wedding anniversary. This same stratagem had also worked for her previous husband, Bobby Dean Gilbert, who died in 1989 in a collision between a trailer truck carrying a load of Christmas trees – Frasier firs, primarily – and the Gilberts' rattletrap 1978 Toyota Corolla.

HASHMAL: Both husbands were born on the same day?

RAPHAEL: No. *No!* Listen. This accident occurred on a

fog-blanketed switchback of a north Georgia mountain, and Bobby Dean died instantly, impaled boccally by the trunk of a Frasier fir and thoracically by the Corolla's steering column.

HASHMAL: (*Shuddering*) Praise God our basic incorporeality frees us from any fear of impalement. (*Arches an eyebrow*) Or we'd play hell dancing on the heads of pins, wouldn't we?

RAPHAEL: (*Impatiently*) Angel Marie, on the other hand, survived the accident, but with crippling injuries from which she still quietly struggles to recover. Her survival is owing to the professionalism of the Georgia Highway Patrol and a pair of Emergency Medical Service personnel who drove her to the county hospital.

A few weeks later, as a physical-therapy patient in the Cobalt Springs Rehabilitation Center here in Ackley, she met Philip Hembree, driving instructor for (A) the resident disabled and (B) the teenage progeny of the Center's senior medical and administrative personnel. Blessedly, Angel Marie fell in category A. Philip found her a much less demanding, and exasperating, student than the overweight male quadruple amputee, Carrol Bricknell, who could negotiate Ackley's back roads only with the aid of an experimental, voice-activated computerized guidance unit and a strap-on chin pointer that its manufacturer refers to whimsically as either a 'directional diviner' or a 'unicorn wand'. So, as you can imagine, Philip was predisposed to welcome Angel Marie into his customized, state-provided instructional vehicle as a student. In fact, he –

HASHMAL: Forgive, but these proliferating details overwhelm me. Of what sin of omission or commission is

Sariela guilty? Has she somehow sabotaged the well-being or happiness of the Hembrees?

RAPHAEL: Oh, no. Far from it.

HASHMAL: What, then?

RAPHAEL: The trouble lies in Sariela's untoward response to a very specific, and somewhat delicate, manifestation of the Hembrees' admittedly exemplary mutual regard. I dilate on the human beings under her novice protection to give you a clearer insight into her anomalous attitudes and behavior. *Must* I cut to the vulgar chase? Or may I give you all the facts necessary to reach an informed and sagacious judgment?

HASHMAL: Pardon my impatience. Enlighten me fully.

RAPHAEL: Technically, Sariela served as Angel Marie's guardian. She replaced the quasi-disgraced Cristiana, who only by her pinion tips contrived to save her ward's life in that wreck with the Christmas-tree truck. Cristiana, I regret to report, has since lapsed into a vegetative spiritual funk – but that's another story. Sariela, despite her posting as Angel Marie's protector, had a sidelong responsibility to Philip, a professed agnostic, and this extra duty made her the *de facto* guardian of the Hembrees as a couple.

HASHMAL: Yes, yes. I understand.

RAPHAEL: Philip's agnosticism denies him a separate angel, of course, but his 'goodness' – a state without eternal heavenly imprimatur, albeit one that usually elicits unofficial seraphic approval of a conditional sort – did, in fact, put him in line for collateral protection. We hope to win him *through* Angel Marie, for, in the Apostle Peter's take on such matters, 'Even if some do not obey the word, they, without a word, may be won by the conduct of their wives . . .' At which point, of course, we would delightedly grant the redeemed man a guardian exclusively his own.

HASHMAL: I have another appointment two decades into the next millennium. Could we speed this *a bit*?

RAPHAEL: Sure. (*Aside*) But visit a haberdasher before you go to keep it. (*To* HASHMAL) At the Cobalt Springs Rehabilitation Center Philip chastely courted Angel Marie through the latter two years of her convalescence, physical therapy and fight for psychosomatic wholeness. He entered the relationship a long-term bachelor and, in his own self-mocking phrase, a 'recidivist virgin', whatever degree of celibacy *that* implies. The result was – once Angel Marie had placed her late spouse at a healthy psychological remove, and Philip and she had fallen in love and married – their union had the recurrent, uh, libidinous enthusiasm one would expect in the conjugal relations of much younger adult lovers. You see, from the vantage of a woman once satisfactorily yoked to an athletic hedonist – namely, Bobby Dean – Angel Marie had much to teach Philip, even while recovering from her severely crippling injuries. Philip, in turn, had much to offer Angel Marie from the hands-on perspective – metaphorically extended to the act of erotic intercourse – of a driving instructor for the 'physically challenged'.

HASHMAL: You're blushing.

RAPHAEL: That's impossible.

HASHMAL: Perhaps you're right. Go on.

RAPHAEL: The early weeks of the Hembrees' marriage – the past four months, in fact – exposed Sariela to such a repeating commotion of eroticism, whether obstreperous or tender, quick or protracted, that it at first unhinged and eventually totally transfigured her.

Sariela, rather than formulating strategies to protect the couple from accidents, evildoers or harmful individual or joint decisions, began to obsess on the apparent joys of, well, *carnality* – especially in the divinely sanctioned context of marriage. For these reasons, I guess, Sariela gave herself over to a most unangelic pornographic voyeurism.

HASHMAL: My God! Didn't you reprimand her?

RAPHAEL: Despite her preoccupation, she managed to hold the Hembrees entire, as individuals and as a couple.

HASHMAL: Of course she did. Barring unwanted pregnancies, communicable diseases and mattress fires, bed is a haven from danger. But surely you took steps, however feeble, to reclaim Sariela from her obsession?

RAPHAEL: What would you have done?

HASHMAL: (*After thinking this over*) Summoned counselors, persons of good judgment and experience, to expostulate with her, to expatiate upon the pitfalls of –

RAPHAEL: And so I did.

He snaps his fingers, and a bewigged and somewhat bemused male figure, in the garb of an eighteenth-century British gentleman, appears on the dance floor. No one else in the place pays the newcomer any heed.

RAPHAEL: (*Tendering introductions*) Hashmal, Philip Dormer Stanhope, Fourth Earl of Chesterfield. Lord Chesterfield, Hashmal the Dominion. Sorry to yank you so unceremoniously out of the afterlife again, but my colleague here has questioned the course I pursued in attempting to treat Sariela's unseemly variety of spiritual dysfunction.

CHESTERFIELD: Ah, yes. Sariela. A charming sprite. (*He approaches the table*) Altogether charming.

RAPHAEL: I summoned you to counsel her, sir, because

in your earthly incarnation you once made a rather witty, not to say astute, observation about the manifold disadvantages of human reproductive liaisons.

CHESTERFIELD: Sex?

RAPHAEL: (*Distastefully*) As you prefer.

CHESTERFIELD: (*Quoting himself*) 'The cost is exorbitant, the pleasure is momentary, and the position is ridiculous.'

RAPHAEL: That's it.

CHESTERFIELD: And, just as you wished, Your Seraphacy, I took that very epigram to Sariela.

HASHMAL: (*Fascinated*) And how did she respond?

RAPHAEL *snaps his fingers again, and* CHESTERFIELD *vanishes, demanifesting without so much as a hollow pop.* RAPHAEL *snaps them yet again, and* SARIELA *materializes in the center of the grungy dance floor. The jukebox plays 'God Didn't Make Honky-Tonk Angels'.*

SARIELA *stands nearly six feet tall, her svelte body draped in a flowing, snow-white robe. She has a noble, startlingly beautiful face — that of either a somewhat feminine man or a rather masculine woman — and her wings sprout from her shoulder blades like impotent, if shapely, nubs.*

SARIELA: 'The best is free of either payment or guilt; one may protract or re-experience the pleasure; and imaginative partakers may vary the position.'

RAPHAEL: God have mercy.

HASHMAL: (*Caught off-guard*) How clever! (*Recovering*) But how crass. Never do I pity the Almighty's fallen creatures more than when I hear tell of them in the reason-annihilating throes of recreational passion. And you, Sariela, have fallen prey to the meretricious allure of an activity that even Lord Chesterfield, as a frail mortal, had the wisdom to adjudge specious and demeaning?

SARIELA: (*Aloof*) I confess it. Also that it profoundly irks me I can't indulge.

RAPHAEL: (*To* HASHMAL) She's bright. Her counter to Lord Chesterfield's *bon mot* was virtually instantaneous.

HASHMAL: (*To* SARIELA) I congratulate you on your quick thinking, if not your tact.

SARIELA: Each parry of my tripartite reply sprang entire from the Chesterfieldian clause that it contradicts. He smoked me out.

HASHMAL: I take it you don't like the man.

SARIELA: Despite Samuel Johnson's ill-tempered diatribes against him, Lord Chesterfield was – and remains, even in God's unimpeachable Heaven – the perfect gentleman. But that doesn't negate my view that as a living human being he scantly deserved the functional genitals vouchsafed him.

RAPHAEL: Child, come over here. Sit down with Hashmal and me. Have a glass of wine.

SARIELA: I'd prefer ouzo, for all the nonexistent kick it affords intelligences without digestive tracts.

RAPHAEL: Come on. Don't quibble over drinks.

He pats the table. SARIELA *stalks over to it, scrapes a chair away from it, twirls the chair around and straddles the chair like a chip-on-the-shoulder cowpoke.*

SARIELA: I'm not really quibbling over booze, I'm grousing about our asensual incorporeality.

HASHMAL: Oh. I see. Of course.

RAPHAEL: (*Shouting*) Bartender, another Michelob Dark, a glass of zinfandel, and an ouzo for the lady.

BARTENDER: (*Shouting back*) You got it, Raffy!

HASHMAL: 'Raffy'?

As the angels talk, the BARTENDER *prepares their drinks, sets them on a cork-bottomed tray and eventually sends little* AUBREY *across the room to them with the tray.*

RAPHAEL: I've made dozens of trips to Ackley over the past couple of months. What's so heinous about some friendly banter with the local tavern-keeper?

HASHMAL: Nothing. Not a thing.

SARIELA: I'd like to taste what I eat and drink. I'd like to process my food and liquids internally. I'd like to excrete them, once processed. Not to put too fastidious a label on it, I'd also like to screw.

HASHMAL: (*Off-guard again*) Who?

SARIELA: 'Whom', I think you mean. Anyone. Well, *almost* anyone. Almost anyone with the requisite anatomical parts and the tactile sensitivity to enjoy the performance and to impart gratification in turn – if, that is, I were so constituted as to experience such pleasures.

AUBREY *arrives with the drinks, distributes them, gives a mannerly, if awkward, bow, then retreats.*

SARIELA: (*Nodding at* AUBREY) Even that living pre-pubescent facsimile of a Renaissance *putto* has more erogenous impulses and tissues than we do. It's outrageous.

RAPHAEL: (*To* HASHMAL) You see? She has a virulent case of spiritual dysfunction, with counterangelic longings of such insistent strength, that – were she to publish her discontent in Heaven – she could wreak havoc among all nine orders.

SARIELA: Hogwash.

RAPHAEL: (*To* SARIELA) Do you deny that you suffer from an uncommon – for angels – spiritual dysfunction?

SARIELA: Do you deny that we have 'genitals', albeit ones that generate neither offspring nor waste, so that we would do better to call them 'naturalia', 'privates' or even 'doodads'?

HASHMAL: (*His interest wholly engaged*) Why, I never think about them at all.

SARIELA: And why should you? They don't *do* anything. We can neither squirt nor swyve. Yours may swing a little, guys, but mine merely – I don't know, *reside*. It's a joke. A sick, sad, unfunny joke.

RAPHAEL: Sariela, they exist at all only when we incarnate as emissaries to humanity. Why rail against their absence of functionality when, ordinarily, we have our essence as bodiless spirits about the Holy Throne?

SARIELA: Because the Occupant of that Throne should have made us, even in our roles as emissaries, as sexless as kewpie dolls. Instead He made me, in my guise as a guardian, with what I now recognize as a nearly perfect physical simulacrum of the quiff of an adult human female. (*She starts to hike up the hem of her robe*) Look.

RAPHAEL: No! Please, no! We believe you.

HASHMAL: 'Quiff'?

SARIELA: (*Desisting*) You guys could show me yours. I wouldn't mind. All I've had to go by – the Hembrees being my first assignment and my access to photographic representations virtually nil – is Philip's endearing set: so soft in repose, so salient in arousal.

RAPHAEL: *Sariela!*

SARIELA: Why this avoidance? This shame? This Puritanical squeamishness?

HASHMAL: I don't think that's wholly fair. After all, *I'm* wearing a codpiece.

SARIELA: All right, then. Unbutton it. Snap it out.

HASHMAL: (*Flustered*) No, thank you. I couldn't.

RAPHAEL: Such prurient curiosity ill serves you, Sariela.

But I'd argue that our 'shame' — a decent, angelic shame — stems from sympathy for our fallen wards.

HASHMAL: (*To* RAPHAEL) Or maybe from the realization that our equipment has only a place-holding, or a representational, function. That *is* a downer.

SARIELA: Crap. (*She knocks back the shot glass of ouzo, that* AUBREY *brought her and runs her tongue around her lips. Sensually.*) Double crap.

RAPHAEL: Why these mad physical desires? Why such sighing and panting? Sariela, you have in you the distilled essence of pure spirit, whatever your current status as a guardian.

SARIELA: And yet I want . . . I want *to get it on*. The Hembrees have corrupted me past recall or liberated me to joys I'm helpless to know — except, that is, in the witnessing, the hearing and the heat of my fancy, where such joys, worse luck, seem only to carbonize and drift away.

The jukebox plays Hank Williams's 'I'm So Lonesome I Could Cry'. A man and a woman at the back of the room get up, clasp each other and shuffle about the floor, more like shadows than distinguishable human beings. SARIELA *stands.*

SARIELA: (*Enraged*) How can you dance to that song? (*The couple ignores her*) Two people dancing together are lonesome only on sufferance! Stop it! (*A beat or two, then*) I said, *Stop it!*

*The couple goes on dancing. The three angels watch in a mood of perplexity (*RAPHAEL, HASHMAL*) or of raw disgruntlement (*SARIELA*). The song ends, the man and the woman sit back down, the jukebox lever-locks an old Jim Reeves 45-rpm disc into play position: 'Welcome to My World'.*

SARIELA *paces beside the table, methodically rather than feverishly — in the same studied way that she wrings her hands and clenches her jaw.* RAPHAEL *and* HASHMAL *regard her with abashed wonder. At one point, they exchange a helpless shrug. Finally,* SARIELA *slams herself back into her chair and stares glassily out over the audience.*

SARIELA: You guys're firing me, aren't you?

RAPHAEL: Unless you can quell this morbid infatuation with the concupiscent, we'll surely post you back to Guardian Dispatch Central for, well, retraining.

SARIELA: Mothballing, you mean.

RAPHAEL: Nonsense. You can't –

SARIELA: Endless spiritual storage. Eternity will closet, then disassemble and then wholly absorb me.

HASHMAL: Never. Never. We *love* you, Sariela.

SARIELA: Not as Philip Hembree loves his Angel Marie. Or vice versa.

RAPHAEL: Vice – animal frailty – has more to do with it than you seem willing to admit.

SARIELA: (*Acidly quoting*)

Love not the Heavenly Spirits, and how their love
Express they, by looks only, or do they mix
Irradiance, virtual or immediate touch?

RAPHAEL: I beg your pardon.

HASHMAL: (*Enthusiastically*) Adam's appeal to Raphael – to *you*, Your Radiant Seraphacy – toward the end of the eighth book of Milton's *Paradise Lost*.

SARIELA: (*To* RAPHAEL) It made you blush, for your smile 'glowed/Celestial rosy-red, Love's proper hue', and you said to Adam, 'Let it suffice that –'

RAPHAEL: You suppose me, after all these countless aeons, a halo-bearing illiterate? I *know* what I said.

(*He rises and strides about in peeved majesty*) Through Mr Milton's cheeky ventriloquism, I replied:

. . . Let it suffice thee that thou know'st
Us happy, and without love no happiness.
Whatever pure thou in the body enjoy'st
(And pure thou wert created) we enjoy
In eminence, and obstacle find none
Of membrane, joint, or limb, exclusive bars;
Easier than air with air, if spirits embrace,
Total they mix, union of pure with pure
Desiring; nor restrained conveyance need
As flesh to mix with flesh, or soul with soul.

HASHMAL: (*Clapping mildly, once*) Bravo.

RAPHAEL: Stifle it. (*To* SARIELA) Earlier in this same passage, my namesake cautioned Adam to remember – as I caution you, Sariela – that

. . . Love refines
The thoughts, and heart enlarges, hath his seat
In reason, and is judicious, is the scale
By which to heavenly love thou may'st ascend,
Not sunk in carnal pleasure, for which cause
Among the beasts no mate for thee was found.

SARIELA: Then the beasts among whom no mate was found for *me*, a guardian spirit, are those same dear, lascivious monkeys whom you posted me to defend. Is that it?

RAPHAEL: Exactly, my pretty picket.

SARIELA: Fine. But the ache persists. The hunger too. In recesses I fear inaccessible.

RAPHAEL: (*To* HASHMAL) You've got an appointment elsewhere, I believe.

HASHMAL: I do?

RAPHAEL: So you said. Feel free to depart for it.

HASHMAL: (*Somewhat bemusedly*) Thank you. (*He demanifests, promptly and entirely*)

Meanwhile, RAPHAEL *swings around* SARIELA'*s chair, stalks to the bonsai apple tree, pulls from it a small crimson fruit and extends the fruit to* SARIELA.

RAPHAEL: Here. For your ache. For your hunger.

SARIELA: (*Examining it*) I wouldn't have supposed apples in season. And the hunger of which I spoke doesn't submit to *this* sort of feeding.

RAPHAEL: Taste it. Take a bite.

SARIELA: A bite will engulf it.

RAPHAEL: Please. For me.

SARIELA *takes a bite. This bite does encompass the tiny apple. She marvels at her empty hand and savors the fruit's peculiar taste. Then she swallows and smiles.*

SARIELA: Yes. I see.

RAPHAEL:

Whatever pure thou in the body enjoy'st
(And pure thou wert created) we enjoy
In eminence, and obstacle find none
Of membrane, joint, or limb . . .

SARIELA: (*Radiant*) I understand. But show me. No one has ever showed me.

RAPHAEL: An anomalous — indeed, an unforgivable — hole in your education.

SARIELA: Fill it. Please.

RAPHAEL: Immediately. But not here.

He takes SARIELA'*s hand and guides her to her feet. Then, as the two of them tower in the center of the dance floor, he clicks his heels together three times.*

RAPHAEL: (*After clicking his tongue three times*) Presto, Sariela: the Rapture!

These two angels vanish, hand in hand, from the Cat's Eye. Over the dying strains of 'Midnight Train to Georgia' we catch a brief riff of laughter from the departing SARIELA. *Then the dance floor stands empty, and the only audible sound is that of* AUBREY's *toes kicking the turquoise Chevy.*

A door to the right of the car bar opens, and a man in his mid-thirties wrestles a wheelchair containing a smiling young woman over the Cat's Eye's threshold. Every patron at the bar looks toward the newcomers, including AUBREY, *who stops kicking the bar's body metal.*

BARTENDER: (*Affectionately*) Hey, Phil! Hey, Angel!

ANGEL MARIE: Hey, Troy.

PHILIP: How goes it, Troy?

BARTENDER: Can't complain. The usual?

ANGEL MARIE: Sure. And rack up some songs by the King.

BARTENDER: You got it.

PHILIP *wheels* ANGEL MARIE *past the bar, tilts her chair so that it can roll on to the dance floor and pushes her to the table where the three angels sat. Here he parks her and sits down in* RAPHAEL's *former spot.* AUBREY *carries the Hembrees a couple of amber long-necks, while the* BARTENDER *leaves the bar to feed the jukebox a handful of coins.*

BARTENDER: (*Over his shoulder*) Y'all trust me to do this?

PHILIP: (*Nuzzling* ANGEL MARIE, *prompting a low giggle*) Why shouldn't we?

BARTENDER: It's out of my era. I'm a Travis Tritt kind of guy. (*To* ANGEL MARIE) Hey, darlin', need a bodyguard?

ANGEL MARIE: Got one. Got one real close.

BARTENDER: I'd say. Well, Aubrey and me're real proud to have you all here.

ANGEL MARIE: (*Glancing at him*) You are? Why?

BARTENDER: The head-in-the-cloud riff-raff leaves and the bona fide class comes in.

ANGEL MARIE: What?

AUBREY *pulls a fruit off the bonsai apple tree and hands it to* ANGEL MARIE, *who gives* AUBREY *an appreciative buss and takes a dainty bite of the apple. The* BARTENDER *comes over, picks up* AUBREY *and totes him back down to the bar.*

From the jukebox, 'Love Me Tender'. A man and a woman get up from a shadowy rear table, embrace each other and begin to shuffle about the floor. ANGEL MARIE *takes what's left of her apple and feeds it to* PHILIP.

PHILIP: Mmmmm. Delicious.

ANGEL MARIE: Even half-bitten?

PHILIP: (*Nuzzling her*) Even half-bitten.

The lights slowly fade. Soon about all we can see is ANGEL MARIE *outlined in her wheelchair and* PHILIP's *silhouette leaning into hers. The King continues to croon, the anonymous couple to hitch around on sawdust . . .*

Real Messengers

JOHN BRUNNER

> [In the nineteenth century] Children were not
> exempted from this severe knowledge of guilt.
> It was believed they were so steeped in origi-
> nal sin that it was most inexpedient to indulge
> them.

Unobserved – save perhaps for the guardian angel that, according to Aunt Eunice, kept the record of his deeds and thoughts whereby he would be measured and found wanting on the Judgment Day – Hadrian set his jaw against the pain in his joints and made the best dash he could from the shrubbery to the corner where the wall of the house met that of the carriage shed. Here there was a downpipe feeding to an oaken water butt. Higher up, the pipe passed within arm's reach of the window of the spartan room his aunt allotted him: always open for the sake of fresh air save when it rained, but barred to stop him climbing in or out.

Not that he would have had the strength to do so.

Hidden from casual view by the pipe, a rope hung down that ended in a bag made from scraps of sacking, mistakable for an abandoned bird's nest or the like. Hastily, ignoring his never-ceasing discomfort – petty next to what Our Lord had suffered, as his aunt so often stressed – he transferred to the bag flowers gathered in what he privately thought of as the Wilderness, a neglected patch of copse at the far end of the grounds. There weren't many, for summer was drawing to its close. But he had eked them out with sprays of berries.

It would have been more than his life was worth to raid the roses and hydrangeas in the actual garden.

Then, having rinsed his hands in a splash of water from the barrel and rubbed, albeit ineffectually, at a muddy mark on the left knee of his breeches, he stole into the house through the tradesmen's entrance.

There was no sign of Mrs Winter, the cook-general, either in the kitchen or in the pantry. When he slunk through the green baize door dividing the servants' wing from the front hall he realized why. In the morning-room Aunt Eunice was casting over her accounts and issuing instructions about future expenditure.

Which would not include coals to warm Hadrian's room. Which would not include cakes or pies or fruit to set before his place at table. Privation, as she so often emphasized, was good for the soul.

One had to presume that her own soul had endured as much good as was necessary to perfect it.

If only Mrs Winter were not so spineless! If only she could be more like her sister Mrs Chalk, who was housekeeper to Dr Mostyn down in the village – change that to *had been*, for the kindly but vague old gentleman's funeral was a month in the past. When she came to call she never failed to bring a treat for Hadrian, be it no more than a crust enfolding a smear of jam or a grating of cheese . . .

Thinking about food, though, always threatened to make him moan aloud, and he had no wish to attract his aunt's attention.

Severity and deprivation were character-build-
ing. It was a parent's duty to see the child did
not pay too much attention to sensual
delights.

Gritting his teeth, concentrating on the distraction he
could look forward to within a few minutes, the boy
struggled upstairs with much recourse to the banister.
At the main landing, where his aunt turned right on her
way to bed, he turned left to the servants' wing and
then left again, down a narrow passage that led solely to
his room above the carriage shed. Its floorboards were
bare and gapped. Its fireplace had not warmed to a
flame in years. Its window was innocent of curtains. Its
furniture consisted of a wood-and-webbing bedstead
with a lumpy flock mattress; a chair that also served to
hang his day-clothes when he donned his nightshirt; a
cracked and warped deal wardrobe for attire not presently being worn, whose door would rasp open unex-
pectedly at any small-hours change of temperature and
wake him sweating with its groan; a wash-stand where-
on reposed a chipped bowl and a ewer he must himself
fill on retiring, knowing the contents had to suffice for
both evening and morning ablutions; and an ancient
vanity table with a fly-specked tilting mirror, five
drawers – two to either side and a wide shallow one
across the centre that would no longer open – and two
tarnished brass candle-holders.

And, on the reverse of the mirror . . .

Hadrian closed the door and hobbled to the window.
Stretching, he drew up the rope. He extracted the pitiful
parody of a bouquet from the sacking, then let the latter
drop to the carriage-shed roof, where it was invisible at
ground level. From the candle-holders he removed their

withered contents and sent them after the rope's end. Then he arranged the fresh offerings, adding from his ewer the splash of water he had saved after rinsing his mouth this morning.

He was not allowed to brush his teeth. He had told his aunt how his gums bled, and she blamed it on the use of a brush and ordered him to make do with cold water and a pinch of salt – 'Only a pinch, mind!'

Yes, aunt.

From the right upper drawer of the vanity table, which he no longer thought of by that name but termed his altar, Hadrian withdrew a Bible inscribed to him by his parents on the occasion of his christening. It fell open at a passage in Luke xv that had come more and more to obsess him. His eye flew instantly to the line, 'the husks that the swine did eat . . .' A grumble of hunger resounded in his own belly. (His aunt forbade the word as vulgar; the Bible used it, though, so inside his head he did the same.) Glancing toward the Wilderness, visible from here, he wondered how long it would be before autumn accorded him beechmast.

He was so hungry! He had been hungry for so long! And he hadn't been prodigal, truly he hadn't! Surely Jesus, surely even Aunt Eunice, must admit that! What had he ever had to be prodigal with?

But Jesus had fasted forty days and nights. He must endure.

Resolute, he turned the mirror over. To its wooden back was pinned a crucifix with one hand broken, chance-found on a rare trip into town: he scarce remembered how – save that it had been dropped so as to incur the damage or discarded because of it – nor by what device he had smuggled it home. It was made of a substance pretending to be ivory, some patent compound painted in a factory, the like of thousands no doubt, yet affecting for its message of eternal verity. His eyes filled with tears, blurring that drawn face, its forehead arun with blood from the crown of thorns, that mouth which but a moment since had uttered those imperishable words, 'Father, forgive them, for they know not what they do.'

Lord Jesus, please forgive my aunt!

Hadrian always prayed that first, and hoped he meant it even though he no longer believed that an angel was on unwearying patrol inside his head – at least, not very much.

But why must I be so hungry and so weak when she is fat? Did You not promise that if the hungry call on You they will be filled?

There was a creak beyond the door. Terror erupted in his mouth like, and bringing with it, bitter bile.

Would that what he had heard might prove no more than another sign of the way this old house was settling on its old foundations! But it was not to be; he could detect the dry scrape, like a monstrous insect rustling its wings, of a crinoline skirt brushing against the sides of the passage.

Slowly, as in a nightmare, he turned to face the door when it should open. For a moment he dared to imagine that his aunt might at least approve his devotion to Our Saviour, inasmuch as she enforced on him and Mrs Winter daily prayers and demanded church attendance twice each Sunday, but the moment he saw her look of satisfaction he realized that hope also was futile.

Carnal indulgences such as lollipops were pun-
ished by doses of rhubarb and salt. It was

often thought wise to allow children to go
hungry.

Hadrian's mouth was too dry for speech as Aunt
Eunice advanced on his altar. Forced back to avoid
treading on her gown's hem, he shook and wavered and
eventually moaned. She disregarded him except to say,
'So this is how you misapply your time, you shameless
idolator. Bowing to graven images!'

Gulping air, he wanted to retort, 'That's blasphemy!'
But failed.

'Oh, I'm sure you'd love to defy me and ask how
time spent in prayer can be called misapplied!'

That was so uncannily accurate, Hadrian recoiled as
from a blow.

She removed the flowers and berries from the candle-
holders with an exaggerated grimace and tossed them
on the floor.

'But I can answer you. It's because you don't pray
from honest love of God. You do it out of vanity and
self-indulgence. You do it to compare your trivial suffering with the transcendental agony of Jesus. Stop
blubbering!'

The boy tried, he honestly did try, and yet he failed.
He was so weak in flesh, it rendered his spirit fallible as
well. So he excused it to himself.

'I knew my poor dead sister was wrong to afflict you
with the name of a pope, dreadful outlandish name that
it is. Now take this Papist rubbish out of doors and burn
it. Ask Mrs Winter for coals from the range – humbly,
mind! After that beseech her to provide plain bread and
water for you at every meal for a week, to aid you on
the path of repentance. And never let me catch you at
such heresies again.'

Where was the angel this loathsome woman said was ever at his side? How could he permit such wickedness? Must angels not be just another lie? With a final pathetic attempt at remonstrance he blurted, 'Aunt! I never imagined you would destroy a representation of Our Lord!'

'Nor would I,' said she with a curl of her lip. 'It is not I who shall do it. It is you, who are yourself a brand to the burning. Now do as you're told!'

Forcing her way back through the door, she snagged her hoop-wide skirt on a splinter. It tore. A glance down, an exclamation of suppressed fury were succeeded by a glower at Hadrian, hoping to catch him in a bout of *Schadenfreude*. He had found his own way to the term. Aunt Eunice did not approve of the time he spent with books, especially in foreign languages, but it had been a condition of his father's will that he inherit his progenitor's library, and while she might discourage his use thereof she could not altogether interdict it. Not that he always understood what he read; however, there were certain usages that life illustrated for him.

But he was too feeble and heartsick to betray signs of the reaction his aunt was eager to rebuke him for.

It was only later, while he was presiding over the little pyre to which he had perforce consigned the crucifix, that presence of mind returned to him. Never had he prayed with such fervour and commitment as when he called on Jesus to avenge this insult, or if Jesus was too busy, then the angel alleged to companion him. The word 'angel' came from the Greek for 'messenger' – he knew that from the dictionary – so logically angels ought to relay prayers. But when the pyre had been reduced to embers and a wisp of smoke, no lightning had struck. The house still stood, four-square. There still wafted tantalizing odours from its kitchen.

And he had been condemned to bread and water.

In absolute despair he fled towards the Wilderness and there collapsed, moveless save that his body heaved with sobs.

> When the Brontës pleaded for more to eat, they were lectured on the sin of caring for carnal things and of pampering greedy appetites.

It was a long while before Hadrian realized where he had fallen. He roused slowly and stared around. What had tripped him was a tree stump long known but in his stumbling flight overlooked. It formed the focus of a little glade, maybe eight or ten feet across. And it was loud, for some animal had died on the far side of the stump and in putrefying summoned swarms of flies.

Awkwardly he pushed himself up from prostration and found with sudden insight that he was kneeling. He was kneeling before the stump. Objects reposed on its flat top: fading petals, a few of the first leaves to fall. Some were prettier and more colourful than what he had found to offer Jesus.

Who was in any case a liar and a cheat. He hadn't struck Aunt Eunice dead for ordering the burning of the crucifix. He hadn't filled the hungry. He had left his poor unhappy worshipper to weep and moan and –

And change his faith.

Slowly, but with growing resolution, he nodded new understanding. The clues – no, the proofs – were all around him. The best and clearest consisted in the flies. Was not God's rival called the Lord of Flies? He heard himself utter a little crazy chuckle. At least Beelzebub's messengers could be seen and heard. Moreover – staring, he actually *saw* them for the first time in his life – they were rather handsome, armoured in metallic green and blue.

But he'd never *seen* a messenger from Jesus.

Clumsy for the pain in his joints, Hadrian forced his scrawny body upright. From now on, he vowed, this would be the altar to which he carried offerings. It was a good and fitting place. Some day, if he prayed hard enough, he might witness Aunt Eunice devoured by flies like these. That would be a suitable fate. Yes: with flies crawling on her face, supping at her eyes and laying maggots in them, and not just her face, but . . .

Well, the rest of her. The rest, so efficiently hidden it might not, in fact, be flesh and blood.

Before heading back to the house, where supper waited (for him one wedge of dry bread and a glass of water), he made his first sacrifice to his new lord. He could think of nothing more apt than something of himself, so he opened his breeches and pissed on the stump.

From the edge of the little clearing he glanced back and was cheered to see that several of the flies from the rotting carcass had already diverted to investigate this new attractive smell.

He laughed, and was glad, it having been a long while since amusement stirred him.

But at supper with his aunt he was careful not even to hint at a smile.

> The food at boarding schools was generally appalling; the boys at Radley College were obliged to grub for bulbs in the garden to supplement their diet.

Very quickly Hadrian established a routine. He would excrete on the stump beside the carcass, thus ensuring more flies would gather – not that his current diet yielded much residue – and then whisper to them, convinced they would carry his message to their lord. To some he would say, 'Soften Mrs Winter's heart'; to others, 'Let me find food'; and to by far the most, 'Kill my aunt!'

After which he would kneel with eyes closed and fists clenched, staring blindly at the red of hate behind his lids.

And then eventually he would have to go away.

It was on the third day that, fearing in premature disappointment he must bring more desirable offerings and wondering whether he might spot a dead bird or animal, he followed some stray flies away from the stump. After a dozen paces he noticed many small bulges raising the leaf-mould. Poking at them, he abruptly realized: here were mushrooms.

Mushrooms! Mrs Winter never served them, but – for a change – that could scarcely be because Aunt Eunice forbade her. At any rate he recalled how she had tucked into them on occasional visits to his old home while his parents were alive, and how delicious they had tasted, fried in dripping or grilled with bacon. His mouth flooded at the memory. Tomorrow – no, in two days' time, perhaps three – he would steal into the kitchen, filch butter or lard, cook his booty with the door and window open to disperse the smell . . .

And he had been led hither by the flies.

'Better than Jesus!' he whispered defiantly to the air. 'You actually answer people's prayers!'

The following day his discoveries had begun to develop the proper mushroom shape, though their pale, whitish tops were still too convex. The day after, their ripening was nearly complete but they were still small. Fighting hunger with all the strength remaining to him, Hadrian put off the harvest yet one day longer in hope of reaping the maximum benefit.

And next morning, so pain-racked now he had to stop and rest every few paces, he carefully picked the mushrooms, making sure he secured the whole of the stems as well as the caps, and hirpled them back to the house. Mrs Winter would be busy upstairs airing bedding, for the day was fine; his aunt had just received the latest catalogue from Mudie's and was certain to be conning it — there might never befall a better opportunity.

Cautiously, having set the mushrooms on the kitchen table, Hadrian sought a frying-pan and located one on a low shelf. Clutching it, he straightened, turning as he rose . . .

And felt his left ear nipped as by a lobster's claw.

'So that's your game, is it?' rasped Aunt Eunice. 'Mushrooms! *Mushrooms!* A delicacy you planned to reserve for your greedy self, without offering so much as a morsel to the person who affords you lodging and does her utmost to tame your rebellious and ungrateful spirit!' Turning where she stood: 'Had you foreknowledge of this felonious behaviour, Mrs Winter?'

She should have been in one of the bedrooms, but she was here behind his aunt. Hadrian felt sure he would faint presently.

'N-no, ma'am!' whimpered the cook-general.

'I trust not, indeed! You wouldn't wish to lose your place, would you? As you most certainly shall if I catch you aiding and abetting this miscreant. Cover those mushrooms to keep the flies off and dress them for my dinner. This villain's reward shall be to watch his haul being consumed – not that I expect the sight to soften his recalcitrant heart. To your room, sirrah! And stay there until I send for you!'

She ate all the mushrooms, every shred, pronouncing them delicious, and wiped the juice up with a slice of bread. Timidly Hadrian hinted that he would not refuse a drop to moisten his own crust, but she snorted and rang for Mrs Winter to clear away.

I want you to be consumed by flies. And worms, and slimy mould!

But he kept his pale face as still as had been that of the crucifix, and directly after grace he returned to his room without bidding. He felt very tired, and eventually lay down and dozed off.

> As a child, Augustus Hare was vilely treated,
> mainly at the instigation of his religious crazed
> Aunt Esther, whom he described as the Inquisi-
> tion herself.

When he was woken – by Mrs Winter shouting her way along the passage – it was night, though half a moon beamed from a cloudless sky. Stiffly he sat up as the door was flung open. He heard: 'Bear this note to the doctor! Your aunt is ill!'

What? I can't believe it! Oh, wonderful! And Dr Mostyn is dead so he can't help her!

Striving to conceal jubilation, he pointed that out, but Mrs Winter interrupted. 'No, my sister told me. The new doctor has arrived – he moved in yesterday. Come on, stir your stumps! You'll not need a lantern with this moon.'

Sickly Hadrian drew on his boots.

The doctor's house was dark when he reached it — having done his best to hurry even though the temptation was to dawdle and delay assistance for his aunt now he no longer feared his guardian angel — but in response to his lifting-dropping of the knocker Mrs Chalk opened the door on a chain and blinked at him in the yellow glow of an oil-lamp.

'Why, it's Master Hadrian! What brings you at this hour? Saints alive! Doctor! *Doctor!*'

For the boy had slumped unconscious on the step.

> She shut Augustus to sleep in two dismal uncarpeted rooms, looking out into the courtyard of a howling dog. He had no hot water, no heating, his chilblains worsened and his beloved cat Selina was hanged by the potty Aunt Esther in the name of some religious moral or other.

Hadrian woke to twilight seeping through drawn curtains. He lay in a clean, soft bed amid a confusion of trunks and boxes, suggesting that new residents had taken over too recently to have unpacked. Unfaded patches on the wall showed where pictures had been removed after long tenure. That was enough to remind him where he had come to last night.

He had been roused by the click of the door. Mrs Chalk was admitting, presumably, the new doctor. He seemed absurdly young compared with grizzled Dr Mostyn with his toll of years.

'Ah, you're awake. Good morning. I'm Dr Bond.'

Hadrian muttered a few half-audible words, trying to sit up despite feeling as lax-limbed as he was light-headed. The doctor checked him with a gesture.

'You must rest until you're better,' he decreed. 'I've heard about the way your aunt treated you, and it was nothing short of a disgrace. Why Dr Mostyn never . . .'

Hadrian didn't catch the remainder. Suddenly he was giddy from not inanition but anticipation. Dr Bond had used – had he not? – the past tense.

'I said: do you know what's wrong with you?' The words he hadn't registered were being repeated, louder. Hadrian shook his head, trying not to betray his delight.

'Your gums bleed, correct? You bruise easily? Your joints ache?'

This time a nod.

'You have scurvy,' Bond said in disgust. 'And the way that woman starved you, it's no wonder. But we'll see you well soon enough. I've sent my coach-man to find watercress and lemons. Meantime Mrs Chalk is brewing up beef tea. Is it not yet ready, Mrs Chalk?'

'Soon as it is I'll bring it,' was her composed reply.

'You'd best stay here for a few days,' the doctor continued. 'When you're up to it I'll send you home. But you needn't be afraid. I've given Mrs Winter a piece of my mind that she won't forget in a hurry.'

Hadrian could contain himself no longer. 'Is Aunt Eunice dead?'

Bond blinked. 'Hasn't anybody told you? Yes, she is – and, so I'm informed, through her own fault. I gather you were so hungry yesterday you picked some wild mushrooms and she insisted on eating the lot.'

Hadrian's voice was instantly hoarse. 'They were toadstools?'

'Among the most dangerous kind. They take hours to show an effect, but when they do it's already too late. You're lucky to be alive.'

Lord of Flies, your messengers bore you my prayer and you listened, you listened!

Under the bedclothes he clenched his fists in sign of worship.

But yesterday I'd have counted myself lucky not to be alive . . .

Muzzily he tried to figure out the logic of what had transpired, but he was too weak and too confused.

Dr Bond turned to the door, instructing Mrs Chalk to see whether the beef tea was ready and deliver lemonade as soon as the coachman returned. She departed. About to follow, struck by a sudden thought, Bond hesitated. 'Life under your aunt's thumb must have been a foretaste of hell. You didn't by any chance –?' But he broke off, shaking his head.

'Please finish,' Hadrian invited.

'I was about to ask: did you know what you were picking? But it's a silly question. You were planning to eat the things yourself, weren't you? It was just your aunt's greed that made her appropriate them.' Dr Bond spread his hands and smiled. He was rather a nice-looking young man, Hadrian decided. 'It was a silly question, wasn't it?'

The boy smiled back. 'I'm afraid so, sir. I don't know anything about fungi. I was just so hungry, you see.'

'Yes, I thought that must have been the way of it . . . Well, I'll leave you in peace. Sleep as much as you can. It'll help to build up your strength. I'll see you later.'

'Just a moment, please.'

'Yes?'

'You said "among the most dangerous kind". Does that mean you know what sort, or are you just going by what happened?'

'As luck would have it, I dare think I have identified

the species. It's not a common one, but I located another stand close by the one you found, so I brought back samples to compare with a book I own, and they match the plate depicting *Amanita virosa*.' He added after a pause, 'You may judge how deadly that is from its English name.'

'Why, what can it be called?'

'Destroying Angel . . . Ah, I hear Mrs Chalk coming back. Don't forget what I said about plenty of sleep. Before you go home –'

But Hadrian wasn't listening. He was silently pledging life-long fealty to Beelzebub who commanded real messengers that did real things.

All quotations are from Consuming Passions *by Philippa Pullar (Hamish Hamilton Ltd, 1970).*

The Visit

KATHRYN PTACEK

The first day I noticed the angel it was snowing.

Snow and angels went together, I thought, as I looked out of the window into the backyard. But in October?

It was two-thirds of the way through the month, and the weather had been peculiar all year long for this part of the south-west, so why not expect heavy snow in October? At least it wasn't July. Now *that* would have been ridiculous.

I stood watching the angel, who was busy darting through the drifting flakes, looking as if he – or was it a she, or possibly an it? Had some ecumenical council somewhere determined the sex of angels? And just how was that done anyway? – wanted to pick up his robes and roll and roll and roll.

The ground wasn't quite white yet, so the angel would probably get more dirt than snow on his flowing robes.

Angels with dirty faces, I thought, the old movie title floating into my mind.

After a while the snow stopped. There was hardly more than half an inch coating the ground, and the angel stopped his dancing, or whatever it was, and turned to gaze at me through the window.

Involuntarily I stepped backward. Then I realized what I was doing and gave a little laugh. The angel could have seen me at any time. Why did it bother me now? I'd been standing in front of the picture window for an hour.

Framed.

Outlined.

Vulnerable.

I shifted uncomfortably. There was no reason to be afraid of an angel, after all.

The second day I saw the angel the wind was blowing, propelling the clouds through the turquoise sky as if they were mere pieces of fluff. The day was warmer than the previous one, and there was the smell – the tease – of rain in the air. I watched the angel dance in the wind, rainbow raiment twisting this way and that with the air currents, long coppery hair spinning outward from his head.

I thought of all the phrases that involved angels: your guardian angel watches over you, my mother always insisted; be an angel, my maiden aunt said to coax me to do something I didn't want to do; how many angels can dance on the head of a pin? ran the old religious debate. 'Angel of the Morning' . . . a song; 'Teen Angel' . . . another one. An angel on Broadway meant someone who supplied the money for the production of a play or musical. Angel dust . . . used to be good stuff, now it was a drug. You lay down in the snow and moved your arms and legs vigorously and 'made' an angel.

Angels to the left, angels to the right, angels, stand up, sit down, fight, fight, fight.

I smiled briefly, then wondered if my thoughts verged on the heretical. I didn't think Father Sanchez would approve much, but then Father Sanchez hadn't approved of much of what I'd done, starting with when I left the Church at the age of eighteen. He hadn't approved of

Andrew or our marriage or what came after. He had approved of Patrick, though, and that had been good. But then Patrick –

No, I told myself. I didn't want to think of little Patrick or Andrew. That way lay madness. Or at least more pain, pain that I couldn't control, pain that racked my mind and soul. And hadn't I, through sheer force of will, driven that pain from my heart? Hadn't I built walls around myself so that I could retreat to this neutral spot and think of nothing, feeling nothing?

Hadn't I?

I watched a few minutes longer, then slowly backed away, never turning my back on the creature that danced in the wind.

I didn't know why the angel made me uneasy, but he did. Maybe even a little fearful.

Angels were good, weren't they? They were *godly* creatures, after all.

I remembered that when I was a little girl, long before I went to school, I contracted chickenpox so severely that I had almost died. My mother told me later that I had insisted that I saw someone – something – in the corner, an angel, perhaps, 'come to take me away'. She always dismissed it as a mere fever dream. But what if it were true? I wished I'd asked my mother about it when I was older, but I left home for college, and then later my parents had died in a car crash, and so much had been left unsaid, unfinished, between them and me.

Come to think of it, they probably wouldn't have approved of Andrew either.

I breathed deeply and thought I felt a pain in my chest. Nothing physical, I assured myself; just some little shard left over from the breaking of my heart.

Outside, the angel whirled and twirled, and my attention returned to him.

Angels . . .

Angel-food cake . . . angelfish . . . angel-hair pasta . . . Los Angeles, the City of Angels . . . there were so many phrases, so many times that angels touched our lives. If you had an angel on your shoulder, you were lucky.

The third day I saw the angel it was raining.

Water gushed from the leaden sky, drenching the poor creature. His – her – its hair lay in strings across its thin face. The robe, once so beautiful, sagged around the creature's asexual body, and even the feathers of its magnificent wings drooped.

It stared at the house . . . at *me* . . . as if the rain and its miserable condition were all my fault.

I ached for it. It looked so lonely. Like me. Should I invite it in for a cup of tea and a chance to dry off? What would happen if I went to the back door and called to it? Did I want to know?

Yes.

No.

Yes.

I walked into the kitchen and stood there, my fingers resting lightly on the knob, and thought about what lay beyond.

Something . . . unknown.

Something . . . marvelous.

Something . . . angelic.

Something wonderful to touch my life . . . finally.

I'd better do something before I chickened out.

I whisked the door open and stared out into the pattering rain, but the angel was gone.

★

He didn't show up the next day, nor the next. A week later he was still missing.

Or whatever you wanted to call it. And I felt the loss far more than I wanted to admit. I had been alone for years now, since Patrick, since Andrew, and I had grown accustomed to it, and it didn't bother me.

Or so I had thought.

But now it got to the point where I would get up at different times of the night to check my moonlit yard to see if the angel was there.

But he wasn't.

I was relieved, and yet ... there was a hint of disappointment.

The mornings were grey.

Imagine, though, I told myself as I checked in my car's rear-view mirror to see that my lipstick hadn't transferred to my teeth, if I'd mentioned the angel to anyone at work. Imagine if some of them had come home with me to see the angel. Imagine when the angel didn't show up.

The guys in white suits would come for me with butterfly nets, I told myself, and laughed nervously, the sound too loud in the car's confined space.

When I got to work I hiked my way to the building from the lower lot. I always parked down there to force myself to walk those extra yards. I waved off-handedly to a cluster of fellow workers who greeted me, and I smiled politely, although I didn't really hear what any of them said. I had worked here, shuffling bureaucratic papers in this state government office, away from the public and all of the people there and their pitiful stories, for nearly a decade now, and I didn't think I knew anyone here better than I had the first time I walked through the door.

My walls kept them out.

My walls kept me in.

Once in my cubicle, I reached for the morning paper and scanned the headlines of the front section.

I was searching, as I had been since first I'd seen the exquisite angel that snowy morning, for some mention in the local newspaper.

Nothing.

Not even a paragraph buried in the back section, right before Classified.

Or possibly they weren't admitting it. Or else they *had*, and the men with the butterfly nets had already come for them.

Still it would have been comforting to see some reference, no matter how small, to another sighting . . . somewhere, anywhere. Some little blurb to reassure me that I really wasn't losing it.

How nice it would be to see something like 'Penny Warren of Pennsauken today reported seeing an angel. Ms Warren invited the angelic visitor in for decaf and doughnuts, whereupon the angel bestowed her with many wondrous gifts and then left, declaring that Ms Warren's homemade doughnuts were the best he'd ever tasted.'

Then I could call up Penny Warren back in Pennsauken, and we could chat about our mutual strange experience, and there would be some comfort in knowing . . . knowing that I wasn't alone.

But angels wouldn't come in and chow down on glazed and raspberry-filled doughnuts.

Would they?

And what kind of wondrous gifts would an angel give someone? Long life? Wealth? Health? For God's sake, I told myself, *angels* aren't *genies*.

Or maybe angels brought the gift of removal of memories? I wouldn't mind that. Memories brought pain, and pain brought awareness, and –

No. The walls slid down silently, and I forced myself to smile, alone in my cubicle. My practiced smile, my friendly yet impersonal smile, my smile that said nothing is affecting me, I'm quite all right, thank you.

But it really didn't matter, did it? No one else had seen the angel, an angel . . . any angel. Only I had. Or perhaps others had seen them but said nothing. They didn't want the butterfly nets coming after them.

An angelic visitation.

I was far from being a saint or a virgin, so I wondered that an angel would call on me. He hadn't spoken to me, though, so was it a *real* visitation? I wished that I still went to church, that I could talk to Father Sanchez or someone about this. Was I blessed by this event? How should one feel when one was blessed? I didn't feel any different. Or did I? I patted my hair, aware for the first time that I did this too often.

But, I thought and took strength in that thought, I might not be alone. Perhaps the angelic visitations numbered in the dozens . . . the hundreds . . . the thousands.

Literally an angelic invasion. Hundreds and hundreds of celestial beings sprinkled through this country and others. Maybe it signified the coming of better times, the coming of the end of the world. Maybe it meant nothing.

Maybe it meant ultimately that we weren't alone, that someone waited.

Maybe it didn't mean that at all.

I sighed, shoved the paper aside and got to work. I had too much to do that day without dreaming about angels and such nonsense. I focused on the numbers and not the pitiful excuses, and told myself for the millionth time that I really enjoyed my work.

Only once more that day, and that was right before lunchtime, did I think of the angel, and that was to tell myself that I would be better prepared next time – next time I'd have my camera at hand. I'd take a photograph of the angel, and then I'd have the film developed, and there, that would prove that I was seeing an angel.

Prove to whom? I asked myself.

Prove to myself, but by now I was wondering if I had really seen it.

But I *had* seen the angel because the very next day it was back in my yard.

It just stood there in the yard, not doing anything. It wasn't dancing. Just standing. The wind didn't blow; there was no snow or rain. It was a perfect October day, with the sky overhead a rich turquoise.

The angel was staring at my house, staring at *me*, I decided, and I wanted to be somewhere else.

I was nervous and wanted to stay away from the window, but I couldn't. All I could think of was the angel. I had to go to work but couldn't. I couldn't bring myself to go out of the door. Even though the angel was in the back yard, he might come around to the front yard. He might block the driveway. I might hit him with my car. What happened if you accidentally killed an angel? I frowned. Wasn't there a story a long time ago about something like that? I couldn't remember, but I figured it couldn't have had a pleasant ending. They rarely did.

I could still remember the sound the car made that day . . . that gentle *thump* . . . and then I slammed on the brakes and I was out on the driveway in an instant, and there was the little broken body of Patrick who had been playing under the car. I would have known that too if Andrew and I hadn't been fighting as usual, if I hadn't stormed out of the house, hadn't thrown the car in reverse without checking . . . checking as I always did.

Except that day.

I couldn't face the car today.

Too many memories, and my wall seemed to be crumbling in spots.

So I called in sick, and spent most of the day flitting from window to window, looking out. The angel was there all day too, just standing and looking.

Gooseflesh erupted on my skin, and I rubbed my upper arms.

I tried to read some of the books that had been piling up by my couch but couldn't concentrate. I tried to watch some soaps on the television, but all I saw was the angel standing there.

Finally, I stood and told myself that this was nonsense and that I had to face this thing once and for all. I didn't have any home-made doughnuts, but I had a box of ginger snaps. Maybe he'd like a couple of those.

I went to the back door and opened it. If I expected a gust of wind or something equally dramatic at that moment, then I was disappointed.

The angel continued to look at me.

I smiled.

The angel smiled back.

I breathed a sigh of relief. This wasn't so bad after all.

'I would like to invite you inside,' I called, using my friendliest tone, and I smiled my bureaucratic smile because I no longer knew how to smile otherwise. 'There's so much to speak of.'

'So much,' the angel echoed.

He glided toward the house, toward me, and it wasn't until he was on the patio and only a few feet away, that I saw his eyes weren't the heavenly cerulean blue I had envisioned but rather a flat *dead* black; and his skin wasn't porcelain-white but rather the pasty color of something diseased.

It took a few seconds before I recognized Patrick.

I think I said, 'God help me,' but by then it was too late.

Part-singing

NINA KIRIKI HOFFMAN

'But I don't want to go caroling,' Molly told her older sister Serena. Molly pulled her legs up on to the canopy bed and wrapped her thin arms around them. 'I don't want to do anything Christmas-like this Christmas.'

'It's Christmas Eve. We always go caroling Christmas Eve, and you know it. You've been moping long enough,' said Serena. She paced across to Molly's dresser and fiddled with the pink hair-brush, tugging long, dark-gold hairs from it, holding them up for a moment, then dropping them in the waste basket. 'So he's dead. You've got to accept it and go on instead of staying stuck.'

'Puh-lease, spare me the clichés.' Molly ran her hands through her caramel-colored hair, then pulled her hair forward so it covered her face. 'Excuse me if I have things to do in my own room and don't feel like spending time with the rest of you drones. Like, you're all so fascinating!'

'Well, we are,' Serena said. 'You're just being a gloomy little brat.'

'Isn't that my job?'

Serena stared at Molly's hair-concealed face. At twenty-one Molly was the youngest, and maybe it *was* her job to be an unbearable brat. Even though all five of the siblings were in their twenties, they maintained the roles they had learned before they turned ten. It might have helped if one or more of them had moved away from home, but somehow no one ever did. 'And it's my job as the oldest to try to get you to come back to the family,' Serena said. 'All this posturing had a certain charm when you started it, but that was five months ago. We're bored with it now. Come up with some other act.'

Molly leaned over until she fell to her side on the bed, still curled up. She chewed on a lock of hair. She knew she would have been bored with her own moping if she were someone else watching it, but what she couldn't seem to convince anybody of was that she really *didn't* feel good, and it wasn't going away. She wasn't sure if she would ever feel better. Her family thought she was just being dramatic, but she really had loved Harold. She hadn't known him very well, but he had told her many amazing things, and he was on his way to making her believe them when he had died.

He had told her she could come live with him. He had told her it was normal for people her age to move out of their parents' houses. He had told her she could get a job and support herself. He had said all these incredible things as if they were perfectly sensible. He had even taken her to his apartment and showed her how he lived, let her search each room for evidence that he had a sibling or a parent or an aunt in residence; it certainly looked as though he lived alone, even though he had a guest room into which he said she could move.

Harold. Harold had promised her a new life. Harold hadn't treated her like a colossal brat and a pain who had to be ordered around all the time or nagged or manipulated into doing things 'for her own good'. He told her she was an adult and could make her own decisions. When he had said things like that, she had felt terrified and excited, as if she were considering a new religion.

They had gone to thrift stores together, and when she found a shirt her mother would never in a million years have let her wear – a shiny yellow shirt of some slippery material, a shirt that for some reason Molly loved – Harold had told her she could buy it and wear it. She never wore it at home. She was sure that if she ever took that chance, the family would inundate her with criticism, maybe even tear the shirt right off her and rip it into shreds. But she kept it at Harold's apartment and sometimes wore it when she and Harold went out for coffee. He said it made her eyes greener. He said very few people could wear yellow like that, but she could. He told her she looked terrific. She played the I-believe-you game for as long as she was with him. It made her feel strange and brave and different.

Since his death she had found that all she wanted to do was lie in her room and dream about all the things he had told her. Even the silliest small things, like 'Why don't you try this one?' or 'You could have a bite of my dessert to see if you like it.' Before she met Harold she had never ordered anything new off a menu, always something she had tasted before. He took her to Thai and Vietnamese and Japanese restaurants where there was nothing familiar on the menu. Sometimes she didn't like what she had ordered, but sometimes she did. He never said she had to eat it all if she didn't like it, even though often he was paying for it.

She used to wonder how she had gotten lucky enough to meet Harold in her art class at junior college, and then have him actually press past all her resistance and barriers to ask her for a date, and to contradict her own programming and say yes.

Now she wondered if she had been lucky at all to have known him and lost him.

'If you don't come caroling with us,' Serena said, 'mom said I could cut your hair off. All of it. I'll use daddy's Norelco. I know you don't get out much, but just think if you had no hair. You'd never leave your room at all.'

'Mom did not say that!'

'Ask her.'

Molly parted her hair and stared at her sister, who was leaning against the wall and studying the ceiling, the pink hairbrush still in her hand. It didn't sound like something mom would say, but Molly had never resisted family plans to this extreme before. Like the rest of her siblings, she had learned that things were much more comfortable if she followed mom's and dad's suggestions. 'Would you do something like that?'

Serena's eyes looked into Molly's. 'Sure,' she said, without even the hint of a smile. 'I might even enjoy it. You're driving me crazy.'

'I'm not doing anything to you.'

Serena hunched her shoulders. 'You are. You're stretching the – the unit. You're throwing us all off-balance. Besides, we really need a soprano.'

Mom and dad had forged them into a tight, precise vocal group even before their voices had changed, had run them through the rigors of sight-reading and harmonizing, made them practice year round even when they were children, found outlets for them to perform – at mall openings, parties, churches, charity events. Group singing was part of the fabric of tradition that bound them all together.

Serena was an alto; Tim was a tenor; Karen was almost a soprano; and Brian was a bass. It was true, only

Molly had that high, clear soprano, but they could sing the carols straight, without parts, for one year or have the men take the melody and women the harmony or something. They were all flexible and adept.

'I'm going for the Norelco,' said Serena.

Molly closed her eyes for a second, thinking about Harold. Then she sat up. 'OK. All right. Leave me alone.'

'Be in the front hall at ten minutes of seven,' said Serena, 'if you want to keep your hair.'

First they went to the Golden Years Retirement Home. Every year it was their first stop, while they still had plenty of voice left. Mom and dad had established the tradition when the children were still too young to go out alone. 'Serve your community now, and it will serve you later,' dad always said. 'Serve your family now, and it will always be here for you,' he also said.

Molly had liked singing in the retirement home because the activities director gave them candy afterward.

It was when she was singing, 'Glo-o-o-o-o-ria,' and looking out over the listening seniors sitting in chairs that Molly first saw the shadow. She was smiling at an old lady with improbable yellow hair and lots of eye make-up and a bright-yellow jacket – it made Molly think of her precious secret yellow shirt – when she saw a shadow behind the lady that nothing was casting. In fact, it stood against the window that the westering sun shone through. A faint stain on the air, that was all, at first.

'In excelsis Deo,' sang Molly, looking elsewhere, spying a small, elfin man with glasses and a big grin. She remembered him from last year. He had invited her to go out to dinner with him, told her to call up the retirement home and ask for Ken. He had frightened her. That was before Harold. Every suggestion that she spend time away from her family had scared her then. She wondered what she would do if he asked her this year.

When she glanced back the shadow was darker, and there was something familiar in its outline.

'Shepherds, why this jubilee?' she sang, staring at the shadow, which grew darker and took on solidity. 'Why these songs of happy cheer?'

A face emerged from the shadow. Harold's face, his glasses gleaming, his mouth smiling.

'What great brightness did you see?' Molly sang, her voice fading. Karen nudged her, and, startled, she glanced at her sister, took a deep breath and jumped on the next line. 'What glad tidings did you hear?'

Harold stood, quiet and shadowy, through the rest of the performance. Molly still looked at other people, but her eyes always came to rest on him. She felt a strange stirring in her chest. She wasn't sure if she was hallucinating Harold or actually seeing him; none of her brothers or sisters seemed to notice him, and none of the older people in the room reacted to him either.

What if he were really there, though?

If he wasn't, why was she conjuring him up?

When they had run through their half hour of allotted carols and took the synchronized bow their parents had drilled into them, to a smattering of applause, the loudest coming from the activities director, the shadow that was Harold came closer.

Molly glanced at Karen, then at Harold, wondering if Karen would notice. Molly had never introduced Harold to her family. She had always been afraid that if they met him, if they knew him, they would somehow take him away from her. Her mother had removed most of her schoolfriends when Molly had brought them home after class, enchanting them until they said to Molly, 'What a great mother you have. You're so lucky! I wish my mother was like yours!' All her friends wanted to do was visit her mother; and if Molly tried to complain about anything going on at home, they no longer believed her.

Harold had been her refuge and her sounding board, even before she knew she had something to say. He had asked her real questions, drawn her out, then told her that some of the things she had always believed might be wrong.

'It's been our pleasure,' Serena said to their audience. 'See you next year, and merry Christmas!' They struck up 'We Wish You a Merry Christmas' as they filed out, lockstep. Harold matched Molly's stride, sneaking smiles at her.

'Now, we want our figgy pudding,' Molly sang to him, her voice wavering a little, as they all slipped out of the door. It was just as well, really, because singing 'We won't go until we get some' was counter-productive; nobody had ever explained what figgy pudding was, and nobody ever offered them any despite their insistence. What if somebody suddenly offered them some figgy pudding? What if it was horrible stuff?

'Save your voice,' said Karen, nudging her. Molly broke off in mid-note and followed her siblings into the van. She climbed into the very last bench, alone – or nearly alone, because Harold came too. Karen almost shut the door on him.

'Children's ward next,' Brian said. 'Anybody need a cough drop?'

'Harold,' Molly whispered under cover of the engine starting.

His shadow was a strange presence beside her, dark except for its face, like a mask on a pine tree.

He glanced at her. Light glinted from his glasses. He said nothing.

Molly felt a deep chill. She wanted to reach out to him but was afraid her hand would go right through him. What was he doing here? Here, in the midst of family, where she had never wanted him to be?

'I miss you,' she said. 'I miss you so much.'

He didn't smile or frown. He just watched her, with his serious, I'm-thinking-hard-about-this look.

She hugged herself. She wasn't sure it was any better being able to look Harold in the eye than it had been when she was just missing him hopelessly. Somehow it hurt more, the way the smell of something delicious coming from a restaurant could torture one when one had no money.

When they reached the hospital, Tim yelled at her for not climbing out immediately; she was still waiting for Harold to move. He thinned and vanished, and she scooted out of the van, feeling as if her feet touched air instead of ground.

'You look pale, Molly,' Karen said. 'You feeling all right?'

'I wish I'd never come,' said Molly.

'We need you,' Karen said.

'I don't know,' Molly said.

'You need a glass of water? An aspirin?' asked Serena.

'Peanuts?' Tim said.

'Let's just sing and get it over with,' said Molly.

'Nice attitude,' Brian said, frowning.

Molly shrugged.

Brian led the way to the elevator and they rose to the fifth floor, where the ward was expecting them; all the mobile children had been gathered in the activity room.

They went through half their repertoire before Molly saw Harold again, lurking behind a pale bald child seated in a wheelchair.

'Shepherds, why this jubilee?' Molly sang, the melody clear and carrying in her voice as the other three wove harmonies around it.

Molly, why not come with me? Harold sang, his words twining with hers; she could only hear them because the ones she was singing had ceased to have meaning for her.

'Why these songs of happy cheer?'

There is nothing for you here, Harold sang along with her.

'What great brightness did you see?'

They just use you, can't you see?

'What glad tidings did you hear?'

Leave them; you'll have less to fear.

'Glo o-o-o-o-o o-o-o-o-o o-o-o-o-o-ri-a . . .'

You need to get away, need to get away, need to find yourself someday . . .

'In excelsis Deo . . .'

Molly, let me help you . . .

His voice wove with hers in a new way. His voice was not a perfectly edged precision instrument like the voices of her siblings but a little rough, a little off-key, and yet blending with hers so that hers sounded different and new to her. Somewhere in the harmonics, or the undertones, possibilities and promises chimed.

Come, far away from here, there is room out there for the things that you can do . . . There's a life you don't know, he sang.

Then the song was over.

Harold stood silent as she and her brothers and sisters sang 'Joy to the World'. She sang, and she listened, and she thought how fine a thing it was that she and her siblings had this shaped and crafted art, that music was alive while it was being sung, taking on an identity all its own, but without even one of them it would be only half as good. The year Karen had had laryngitis, and they sang without her, their carols had been without soul; the vital spirit that filled Molly when she knew they were all in tune and on time would not come alive. They were all together, and Molly was comfortable in the midst of them. It felt right to be here.

She didn't even have to think very much about what she was doing; her body had been taught and rehearsed into this function, and it was a wonderful thing to see and hear when she watched and listened to her siblings, and a wonderful thing to be on the inside. Nothing to fear; serene contentment, a sense of perfection and accomplishment, of knowing every minute that this was a job she knew and loved and that she could trust the others to carry out their parts with equal perfection.

She would never find other people she could do this with, she was sure of it, not with their history and commitment and dedication. She had never seen another family who had done what she and her siblings did. What could ever compare with this?

'It came upon a midnight clear, that glorious song of old,' they sang.

Molly, you are in prison here, although the bars are gold, Harold sang.

'From angels bending near the earth,' Molly sang, and her voice faltered. What was Harold if not an angel bending near the earth?

The others sang on without her, though Karen nudged her; they tried to capture the power of the carol, Karen assuming the melody and the others filling in, but something was missing.

Molly was missing.

Without her, there was no magic.

Her golden prison of music, whose bars caressed her, whose sounds fed her something essential, was something she couldn't live without.

'Peace on the earth, good will toward men, from Heaven's all-glorious King/The world in solemn stillness lay to hear the angels sing.'

Say no, my love, trust me and then you'll do this important thing./It's time to let this prison go and find your own bright wings.

Molly felt tears forming, hot and wet, in her eyes. She thought of one night when she sat all alone in Harold's apartment while he went out to pick up Chinese take-out. She had sat there on a couch in the silence, with none of the house-awareness she felt at home; at home she had a sense of where everyone was in the house, what they were doing, if a moment was coming when she would want to, or be expected to, join them for a meal, for television, for singing practice or just to talk. She sat and tasted the light, heady wine of no demands and no expectations, of no one even knowing where she was.

In that moment she had felt there were a million possibilities just waiting for her to pick one of them. She could get in her car and drive to someplace she'd never been, where no one knew her or wanted anything from her. She could take a nap; she could stand on her head; she could draw, or bake, or dance naked through the apartment.

She had gone to the window and looked out at the city night, and she had sung a song she had heard on the radio, the kind the family would never, ever sing, and she had listened to her voice alone, its sound a pure golden thread soaring to each note without scooping or wobbling or effort, each word clear and full and startling. There was none of the spirit that filled the music when she sang with her siblings, but something else was there.

Brian gripped her shoulder from behind. She glanced back at him, felt a tear streak down her cheek. He stared into her eyes, his own at first angry, then troubled, then just sad. She felt a twisting in her gut, sensed that she was cutting some thread that held her up, as though she were a marionette; and yet she did not collapse. She was still standing.

'It's been our pleasure,' Serena said to the children, her voice faltering a little. 'See you next year, and Merry Christmas!'

Brian squeezed Molly's shoulder. She wiped her eyes and faced front, joining with the others in 'We Wish You a Merry Christmas'.

She felt each word as it moved over her tongue, thinking it was a way of saying goodbye to her siblings, a way of saying hello to standing alone.

And a happy new life, Harry sang to her, with her, his voice not quite in tune and yet strong and steady, full of furry tones she never heard in the voices of her brothers.

'And a happy new life,' Molly whispered.

Gordy's A-OK

STEPHEN LAWS

He's nine years old but looks younger. A band of
freckles darkens the bridge of his nose and dots his
cheeks. His eyes are a kind of faded blue – almost the
same colour as the sky above him as he wheels in a
crazy arc on the rough wooden swing in the garden.
His name is Gordy, and his mouth is opened wide in a
silent, exhilarated shout of happiness as he embraces the
clouds. It's a familiar expression that seems to say: *It's
great to be alive*.

Which is crazy, of course.

He leans back in the small wooden seat as the swing
reaches the apex of its new ascent and then hurtles
backwards again. He adjusts his position and frog-kicks
his legs for greater impetus and height on the next
return. His jeans have ridden up almost to his knees,
revealing scabbed shins. They're the same jeans he was
wearing on the day when . . . but I cancel that thought
as he swings even higher and makes me afraid that he
might go too far and fall. I move forward in alarm but
check myself before I can do anything. After all, how
could he hurt himself even if he fell? He can't be hurt
now.

Which is also crazy, of course.

Gordy's feet scrape the ground as he swings back
again, the impact rattling the tightly clutched seat chains.
He throws his head back and laughs his silent laugh
again.

I turn from the garden, where I've been watching him now for fifteen minutes, and walk slowly back across the patio, noticing from the corner of my eye the slight twitching of a curtain in the living room of our ever-watchful neighbour Mrs Grant, who lives alone in the large white house beyond the fence. Maybe she's been watching Gordy.

But that's even crazier, of course.

I reach the French windows and enter the house, gathering the kids' plates up from the kitchen table and dunking them in the sink. I pause to look up through the kitchen window as Gordy continues his silent assault on the sky (*Or is it surrender?* I ask, not really understanding why that thought should come to me.)

'Why is it always during the school holidays, Gordy?' I ask myself quietly as I begin the washing up.

Dennis has taken the kids to the pictures after failing to live up to three previous promises. But it's not such a chore, since he enjoys the kids' movies just as much as the kids do themselves. Barry is the same age as Gordy and about the same size, but he's heavier and has ginger hair like his dad. He has a brace on his teeth, likes fast bikes and comics and is a secret founder-member of the gang that smokes sly cigarettes in the small quadrangle, screened from the rest of the schoolyard. It's a precarious occupation for him, I think, because his sister – my daughter Janet – goes to the same school and hounds him continually with threats of 'telling on him' and horror tales about the dreaded weed. She's seven, doesn't like dolls but loves cartoons, Cherry Surprise chocolates and Mark Pagett from No. 7 Burlington Terrace. (I've seen the unposted love letters lying on sofas, chairs and even one day in the fridge, of all places. Cold hands, warm heart? I don't know.) Anyway, she's beautiful now and she'll be even more beautiful when she's older, which makes me wonder if Mark Pagett of No. 7 Burlington Terrace will regret his rejection of Janet's advances after he's reached the age when such things aren't regarded as 'soft' any more.

The swing chain rattles again, and I look up to see Gordy twist out of his seat in mid-air and land agilely in the garden, deliberately rolling over and over on the ground. He begins to practise handstands. I stand and watch for a while and then return to swabbing the dishes.

I married Dennis, the oldest brother in the Baxter family, ten years ago. We get along just fine. There was a rough patch five years ago when we seemed to just get on each other's nerves all the time, but that's all resolved now – every marriage has its problem patches – and we're really happy. Well, let's put it this way: the relationship is happy, we love each other and the kids. Everything on that side of things is fine.

But I'm not really happy in myself, if you know what I mean. And it has to do with that nine-year-old freckled kid out there who is walking on his hands and who now leaps back to his feet and begins to climb the tree at the bottom of the garden. There's a frisbee snared in the upper branches, which we've been trying to retrieve for the past six weeks with thrown stones and a clothes prop. Climbing is out of the question, of course – it's much too high and dangerous. Gordy scrambles upwards, and I know that he's going to try to reach it. Again I check the impulse not to bang on the window glass and tell him to come down before he hurts himself. But, of course, I'm being stupid. He won't fall out of the tree, and even if he does, it won't matter.

I love Gordy. I always will. And perhaps that's the reason why things are the way they are. Perhaps that's why he comes. This makes me wonder whether my love is like a chain that holds him here, and it can't be right if I'm keeping him here against his will.

Then I look at his face again and I think: *No, that's not really it. He wouldn't be here if he didn't want to be. Just look at his face. He's smiling, always smiling.*

Of course, I start to cry, which is the worst thing I can possibly do. Every time I cry, every time I try to speak to him and ask him what it's all about, he goes away.

I try to stop myself. I choke it back, but as I look up I see that Gordy, who never, ever looks at me or recognizes my presence, has heard or sensed me. He freezes in the tree, a small hand clutching up for the frisbee, fingers only inches away. He makes a half-turn of his head in my direction (but not *at* me, you understand) then pulls his hand back.

I realize now that it's too late and that this will be the end of his visit today.

He goes away.

The tears really flow now while I busily dry the dishes on the draining board, as if wiping them dry can dry the tears themselves. It doesn't work, of course.

'Why, Gordy? Why?' I ask, as if he was still here to answer me.

When I feel a little better I move into the living room, wondering if Gordy will be back again tomorrow – there never seems to be a set pattern for his visits. I find my magazine and slump on to the sofa. A box of chocolates lies open on the coffee table, with the Cherry

Surprise missing from its tray, while the television has been playing to a lost audience. But the quiz-show host, who beams at me from the screen, doesn't seem too bothered. I begin to read my magazine, and it's only when I've read the same paragraph six times without taking anything in that I realize my mind is too absorbed in other things to allow for light reading. Nevertheless, I do my best not to think about Gordy and flip through the pages of the magazine.

'. . . the latest design from La Frolière is perhaps a little too outrageous for even the most extroverted, but sales of this new line have indicated . . .'

Why, Gordy? Why?

'Dear Jane, I am writing to you because of my mother-in-law. Ever since I married my husband, John, three years ago, I have been increasingly concerned . . .'

And why only during the school holidays? Is it because the kids are around the house more often during the day? Is that it?

'. . . the film is an adaptation of the bestseller by Joseph Wambaugh and is the first starring role for Brooke Matthews, whose previous minor roles in . . .'

Why can't I even speak to you, Gordy? Why do you always go away when I try?

The next day is Saturday, and both of the kids are re-enacting the key scenes from the movie they saw with Dennis, up and down the stairs, over the furniture and under my feet. Dennis can sense that I've had a bad night (sleep did not come easily) and that I'm on edge this morning. He takes charge of the chores and bundles the kids out into the garden without having to ask how I'm feeling.

We talk small talk for a while. We're going out with

friends this evening, and Dennis has just telephoned to fix the final details of where we're meeting and who's catching up with us later on at the restaurant. I'm talking about what to wear, and he's telling me that the 'kid-sitting' arrangements are fine now.

We're saying all of these things to each other, but what we're really saying between the lines is:

Are you OK, Anne?

Fine.

You're not feeling good today. I can tell.

I'm going to be fine, Dennis. Just give me a little time.

You're feeling strained again, I know. What can I do to help?

Nothing. Really. Just a little time is all I need.

Dennis has got some work to do about the house this morning, while I've arranged to meet Geraldine for shopping. We'll have coffee, and she'll tell me all about her problems at home. But I'll probably not be able to concentrate on Geraldine's problems today.

There is a rattle and clatter from the garden and I look up quickly, heart pumping, expecting to see Gordy on the swing, swooping backwards and forwards with that beautiful smile on his face. But it isn't Gordy, it's Barry, and the disappointment I feel makes me terribly ashamed. It's as if I'd rather see Gordy than my own son out there.

Dennis encircles my waist from behind and presses his chin down on to my shoulder. The bad feeling disappears for a while. I smile and kiss him, then gather up my shopping bag and coat.

When I get home and begin unpacking the shopping on to the kitchen bench, I look out of that window again, and this time I do see Gordy.

He's standing by the fence, arms hooked through the tines and lifting his feet up to his chest – one-two, one-two. Barry and Janet are squabbling over the lost frisbee up in the tree again. It's Barry's frisbee, and they have been taking turns in throwing things at it. When it is Janet's turn, a freak gust of air carries it away into the uppermost branches. They both move to the base of the tree, only ten feet or so from Gordy, who is still preoccupied with his one-two, one-two, but don't see him. And Gordy, apparently, doesn't see them.

The kids' argument is becoming too heated. I bang on the window, and they look around. Gordy must know that the knocking is for the kids' benefit, so he doesn't freeze and then go away. Dennis leaves the pine bench on which he's been working and goes out into the garden to see if he can settle them down. He joins them at the foot of the tree, hands on hips, looking up and trying to decide on a new course of action to retrieve the frisbee.

Gordy begins to cartwheel over the grass and comes within inches of Dennis, but he never sees him.

Then I get to thinking about that day again, and this time the memory is too strong to be resisted or denied.

He was nine years old when it happened, wearing the same clothes he's wearing today, the same jeans, the same sandshoes.

The first things I saw when I pushed through the crowd on the pavement were the fish and chips he'd just bought for supper from the shop on the other side of the road. For some reason, it's the memory of that supper and the scattered newspaper in which it was wrapped, trodden underfoot by a gawping crowd of passers-by, that is the most unbearable. Gordy himself seemed untouched – as if he'd just decided to go to sleep in the middle of the road, face resting lightly on the

tarmac and with the same expression I'd seen on his face a
hundred times before when I'd tiptoed into his bedroom.
Innocent, open-mouthed and face down on his pillow, lost in
the land of Nod. That's the way he looked then, as if he were
at home in bed.

I was twelve. And it was my fault for what happened,
because I'd sent him to the fish-and-chip shop that night
while I stopped to talk to my friend on the street
corner. Gordy, you see – Gordon, that is – was my little
brother.

He started to come again just after I married Dennis.
That would be . . . let's see . . . when I was nineteen. I'm
twenty-nine now. I probably don't have to tell you
what I thought when he first started to appear – you can
no doubt guess. But Gordy's real, of course. Real in the
sense that he comes to me during the school holidays
even though no one else can see him. Not Dennis – not
Janet – not Barry – not even nosy Mrs Grant.

I've also learned that I can't approach him or speak to
him because he always disappears if I do that. And when
I cry, of course, this is worst of all.

'Why do you come, Gordy?' I mumble under my
breath, for fear of being heard. 'What are you trying to
tell me?'

Yes, I'm sure that he's trying to tell me something.
He knows I'm here, even though he never looks directly
at me. It's as if a direct confrontation or recognition
might somehow sever the strange laws that enable
Gordy to be here so long after that terrible accident.
Sometimes, though, I can tell that he's watching out of
the corner of his eye, as if entreating me to acknowledge and realize . . . something, I still don't know
what.

Of course, Dennis and the kids know nothing about

this. No one knows. How could they possibly understand?

Dennis has persuaded the kids that the frisbee is a lost cause and bundles them indoors and upstairs to tidy up their bedrooms, leaving me alone. The shopping's unpacked, so I wander out into the garden.

Gordy's gone again. This isn't surprising, but I feel sad that I haven't had a chance to watch him playing for as long as I'd like. I walk over to the swing and sit on it, holding the chains and swaying slightly back and forth, listening to the hollow screech of the chains on the metal poles. I'm thinking of that mysterious something that I know is the reason for Gordy's appearances, just as I've thought about it these long years gone by. Today is like any other day; there's no real reason to suppose I'm ever going to find out what he wants me to know, but somehow I've got this feeling that I might just be closer to the truth on this Saturday than I've ever been before. If only Gordy had stayed a little longer and given me a chance to watch him and think . . .

I rise from the swing and walk towards the tree, arms folded before me, wondering when he'll next appear. Someone is whistling somewhere. The kind of high-pitched, shrill whistle that can only be made by using two fingers in your mouth. I look back at the house to see who's making the sound, but there's no sign of Dennis or the kids. Again the whistling, and I look over the fence on to the pathway but see no one. When the whistling comes yet again, I'm starting to feel irritated. It is very shrill, making my eardrums vibrate, and it seems very close. But there is no one to be seen.

I look up.

Gordy is sitting in the top branches of the tree, one hand held to his mouth. I resist the urge to yell at him to come down before he falls and breaks his neck. But as I've said before, this would be a crazy thing to do. Instead I let my pleasure in knowing that he hasn't gone away yet take over.

Then, it hits me. Gordy is the whistler. Yet in ten years he's never made a sound before.

My heart is really hammering now as I strain to look up at him in the tree. Is it just a trick of the light, or is he really looking *directly at me* with that great big, beaming smile? I take a couple of steps back, shading my eyes with my hand, and now I'm sure – yes, I'm sure. There's a feeling of joy inside me, the kind of joy that hurts your throat, to know that finally, after all these years, Gordy is actually looking at me and recognizing me.

'Gordy! Gordy! Gordy!' I shout. And that's all I can find to shout as he takes his hand from his mouth and waves at me. I wave back furiously, not ever wanting him to go away again. But as we wave, and our eyes drink each other in, something happens.

Don't ask me how it happens, but it does. I suddenly realize things that I've never realized before. It's as if Gordy is telling me things, true things that can't be denied. He's not speaking to me, though; he's just looking at me, smiling. And I listen and understand, although *listen* isn't the right word. I just know.

I know now that I can't blame myself for what happened. An accident can happen any time, anywhere, and just because I'd sent Gordy for supper that night, it didn't make me responsible for what happened. There's been a shadow on my life all these years. It's never allowed me to be really happy.

Gordy says, although *says* isn't the right word, that I've spent too long being unhappy, and it's time to stop.

He says that it would have been better if I'd come to these realizations myself. But I've been incapable of it; that's why he's been coming, although he wasn't allowed to acknowledge my presence or speak to me.

And why in the school holidays? Well, of course, that's when the accident happened. That's when I feel really bad and need Gordy the most.

Gordy is telling me that the simple things are the best things. Love is a simple thing. The simplest and best thing. Gordy tells me that grief is normal and necessary but it shouldn't last for so long.

It's time to let go, says Gordy. Time to stop feeling pain. Keep our love because death can't end it. He raises his hand, and I can see that he's holding something in it. It's the frisbee.

He smiles again and then makes the sign with his other hand, a sign which he used to make all the time when he was alive and which, until now, I'd forgotten about. He pinches his thumb and forefinger together in a circle and holds it in a salute to me. He doesn't speak, but I can still hear the familiar phrase in that silly pseudo-American accent, which used to make the whole family fall about laughing whenever he used it.

'Gordy's A-OK!'

He smiles again and throws the frisbee, which sails gracefully down from the tree towards me. Suddenly it becomes terribly important that I catch the frisbee and don't drop it. But I don't really have to try because the frisbee dips down towards the ground and then floats up on an up-draught of air right into my hands.

I look up again. Gordy smiles.

And then he's gone.

Only this time I know he won't be back. That

knowledge doesn't make me sad because now I know that everything's OK.

Dennis and the kids come running out of the house because they heard me shouting earlier. Their look of concern changes when they see the frisbee in my hands. Dennis asks me how I did it, and I tell him that the wind blew it out of the tree. But I know by the look on his face that he can sense that something else happened. Something important. He kisses me but doesn't ask, and we both feel good.

I give the frisbee to the kids, but somehow that piece of ordinary round blue plastic now seems to be much, much more than just a frisbee. And my giving it to the kids seems important, though I don't know why.

The kids run away, squabbling over it. A warm wind caresses the upper branches of the tree as if something has flown away. I look up and feel for the first time that I can live my life without an awful shadow hanging over it.

Gordy's A-OK.

And that's fine by me.

The Realms of Glory

JUDITH MOFFETT

Mattie was canning peaches in a boiling-water bath, sweat dripping off the end of her nose, pink-rimmed glasses in danger of sliding completely off her face into the canner, when the whole kitchen flashed with brilliance and a loud voice pronounced: 'HAIL, O THOU BLESSED OF THE LORD!'

Mattie jumped. She put down her paring knife, pushed her glasses back up where they belonged and turned to stare at the intruder.

Between the kitchen table and the groaning refrigerator, feet just touching the linoleum, stood a man in a long white robe. One of his hands was holding a branch covered with peach blossoms straight up in the air. Except for his soft, shoulder-length blond hair, he was a dead ringer for Billy Keith Waller, who lived over on 33rd Street and ran the Friday-night fish fry for the Knights of Columbus in spite of being a deacon at the Baptist Tabernacle. Mattie looked the intruder up and down. 'Well if *you* don't look like one blame fool, Billy Keith. Tryin' ta git yersef arrested?'

After a little nonplussed pause, the bright figure brandished his flowery bough and tried again: 'HAIL, MATTIE PEAKE! THOU ART BLESSED OF THE LORD. I AM COME WITH A MESSAGE FROM THE MOST HIGH.'

Mattie turned her back on him, pushed up her glasses, picked up her paring knife and a big fuzzy peach from the basket. 'That the best you two could come up with? I'd be mortified, Billy Keith, I would really. Now go 'way. I got my work to do.' She ran the knife around the seam, pulled the peach apart, nipped the skin between her thumb and the blade and deftly pulled it free.

There was another short pause. 'I BEAR A MESSAGE FROM THE LORD OF HOSTS. I AM NOT THE BILLY KEITH OF WHOM YOU SPEAK,' the being intoned sternly.

Mattie whipped around and made a swipe at the wig with her peach-juice-covered left hand. The hand went right through the figure's head.

'Hunh!' said Mattie. Eyebrows raised, she passed her hand back and forth through the figure at head level. She stepped back, dried her hands on her apron and planted her fists on her skinny hips, frowning narrowly. 'One of them holographic projections. Nice to know some people got money to throw around on foolishness.' She turned decisively and picked up another peach.

'MATTIE PEAKE, INCLINE THINE EAR UNTO ME,' said the white-garbed image, beginning to sound a bit desperate. 'BANISH DOUBT FROM THY HEART AND HEAR ME!'

'Who ya tryin' t'impersonate, Billy Keith — the Ghost of Christmas Past?' said Mattie sardonically. 'You an' Bertha musta figured me fer as big a fool as y'all are if ya reckoned I wouldn't know ya in that wig!' She snorted. 'I ain't returnin' to the fold, now, and that's all there is to it! Now git!' She bisected the peach, prised out the stone and pulled the skin off. When she turned to look again, the kitchen was empty.

But only for an instant. Right in front of her eyes, the vision reappeared, still in its white choir robe but without the branch and, more significant, without the long hair. The image floating now just above the floor was bald, with a curly blond fringe around his shiny scalp. Mattie's eyes narrowed; in this 'bald' wig – if it was a wig – the resemblance to Billy Keith Waller was much less marked. 'Mattie Peake, thou seest I am not the man Billy Keith,' declared the robed figure in a less imperious voice. 'The hairs of my head are removed that thou mayest know the truth. I am an angel of the Lord. I am come with a message for thee.'

Mattie rolled her eyes. 'Law, if she ain't up an' hired a actor! Give me strength.' She wiped her face again and pushed a damp strand of iron-gray hair back into her bun. 'So you ain't the same fella in a different wig, eh? Well, I'm afraid you got the wrong party, Mr Holographic Projection from the Most High,' Mattie said drily. 'You want my sister. Now, Bertha's the religious one, as I expect you know. Gives me no peace. You tell Bertha,' said Mattie, 'that I've had just about enough of these shenanigans for one day, and if she expects to eat any peaches this winter, she better stop trying to save my soul and let me git on with it.'

'Moreover,' said the angel, addressing the back of Mattie's print housedress, 'I am no holographic image, and I know not of this Bertha.'

'Unh-hunh,' said Mattie. Her knife swooped, flashed; peach halves plopped into the mixing bowl. The stove timer rang; Mattie twisted the knob up straight and began lifting jars of golden orbs out of a bubbling canner by their necks, using a tool shaped like oversized forceps.

'Thou hast indeed a sister,' intoned the angel. 'Her name is *Fran*. She is a writer of abundant gifts. She will make thee great, and will noise thy name abroad in every land.'

Mattie paused, elbow cocked high, a quart of peaches strangled in the clamp. She set the jar down carefully, lifted out another – the last – and placed it on the folded-up towel with the rest. Then she turned around and faced the angel. 'Bertha Frances,' she said. 'Everbidy calls her Fran but the family and one or two old friends, and nobody thinks she's got a snowball's chance in Hell of makin' it big as a writer. I don't b'lieve you *are* Billy Keith Waller.'

'I am an angel of the Lord,' said the angel with palpable relief.

Mattie snorted. 'Angel of the Lord, my foot. Yer some Baptist Billy Keith lookalike that Bertha sweet-talked into doin' this. Sweet-talked or paid.'

The angel opened his mouth and shut it again, looking extremely put out. His face had gotten very red. Mattie turned back to the stove, picked up some tongs – moving a trace more warily than before – and lifted a clean quart jar out of a steaming cauldron on the back burner, and another, and another, keeping half an eye on the angel all the while. 'If you think yer any good at impersonatin' angels, ya got another think comin'. Now, take makin' fun a Bertha's writin' ambitions. Not even a hardhead like Billy Keith Waller would do that. Lot a foolishness at her age if ya ask me, but she's got her heart set on it. Poems in the church bulletin ever' coupla weeks. Terrible stuff. Means a lot to Bertha, though. Next time ya set up to terrify a body back to the Lord,' said Mattie, 'ya might just show a little more respeck for people's feelin's while yer about it.'

'But I wasn't – I didn't –' the angel sputtered.

'Always did say Christians was a bunch a hypocrites.'

There was a moment of strained silence.

'*This sucks*,' said the angel. He grabbed the front of

his gown in two hands, tore it open down the front seam – Mattie heard the rip of Velcro – and dragged it off.

Mattie smiled a tight, shrewd smile. 'Not a holographic projection, hunh? Not much. You folks must think I was born yesterday.'

The angel seized hanks of his curly fringe in either hand. 'Lady, do me one favor. Shut the hell up about holographic projections. I'm not a holographic projection, OK?'

'You ain't no angel, mister,' said Mattie with asperity. 'That means yer a holographic projection, b'cause there's nothin' else ya *could* be.'

'My name's Bernie Tuckerman,' said the angel. 'I'm from the twenty-second century, and I'm running a Time Window.' He wadded up the gown and threw it toward the refrigerator, where it vanished into thin air. Underneath he was wearing long white underwear, and he was barefoot. 'And you shut up too,' he yelled in the direction the gown had gone. 'I've had enough! We'll have to wipe her, OK?'

Without looking at what she was doing, Mattie began to layer peach halves, cut side down, into the clean jars. 'Who's that yer talkin' to? I still think yer a ho–'

'You can't have a projection without a projector in the place, goddammit!' the angel shouted. 'Not in 2003 you can't. No projector, no holographic image. You got a projector in this kitchen? No? Then give it a rest! You wanted to know who I am, and I'm telling you: Bernie Tuckerman, talking from your future!'

Mattie pursed her thin mouth, considering. 'How do I know yer tellin' the truth about a projector?'

The angel sat down abruptly, legs crossed, elbows on knees, chin on hands. All his fury had turned to gloom.

'Who the fuck cares? What the fuck went *wrong* here's what I'd like to know.'

'Matter of fact,' said Mattie in her sharp voice, but quietly, 'I do b'lieve you.' Surprised at herself, she pushed up her glasses by their plastic bridge and stared at the angel.

'*Now* she believes me,' he said with heavy irony, not looking at Mattie. 'Wonderful.'

The peaches were all packed in the jars. Mattie grabbed a saucepan off the stove, using a pot holder, and poured each jar full of syrup, lifting the squat canning funnel from jar to jar till all were filled. She wiped the rims, popped on the lids and began to tighten the bands. Her movements were smooth and practiced. While she worked the angel sat muttering on her clean kitchen floor, massaging the back of his neck. Mattie craned over her shoulder to look at him. 'What the Sam Hill's goin' on, anyhow?'

'Lady, you wouldn't believe me if I told you.'

Mattie lowered the last newly filled jar into the canner, reset the timer and turned sharply. 'Now looky-here. You 'kspected me to b'lieve you was a *angel*, didn't cha? You think b'lievin' in a angel's easier than b'lievin' in a whatchamacallit, a Time Window?' She sniffed. 'How 'bout *you* doin' *me* a favor?'

Bernie looked up at her askance. 'You got a point, I'll admit.'

Mattie folded up her skinny frame and sat down, tucking the skirt of her dress around her legs. Her glasses fell into her lap. 'Come on, let's have it. What was y'all tryin' to do?'

Bernie Tuckerman stopped massaging his neck and stared at her. 'Ah, what the hell.' He glanced suddenly past Mattie at something she couldn't see and yelled,

'You terminate this connection before I tell you and I'll break your fucking face! They're monitoring me,' he explained. 'They're all freaking because of the fuck-up . . . I have to tell you, you won't remember any of this.'

'Maybe I will an' maybe I won't,' said Mattie. She wiped her face with her apron and put her glasses on. Her eyes, enlarged behind the lenses, glittered with curiosity.

'Believe me, you won't. Oh, well. Makes no difference. To make a long story short, a while back the scientists discovered the Time Window technology. We can tune the transceiver to a particular time and place in the past – *our* past – and look into it easy as looking through a window. The people in the past can see us. We can talk to each other. Great, fantastic! Except scientists have always been afraid that contacting the past might change the future, so this technology is used only under very strict supervision. They're always standing by to erase people's memories if there's a fuck-up, like today. Now, the transceiver's so expensive to run they can hardly ever afford to use it. But everybody's always dying to use it anyway, in spite of all the risk and expense, because it's so fascinating. Still with me?'

Mattie nodded. 'Sure thing.'

'Right. So one day this genius gets this bright idea. Maybe the historical moments when so-called supernatural events are supposed to have taken place were when the Time Window was being used! Maybe we're *supposed* to use it – maybe using it is necessary to make the future follow from the past we know about. So, they figure, this'll be a way to go on with the research. We do a computer search and make a log of all the times somebody saw an angel, or the Virgin Mary, or Christ himself, or whatever – non-Christian religions have their own tradition of spiritual visitation – and we just go back to those times, get me?'

Mattie's eyes were glittering brighter and brighter. She nodded.

'And the way they decided to pay for it was, they had this big ol' lottery, and they sold tickets for a million dollars each.' Mattie blinked. 'So naturally only molto-molto rich people could buy tickets, but they still sold a lot of 'em because it was such a unique opportunity, y'know? Well, it so happens I'm rich – I'm a very wealthy man – and it so happens that I was one of the winners.'

The stove timer buzzed; Mattie jumped up. 'How many winners did they have?'

'Couple of dozen. There was a list of definite supernatural appearances, and then another list of ones they thought were probably just myths – I sure did, I'm Jewish – but some of the winners were Christian Fundamentalists, so they insisted on trying for those questionable ones anyway. The scientists figured, like, if it was a bust, they could always wipe people's memories. You can probably guess what the biggest plums for those types were.'

Mattie sat again and ticked them off on her fingers: 'Gabriel appearin' to *Mary* . . . the angel that appeared to the *shepherds* . . . the multitude of the heavenly *host* . . . an' the angel at the door of Christ's tomb.'

'Right four times,' said Bernie Tuckerman. 'Plus anything from the Old Testament: Jacob wrestling with the angel, and the angel in the fiery furnace and all that. Impossible to get accurate fixes, but that bunch won't take no for an answer. Throwing away your chance, I'd say. Most of the others agreed. They went for the modern appearances – the Virgin and those kids in

Mexico, that sort of thing. And me,' said Bernie. 'I'm the Grand Prize winner. I got the pick of the lot, so I picked you.'

Mattie blinked several times. 'Why?'

'Because,' said Bernie, 'you are supposed to start a religion that's going to determine the entire shape of the future. Your future, my past and present. You're the most important and influential person of your time, and we had the exact coordinates. It should've been a piece of cake. I don't know what went wrong.'

'Why, that's the craziest thing I ever heard,' said Mattie almost indignantly. 'I left the Baptist Church when I was twelve years old. I knew even then they was a bunch a hypocrites. My sister Bertha hounds me night and day about it, talkin' about the peace that passeth understanding an' all. *Peach* that passeth understanding, that's more my way of thinkin'.' She shook her head. 'I wondered how Billy Keith come to have him a piece of a bloomin' peach tree in high summer. Thought maybe he got it flown in from California . . . No, you folks up ahead there made some kinda big-time mistake about *me*.'

'Then it's a mistake that passeth *my* understanding, I kid you not,' Bernie said. 'Hell, everybody knows you left your Church as a child and weren't religious till the angel came. Everybody knows you were canning peaches in Louisville on a hot day in August when it happened. It's a totally known story. After the visitation you started doing a televangelism show, and your sister Fran wrote up an account of what happened, the Bible of the new religion. There's a copy of the Peakist Scripture in every house in the country, maybe the world.'

'The Peakist Scripture. Lord have mercy on my poor

perockatary soul,' Mattie said weakly, for the first time in the entire bizarre proceeding sounding downright shocked.

Bernie looked offstage. 'OK, OK,' he yelled. 'Mattie, they're telling me time's up. And you got to get your memory blanked. Christ,' he said, 'why me? Olivia Delgado does her Virgin-Mary-at-Lourdes number: no problemo. Nigel Hawkesworth does Moroni in a perfect nineteenth-century-upstate-New-York accent: gang-busters.' He stood stiffly, a balding, bare-footed, round-faced, middle-aged figure in a white jumpsuit. 'Me, I spend six valuable months letting my business run itself while I learn everything there is to know about the turn of the twenty-first century in the North American Bible Belt, *and* how to talk like a KJV-type angel, and I get zip.'

Moments later ... Mattie came back into focus as herself to find, to her amazement, that an entire peck of peaches had been transformed into a heap of skins and pits, two dozen beautiful quart jars lined up on towels and a mess of pots and pans. Where had her mind been? She had wool-gathered and sleep-walked through the whole familiar process, scarcely noticing what she was doing. It was a little spooky. Bertha was always complaining her mind was a million miles away, but still.

The lid on one of the cooling jars sealed with a little metallic snap. Mattie stirred, wiped her sweaty face on her apron, pushed up her glasses. She fetched a carton and started to put the sealed jars in for Bertha to carry down to the cellar. She had almost finished when the jar in her hand exploded into fragments of purest peach-golden light, setting ablaze a kitchen suddenly drenched in the fragrance of flowers, and the huge presence, the enormous voice, spoke in her mind.

Steam

IAN MCDONALD

Because Missaluba's father had told her, since the day she was squeezed into the world, that steam was in the blood, Missaluba was therefore not surprised when the locomotive called her name.

– *Missssaluba.*

An easy name for steam-powered piston rods and drive shafts to breathe into Eternity Junction's flint-dry noonday air.

– *Missaluuuuba.*

To ears less attuned than hers to the marshalling yard's night-and-day push and shunt, it might have been just another whistle or sigh from the ore freighter crossing the points on the slow down-line, or a sudden ecstatic ejaculation from the Transpolaris Overnight Mail waiting impatiently at red for a Great Southern grain hauler to clear into a siding. But Missaluba knew every huff and puff, every hiss and piss, every moan and groan in Eternity Junction from the big black-and-gold expresses of Bethlehem Ares Railroads to the meanest wood-burning shunter on Track 29, and never, once, had any of them come out with something that could be mistaken for her name.

– *Missalubaaaaa.*

The third time, that's the witching time. The third time, it's destiny speaking.

Steam in the blood makes you able to hear these things. In her early years, beneath the tracks, Missaluba had imagined steam in the blood to be a medical condition, rather like the bottles of home-brew cola Mr Grampuri sold from the basket on his tricycle to hot and sweaty track workers. Feet frozen in the ice-basket, heads crazy from the noonday sun, shaken and shivered by the jolt of tricycle across Eternity Junction's many tracks, these bottles of innocuous brew became deadly weapons. The zenith of the living dome ceiling glowed with a constellation of embedded bottle caps. Every so often the lumber of a Great Southern 'Mahabharata' or a Transpolaris Traction Tokamak Multiple passing overhead would dislodge a star or two and send them crashing to earth. That, Missaluba still thought, was what steam in the blood was like. Big and hissing and it shot you to the stars.

Forty generations of it, her father told her, pride fizzing in his breast. *While the world was being invented, girl, Salamagundis were a-roddin' and a-railin', throwin' the big fusion powered engines across the airless red desert, iron lions frost-maned with flash-frozen steam and dry ice. Steam, girl, steam. In the blood, girl. In the genes.*

This Missaluba understood unequivocally. To her, it was a function of home laundry. Good sharp creases in Salamagundi Engineer's dress dungarees as he took the Ares Express out of Belladonna's Bram Tchaikovski Station with the tokamaks singing sweet as trained larks. That was what steam in the genes meant.

Perhaps. Perhaps if her mother had not left that Decembuary morning with the frost glinting on Eternity Junction's rails. *No more timetables*, her note had said. *Woman was not made to live by timetables. 22:13 knickers down, 22:14 piston in, 22:15 full throttle, 22:16 whistle . . .* Perhaps if Uncle Billy had refused that last plum brandy and not fallen asleep with his left leg athwart the 27 downline as a 10,000-ton robot ore freighter pulled away from its stand. The dwarf doctors of Belladonna's Sorrowful Street had given him the best tick-tock tin leg their science and his insurance could agree upon, but he never again worked the Solstice Landing Night Unlimited. The *click-tap*, *click-tap*, *click-tap* as he patrolled the sleeping-car corridors disturbed the passengers in their berths. The watchword of the night-train steward is, above all, *discretion*. Perhaps if Uncle Billy had spent less of his time immersed in extended acts of gastronomy that tied up the kitchen and all its resources for hours on end, thus foisting the rest of the domestic maintenance on to woman's shoulders.

Most perhaps of all perhapses; if Uncle Billy had not brought the noisome Cousin Aron into the subterranean dome she and her father called home. Had Cousin Aron been a daughter and not a son, then Missaluba's hopes of being the forty-first Salamagundi to inherit the Engineer's cap, badge and lamp might have survived. But Cousin Aron was a male, and not just any male but a male of the blood and, *as a favoured male*, received Salamagundi Engineer's devout schooling in the catechism of Eternity Junction.

This was the way of it.

First: the crystal lights in the chandelier Salamagundi Engineer had won in a Katerinamass lotto would ring, and jing, and sing.

Second: the hand-painted porcelain model of the Bethlehem Ares 'Catherine of Tharsis' Express he had brought Missaluba from the floating markets of Llangonedd, which was her most treasured possession, would start to creep toward the left edge of the fireplace, and all the dirty crockery and sauce bottles that Uncle

Billy's culinary excursions required would tremble on the table top and huddle together for support.

Third: a shivering, shuddering sound, which became a swelling thundering, which became a shattering roar that shook the entire house and everything in it: at its very ear-splitting peak Missaluba's father would stab his finger at the sound of the many, many wheels passing overhead.

'Eleven seventeen Argyre Express, split at Jones for Deuteronomy and points south,' Cousin Aron would bellow from his cushion in front of the wireless. 'Configuration: 0240 Great Southern "Vishnus" in tandem.'

Except it's the ten fifty-six from Wisdom to Llangonedd through service via Belladonna that's running eight minutes down because of a points freeze-up at Herschel, Missaluba would say to herself as she moved swiftly with her dustpan to sweep up any bottle-top stars that might have been dislodged from the ceiling. She knew the name, number, configuration, time and destination of every train that passed through Eternity Junction. *No one with any feel could mistake two 0440 Bethlehem Ares Class 88s in push-pull configuration for Great Southern Vishnus. And the lead tokamak needs an overhaul.* The knowledge of the autodidact is always the noblest, for it is born out of pure love.

Though her father's disappointment was obvious to everyone but Cousin Aron, Missaluba would keep her right answers to herself because she knew that her father could not see that no amount of education could inspirit someone who might have steam in the genes, in some remote way, but certainly did not have steam in the blood. Cousin Aron's main interest in life was the sweet cotton panties of the Tracklayer's disreputable daughters, who lived geographically behind the water tower and socially below the salt, but Missaluba knew better than to try to convince her father of this.

Boys Drove Trains. Girls, no matter how hot the steam bubbled in their blood, did not. There, that was it said. Thus Cousin Aron took footplate rides with Salamagundi Engineer on the Meridian Night Mail or the Solstice Landing Limited or the Slow Stopper to O and China Mountain and all the world's legendary trains, and Missaluba remained trapped in the ancient terraform bubble with the stink and vapours of Uncle Billy's infusions and steepings and the thoughtless detritus of three single men who have a female in the house. The steam in her blood would boil with every train that thundered overhead until, like one of Mr Grampuri's colas with real coke in it, the explosion blew her up the spiral staircase and out of the jammed open airlock and into the sun-red dust and polished steel of twelve minutes of twelve in Eternity Junction.

Unlike most places in the world, Eternity Junction had happened rather than been invented. That is, some billion and half years before ROTECH laid its manforming hand on the world, a small chunk of asteroidal matter about eighty by forty by twenty metres had wandered into the gravitational bailiwick of the fourth planet from the Sun and expired in a multi-megaton blast on the sands of Syrtis. Even then, God the Panarchic had foreseen the day that a ROTECH survey tracker would come lumbering up over the close horizon and find in the eroded impact crater the perfect marshalling yard for the north-eastern quartersphere rail net.

Then the angels of ROTECH came down from the sky, and when they ascended again there in the crater were domes and homes and signal towers, tracks and rails and switch-overs, grades and points and junctions, a hundred seek-fusion-powered locomotives and generation zero of Salamagundis to master them.

Forty generations later Missaluba Salamagundi was picking her way between the grease monkeys and the snack-vendors' tricycles and the freight forwarders, sweating in their luminous yellow jackets and hard hats, when she heard the engine call her name.

– *Missaluba.*

Calling her through the crowds of licensed mendicants and general goondahs who jogged along beside slow-moving passenger trains, alms bowls upraised to the gold-tinted windows.

– *Missaluba.*

Ducking under the clanking couplings of shunting goods cars from Iron Mountain and Redemption while the tramps and hobos hitchin' rides on the roof to anywhere laughed and whistled and waved.

– *Missaluba.*

Skipping across the heat-warped iron rails, mere centimetres from the cow-catcher of a heavy grain train as the crew whistled more out of recognition of their Missaluba, their mascot, than out of warning.

And there, hard up on the buffers of the furthest siding, she found it.

'Blessed Lady,' she breathed, for, in all the trains she had seen pass through Eternity Junction – which was all the engines in the quartersphere, and then some – she had never, ever seen a locomotive like the one on Track 115. Black it was, with a blackness that swallowed sight when she looked at it straight yet, when she looked at it out of the corner of her eye, seemed to shimmer and twinkle with stars. Long it was: Missaluba counted the paces: twenty, twenty-five, thirty, thirty-five as she analysed the wheel configuration. Streamlined it was, like a thing made to fly, not run, with streaks and straiks and flutings that carried the eye along its sleek fuselage. Beautiful it was: for its front end was sculpted into the shape of a very thin naked woman, cast in bright silver, head and breast out-thrust in the personification of speed. To further amplify the image, her arms were silver-feathered wings which reached back behind her to enfold the boiler and tokamak tubes.

Missaluba ran her hand along the fairings. They were as smooth as a glass of the black, black beer Uncle Billy slid down his gullet as often as his railroad pension would allow. The gleaming drive wheels arced a full metre above her head.

No name. No company colophon, save the yearning angel of speed.

She knocked her knuckle against the pressure vessel: did she hear, did she imagine, a slithering stirring deep inside, like a waking spirit?

Points creaked in the crucible of Eternity Junction; the steady clunk of freight cars shunting was oddly muted. There were no birds flying. Green weeds struggled sporadically from the oily red dirt around the black engine, coaxed to life by drips from leaking piston seals.

Though nothing a train should do could surprise her, Missaluba started at the sudden venting of steam a hand's breadth from her face.

— *Missaluba, come*, the steam had said. Down the track, the engineer's cabin unfolded a flight of steps. *Come, Missaluba.*

None of forty generations of Salamagundis had ever ridden a footplate like the one that opened its doors to welcome the curious Missaluba. There was too much room in the useless places and too little in the important ones. The video-eye monitors were oddly mounted, strangely angled, as if for engineers either very much taller or very much smaller than Missaluba. Readouts and counters displayed the status of energies more esoteric than mere water vapour. The controls seemed made for hands with more fingers than five, or no fingers, and more hands and feet than two. Strangely wise, they felt Missaluba's gaze fall on them and moved, purring, to accept her touch. Missaluba drew back, certain with the certainty that forty generations of steam in the blood imparts – that, had she laid finger to them, the black locomotive would have taken her anywhere in the world she desired. And beyond.

Sensing her unease, the controls withdrew. Time hung suspended on the sharp point of twelve minutes of twelve. No company name, no colophon.

'What are you?' asked Missaluba.

The black engine trembled. Water bubbled deep in its pipes and tubes. A dozen valves fluted open, a dozen tiny geysers of steam spoke with the voice of the piccolo stop of the big calliope that Mr Shoes played with asbestos gloves: – *I am all your prayers answered.*

'Prayers?' asked Missaluba, hopes coalescing into realizations. 'Who are you?'

The valves closed and the bubbling in the pipes became a shuddering rattling like a thousand tea kettles coming to the boil at once. In Eternity Junction there were two kinds of children: the wise and the cooked. Belonging to the former camp, Missaluba understood that the audience was ended. She scrambled down to the oily red grit.

Prayers?

Time heaved at the sharp apex of twelve minutes of twelve and tore itself free.

Prayers.

Missaluba knew better than to expect a sympathetic audience from the Salamagundi males, yet she half hoped that there might be something about her, a luminosity, a smell of the wonderful that they would recognize and would prompt questions and belief. But Salamagundi Engineer was dozing in his chair in front of the plastic jollylogs, far away on the footplate of the imagination, and Uncle Billy was banging his tin shin around the house, furious that his caramelized orange sauce had failed him yet again. Folded into a comfortable corner with cushions and a rising pall of his own farts, Cousin Aron thumbed through *Aircraft Monthly* while All Swing Radio burbled quietly to itself. A train thundered overhead. Bottle-cap stars fell. Without stirring from his chair, Salamagundi Engineer pointed his finger at the ceiling. He did not hear that Cousin Aron made no reply. Missaluba moved to push her beloved china Ares Express back to safety on the mantelpiece before it tumbled fatally to the hearth.

She had half expected it not to be there, that her family's obdurate everydayness had somehow refuted its otherworldliness, but there it stood, the half-glimpsed stars in its carapace echoing the lights of the moonring as Missaluba picked her way across the star-shiny steel rails. Missaluba ran her hand along the straining angel's silver calf-muscle.

'Hello engine. I think I know who you are.'

– *Hello Missaluba*, said the pistons. – *Who am I?*

'You're the angel of steam,' said Missaluba.

Like every other citizen of her world, Missaluba knew about angels. You only had to look up and there they were: choirs and chapters and orders of them, Avatars, Lorarchs, Cheraphs and Archangelsks, forever orbiting by day and night, a great ring of them surrounding the world, singing praise to God the Pan-archic and his servant, ROTECH. Unlike most other fellow Martians, Missaluba knew that occasionally the angels came down out of the moonring and that in those out-of-the-way places where the seams of the world were not as neatly tacked down as in Grand Valley or China Mountain, the fortunate could see them as they went about the Panarch's inscrutable busi-ness. *With her own eyes* she had seen the oily black vapour trails of two low-level avatars come down not half a kilometre from the place where she stood on the top of the crater rim, unfold a bewildering array of arms, hands and fingers, dig up some rusty, long-forgotten scrap of man-forming machinery and return with it to the vault of heaven. And the whole of Eternity Junction had seen that time when the old Transpolaris Traction Type Twelve's tokamak had run wild and the containment field ballooned out like a soap bubble made of lightning and fried the poor engi-neer into something that looked and smelled like the little black bits Missaluba found floating in Uncle Billy's deep-frying fat. People had run for their lives – though they knew no one could outrun a 20-kiloton fusion explosion – when *before their eyes* a hundred tiny trapdoors opened in the pissed-on dirt and twice that many tiny angelettes scurried out of the ground and all over the throbbing locomotive and fixed it, saved the town and everyone in it and disappeared down their tiny burrows again before anyone could even say *What the hell was that?*

'The angel of steam,' Missaluba said again, climbing the steps into the cabin. Hot summer lightning flickered to earth among the impact craters far off across the red desert: in the funeral sidings, pensioned-off doubleheaders creaked at their seams and moaned with hydrogen ghosts.

If angels could be *from* machines, they could as easily be *for* machines. Missaluba's home-brew theology made no distinction between the vivifying spirit in the organic from that in the inorganic. The divine presence rested as comfortably in the fusion tubes and field generators of a Bethlehem Ares Class 88 as in some Cathrinist stylite atop a desert column, hooked into the sky by a score of prayer kites. Trains were naturally divine. Untroubled by geographies of free will, they ran along the steel rails of obedience, forward, back or not at all, and so worshipped the Panarch. Missaluba had no trouble with an angel that dwelled in, and was composed of, steam.

'Are you an avatar or a lorarch?' she asked the controls. 'A cheraph, perhaps, or even an archangelsk?'

The black engine did not speak, but deep in the fusion percolator hydrogen smashed to helium, water flashed to live steam. Pipes thundered, the black behemoth shook as its in-dwelling angel rattled at the confines of the boiler. Missaluba clapped her hands over her ears, and, as it seemed that the angel must break free from its prison in a mushroom cloud of irradiated steam and atomized girl, every valve and every tappet and every cylinder and every seal blew open with the demon shriek of the Train of Damned Souls and poured steam into the cab. Pure steam, white steam, live steam. Searing steam.

Cool steam.

She was not parboiled, her skin peeling away like the shells of the freshwater crayfish the trackside vendors cooked while their customers waited for the signal to change.

Cool steam. Gentle. Steam that smelled of all kinds of

reminiscent things like autumn mornings and warm bathrooms on cold winter nights or Salamagundi Engineer carrying home a pocketful of presents from the other side of the world. Steam that smelled of iron rails, of travel, of cracked leather seats faded by desert sun, of marvellous journeys to wonderful places both physical and metaphysical. Missaluba breathed it in, and it went down into her lungs and out of the bottom of them into the secret heart of her where it became more than just the motive power of a train. It became *time*. It became *history*.

The steam clouded up the windows of her mind, and when she rubbed them she saw not the cab of a locomotive, or Eternity Junction under the desert night, but wings. Wings: diaphanous gossamer membranes the colour of oil in water, beating in a great darkness she now understood was the void of space. Wings such as an angel might own, if an angel were 5,000 kilometres tall, spread to catch the wind from the sun. Something less and something more than an angel, Missaluba realized as her steam-sight moved to the golden tangle of modules and podules and lifters and lighters and docks and bays at the junction of the wings. A SailShip of the Motherworld Praesidium: all of Eternity Junction's 115 tracks could be fitted into the least of its cargo bays, yet it was dwarfed by solar wings wide enough to have wrapped her world like a Katerinamass present. Stars shone through those wings, and the swelling red eye of a world framed in a silver monocle: Missaluba's world, turning within its cincture of mechanical angels, swiftly growing as the SailShip approached.

Her world, but not of her time. Her world as it was when only the will of ROTECH and the spirit of St Catherine moved upon its tholae and paterae, its canyons and shield volcanoes, its dust deserts and its chaotic terrain, its waterless lakes and waveless oceans. Missaluba saw her world's nightside terminator flicker with a hundred brief fireflies: the multi-megaton impacts of cometary heads lobbed by ROTECH down the shallow gravity well. She saw the long polar night burn with the light of ten thousand vanas, orbital mirrors turning the heat of the sun upon the ice cap. She saw brief flashfloods scar the pristine red land and those same sky mirrors cut swathes of melted permafrost the width of continental basins. She saw the wild dust storms trapped and raging within the magnetic fields generated by orbiting hyper-conductors. She saw spirals of cloud spin successions of fronts and rain clouds down from the pole and lighters and lifters running before them, sowing insubstantial veils of carbon-fixing bacteria.

And when the storms had passed, she saw the gentle edge of green advance across the face of the world. Wherever the green passed, the angels of ROTECH came after. Pylons 3 kilometres tall sprang up along the shattered edge of Grand Valley; in the twinkling of an angel's eye busy spinning machines had slung a glass roof 4,500 kilometres long between them. Beneath it forests grew, cows grazed, humans built homes and fought about money.

Another blink of the All-seeing Eye and the trackbuilders had laid a web of shining silver across the greening world and created a race of fire-bellied monsters to bestride it. The great SkyWheel space elevator came spinning across the land, picking people off the SailShips that so thickly crowded the sky that no stars shone through their massed wings, flinging them out at the bottom on to the new world prepared for them. People came out from the glass-roofed hives of Grand Valley and found green plains and land-locked shallow seas and sweeping forests and majestic deserts. By the trainloads they came, by the lighter-load, to hew and build and mend and tend, to live and die and prosper and dwindle, to establish their dynasties and build their gracious cities.

A tear, Missaluba? An honest lump in the throat, sniffle in the nose, water in the eye?

A piece of grit, that's all, a fleck of soot. Must have been in the steam. Can't seem to get it out. Blink. Blink.

Blink. The teeming new world was blinked away and by the power of the black locomotive she was back at the very beginning. She flew alone beneath an indigo sky over a pale-pink rocky desert where nothing lived and nothing breathed and nothing moved but the frozen wind and nothing changed but her own great velocity and the immeasurably slow processes of erosion. After a time that could have been moments or millennia measured against the unchanging desert, she noticed a spot of colour. Drawing closer, she saw that it was a small plastic environment bubble, alone in the wilderness. Drawing nearer still, she saw there were two things inside the bubble: a many-armed robot bearing ROTECH's hand-and-globe symbol on its back, and a coniferous sapling about a metre tall. As she circled the lonely outpost she saw the robot raise its arm and release a spray of mist over the infant tree.

'The Tree of World's Beginning,' Missaluba whispered and the mists and illusions were dissolved away. 'That means you're more than just an angel, you're . . .'

– *I am Kathy Haan, ROTECH employee number 703286543, Taphead Remote Terraforming Division*, the voice of the steam said. – *Aka St Catherine aka Our Lady of Tharsis, aka that stupid bitch who wanted the freedom and spirituality of Mars so much she left her body behind and now she can't go back to it.*

'But you're Our Lady, our saint,' protested Missaluba, horrified that the sanctified could speak of themselves in such everyday, even unhallowed, language.

– *If I'm any kind of a saint, it's an accidental one*, said the black locomotive. – *Just because I move from body to body and have been a lot of places and done a lot of things that look like miracles, which people remember better than the stupid or downright petty things I've done, that doesn't make me any nearer to God the Panarchic than you, Missaluba. A million of those machines you call angels – and who, in honesty, are holier than I can ever be, for they are untroubled by the quandaries of free will – could climb on to each other's shoulders and lock their claws into a great tower of angels taller even than the SkyWheel, and still they would be not 1 centimetre nearer God than when they started, for He is infinitely holy. If a million such towers were piled on top of each other, still they would be no closer. God is perfect.*

Heresy, from the Mother of the World.

'But you gave up your body and entered the taphead network and were enlightened and beatified in search of perfection,' Missaluba but-butted, having learned the mysteries at her mother's knee, before that knee and its partner decided they could have a better time of it in Wisdom.

– *Big mistake, bubbacubba*, said St Catherine of Tharsis. – *It was fine for the first few centuries. The world seemed a bigger place then and got progressively smaller as more and more of it got invented. I could move with ease through the taphead web – at any time there was always some machine that wasn't being guided by a mind back on Motherworld that I could slip into – and there was always something to do, somewhere to go. I had a purpose then, and a place. The irony — you're old enough to appreciate what that is, Missaluba? — was that I was the angel of my own damnation. I came to this world to find spirituality in sterility, to see the footprints of God in the absolute purity of areology and areotectonics and areomorphology. Can you understand what I'm saying, Missaluba?*

Missaluba could not, but she knew better than to shake her head in front of a saint full of super-heated steam.

— As I brought life to it, spirit went out of it. I didn't know then. I thought the spirit of the planet was passing out of the rock into living things — red into green — that was why I grew that Sequoia tree I showed you, which now stands at the centre of the Forest of Chryse. It wasn't until the people started to move out from under the Grand Valley roof that I realized I had worked myself out of a job. I was no longer a player: I was a many-bodied, many-eyed spectator. I know now how God feels: the thrill is gone. All that's left is history, and a ghost in the machine.

A steel shout in the darkness, a yell of steam and wheels: a night express, slamming through Eternity Junction as if it wasn't there. Twenty-three-forty-eight High Plains Flyer, non-stop Deuteronomy to Iron Mountain, Missaluba judged, as unable not to analyse and identify as a pyschologist's dog not to salivate at mealtimes. A single Great Southern 'Vedanta', tuned sweet and tight as an almond. How many times had it woken her in the dark hours: the night train, going *somewhere* fast?

'People made you holy,' said Missaluba, understanding. 'You never wanted to be a saint; all you ever wished was to be unnoticed, unseen, overlooked, forgotten. But they wouldn't let you do that.'

— When you can do things — miracles, though they're just

the appliance of high science — people start to have expectations of you, said the train in doleful blue notes squeezed from its master regulator. *— A terrible burden, expectations you never wanted to have to live up to.*

'Or expectations that no one but you believes,' said Missaluba, understanding now.

— I know, Missaluba, said the voice of the steam.

'Know?'

— That Girls Don't Drive Trains. That Salamagundi Engineer wastes his energies and his dreams on one who does not have steam in the blood, which is just another word for love. Not like you do, Missaluba.

Before Missaluba could squeeze a syllable of surprise out of her open mouth, the train continued. *— Call it another little miracle of St Kathy, call it a call I could not refuse, that I have heard the souls of the locomotives whispering your name up and down the lines: Missaluba Salamagundi, forty-first of the line of Salamagundis, who by all the saints and angels should follow the steam in her blood and become Missaluba Engineer, but won't. And when I asked them why, they all replied: Girls. Don't. Drive. Trains.*

Those arguments. *But it's dirty, child,* her father had told her. *Sweaty, grimy, filthy, oily, steamy. But it's long cold nights up over the pole, child, with the dry ice crystals twinkling high above you and the air so thin every breath is like a stiletto in your lungs, or out across the desert of sand and the desert of stone and the desert of dust and the desert of soda where the heat bakes you in your skin like a thousand-year-old sand-lizard in a lump of clay and the land's like a mirror shining dazzling light into your eyes, a thousand kilometres across the mirror will turn your eyes to coal and your skin to leather, child, so that no man that's worth a spit will ever look at you; there'll be no husbands, no providers, no fathers, no children — all the things that you deserve, child.*

But he could never understand that she did not want those things that men could provide, and desired above all others the things that steam gave, for, despite her youth, she knew that the grander, wider, wonderful world came at a price, and that she had reckoned it up and thought it an acceptable trade.

It's all said and set, child. It's a natural law, like the sun rising, and cows giving milk. Men do men's work, women do women's. Cousin Aron drives trains. You make a home. It's a grand and honourable calling.

– *But steam is in the blood*, said the angel train in a voice very like a devil's. – *It can no more be taken out of you without killing you than that blood. And steam calls to steam, and therefore I have incarnated myself in a locomotive so that I can meet this girl and make her an offer that will benefit both of us.*

'What is this offer?' asked Missaluba, though by dint of that same steam in her blood she knew, had known in some sense since she first heard the angel call her name.

– *A trade, Missaluba*, said the black locomotive in whispers so low as to be almost inaudible. – *You cannot imagine how attractive the life you despise appears to me. No hopes, no aspirations, no expectations: the pure sacrament of merely being. The mystics have always said that God is more easily, and purely, found in the drudgery of the kitchen than the tranquillity of the mountain-top contemplarium. The shame is that it has taken me the better part of a millennium to realize this.*

'You become me,' said Missaluba.

– *And you become me*, said the engine. *Life for life, spirit for spirit, steam for steam.*

'See if we really want the things we wish for,' said Missaluba.

— *Yessss*, said the steam, so gently it was hardly a word at all.

All. Everything. Every silver star embedded in the chalky ceiling. No wonder she hesitated.

'I'll have to go back.'

— *I can understand that*, said the engine, as one who had not, for a thousand years, had anything to go back into.

'I'll have to see.'

— *You have to be sure*, said the Angel of Impetuosity, unsealing doors, unfolding steps.

Missaluba understood a thing that made her more a woman than the first chocolate-coloured smear in her panties. It was that, though her father had taken her dreams and given her a vacuum cleaner for them, though Uncle Billy had tramped all over them with his tin shin, though Cousin Aron had used them to wipe the smegma off his dick, still, she loved them. She had to go back, to be sure.

The house was asleep, doors closed, lights extinguished save a few everglow wall panels. The wireless burbled breathily, slipped off station into some electromagnetic limbo between cosmic hiss and Hamilton Bohannon and his Rhythm Aces. Crushed plastic beer cans rattled and rolled treacherously beneath her feet. The smell of Uncle Billy's evening offering had stolen into the soft furnishings and wall-carpets. Behind palisades of gravy-stained plates, the condiment bottles stood like the towers of a miniature city.

Then she saw it. No attempt had been made to clear up the pieces; it lay where it had fallen. The whiteness of the broken edges of bone china were startlingly white, like snapped teeth.

The porcelain model of the Ares Express 'Catherine of Tharsis' lay smashed in a dozen pieces at the end of

the mantelpiece. Missaluba knelt and picked up the
fragments, trying to fit them together, but the edges
had been chipped by the fall and could never be made
whole again.

They could not have spared five seconds to push it
back from the brink to the safety of the centre.

Without an explanation, without a word, without a
single regret or a tear, she walked away. She closed the
door behind her gently so as not to wake the lightest of
sleepers, but it was enough to dislodge the last bottle
top from the ceiling and send it falling to mundane
earth.

The sky was brightening above Eternity Junction's
eastern lip. The moon-ring was an arc of phosphores-
cence. The black engine woke with a dramatic sighing
of valves, but Missaluba was not fooled. Her mother
had taught her that if the saints sleep, the world unravels.
The stars within its hull seemed very bright. The engine
drew her into its cab.

'I want to do it,' said Missaluba Salamagundi. The
angel in the engine did not speak. From deep in its
tubes rose a seething and bubbling and thundering boil-
ing like none she had heard before. The black locomotive shook to its last weld and rivet; the rumble of the
engines rose to a howl, to a roar, to a scream that few
have heard and lived to report. Missaluba was not
afraid. She had the word of an angel. As the tokamak
containment field swelled to bursting point and tongues
of crazy fusion fire licked along the streamlines and flew
from the silver angel's hair, every valve blew open and
every last breath of steam was released in a wordless
shout like a hundred night-freight whistles blowing at
once.

She should have died then, Missaluba, the meat seared

from her bones. That she did not was proof that she was under the protection of a saint and not a subtle devil.

The black locomotive vanished in a cloud of steam. In the cab Missaluba saw the blinding white fog roil into the face of a young woman and imagined she heard over the dying shriek of emptying steam the words – *Breathe out. Trust me.*

'I trust you,' she said, and she felt the breath rush out through her mouth past the end of those three little words and the steam cloud twist into two thin ropes of vapour and pour in through her nostrils.

'I trust you,' Missaluba said again, as she felt her *girlness* unravel and in through the ragged gaps came a sense of power, of strength, of the need to run and run all the day into the night and through the night into days beyond imagining, and of a star-hot, unquenchable fire in her loins that gave the ability to do this, and a freedom, and a horizon to test it on.

– *I trust you*, said Missaluba Engineer in a hiss of living steam as she found connections to new muscles she had never dreamed she possessed: driving wheels and cylinders and pistons and crankshafts. The black engine creaked on its track, anxious to try its new-found might.

'Go well,' said the girl-Catherine, who had swallowed all the steam in one distilled drop of essential spirit. She stepped down from the cab and Missaluba folded the steps and sealed the doors behind her.

With a flicker of her divine essence, the Catherine-girl knocked down a dozen signals and up a dozen more, sent messages running a thousand kilometres up and down the track that diverted fast and important trains into sidings and told continentsful of signal boxes – *Make way, make way for the Catherine of Tharsis express.*

– *Go well*, said Missaluba. – *Enjoy your life.*

'I'll try,' said the Catherine-girl. 'If you ever get bored, come back and see me.'

Missaluba-engine released the energy that burned inside her in a roar of tokamaks powering up. Black desert birds went flapping from their roosts on the signalling pylons; hobos and goondahs were woken from their sleeping holes as, with a grand huffing and chuffing and spinning of wheels, the black locomotive began to move. Very slowly, very tentatively, like a child's first steps, then with growing confidence and assurance, the black locomotive gathered speed. Points clicked over, Missaluba moved on to the branch line, and on to the slow up-line, passed in front of the halted Dawn Unlimited that nothing, but nothing, stopped and on to the fast up-line.

Whistles blew. The eastern edge of Eternity Junction's crater dipped beneath the sun, and the silver angel on the boiler caught and kindled and burned into gold.

The Catherine-girl waved: the whistles sounded again. Faster now, faster, through the signals, faster faster, past the main control box where bleary-eyed dispatchers leapt from their cracked leather chairs to rub their eyes and stare in amazement, faster faster faster, through the crater wall that had been the edge of Missaluba's world for so long, and out into the great red desert beyond.

The Catherine-girl watched until the locomotive was a shiny black seed beneath a plume of white steam. Then she turned and with inexpressible joy went down to the dome called home and the sacraments of crushed beer cans, dirty plates, soiled underwear, ironing and dusting.

Dust, she reckoned, when it came to it, was very like steam, or spirit.

Even Cousin Aron noticed when the miracles began – little domestic miracles of the healing-sick-radios, fixing-temperamental-washing-machines, curing-cars kind – but Salamagundi said it was just the steam in the blood, boy, the steam in the blood, never realizing how near the truth he was, much less that the saint who inhabited the forty-first Salamagundi was by now growing weary of dusting cleaning washing drying – any God who demanded such a path to Him was not worthy of much consideration – and craved a little diversion. The people of Eternity Junction regularly saw her up on the crater rim at dawn and dusk, looking out across the desert. They thought little of it: Salamagundi's daughter, a little touched, steam in the blood, all that. Had any of them asked what she was doing up there at all times of the day, she would have told them she was looking for a black engine with a silver angel riding it to come back and take her away. This would have proved her craziness (despite the useful miracles), though it was nothing less than the truth. Which only goes to prove that servants of the Panarch may know everything without being wise, for the black train never came back. It had never intended to come back. Every so often a legend would make its way to the girl up on the crater rim: that at dead of night the whistles of a black train could be heard far out across the plains and that all good people would hurry to their homes, for no one dared look upon the Night Train of the Damned as it hauled its carriages, packed with wailing lost souls, to eternal perdition.

But that was only a story.

Synandra

ED GORMAN

> Our cosmology is a double exposure of two
> realities superimposed.
>
> *Philip K. Dick*

*And everywhere that Synandra went, death was sure to
follow.*

In 520 BC *Carthage was a city of nearly a million,
spending all its attention upon the commerce of Negro slaves,
ivory, metal and precious stones. Yet despite all this prosper-
ity, a famine took the city near the end of its reign, a
famine that left men killing their own children to spare
them the cruel death of starvation. An unnamed scribe from
the time described how he one night saw 'a beautiful woman
wrapped in a mist of some kind, who walked the streets
accompanied by a wolf whose fur was the color of swirling
smoke and whose eyes were redolent of midnight
moons'.*

In AD 1348 *the plague reached England and destroyed
half the population; in Europe the toll rose to 25 million
dead. A Dominican friar noted in his journal, 'Every night
I follow her, this woman so beautiful and terrifying, as she
passes among the plague-dead and -dying in the streets,
trailed by the eerie wolf that calls her name in a human
voice. "Synandra! Synandra!" I saw her take a dying
young man to her and kiss him with an eroticism*

that was sinful to behold. I did not realize, not until the young man fell to her feet, that she was not kissing him at all, but rather sucking his soul from him, and ingesting it herself.'

In 1943 a Jew at the Belsen death camp confided to his journal that he had had nightmares for the past few months of 'an astonishingly beautiful woman, her face and body obscured by some kind of mist, pushing my father's perambulator into one of the rooms where the cyanide killed as many as thirty at a time'. A few days after this journal entry the man saw exactly that, his father disappearing down a sloping ramp to the death chamber . . . pushed in his wheelchair by the woman, who was in turn followed by a wolf, 'who was the color of 3:00 a.m. and who evoked in me a chill so terrible that I could not stop from trembling, and could not even cry out a warning to my poor frightened father'.

The smells are what I can never get used to.

I've been time-lining for half my life, thirty-seven years real-time, and no amount of preparatory drugging, no amount of inhalants, can help me. I always spend the first few minutes in a new time-zone letting my sinuses have their way with me – runny eyes, sneezing, a constricted throat. And the foulest smells imaginable stenching my olfactory system.

Today was no different. Fifteen minutes earlier I'd climbed through a hole in the air that was instantly sealed up behind me. I had in my hand a psychID card that identified me as Jason Parks, History Professor from time-zone 2178. As part of my tenure, I'm granted three time-trips a year, usually to zones that I'm studying for discussion in my classes.

But this trip was different. This trip was an emergency. I had just reached time-zone AD 2034.

An early autumn dusk – mauve sky, cool and graying darkness, a sprawl of bright stars, the dying sounds of birds in leafy trees – took the world into night.

I stood on a street filled with buildings that looked about ready for demolition. The Timeline offices are usually hidden in neighborhoods like this one.

I checked the address in my hand and started down the street. Ragged, raw children of all ages bolted from an alley just ahead of me and descended on a new car that had been crazy enough to come through this neighborhood. They swarmed over it, laughing, cursing, screaming, rending it like scavengers tearing a carcass. They started stripping it of everything that could possibly be resold. They let the elderly fat man driving it escape screaming down the block. They didn't shoot him until he was a few hundreds yards away.

I hurried on.

A dozen women shouted all the erotic things they wanted to do to me with their mouths. A beggar threw himself at my feet and beseeched me for money. A madman stood in the center of the sidewalk, slashing his left arm with a razor blade.

The number I wanted was 1204, a narrow building set between two wider buildings. I went up a steep, dark staircase. The smells were overwhelming, vomit, blood, feces, street drugs.

Atop the landing was a long hallway with four office doors on each side. Timeline was on the right, three doors down.

Dirty, dim light shone behind the pebbled glass in the door. The door itself was ajar an inch or so.

Behind me, at the top of the stairs, footsteps sounded.

I ducked inside the Timeline door, closed it, clipped off the overhead light.

In the dusty, fetid darkness of the building, a man walked down the corridor whistling an ancient love song. A Jerome Kern song, in fact, Kern being a popular composer I'd sometimes taught.

The whistling went past the door and on down the hall.

A door was opened with a key that had to be wiggled violently; door was opened, man walked heavily inside, door was closed behind him.

I clipped the light back on, ready to face the Timeline employee at the desk behind me. I'd caught only a momentary glimpse of him. He would certainly be wondering what the hell was going on here. My abrupt entrance had probably frightened him into silence.

So I turned around and faced him.

He was a young, fleshy man, in a dirty white shirt and a pair of heavy, black-rimmed glasses, sitting behind a battered desk that had on it a computer screen far too sophisticated and expensive for a building like this.

He was still silent, but it wasn't me who had silenced him. It was the blaster hole in the middle of his stomach that had done it. Now I was sure that all my suspicions were confirmed. My student assistant Thornburg had indeed stolen one of my time-passes and used hours of my tracking time to figure out where he could best intersect with the creature known as Synandra. I'd become aware of her by accident, by seeing that the same wraith-like woman was present at most of history's great tragedies. Who was she? What was she? I hadn't been able to find out, but I had the feeling that my assistant Thornburg had.

He'd had to check in with the dead young man here

to get instructions about this time-zone — where to eat, what areas to avoid, any notable festivities or holidays coming up.

But, after getting the information, Thornburg had killed him, wanting to erase his presence in this world so that the University would never learn what he was up to. And nobody could track Synandra through him, in case some other professor on some other time-line had also stumbled on her mysterious existence.

I found another chair, pushed the dead man a few feet away and spent the next twenty minutes on the computer.

The dead man had been nice enough to lay out an entire three-day vacation plan for Bob Thornburg, the finale of which was a day-long stay at a resort in the mountains. Thornburg had obviously passed himself off as a tourist.

But there was one address that didn't fit in with a vacation plan, an address, according to the computer map, only a few blocks from here.

This was what Thornburg had really been after. This was where he would find Synandra. And so would I.

In addition to regular academic studies, the University specializes in developing weapons for the government. For instance, it was rumored — though as yet I'd never seen any evidence of it — that a mind-scrub unit no larger than a pistol was now in development. Mind-scrubbing was used on all revolutionaries and on many kinds of sex deviants. At its most powerful, the process utterly erased a person mentally and spiritually; not only was his memory taken away, so were all his or her instincts and proclivities.

There was rumored to be another type of police tool in development too. But I knew this was more than a rumor. I held one in my hand. The scientists on the project called it a dissolver. It could break down molecular structures in a matter of moments.

I pointed it at the head of my friend the dead man and watched him vanish. The only trouble was the smell. It made the street below seem like perfume.

After I had finished with him, I set to work on the computer, destroying it as well. When I got back to the University, I let Timeline know that I'd wiped out all evidence of their existence in this particular time-zone and that they'd have to set up a new office.

Ten minutes later I walked down a narrow street filled with men and women who were falling to their knees and literally tearing off their clothes and ripping out their hair at the bloody roots. A man in flowing white robes and a crown of thorns stood on the back of a flatbed truck. In one hand he held a microphone and in the other a cigarette. He exhorted the people to go out and rob and steal and plunder and murder, if necessary, but to bring back green American cash because wasn't the grand total of tonight's Christ-A-Thon looking particularly woeful? A mostly naked girl, who couldn't have been more than fifteen, shot her hip and pointed seductively to a flashing white sign that read $1,350. 'We need a lot more fucking money than that, my friends,' the guy in the white robes told them in a harsh voice. Meanwhile, the true believers continued to wail and moan and tear at themselves. I suspected that the good reverend had probably given them too much of whatever drug he used on them.

Then into gunfire darkness. A block where all the street lights had been shot out. Where all the house lights and apartment lights were dark. A block where the only illumination was the muzzle-flame of weapons firing back and forth across the street at each other. Some kind of on-going feud.

I ran down the middle of the street, zigging and zagging, keeping my head down, anticipating the awful *thunk* of a bullet ripping into my flesh and tearing up my vital organs as it made its way out the other side.

The street, and the gunfire, fell away, and then I was on some kind of pier, vast black water tinged with moonlight, a foghorn hooting lonely in the midnight distance.

The pier had been on the computer map.

Not far now. Just a few blocks.

Freezing inside my own sweat, I ran along the pier, northward-bound.

At one point the pier jogged left. Remembering the map, I went right, now running down three or four blocks of alleys where huge plump rats ate their way down inside garbage cans, their pointed tails flicking in the night like antennae.

Then I heard the mob.

There's maybe no other sound quite so terrifying. A large group of people driven insane with drugs or drink but, most especially, driven insane with hatred. I've been to Nazi Germany, and I've heard such mobs first-hand. I've also seen blacks lynched in Mississippi at the turn of the century. And elderly white people kicked to death by young blacks in LA.

Mobs always sound the same. Always.

I drew to the head of the final alley and got my first look at them. They carried ball bats and lead pipes and torches whose flames snapped in the wind. They were rich and poor, young and old, black and white. They flung rocks at the windows of the two large Victorian-style houses that sat on the corner. They also hurled an unceasing list of ugly names at the people inside the houses, some of whom could be seen in silhouette at the windows. Even from here, you could tell how frail they were.

The plague had begun to spread in this time-zone, and these were the people singled out for blame.

They lunged as one toward the houses, their voices thunderous beneath the same moon that had witnessed Druid sacrifices and witches burned at Salem and American Japanese in prison camps during World War II.

And once again, Synandra would be pleased. And she would pass through this night, an angel of sorts, eyes alight, sated for the moment by this misery and treachery, her smoke-ghost wolf crying his pleasure too.

I shouted at them to stop but it was already too late. The houses were already in flames and soon enough would come the cries of the dying trapped within the walls.

'She'll really like this very much.'

Somehow, even above the din, I heard the voice and knew who it belonged to even before I turned to face him.

Thornburg.

'I knew you'd catch on eventually,' he said. Handsome, blond and smirky, he looked at me with his usual disdain. 'You think you know about her, Professor, but you don't. You think you understand this –' and here he indicated the mob as they set the second house afire '– but you don't. You think it's about good and evil. But it's not. Not any more. That's where your scholarship is so pathetic, Professor. So pathetic.'

Thornburg considered himself my superior in every

way, including scholarship. 'I'm going to tell you about her, Professor, so I hope you'll listen.'

'It's hard to listen when people are dying in the background.'

'They don't matter,' he said. 'That's what you don't understand.' The smirk again. 'Synandra is several million years old, Professor. The being that created the universe had two trusted allies, whom he'd also created, his son Clotho and his daughter Synandra. But Clotho was jealous of Synandra because he knew that her son would some day come to hold a very special place in the master's mind. And so Clotho found a being who could transform one thing into another, and he forever transformed Synandra's son into a wolf. And then, because he knew that suffering caused his sister such pain, he began destroying that half of the universe which the master had given her. Only reluctantly did she begin to retaliate – by destroying the worlds in Clotho's half of the universe. And, after a time, so violent and all-consuming did her rage become that she forgot all about sparing lives . . . and became just like Clotho himself. She took the same pleasure in destroying his worlds as he took in destroying hers – with plagues and novas and asteroid attacks.' The smirk. 'She uses whatever whim strikes her fancy at the moment. This is the real nature of the universe, Professor, the battle between Synandra and her brother Clotho, and it will continue a billion years into the future.'

'I'm going to stop her,' I said. 'That's why I came here.'

I thought he might respond to that with a joke but instead, as if he'd heard a silent call, he angled his head to the right, and there, far down the alley, she stood, beautiful and glowing beyond description, radiant hair tumbling to naked shoulders, smoke-ghost wolf, her son, crying his pleasure at the sight of the houses burning.

I started to reach for my dissolver but Thornburg put a hard hand on my arm. 'Don't be a fool, Professor. You can't destroy her. She is a force you know nothing about.' He smiled. 'Anyway, in a few minutes you won't remember anything about her. I've taken her name out of all your computers. And now I'm going to take her name out of your memory.'

From his pocket he took a small silver pistol that looked like a miniature blaster. 'You've heard about the mind-scrubber weapons? The tiny ones we're research-ing at the University? Here's the prototype.'

And just then I heard the first sobs and pleas of the men inside the houses as the flames reached them. And I saw a man on fire climb out of a third-storey window and fall through the air. The mob gathered around him and kicked and stoned him to death.

And I saw Synandra, so beautiful inside the mist swirling about her – and the smoke-ghost wolf – begin to walk away down the long, dark alley, satisfied now that their job was done.

They would stay long enough in this time-zone to make sure that millions of other plague victims died in similar ways. And then it would be on to another time-zone.

'You won't have to worry about her any more, Professor,' Thornburg said, as I turned back to him. 'I'm going to follow her from planet to planet, time-zone to time-zone. This is the only history that matters, Professor, the battle between Synandra and her brother Clotho.'

'And the lives they destroy in their selfish little war?'

The smirk. 'As I said, Professor, you won't have to worry about that any more.'

He raised the prototype and shot me with it.

'Nice time-trip?'

'Very nice, thank you.'

His colleague Brendan stood in the doorway of his office.

'I was afraid something was wrong.'

'Oh?' he said.

'You put in for an emergency time-trip.'

He looked up from his computer, startled. 'I did?'

'Uh-huh.'

He shook his head. 'Don't know why I did that. Just took a nice little trip, was all. I must have punched the wrong access code. Hit "Emergency" instead of "Vacation". All I did was relax.'

That was not true, not exactly, because he wasn't sure what he'd done. He had no memory of the forty-eight hours he was gone. But all that could mean was that he hadn't done anything significant enough to remember, right? We like to think we're masters of time-tripping, but we're not, he thought. People still have all sorts of strange reactions to going back and forth in time. He'd obviously just had a strange reaction himself.

The tone rang for class.

'Well, time to go share my wisdom with my students,' Brendan said.

He smiled. 'That shouldn't take long.'

Brendan laughed, and left.

He turned back to his computer, checking messages he'd received while time-tripping.

There was only one, from his assistant Bob Thornburg.

I know this is crazy, Professor Granger, the message began, *but I just couldn't stay away from my fiancée any longer. I've given up my scholarship. By the time you read this, I'll be living with Emmie in Portland. I've enjoyed working with you. I learned a whole lot.*

For a long time he just stared at it. Something about his time-trip and Thornburg . . . Some vague memory that teased him . . .

But, no, he thought, there's no connection. Just another odd reaction to time-tripping itself . . . He looked back at the message and smiled. Who would have thought that such a smug academic as Bob Thornburg had it in him to give up his scholarship and run away for love?

But then, he thought, there are a lot of things about this old universe we don't understand.

After the Elephant Ballet

GARY A. BRAUNBECK

Our acts our angels are, or good or ill,
Our fatal shadows that walk by us still.
John Fletcher (1579–1625)
An Honest Man's Fortune, Epilogue

The little girl might have been pretty once, but flames
had taken care of that: burned skin hung about her neck
in brownish wattles; one yellowed eye was almost completely hidden underneath the drooping scar tissue of
her forehead; her mouth twisted downward on both
sides with pockets of dead, greasy-looking flesh at the
corners; and her cheeks resembled the globs of congealed
wax that form at the base of a candle.

I couldn't stop staring at her or cursing myself for
doing it. She passed by the table where I was sitting,
giving me a glimpse of her only normal-looking feature:
her left eye was a startling bright green; a jade gemstone.
Buried as it was in that ruined face, its vibrance seemed
a cruel joke.

She took a seat in the back.

Way in the back.

'Mr Dysart?'

A woman in her mid-thirties held out a copy of my
latest storybook. I smiled as I took it, chancing one last
glance at the disfigured little girl in the back, then

autographed the title page.

I have been writing and illustrating children's books for the last six years, and, though I'm far from a household name, I do have a Newbery Award proudly displayed on a shelf in my office. One critic, evidently after a few too many Grand Marniers, once wrote: 'Dysart's books are a treasure chest of wonders for children and adults alike. He is part Maurice Sendak, part Hans Christian Andersen, and part Madeline L'Engle.' (I always thought of my books as being a cross between Buster Keaton and the Brothers Grimm — what does *that* tell you about creative objectivity?)

I handed the book back to the woman as Gina Foster, director of the Cedar Hill Public Library, came up to the table. We had been dating for about two weeks; romance had yet to rear its ugly head, but I was hopeful.

'Well, are we ready?' she asked.

'"We" want to step outside for a cigarette.'

'I thought you were trying to quit.'

'And failing miserably.' I made my way to the special 'judge's chair'. 'How many entries are there?'

'Twenty-five. But don't worry, they can show you only one illustration and the story can't be longer than four minutes. We still on for coffee and dessert afterward?'

'Unless some eight-year-old Casanova steals your heart away.'

'Hey, you pays your money, you takes your chances.'

'You're an evil woman.'

'Famous for it.'

'Tell me again: how did you rope me into being the judge for this?'

'When I mentioned that this was National Literacy

Month, you assaulted me with a speech about the importance of promoting a love for creativity among children.'

'I must've been drunk.' I don't drink — that's my mother's department.

Gina looked at her watch, took a deep breath as she gave me a 'Here-we-go' look, then turned to face the room. 'Good evening,' she said in a sparkling voice that always reminded me of bells. 'Welcome to the library's first annual storybook contest.' Everyone applauded. I tried slunking my way into the woodwork. Crowds make me nervous. Actually, most things make me nervous.

'I'll just wish all our contestants good luck and introduce our judge, award-winning local children's book author Andrew Dysart.' She began the applause this time, then mouthed *You're on your own* before gliding to an empty chair.

'Thank you,' I said, the words crawling out of my throat as if they were afraid of the light. 'I . . . uh, I'm sure that all of you have been working very hard, and I want you to know that we're going to make copies of all your storybooks, bind them and put them on the shelves here in the library right next to my own.' Unable to add any more dazzle to that stunning speech, I took my seat, consulted the list and called the first contestant forward.

A chubby boy with round glasses shuffled up as if he were being led in front of a firing squad. He faced the room, gave a terrified grin, then wiped some sweat from his forehead as he held up a pretty good sketch of a cow riding a tractor.

'My name is Jimmy Campbell and my story is called "The Day the Cows Took Over".' He held the picture higher. 'See there? The cow is riding the tractor and the farmer is out grazing in the field.'

'What's the farmer's name?' I asked.

He looked at me and said, 'Uh . . . h-how about Old MacDonald?' He shrugged his shoulders. 'I'd give him a better name, but I don't know no farmers.'

I laughed along with the rest of the room, forgetting all about the odd, damaged little girl who had caught my attention earlier.

Jimmy did very well – I had to fight to keep my laughter from getting too loud. I didn't want him to think I was making fun of him, but the kid was *genuinely* funny; his story had an off-kilter sense of humor that reminded me of Ernie Kovacs. I decided to give him the maximum fifty points. I'm a push-over for kids. So sue me.

The next forty minutes went by with nary a tear or panic attack, but after eight stories I could see that several of the children were getting fidgety, so I signaled to Gina that we'd take a break after the next contestant.

I read: 'Lucy Simpkins.'

There was the soft rustling of movement in the back as the burned girl came forward.

Everyone stared at her. The cumulative anxiety in the room was squatting on her shoulders like a stone gargoyle, yet she wore an unwavering smile.

I returned the smile and gestured for her to begin.

She held up a watercolor painting.

I think my mouth may have dropped open.

The painting was excellent; a deftly rendered portrait of several people – some very tall, others quite short, still others who were deformed – standing in a semicircle around a statue that marked a grave. All wore the brightly colored costumes of circus performers. Each face had an expression of profound sadness; the nuances were breathtaking. But the thing that really impressed me was the cloud in the sky; it was shaped like an elephant but not in any obvious way: it reminded you of summer afternoons when you still had enough imagination and wonder to lie on a hillside and dream that you saw giant shapes in the pillowy white above.

'My name is Lucy Simpkins,' she said in a clear, almost musical voice, 'and my story is called "Old Bet's Gone Away".

'One night in Africa, in the secret elephant graveyard, the angels of all the elephants got together to tell stories. Tonight it was Martin's, the Bull Elephant's, turn. He wandered around until he found his old bones, then he sat on top of them like they were a throne and said, "I want to tell you the story of Old Bet, the one who never found her way back to us."

'And he said:

In 1824 a man in Somers, New York, bought an elephant named Old Bet from a traveling circus. He gave her the best hay and always fed her peanuts on the weekends. Children would pet her trunk and take rides on her back in a special saddle that the man made.

Then one day the Reverend brought his daughter to ride on Old Bet. Old Bet was really tired, but she thought the Reverend's little girl looked nice, so she gave her a ride and even sang the elephant song, which went like this:

> I go along, thud-thud,
> I go along.
> And I sing my elephant song.
> I stomp in the grass, and I roll in the mud,

And when I go a-walking, I go along
    THUD!
It's a happy sound, and this is my happy song:
Won't you sing it with me? It doesn't take
    long.
I go along, thud-thud,
I go along.

Old Bet accidentally tripped over a log and fell, and the Reverend's daughter broke both of her legs and had to go to the hospital.

Old Bet was real sorry, but the Reverend yelled at her and smacked her with a horse whip and got her so scared that she ran away into the deep woods.

The next day the Reverend got all the people of the town together and told them that Old Bet was the Devil in disguise and should be killed before she could hurt other children. So the menfolk took their shotguns and went into the woods. They found Bet by the river. She was looking at her reflection in the water and singing:

I ran away, uh-oh,
I ran away.
And I hurt my little friend.
I didn't mean to fall, but I'm clumsy and old,
I'm big and ugly and the circus didn't want me
    any more.
I wish they hadn't sold me.
I want to go home.

The Reverend wanted to shoot her but the man who'd bought her from the circus said, 'Best I be the one who does the deed. After all, she's mine.' But the man wasn't too young either and his aim was a bit off, and when he fired the bullet it hit

Old Bet in the rear and it hurt and it scared her *so much*! She tried to run away, run back to the circus.

She didn't mean to kill anyone, but two men got under her and she crushed them and her heart broke because of that. By now the judge had come around to see what all the trouble was, and he saw the two dead men and decreed right there on the spot that Old Bet was guilty of murder and sentenced her to hang by the neck until she was dead.

They took her to the rail yard and strung her up on a railroad crane, but she broke it down because she was so heavy. They got a stronger crane and hanged her from that. After three hours, Old Bet finally died while five thousand people watched. She was buried there in Somers and the man who bought her had a statue raised above the grave. Ever since, it has been a shrine for circus people. They travel to her grave and stop to pay their respects and remember that, as long as people laugh at you and smile, they won't kill you. And they say that if you look in the sky on a bright summer's day, you can see Old Bet up there in the clouds, smiling down at everyone and singing the elephant song as she tries to find her way back to Africa and the secret elephant graveyard.

Then it was morning, and the sun came up, and the elephants made their way back to a place even more secret than the elephant graveyard. They all dreamed about Old Bet, and wished her well.

'My name is Lucy Simpkins and my story was called "Old Bet's Gone Away". Thank you.'

The others applauded her: softly at first, as if they were afraid it was the wrong thing to do, but it wasn't long before their clapping grew louder and more ardent. Gina sat forward, applauding to beat the band. She looked at the audience, gave a shrug that was more an inward decision than an outward action, and stood.

Lucy Simpkins managed something like a smile, then handed me her watercolor. 'You should have this,' she said, and made her way out of the room toward the refreshment table.

As everyone was dispersing, I took Gina's hand and pulled her aside. 'My God, did you hear that?'

'I thought it was incredibly moving.'

'*Moving?* Maybe in the same way the last thirty minutes of *The Wild Bunch* or *Straw Dogs* is moving, yes, but if you're talking warm and fuzzy and *It's a Wonderful Life*, you're way the hell off-base!'

Her eyes clouded over. 'Jesus, Andy. You're shaking.'

'Damn straight I'm shaking. Do you have any idea what that girl has to have been through? Can you imagine the kind of life which would cause a child to tell a story like that?' I took a deep breath, clenching my teeth. 'Christ! I don't know which I want more: to wrap her up and take her home with me or to find her parents and break a baseball bat over their skulls!'

'That's a bit . . . strong, isn't it?'

'No. An imagination that can invent something like that story is not the result of a healthy, loving household.'

'Don't be so arrogant. You aren't all-knowing about these things. You don't have any idea what her family life is really like.'

'I suppose, Mother Goose, that you're more experienced in this area?' I don't know why I said something like that. Sometimes I'm not a nice person. In fact, sometimes I stink on ice.

Her face melted into a placid mask, except for a small twitch in the upper left corner of her mouth that threatened to become a sneer.

'My sister had epilepsy. All her life the doctors kept changing her medication as she got older – a stronger dose of what she was already taking or some new drug altogether. Those periods were murder because her seizures always got worse while her system adjusted. Her seizures were violent as hell, but she refused to wear any kind of protective gear. "I don't wanna look like a goon," she'd say. So she'd walk around with facial scrapes and cuts and ugly bruises. She sprained her arm a couple of times and once dislocated her shoulder. People in the neighborhood started noticing, but no one said anything to us. Someone finally called the police and Child Welfare. They came down on us like a curse from heaven. They were, of course, embarrassed when they found out about Lorraine's condition – she'd always insisted that we keep it a secret – but nothing changed the fact that people who were supposedly our friends assumed that her injuries were the result of child abuse. Lorraine had never been so humiliated, and from that day on she saw herself as being handicapped. I think that, as much as the epilepsy, helped to kill her. So don't go jumping to any conclusions about that girl's parents or the life she's had because you *can't know*. And anything you might say or do out of anger could plant an idea in her head that has no business being there.'

'What do you suggest?'

'I suggest that you go out there and tell her how much you enjoyed her story. I suggest we try to make her feel special and admired because she deserves to feel that way, if only for tonight.'

I squeezed her hand. 'It couldn't have been a picnic for you, either, Lorraine's epilepsy.'

'She should have lived to be a hundred. And just so you know – this has a tendency to slip out of my mouth from time to time – Lorraine committed suicide. She couldn't live with the knowledge that she was a "cripple". I cried for a year.'

'I'm sorry for acting like a jerk.'

She smiled, then looked at her watch. 'Break's almost over. If you want to step outside and smoke six minutes off your life, you'd better do it now. I'll snag some punch and cookies for you.'

I couldn't find Lucy; one parent told me she'd gone into the restroom, so I stepped out for my smoke. The rest of the evening went quickly and enjoyably. At the end of the night, I found myself with a tie: Lucy Simpkins (how could I not?) and my junior-league Ernie Kovaks who didn't know no farmers.

Ernie was ecstatic.

Lucy was gone.

I have only the vaguest memories of my father. When I was four, he was killed in an accident at the steel mill where he worked. He left a handful of impressions: the smell of machine grease, the rough texture of a calloused hand touching my cheek, the smell of Old Spice. What I know of him I learned from my mother.

His death shattered her. She grew sad and overweight and began drinking. Over the years there have been times of laughter and dieting, but the drinking remained constant, evidenced by the flush on her cheeks and the reddened, bulbous nose that I used to think cute when I was a child because it made her look like W. C. Fields; now it only disgusts me.

After my father's death, nothing I did was ever good enough. I fought like hell for her approval and affection but often settled for indifference and courtesy.

Don't misunderstand: I loved her when she was sober.

When she was drunk, I thought her the most repulsive human being on the face of the earth.

I bring this up to help you make sense of everything that happened later, starting with the surprise I found waiting on my doorstep when, after coffee and cheesecake, Gina drove me back to my house.

Someone on the street was having a party, so we had to park half a block away and walk. That was fine by me; it gave us time to hold hands and enjoy the night and each other's company. The world was new again, at least for this evening –

– which went right into the toilet when something lurched out of the shadows on my porch.

'Been waitin' here . . . long time . . .' Her voice was thick and slurred, and the stench of too much gin was enough to make me gag.

'Mom? Jesus, what are you –' I cast an embarrassed glance at Gina – 'doing here?'

She pointed unsteadily to her watch and gave a soft, wet belch. 'S'after midnight . . . s'my birthday now . . .'

She wobbled back and forth for a moment before slipping on the rubber WELCOME mat and falling toward me.

I caught her. 'Oh, for chrissakes!' I turned toward Gina. 'God . . . I don't know what . . . I'm sorry about . . .'

'Is there anything I can do?'

Mom slipped a little more and mumbled something. I hooked my arms around her torso and said, 'My . . .

dammit ... my keys are in my left jacket pocket. Would you −?'

Gina took them out, unlocked the front door and turned on the inside lights. I spun Mom around and shook her until she regained some composure, then led her to the kitchen, where I poured her into a chair and started a pot of coffee. Gina remained in the front room, turning on the television and adjusting the volume, her way of letting me know she wouldn't listen to anything that might be said.

The coffee finished brewing and I poured a large cup for Mom. 'How the hell did you get here?'

The shock of having someone other than myself see her in this state forced her to pull herself together. When she spoke again, her voice wasn't as slurred. 'I walked. It's a nice ... nice night.' She took a sip of the coffee, then sat watching the steam curl over the rim of the cup. Her lower lip started to quiver. 'I'm ... I'm sorry, Andy ... didn't know you were gonna have company.' She sighed, then fished a cigarette from the pocket of her blouse and lit it with an unsteady hand.

'Why are you here?'

'I just got to ... you know, thinking about your dad and was feeling blue ... 'sides, I wanted to remind you that you're taking me out for my birthday.'

My right hand balled into a fist. 'Have I *ever* forgotten your birthday?'

'No ...'

'Then why would I start now?'

She leaned back in the chair and fixed me with an icy stare, smoke crawling from her nostrils like flames from a dragon's snout. 'Maybe you think you've gotten too good for me. Maybe you think because I wasn't a story

233

writer or artist like you, you don't have to bother with me any more.'

Time to go.

'Sit here and drink your coffee. I'm going to walk my friend to her car, and then I'll come back and take you home.'

'Didn't get it from me, that's for damn sure . . . does you no good anyway . . . drop dead at forty-five and no one'll care about your silly books . . .'

I threw up my hands and started out of the kitchen.

'What's this?' she said, pulling Lucy's watercolor from my pocket. 'Oh, a picture. They used to let us draw pictures when I was in the children's home . . . Did I ever tell you about —'

She was making me sick.

I stormed out of the kitchen and into the front room in time to see Jimmy Stewart grab Donna Reed and say, 'I don't want to get married, understand?'

'Don't worry,' said Gina. 'They get together in the end.' She put her arms around me. I felt like Jason being wrapped in the Golden Fleece.

'I'm so sorry about this,' I said. 'She's never done this before.'

'Never?'

I looked into her eyes and couldn't make any excuses. 'I mean . . . she's never come *here* drunk before.'

'How long has she been this way?'

'I can't ever remember a week from my life when she didn't get drunk at least once.'

'Have you ever tried to get her some help?'

'Of course I have. She tries it for a while but she always . . . always —'

'I understand. It's OK. Don't be embarrassed.'

That's easy to say, I thought. What I said was: 'I appreciate this, Gina. I really do.' I wished that she would just leave so I could get the rest of this over with.

She seemed to sense this and stepped back, saying, 'I guess I should, uh, go –'

A loud crash from the kitchen startled both of us.

I ran in and saw Mom on the floor; she'd been trying to pour herself another cup of coffee and had collapsed, taking the coffee pot with her. Shattered sections of sharp glass covered the floor and she had split open one of her shins. Scurrying on her hands and knees, she looked up and saw me standing there, saw Gina behind me and pointed at the table.

'W–where did you . . . did you get that?'

'Get *what*?'

'Th–that goddamn . . . picture!'

I moved toward her. She doubled over and began vomiting.

I grabbed her, trying to pull her up to the sink – making it to the bathroom was out of the question – but I slipped and lost my grip.

Mom gave a wet gurgling sound and puked on my chest.

Gina came in, grabbed a towel and helped me get her over the sink –

– and Mom gripped the edge, emptying her stomach down the drain.

The stench was incredible.

Feeling the heat of humiliation cover my face, I looked at Gina and fumbled for something to say, but what *could* I say? We were holding a drunk who was spewing all over –

What could you say?

Gina returned my gaze. 'So, how 'bout them Mets, huh? Fuckin-A!'

That's what you could say.

I didn't feel so dirty.

Gina surprised me the next morning by showing up on my doorstep at eight thirty with hot coffee and croissants. When I explained to her that I had to take Mom's birthday cake over to her house, Gina said, 'I'd like to come along, if you don't mind.'

I did and told her so.

'Come on,' she said, taking my hand and giving me a little kiss on the cheek. 'Think about it. If she's hung over and sees that I'm with you, she might behave herself. If she doesn't behave, then you can use me as an excuse not to stick around.'

I argued with her some more. She won. I don't think I've ever won an argument with a woman – they're far too sharp.

Besides an *ersatz* apology ('I feel so *silly*!') and a bandage around the gash on her shin, Mom showed no signs that last night had ever happened. Her hair was freshly cleaned, she wore a new dress and her make-up was, for a change, subtly applied. She looked like your typical healthy matriarch.

We stayed for breakfast. Gina surprised me a second time that morning by reaching into her purse and pulling out a large birthday card that she handed to Mom.

Well, that just made Mom's day. She must have thanked Gina half a dozen times and even went so far as to give her a hug, saying, 'I'm glad to see he finally found a good one.'

'Blind shithouse luck,' replied Gina. She and Mom

got a tremendous guffaw out of that. I gritted my teeth and smiled at them. Hardy-har-har.

'So,' Mom said to Gina, 'will you be coming with us?'

'I don't know,' Gina replied, turning to me with a Pollyanna-pitiful look in her eyes. 'Am I?'

'You stink at coy,' was my answer.

'Good!' said Mom. 'The three of us. It'll be a lot of fun.'

'Have you decided where you want to go?'

'Yeee-eeessss, I have.'

Oh, good. Another surprise.

'Where?'

She winked at me and squeezed Gina's hand. 'It's a secret. I'll tell you when we're on our way.' This was a little game she loved to play – I-know-something-you-don't-know – and it usually got on my nerves.

But not that morning. Somehow Gina's presence made it seem as if everything was going to work out just fine.

Our first stop was the mall, where Gina insisted on buying Mom a copy of the new Stephen King opus and paying for lunch. After we'd eaten Mom looked at her watch and informed us it was time to go.

'Where are we going?' I asked as we got on the highway.

Mom leaned forward from the back seat. 'Riverfront Coliseum.'

'*Cincinnati?* You want to drive three hours to –'

'It's my birthday.'

'But –'

Gina squeezed my leg. 'It's her birthday.'

I acquiesced. I should have remembered that no good deed goes unpunished.

★

'A *circus*!' shouted Gina as we approached the Coliseum entrance.

I slowed my step, genuinely surprised. I have been to many circuses in my life, but never with my mother – I always thought she'd have no interest in this sort of thing.

'Surprised?' said Mom, taking my arm.

'Well, yes, but . . . why?'

Her eyes filled with a curious kind of desperation. 'All our lives we've never done anything *fun* together. I've been a real shit to you sometimes, and I'll never be able to apologize enough, let alone make up for it. I've never told you how proud I am of you – I've read all your books. Bet you didn't know that, did you?' Her eyes began tearing. 'Oh, hon, I ain't been much of a mother to you, what with the . . . drinking and such, but, if you'll be patient with me, I'd like to . . . to give it a try, us being friends. If you don't mind.'

This part was familiar. I bit down on my tongue, hoping that she wasn't going to launch into a heartfelt promise to get back into A A and stop hitting the bottle and turn her life around, blah-blah-blah.

She didn't.

'Well,' she whispered. 'We'd best go get our tickets.'

'Do we get cotton candy?' asked Gina.

'Of course you do. And hot dogs –'

'– and cherry colas –'

'– and peanuts –'

'– and an ulcer,' I said. They both stared at me.

'You never were any fun,' said Mom, smiling. I couldn't tell if she was joking or not.

'I never claimed to be.'

Gina smacked me on the ass. 'Then it's about time you started.'

It was a blast. Acrobats and lion-tamers and trained seals and a big brass band and a sword-swallower, not to mention the fire-eating bear (that was a real trip) and the bald guy who wrestled a crocodile that was roughly the size of your average Mexican chihuahua (A DEATH-DEFYING BATTLE BETWEEN MAN AND BEAST, proclaimed the program: 'Compared to what?' asked Gina. 'Changing a diaper?'), all of it was an absolute joy, right up to the elephants and clowns.

Not that anything happened with the elephants; they did a marvelously funny kickline to a Scott Joplin tune, but the sight of them triggered memories of Lucy Simpkins's story. I looked at Gina and saw that she was thinking about it as well.

Mom thought the elephants were the most precious things she'd ever seen – and since she used to say the same about my baby pictures I wondered if my paranoia about my nose being too large was unjustified after all.

At the end of the show, when every performer and animal came marching out for the Grand Finale Parade, the clowns broke away and ran into the audience. After tossing out confetti and lollipops and balloons, one clown ran over to Mom and handed her a small stuffed animal, then, with a last burst of confetti from the large flower in the center of his costume, he honked his horn and dashed back into the parade.

I looked at Mom and saw, just for a moment, the ghost of the vibrant, lovely woman who populated several pages of the family photo albums. In that light, with all the laughter and music swirling around us, I saw her smile and could almost believe that she was going to really change this time. I suspected that it might just be wishful thinking on my part, but sometimes a delusion is the best thing in the world — especially if you *know* it's a delusion.

So, for that moment, Mom was a changed woman who might find some measure of peace and happiness in the remainder of her life, and I was a son who harbored no anger or disgust for her, la–dee–da.

It was kind of nice.

We made our way through the crowd and toward the exit. I don't like crowds and soon felt the first heavy rivulets of sweat rolling down my face.

Gina sensed what was happening and led us to a section near a concession stand where the crowd was much thinner.

As I stood there, catching my breath, Gina nudged Mom and asked about the stuffed animal. Mom looked at it then for the first time.

'Oh my. Isn't that . . . something?' She was smiling, yet she cringed as she touched the tiny fired–clay tusks of the small stuffed elephant in a ballerina pose, wearing a ridiculous pink tutu. Cottony angel's wings jutted from its back.

'That's *adorable*.' Gina laughed.

'Yes . . . yes, it is,' whispered Mom. Her smile faltered for just a moment. I have seen my mother worried before, but this went beyond that; something in her was genuinely *afraid* of that stuffed toy.

'Janet Walters!' shouted a voice that sounded like old nails being wrenched from rotted wood.

Mom looked up at me. Walters was her maiden name.

'What the —?'

The nun came toward us.

That in itself wasn't all that unusual; it was easy to

assume that the nun was here with some church group. What *was* unusual was the way this nun was dressed; pick your favorite singing sister from *The Sound of Music* and you'll have some idea. Nuns don't have to dress this way any more, but this one did. The whole outfit was at least fifty years out of date. Her stockings were four times too heavy for the weather, and her shoes would have looked right at home in a Frankenstein movie.

Sister Frankenstein barreled right up to Mom and grabbed her arm. 'Would you like to hear a story?'

Mom's face drained of all color.

I didn't give a good goddamn if this woman was a nun. 'Excuse me, Sister, but I think you're hurting –'

Sister Frankenstein fixed me with a glare that could have frozen fire, then said to Mom: 'He was led across the railroad yards to his private car. It was late at night. No train was scheduled, but an express came through. A baby elephant had strayed from the rest of the pack and stood on the tracks in front of the oncoming train, so scared it couldn't move. Jumbo saw it and ran over, shoved the baby aside and met the locomotive head-on. He was killed instantly and the train was derailed.'

My mother began moaning soft and low, gripping the stuffed toy like a life-preserver.

Sister Frankenstein let fly with a series of loud, racking, painful-sounding coughs and began to stomp away (*I go along, thud-thud*), then turned back and said, 'Only good little girls ever see Africa!'

A crowd of teenagers ran through and the nun vanished behind them.

I was reeling; it had happened so *fast*.

Mom marched over to the only concession stand still open –

– which sold beer.

She took the large plastic cup in her hands and said, 'P-please don't start with me, Andy. Just a beer, OK? It's just a beer. I need to . . . to steady . . . my –'

'Who the hell *was* that?'

'Not now.' She tipped the cup back and finished the brew in five deep gulps.

Gina took my hand and whispered, 'Don't push it.'

Right. Psycho Nun on the Rampage and I'm supposed to let it drop.

Gina raised an eyebrow at me.

'Fine,' I whispered.

Mom fell asleep the minute we got in the car and didn't wake up until we hit Columbus.

Mom took her mail from the box, then insisted we come in for a slice of cake.

As I was pouring the coffee, Mom opened a large manilla envelope that was among the mail.

Her gasp sounded like the strangled cry of a suicide when the rope snaps tight.

I turned. 'What is it?'

Gina was leaning over her shoulder, looking at the large piece of heavy white paper that Mom had pulled from the envelope.

'Andy,' said Gina in a low, cautious voice. 'I think you'd better take a look at this.'

It was a watercolor painting of the center ring of a circus where a dozen elephants all wore the same kind of absurd pink tutu as the stuffed toy, all had angel's wings unfurling from their shoulders and all were dancing through a wall of flames. The stands were empty except for one little girl whose face was the saddest I'd ever seen.

There was no doubt in my mind – or Gina's, as I later found out – about who had painted it.

There was no return address on the envelope, nor was there a postmark.

After a tense silence, Mom lit a cigarette and said, 'Would you two mind . . . mind sitting with me for a while? I got something I need to tell you about.

'When I was six years old the county took me and my three brothers away from our parents and put us in the Catholic Children's Home . . .'

I faded away for a minute or two. I'd heard this countless times before and was embarrassed that Gina would have to listen to it now.

Most of what Mom said early on was directed more toward Gina than me. The Same Old Prologue.

In a nutshell:

Mom's parents were dirt-poor and heavy drinkers, both. Too many complaints from the school and neighbors resulted in a visit by the authorities. My mother and her brothers remained under the care of the Catholics and the county until they were fifteen; then they were each given five dollars and a new set of clothes and pushed out of the door.

'There wasn't really much to enjoy except our Friday art classes with Sister Elizabeth. If we worked hard, she'd make popcorn in the evening and tell us stories before we went to bed, stories that she made up. There was one that was our favorite, all about these dancing elephants and their adventures with the circus. I don't know why I was so surprised to see Sister Elizabeth tonight; she always loved circuses.

'She'd start each story the same way, describing the circus tent and giving the names of all the elephants, then she'd make up a story about one elephant in particular. Each Friday it was a new story about a different elephant. The stories were real funny and we always got a good laugh from them.

'Then she got sick. Turned out to be cancer. She kept getting sadder and angrier all the time, so we started to draw pictures of the elephants for her, but it didn't lift her spirits any.

'The stories started getting so ... bitter. There was one about an elephant that got hanged that gave some of the girls bad dreams for a week. Then Sister quit telling us stories. We heard that she was gonna go in the hospital, so we bought her flowers and asked her to tell us one last story about the elephants.

'God, she looked so thin. She'd been going to Columbus for cobalt treatments. Her scalp was all moist-looking and had only a few strands of wiry hair, and her color was awful ... but her eyes were the worst. She couldn't hide how scared she was.

'She told us one more story. But this one didn't start with the circus tent. It started in Africa.'

I leaned forward. This was new to me.

'I never forgot it,' said Mom. 'It went like this.

'The elder of the pack gathered together all of the elephants and told them that he had spoken with God, and God had said the elder elephant was going to die, but first he was to pass on a message.

'God had said there were men on their way to Africa, sailing in great ships, coming to take the elephants away so people could see them. And people would think that the elephants were strange and wonderful and funny. God felt bad about that "funny" part, and He asked the elder to apologize to the others and tell them that as long as they stayed good of heart and true to themselves, they would never be funny in His eyes.

'The elder named Martin the Bull Elephant as the new leader, then lumbered away to the secret elephant graveyard and died.

'The men came in their ships and rounded up the elephants and put them in chains and stuffed them into the ships and took them away. They were sold to the circus where they were made to do tricks and dances for people to laugh at. Then they were trained to dance ballet for one big special show. The elephants worked real hard because they wanted to do well.

'The night of the big show came, and the elephants did their best. They really did. They got all the steps and twirls and dips exactly right and felt very proud. But the people laughed and laughed at them because they were so big and clumsy and looked so silly in the pink tutus they wore. Even though they did their best, they felt ashamed because everyone laughed at them.

'Later that night, after the circus was quiet and the laughing people went home, the elephants were alone. One of them told Martin that all of their hearts were broken. Martin gave a sad nod of his head and said, "Yes, it's time for us to go back home." So he reached out with his trunk through the bars of the cage and picked up a dying cigar butt and dropped it in the hay and started a big fire.

'The elephants died in that fire, but when the circus people and firemen looked above the flames they saw smoke clouds dancing across the sky. They were shaped like elephants and they drifted across the continents until they reached the secret elephant graveyard in Africa. And when they touched down, the elder was waiting for them, and he smiled as an angel came down and said to all of them, "Come, the blessed children of my Father, and receive the world prepared for you . . ."'

She cleared her throat, lit another cigarette and stared at us.

'That's *horrible*,' said Gina.

'I know,' whispered Mom. 'Sister Elizabeth didn't say anything after she finished the story, she just got up and left. It really bothered all of us, but the Sisters had taught us that we had to comfort each other whenever something happened that upset one or all of us. They even assigned each of us another girl that we could go to if something was wrong and there wasn't any Sisters around. Sister Elizabeth used to say that we were all guardian angels of each other's spirits. It was kinda nice.

'The girl I had, her name was Lucy Simpkins. She'd been really close to Sister, and I think it all made her a little crazy. On the night Sister Elizabeth died, Lucy got to crying and crying until I thought she'd waste away. She kept asking everyone how she could go to Africa and be with Sister Elizabeth and the elephants.

'Everyone just sort of looked at her and didn't say anything because we knew she was upset. She was a strange girl, always singing to herself and drawing . . .

'She never said anything to me. Not even when I went to her and asked. At least, that's how I remember it.

'You see, some time during the night she got out of bed and snuck down to the janitor's closet, found some kerosene and set herself on fire. She was dead before anyone could get the flames out.'

Mom rose from the table, crossed to the counter and looked at her birthday cake. 'I never told anyone that before.'

She took a knife from the cutlery drawer and cut three slices of cake. We ate in silence.

She went to bed a little while later, and Gina came over to my place to spend the night.

At one point she nudged me, and said, 'Have you ever read any Ray Bradbury?'

'Of course.'

'Don't you envy him? There's so much joy and wonder in his stories. They jump out at you like happy puppies. They make you believe that you can hang on to that joy for ever.' She kissed me, then snuggled against my chest. 'Wouldn't it be nice to pinpoint the exact moment in your childhood when you lost that joy and wonder, then go back and warn yourself as a child? Tell yourself that you mustn't ever let go of that joy and hope. Then you wouldn't have to worry about any . . . regrets coming back.'

'I think it's a little late to go back and warn Mom.'

'I know,' she whispered. 'You really love her, don't you? In spite of everything.'

'Yes, I do. Sometimes I've wished that I didn't — it would have made things easier.' I tried to imagine what my mother must have been like as a child but couldn't: to me, she was always old.

'I can't do this to myself, Gina. I can't start feeling responsible for the way her life has turned out. I've done everything I'm capable of, but it seems as if . . . she doesn't *want* to be happy. Dad's being alive filled some kind of void in her, and when he died something else crawled into his spot and began sucking the life out of her.

'I remember once reading about something called "The Bridge of the Separator". In Zoroastrianism it's believed that when you die you meet your conscience on a bridge. I can't help but wonder if . . .'

'If what?'

'I used to look at Mom and think that here was a woman who had died a long time ago but just forgot to drop dead. And maybe that's not so far from the truth. Maybe the really *alive* part of her, the Bradbury part of joy and wonder and hope, died with my father – or maybe it died with Lucy and that nun.

'Whatever the reason, it's dead and there's no bringing it back, so is it so hard to believe that her conscience has gotten tired of waiting at the bridge and has decided to come and get her?'

I awoke a little after five a.m. and climbed quietly out of bed so as not to wake Gina. I stood in the darkness of the bedroom, inhaling deeply. Something smelled.

I puzzled over it –

– sawdust and hay, the aroma of cigarettes and beer and warm cotton candy and popcorn and countless exotic manures –

– I was smelling the circus.

The curtains over the bedroom window fluttered.

The circus smell grew almost overpowering.

I put on my robe and crossed to the window –

– pulled back the curtains –

– looked out into the field behind my house –

– where Lucy Simpkins stood, her sad, damaged hands petting the trunk of an old elephant whose skin was mottled, gray and wrinkled. Its tusks were cracked and yellowed with age. When Lucy fed it peanuts, its tail slapped happily against its back legs.

A bit of moonlight bounced off Lucy's green eye and touched my gaze. The old elephant looked at me through eyes that were caked with age and dirt and filled with the errant ghosts of many secrets.

My first impulse was to wake Gina, but something in

Lucy's smile told me that they had come to see only me. I went downstairs and out of the back door.

I became aware of the damp hay and sawdust under my feet. If I had thought this a dream, a small splinter gouging into my heel put that notion to rest. I cried out, more from surprise than from pain, and shook my head as I saw blood trickle from the wound. Leave it to me to go out in the middle of the night without putting on my slippers.

Lucy smiled and ran to me, throwing her arms around my waist, pressing her face into my chest. I returned her embrace.

She led me to the elephant.

'I thought you might like to meet Old Bet – well, that's what I call her. To Sister Elizabeth, this is Martin.'

'And to my mother?'

'This would be Jumbo. Everyone has a different name for it.'

The elephant wound the end of its trunk around my wrist: How'ya doin'? Pleased to meet you.

I fed it some peanuts and marveled at its cumbersome grandeur. 'Is this my mother's conscience?'

Lucy gave a little-girl shrug. 'You could call it that, I guess. Sister Elizabeth calls it the "carrier of weary souls". She says that when we grow too old and tired after a lifetime of work, then it will lift us on to its back and carry us over the bridge. It will remind us of all we've forgotten. It knows the history of the whole world, everyone who's lived before us and everyone who will come after us. It's very wise.'

I stroked its trunk. 'Have you come to take my mother?'

Lucy shook her head. 'No. We're not allowed to take

anyone – they have to come to us. We're only here now to remind.'

She tapped the elephant; it unwound its trunk from my wrist so she could take both of my hands in hers. I was shocked by their touch; though they looked burned and fused and twisted, they felt healthy and normal – two soft, small, five-fingered hands.

Her voice was the sound of a lullaby sung over a baby's cradle: 'There's a place not too far from here, a secret place, where all the greatest moments of our lives are kept. You see, everyone has really good moments their whole life long, but somewhere along the line there is one moment, one great, golden moment, when a person does something so splendid that nothing before or after will ever come close. And they remember these moments. They tuck them away like a precious gem for safekeeping. Because it's from that one grand moment that each guardian angel is born. As the rest of life goes on and a person grows old and starts to regret things, something –' she gave a smile '– *reminds* them of that golden moment.

'But sometimes there are people who become so beaten-down they forget they ever had such a moment. And they need to be reminded.' She turned toward the elephant. 'They need to know that when the time comes, and Old Bet carries them across the bridge, that moment will be waiting, that it will be given back to them in all its original splendor and make everything all right. Again. For ever.'

'And Mom has forgotten about her . . . moment?'

'So have you. You were there. You remember it. You don't think you do, but . . .'

'I don't –'

'Shh. Watch closely.'

The elephant reared back on its hind legs and trumpeted. When it slammed back down, its face was only inches from mine. Its trunk wrapped around my waist and lifted me off the ground until my eyes were level with one of its own –

– which was the same startling jade-green as Lucy's.

I saw myself as clearly in its gaze as in any mirror, and I watched my reflection begin to shimmer and change: me at thirty, at twenty-one, then at fourteen and, at last, the six-year-old boy my father never lived to see.

He was sitting in his room – a large pad of drawing paper on his lap, a charcoal pencil clutched in his hand – drawing furiously. His face was tight with concentration.

His mother came into the room. Even then she looked beaten-down and used-up and sadder than any human being should ever be.

She leaned over the boy's shoulder and examined his work.

'Remember now?' whispered Lucy.

'Yes . . . I'd kept my drawing a secret. After Dad died, Mom didn't spend much time with me because . . . because she said I looked too much like him. This was the first time in ages that she'd come into my room. It was the first time in ages I'd seen her sober.'

The woman put a hand on the little boy's shoulder and said something to him.

My chest hitched.

I didn't want to remember this; it was easier to just stay angry with her.

'What happened?'

'She looked through all the drawings and . . . she started to cry. I was still mad as hell at her because of the way she'd been treating me, the way she never hugged me or kissed me or said that she loved me, the way she spent all her time drinking . . . but she sat there with my drawings, shaking her head and crying and I felt so embarrassed. I finally asked her what the big deal was and she looked up at me and said . . .'

'– said that you had a great talent and were going to be famous for it some day. She knew this from looking at those drawings. She knew you were going to grow up to be what you are today. She told you that she was very proud of you and that she wanted you to keep on drawing, and maybe you could even start making up stories to go with the pictures –'

'– because she used to know someone who did that when she was a little girl,' I said. 'She said that would be nice because . . . oh, Christ! . . . it would be nice if I'd do that because it would make her feel like someone else besides her was remembering her childhood.'

Old Bet gently lowered me to the ground. My legs gave out and I slammed ass-first into the dirt, shaking. 'I remember how much that surprised me, and I just sat there staring at her. She looked so proud. Her smile was one of the greatest things I'd ever seen and I think . . . no, no, wait . . . I *know* I smiled back at her.'

'And that was it,' said Lucy. 'That was her moment. Do you have any idea how much it all meant to her? The drawings and your smile? When you smiled at her she knew for certain that you were going to be just what you are. And, for that moment, she felt like it was all because of her. The world was new again.' She brushed some hair out of my eyes. 'Do you remember what happened next?'

'I went over to give her a hug because it felt like I'd

just gotten my mother back, then I smelled the liquor on her breath and got angry and yelled at her and made her leave my room.'

'But that doesn't matter, don't you see? What matters is the moment before. That's what's waiting for her. That's what she's forgotten.'

'Jesus . . .'

'You have to remember one thing, Andy. It wasn't your fault. None of it. You were only a child. Promise me that you'll remember that?'

'I'll try.'

She smiled. 'Good. Everything's all right then.'

I rose and embraced her, then patted Old Bet. The elephant reached out and lifted Lucy on to its back.

'Are you going back without Mom?' I asked.

She *tsk*-ed at me and put her hands on her hips, an annoyed little girl. 'Dummy! I told you once. We aren't allowed to take people. Only remind them. Except this time we had to ask you to help us.'

'Are . . . are you her guardian angel?'

She didn't hear me as Old Bet turned around and the two of them lumbered off, eventually vanishing into the layers of mist that rose from the distant edge of the field.

The chill latched on to my bones and sent me jogging back inside for hot coffee.

Gina was already brewing some as I entered the kitchen. She was wearing my extra bathrobe. Her hair was mussed and her cheeks were flushed and I'd never seen such a beautiful sight. She looked at me, saw something in my face and smiled. 'Look at you. Hm. I must be better than I thought.'

I laughed and took her hand, pulling her close, feeling the warmth of her body, the electricity of her touch.

The world was new again. At least until the phone rang.

A man identifying himself as Chief Something-or-other from the Cedar Hill Fire Department asked me if I was the same Andrew Dysart whose mother lived at –

– something in the back of my head whispered *Africa*.

Good little girls. Going home.

My new book, *After the Elephant Ballet*, was published five weeks ago. The dedication reads: 'To my mother and her own private Africa; receive the world prepared for you.' Gina has started a scrapbook for the reviews, which have been the best I've ever received.

The other day when Gina and I were cleaning the house ('A new wife has to make sure her husband hasn't got any little black books stashed around,' she'd said) I came across an old sketch pad: MY DrAWiNG TaLlAnt, bY ANdY DySArT, age 6. It's filled with pictures of rockets and clowns and baseball players and scary monsters and every last one of them is terrible.

There are no drawings of angels.

ANdY DySArT, age 6, didn't believe in them because he'd never seen proof of their existence.

In the back there's a drawing of a woman wearing an apron and washing dishes. She's got a big smile on her face and underneath are the words: MY mOM, thE nICE lAdy.

The arson investigators told me it was an accident. She had probably been drinking and fallen asleep in bed with a cigarette still burning. One of them asked if Mom had kept any stuffed animals on her bed. When I asked why, he handed me a pair of small, curved fired-clay tusks.

On the way to Montreal for our honeymoon, Gina took a long detour. 'I have a surprise for you.'

We went to Somers, New York.

An elephant named Old Bet actually existed. There really is a shrine there. Circus performers make pilgrimages to visit her grave. We had a picnic at the base of the gorgeous green hill where the grave lies. Afterward I lay back and stared at the clouds and thought about guardian angels and a smiling woman and her smiling little boy who's holding a drawing pad and I wondered what Bradbury would do with that image.

Then decided it didn't matter.

The moment waits. Still.

I go along, thud-thud.

For my mother

Cherub

GARRY KILWORTH

Harry Meeker stood shivering in the cold wind which swept around the corner of the Royal Festival Hall. His raincoat sagged deeply on one side. In the left pocket was the gun, which he had hardly touched since it had been given to him by John-the-Butcher. Harry didn't want to touch the gun. He hated the feel of the weight and the way it knocked against his thigh every time he moved.

Harry stared out moodily over the River Thames, watching the occasional boat drift up or down, sometimes encrusted with coloured lights, sometimes blacked out except for the mandatory port and starboard lights. The first were usually full of noisy people, the second silent and mysterious. Harry wished he were on any one of them, heading for an unknown destination, somewhere where he couldn't be found.

Suddenly, doors flew open and the building began to disgorge its patrons. People came out, some in evening dress, some not, to fill the precinct outside the hall. Harry went rigid with tension and peered into the chattering crowds as they swept past him, looking for Chas McFey. Harry hoped he wouldn't see him, though he knew the consequences of failure. It didn't bear thinking about: someone waiting in the shadows to blow *his* brains all over his coat collar.

At that moment he caught sight of Chas, all spruced up in black-tie gear, walking with his wife on his arm.

Harry's cold but sweaty hand closed around the butt of the gun in his pocket. His legs started shaking. He couldn't do it here, of course, in front of all these witnesses. It would be necessary to follow Chas and do it in some quiet street. Chas lived only walking distance from the South Bank: there would be no car or cab.

Somehow Harry got his legs to move, and he followed the couple down a series of steps to the streets below. Chas and his wife turned into York Road at the bottom, and along, and then finally into Leake Street, a small quiet area. Harry tried to pull out the gun, but it caught on the lining of his pocket, and it took him at least a minute to untangle it. When he managed to free it, Chas was almost at his house. Harry ran forward, his hand trembling violently, and pointed the gun.

'Chas!' he croaked.

Both Chas and his wife turned and stared, wide-eyed, into Harry's face. For some reason they didn't look at the gun and he wondered if they had even seen it. Harry knew that he would have to kill both of them. He tried to pull the trigger, but his finger was somehow locked. His heart was pounding so fast he wondered if he was going to have a heart attack. He felt sick and faint, wanting to vomit.

'Harry?' Chas said, finally looking down at the gun.

Harry's arm hurt where the muscles were cramping with the tension. There was no way he could pull that trigger. Wincing with the pain, he gradually lowered the weapon.

'I can't do it,' he moaned. 'I just can't do it.'

And still Chas and his wife were no help. They stood there, looking shocked. Then suddenly Chas's wife started screaming — her screams would have penetrated Hitler's bunker — and Harry started running.

He ran all the way back down to the river, stood for a moment on the walk, then threw the gun into the water.

Then he started walking, his hands buried deep in his pockets, towards Blackfriars Bridge.

'I've bloody had it now,' he kept telling himself. 'I'm in the shit right up to my neck now.'

John-the-Butcher had ordered Harry to top Chas McFey, had thrust the gun into his hand and said, 'Get rid of the bastard, Harry, and we'll forget what you owe.' Harry did indeed owe the Butcher a substantial amount, for Harry was a gambler with an extraordinary talent for losing. Harry could bet on a fixed race and the horse would fall over and break its neck right before the finish line. That was how good Harry was at losing.

But Harry was *just* a gambler. He didn't steal, commit violent acts or kill people. The Butcher did all those things. All Harry ever did was lose on the races and borrow more money. That wasn't an offence against anyone, not society, not even Butcher John. What *was* a crime was not paying his debts on time, and though the law of the land was fairly lenient in such cases, the Butcher saw it as a crime of the most heinous nature. Raping the Butcher's grandmother would not have been as serious as failing to pay him what you owed.

So John-the-Butcher wasn't *asking* Harry to kill Chas McFey. He was *telling* him. Now Harry would be lucky if the Butcher didn't top *him* for not doing what he was told. At the very least the Butcher's boys, Dave and Phil, would put Harry's legs over a kerb and jump on them, several times, until the bones were in splinters. Harry's stomach churned at the thought. Harry sweated. Harry's brain buzzed with fear.

As he walked through Blackfriars, after crossing the

bridge, Harry came across a small chapel. The doors were open. On impulse he went inside and sat down in a pew. Not being a religious man, he didn't know what to do at first, but gradually he managed to start praying. He prayed for all sorts of things, from John-the-Butcher getting a cardiac arrest to God providing him, Harry, with a guardian angel.

'I think I've earned it, Lord,' whispered Harry. 'I saved a man's life tonight . . . at the expense of my own. I mean, doesn't it say somewhere something about it's the greatest thing you can do, give up your life for your friend? I did that tonight. You owe me, Lord . . .' This sounded a little impertinent, so Harry added, 'In a manner of speaking. In return, I promise to be good, always.'

After his amen Harry waited around to see if anything was going to happen, then sighed and left. He had never had much faith in mumbo-jumbo, but it was worth a try. As a child he had been sent to Sunday School to get him out of his mother's hair for a morning. In those days he had been pretty impressed with things like miracles. Now there was only the reality of the Butcher and Harry's own vivid imagination.

'I did let Chas live though,' he murmured, 'and I'm glad.'

He saw no point in hiding. The Butcher would eventually find him. So Harry went straight back to his flat in Camden.

As he put the key in the lock, Harry could smell burning.

'Must have left the gas hob on,' he muttered.

When he entered the hallway, it felt very warm. He frowned. There was a kind of roaring sound coming from the living-room. Surely the Butcher's men hadn't been round already? It was too soon for them to have heard. Yet it seemed that his living-room was on fire.

Harry went forward cautiously. The living-room door was partly ajar, and he pushed it open and peered inside. The next second he jumped back, slamming against the hall wall, his eyes starting from his head.

'JESUS CHRIST!' he screamed.

His breath came out in quick gasps, robbing him of oxygen. His heart was stuck somewhere in his windpipe, choking him. Fear was like a flood sweeping through him.

There was a monster in the corner of his living-room, breathing fire.

Harry stared at the creature, which did not move.

The thing was crouched there, but if it had stood up, Harry guessed it would be about twelve feet tall. It was indeed monstrous, with a huge body covered in eyes and tiny wings. There was a semblance of human shape about it, though it seemed more head than anything else. Its beak-like mouth was cavernous, and its enormous claw-feet spread out across the carpet. The whole creature was grotesque, like something that had stepped out of a nightmare, and it was *alive*.

'Oh, Jesus . . .' groaned Harry.

The creature's head turned at this word and it seemed to be staring at Harry with quite a few of its eyes.

It was not exactly *breathing* fire, as Harry had first thought, but was flailing the air with a fiery sword. It never stopped. It was like a demonstration by an Oriental juggler spinning flaming brands, very skilfully, in order to create a circle of fire. Harry could feel the heat of the sword and hear the roar of its burning. Yet it seemed not to start any secondary fires in the room.

Even through his terror it struck Harry that if John-the-Butcher's men came to the flat, they would have to deal with this monster as well as Harry himself. Harry was inclined to think that the monster would not be easily subdued. It appeared to be the kind of creature that might put up a bit of a fight, get a little angry, if someone annoyed it. This gave Harry a modicum of comfort. Gradually, as it became apparent that the creature was not going to attack him, a calmness of spirit crept over Harry and he began to relax.

Exhausted, both by the night's events and by the heat, Harry slid down the wall to the hallway floor, where he lay in a pool of sweat and drifted off into a fitful sleep, the catherine wheel of fire still flashing and roaring before his eyes.

When he woke, at five in the morning, the monster was still there, still swishing about him with his flaming sword, still creating wonderful fire patterns in the air. Its grotesque crouched form filled a good third of Harry's small room.

'Mornin',' croaked Harry, his throat parched. 'Haven't you got the cramps yet?'

When the monster didn't answer, Harry went to the bathroom, had a drink of water, stripped, took a shower and came out feeling refreshed. He went to his bedroom and dressed in clean clothes, lit a cigarette, then picked up the phone and dialled.

'Cynthia? Yes, I know what time it is, but you haven't seen what I've got here ... No, I'm not being coarse − I mean in my living-room. It's a sodding great monster − well, I'm sorry, I know you don't like swearing but there's no other way to describe it. It's − it's − well, I really *can't* describe it − all right, I will ...' And he told her what the thing looked like, what it was carrying and what it was doing with it.

'You see why I'm ringing you? It seems harmless enough, but I need you to find out what it is. Can you come over? Bring a couple of books. We'll go through them together. OK, see you in a bit. Sorry about waking you – yeah, OK. 'Bye.'

Harry put down the phone. Cynthia was his occasional girlfriend and a school teacher. If she couldn't find out what the thing was, nobody could. Cynthia was bright.

Harry went into the living-room and sat in a chair and stared at the creature. The creature stood, waved its flaming sword, and stared at Harry. It was a woefully uneven contest.

Cynthia naturally went into hysterics at first, saying she thought Harry had been hallucinating, or had the DTs or something normal, but she never expected to see a definite, real, honest-to-God monster in his living-room. Harry told her he had got used to the creature now and just wanted to know what the hell it was so he could decide what to do about it.

Cynthia had brought some books with her, thinking she might have to humour him, so when she had calmed down, about an hour later, they went through them together. The books she had brought were full of mythological and fabulous beasts, like the basilisk, the gryphon, the senmurv, dragons, Tengu, Garuda . . .

'That's a bit like him, that Garuda thing,' said Harry.

Cynthia studied the creature in Harry's living-room corner and then the picture of Garuda, the Indonesian god.

'Nothing like it,' she said. 'You should be wearing your glasses.'

She continued to search through the books, while

Harry made her a cup of tea, then she suddenly shrieked.

He came running into the living-room, thinking the beast was devouring or ravishing her, only to find her holding up a picture with the word CHERUB beneath it.

'A *cherub*?' Harry cried, amazed. 'I thought cherubs were plump little babies with wings.'

'That's how Renaissance artists depicted them, but this is drawn from a description in the Bible.'

'Read me what it says underneath,' said Harry, squinting at the monster.

Cynthia read. '*A cherub is a divine being that belongs to the ranks of angels, a multi-eyed, multi-winged giant. One of the functions of the cherubim is to serve as guardians. Their weapon is the ever-turning flaming sword. See Genesis 3:24.*'

'A guardian angel?' cried Harry.

Cynthia nodded. 'You've got it.'

'That's it, then,' breathed Harry. 'I prayed for a guardian angel and I got one. Why doesn't that sword thing set light to my curtains?'

'It's probably *holy* fire,' explained Cynthia, practically. 'Not ordinary fire.'

'Oh,' replied Harry, still just as confused. 'You mean it's sort of different.'

'It probably burns demons and evil things, but not ordinary mundane stuff.'

'Oh,' said Harry again.

He went up as close to the cherub as he dared and stared at it in wonder. It stared back at him, many, many times over, and its beak opened slightly, its hundreds of small wings fluttered, its feet moved a fraction. Even though it continued to twirl its sword, Harry believed it had responded in some way, had acknowledged his presence.

'This is my angel,' he murmured. 'I was sort of expecting the traditional type – you know, Cynth, the ones with feathery wings and white shifts? I thought if one came, it would protect me against bullets and stuff, stepping in and snatching them out of the air, that sort of thing. But this,' he paused again to look the cherub up and down, as it twirled its roaring sword like a juggler, 'this will probably eat the Butcher whole.'

'What about taking me to breakfast somewhere?' said Cynthia. 'After all, you got me up early.'

'Right,' said Harry. 'Let's go.' He took her arm and steered her towards the door. The cherub lumbered after them, filling the hallway, still swishing its sword around, knocking lamp shades and chipping a hat rack.

'Be careful with that thing,' warned Harry, half-turning. 'The landlady will have my guts if you damage anything.'

They all stepped outside the front door, one after another. The cherub stretched to its full height and looked formidable. Dogs ran on sight of it. Cats arched and spat. Birds looked as if they felt inadequate.

It was now eight o'clock in the morning. They wandered along the grey street, Harry and Cynthia holding hands and the cherub walking massively three steps behind them, slicing bits off the overhanging branches of trees. People on their way to work stopped and stared, and pointed. Children on their way to school shrieked and pointed. A police car stopped alongside. The cop in the passenger seat wound down his window carefully, staring fixedly first at the cherub and then at Harry and Cynthia. He pointed.

'You can't bring your friend along here, squire,' said the copper. 'Not while he's waving that thing.'

'Nothing to do with me,' lied Harry, uncomfortably.

'Why's he following you two then?' asked the other policeman at the wheel of the car.

'We weren't aware that he was,' said Cynthia. 'I – I think it's someone dressed up for an advertisement, like the Burger Turkey. You know, advertising fast food.'

Harry walked on quickly with Cynthia trotting at his side. The cherub kept pace with them. The two policemen tried to have a word with the cherub but were ignored. They barked into their radio mike and started the siren.

Harry and Cynthia ducked into a Tube station. The cherub was right behind them. It crashed through the turnstile after them and on to the crowded platform. People made space for them. When the train arrived there was a crush inside. Harry and Cynthia managed to squeeze in, making two more. The cherub miraculously made it three. People were instantly squashed into unfriendly packs, cheek to jowl, lip to shoulder.

The whirling sword was given flailing space, ignored only by the skinhead buried in the tabloid, whose knees were spread wide and whose elbows demanded both seat rests. Not one person spoke or made eye contact except for the carriage's one token schizoid, who glowered and muttered defiantly at the cherub and everyone else, daring someone to meet his glare. The majority of the passengers suffered, as always, in silence, a story under their belts for when they reached the sanctity of the office.

'You'll never guess what some bloke brought on the Tube this morning – bloody great thing with a flaming sword yea long . . .'

Harry and Cynthia left the Tube, went up to street level and found a restaurant serving breakfast. The cherub stumped after them, ducking to get through the door. Its myriad wings fluttered, its manifold eyes took in every nook and cranny of the room. Harry had to give the cherub its due: it was more effective than a gross of secret service agents when it came to protecting its charge.

Fresh coffee aroma had a calming effect on Harry's nerves.

When they sat at a corner table, the cherub stood near by, as if ready to assist the chef with any flambé dishes. A waiter's eyes bulged, and he called the manager. The room began to get warm and people left, in the middle of their breakfasts. The manager came and remonstrated with Harry.

'A restaurant is not the place for circus freaks,' said the manager.

'We could have you for that,' replied Cynthia. 'That's prejudice, that is, and it's not politically correct.'

'I don't care whether it's politically *insane* – you're ruining my trade,' hissed the manager.

'I don't think you can refuse to serve us just because our – our companion is vertically disadvantaged.'

'He's not just too *tall*,' growled the manager, 'he's a bloody mutant – get him out of here.'

The two of them left the restaurant with the guardian angel in tow, but it was the same everywhere. People scattered and screamed, ran in dread or stared curiously with open mouths. No restaurant would serve the couple with the monstrous figure trailing them like a nightmarish fire-wielder. The managers began ringing each other up, warning of an approach.

In the street no one would come near the trio except

for a lone drunk, who staggered up to the cherub and asked for light for his cigarette.

The police caught up with them in the end but could do nothing with the creature. When one of the cops tried to arrest Harry, the cherub leapt forward with alarming alacrity and seemed about to take off the policeman's head, so the law decided to call in the army. After a while an anti-terrorist squad arrived, while the police kept the trio ringed on a bench in a private park belonging to London University. The squad commander assessed the situation, then told the police that if they wanted someone killed, his men would do it cleanly and efficiently, but the case did not seem to warrant such drastic action.

The police agreed, and all the officials left after giving Harry a severe warning.

'If that thing starts wandering about the streets again,' said a police chief, 'I'm holding you responsible . . .'

'I'm off home,' said Cynthia. 'I'm starving. I'll be back later, Harry. Would you like a picnic?'

'Yes, that would be nice,' Harry said, distantly.

Harry was left sitting on the park bench with the cherub standing by, entertaining a crowd of spectators on the other side of the fence with its flaming sword. Eventually this showy but rather repetitive exhibition began to bore the crowd, who yelled for some more tricks, which were never forthcoming.

They too finally drifted away.

Harry remained alone among the trees of the park. The day wore on, and he began to get really hungry. Also there was a horse running in the 3.30 at Epsom, which he was certain would solve all his financial problems. Still, he stayed where he was because if he started walking the whole business with the police and the army would erupt again. If he remained in the park, there seemed to be an unspoken agreement that the law would leave him alone. He hoped Cynthia would return later with a sandwich and a flask of tea, and maybe the *Racing Times*.

While he was sitting there, John-the-Butcher arrived with two heavies, one at each shoulder.

'A little bird told me you was here. You've been a naughty boy, Harry,' said Butcher John, hunching his shoulders inside his overcoat. 'You better tell your mate here to scarper, while we talk business.' The Butcher stared at the cherub for a minute, then shivered. 'Ugly-looking bastard, ain't he? Get rid of 'im before Dave and Phil have to sort him out.'

'No,' said Harry, defiantly, staring at Dave and Phil, the Butcher's two henchmen. 'My guardian stays where he is.'

Dave and Phil flexed inside their windcheaters, then came forward, their fists bunched. The cherub stepped in front of Harry and seemed prepared to protect him. The two men stopped in their tracks. Phil ran his hand over his shaven scalp. Dave sniffed noisily.

'Like that, is it?' said Phil, raising his eyebrows. An iron rod slipped down out of his coat sleeve neatly into his right hand.

Dave sniggered and reached inside his jacket, producing a butcher's knife.

'Wanna change your mind, Harry?' asked Butcher John.

'No,' said Harry.

Dave and Phil came forward again, Dave slicing the air with the knife, Phil whirling the iron bar round his head. They seemed to be competing with the cherub. The cherub skipped forward, as agile as a Thai dancer, and, with a spectacular flourish, ran Dave through the chest with the flaming sword. Dave dropped to the ground with a little sigh, dead as Smithfield pork.

Phil cried, 'You done for my mate, you bastard . . .'

Then he too was impaled on the flaming sword with no less an impressive swish and thrust of the weapon. The blade went through him like a hot skewer through lard. Phil gave a surprised little shudder and fell beside his mate.

On the cherub the multitudinous wings fluttered with each killing stroke. The cherub's ten thousand eyes seemed to close simultaneously in a half-smile. This was obviously its *raison d'être*. All its training had been channelled towards these needle-point moments when the ever-turning sword was put to efficient and piercing use.

Harry pondered on the fact that if JFK's bodyguards had been just one tenth as well trained as the cherub, the great President would probably be alive and still fornicating today.

Despite his horror, Harry was interested to see sort of neat little burn holes, still flaming, in the middle of the hoodlums' chests. Then the bodies swiftly shrivelled into crisp burned wads that flaked off and blew away on the breeze. Soon there was nothing left but a stain on the grass.

John-the-Butcher's eyes were starting out of his head.

'You sod,' he whispered. 'Why couldn't you have done that to Chas McFey and his missus?'

'*I* didn't do it,' said Harry. 'It was my guardian angel. Dave and Phil attacked him. He was only defending himself.'

'I thought angels had wings and stuff like that.'

'He's got wings,' protested Harry. 'Lots of them.'

'Not little sparrow jobs – two big ones in the proper place on its back.'

'Not this kind. This is a cherub – I know you thought cherubs were sweet little babes . . .'

'Not a bit of it, pal. The wife calls her nephews "cherubs", and they're nasty little bastards. They'd destroy a Churchill tank if you took your eyes off 'em for a second.'

John-the-Butcher moved cautiously forward, peering hard at the cherub.

'Be careful,' said Harry.

'I ain't goin' to do you, I'm just getting a closer look at this thing. Where did you get it from? What did you say it was? A cherub?'

'That's right,' replied Harry.

The Butcher said, 'Do they all look like him?'

Harry thought about the books he had seen earlier. 'Well, the next biggest size up is a seraph. They've only got six wings, but they're quite a lot meatier. They don't have flaming swords, but they do have these terrible feet.'

'A seraph sounds more my mark,' said John-the-Butcher, moving even closer to peer at the cherub's muscles. 'I'm not struck on the flaming-sword stuff. It's a bit conspicuous and, what's more, bloody unnecessary with a bloke this size, ain't it? I mean, all that ruddy twirlin' . . .'

'Don't get too close!' warned Harry. 'That's *holy* fire. You're an evil bugger, John. You'll go up in –'

But it was too late. The sword touched John-the-Butcher's hair, and he exploded immediately in a ball of flame with a loud *whumph*. The heat from the burning Butcher singed Harry's eyebrows. In two seconds flat there was nothing but ashes on the ground. The ashes blew away on the wind. Harry wondered whether the police would arrest him as an accomplice to murder, but he realized subsequently that no one had seen, and there was nothing left of the three crooks to prove they had been there at all. Certainly they would not be missed.

A short time later Cynthia came to the park with a flask of coffee and some roast-chicken sandwiches.

'Hi,' she said. 'It's still with you, then?'

The cherub was doing a deft under-arm pass with its sword at that moment.

'Yes,' replied Harry, a little gloomily.

Cynthia said, 'Why so glum? At least it's protecting you from John-the-Butcher.'

'Erm, I don't think I need a guardian angel any more – the Butcher's gone away.'

'Oh,' said Cynthia, surprised. 'Where?'

'Somewhere warm. Look, how am I going to get rid of this thing, Cynth? I've tried praying. That doesn't work.'

'I've been thinking about that. The trouble is, you're basically a *good* person, Harry. Guardian angels look after good people. You've got to become wicked if you want it to go.'

'What sort of wicked?'

'Well, let's take the Ten Commandments – you need to break some of the rules.'

'Thou shalt not kill? That sort of thing? Well, I'm not killing anyone, so that's out. I'm not married, and I don't know any married women, so adultery's out too. I certainly don't wish to dishonour my father and my mother, so what else is there? I don't want to steal anything either: that's not just one of the Ten Commandments, it's also a crime. No point in getting rid of the cherub if I'm just going to end up in jail.'

'Um, graven images? No, a bit old-fashioned. Thou shalt not bear false witness?'

'I dunno what that means, really. Sounds a bit like fixing a gee-gee and then telling everyone else to bet on it to make the odds on the second favourite go up. I can't do that. It's against my professional ethics.'

'What about coveting?'

Harry shrugged. 'I thought that had to do with wanting next-door's wife. She's sixty-five, and, frankly Cynth, the thought turns my stomach. I couldn't even fake it.'

The whirling, flaming sword was distracting him, flaring through the evening air above his head. The cherub was a liability, and with all those eyes it didn't miss a trick. Harry couldn't even touch Cynthia without it blinked and stared with at least a few hundred of them. It was most disconcerting and certainly not conducive to a good sex life.

'Well, there's also menservants, oxen, asses, anything that's your neighbour's.'

'Don't really want any of those either,' said Harry, feeling depressed. 'I wouldn't mind his red Porsche, but that's not the same thing, is it?'

'Do you really, really, *really* envy him his car?'

'Of course I do – who wouldn't? I sometimes imagine it's mine and . . . and . . .'

'And what, Harry?' asked Cynthia, huskily.

'And – you know, I told you. You and me, on the back seat – it's leather upholstery, you know.'

Harry went all hot as he thought about it, and when he looked up, the cherub had gone.

'Blimey,' he said, surprised. 'Is it that easy?'

'It is for *you*.' Cynthia smiled. 'You're such a nice man, Harry. It doesn't take much for you to be wicked.

Here, I've brought you the *Racing Times*. There's a horse running in the two o'clock tomorrow at Haymarket called Guardian Angel.'

'Really?' Harry took the paper eagerly.

'But, Harry . . .'

He looked up. 'Yes?'

'Don't bet more than you can afford?'

Harry sighed and nodded. 'Right, Cynth.'

Later, as they boarded the Tube train, a man got in after them with a seven-foot demon at his heels. He was a small, mild-looking man with round glasses and a little wispy moustache. He looked very miserable. They all travelled in silence for a while, the demon seemingly happy to study a group of skinheads who had suddenly gone remarkably quiet.

Harry glanced at the ferocious-looking demon, then at the mild little man, and said, 'Boy, are you in trouble.'

'I know,' sighed the little man.

'It's much harder to *keep* the Ten Commandments than *break* them.'

'I know, I know,' sighed the little man.

The demon just grinned and kept his peace.

Angel Blood

BRUCE D. ARTHURS

I didn't see the angel fall. Nor did anyone else, apparently. There were no phone calls or visits from authorities, investigating an apparent downed aircraft on their radar. No helicopters or airplanes flying over my house. Not at first.

I try to imagine what the angel must have looked like as it fell. Was it still alive? Did it feel the cold of the dark, frigid atmosphere? Did ice gather on its wingtips? Did its luminous blood leave thin, evanescent contrails of light in the air? Was it deliberately aiming for my swimming pool?

I wish I hadn't drained the pool for the winter.

The angel cracked the plaster and concrete when it hit the dry bottom of the pool. The *WHOOMPH!* of its impact startled me awake.

'Kelly —?' I started to say, then remembered. I took the gun from the nightstand drawer and went to investigate.

The back porch was dark, but there was a glow from the bottom of the pool. I approached slowly, and stopped at the edge.

The angel oozed its bright blood from nose and mouth and ears. It cried dead, luminescent tears. The underside of its twisted and broken wings were webbed with trails of angel blood from the thousand eyes there.

The pool is thirty-two feet long; the angel filled almost half its length. A small puddle of light was forming beneath the gash in its side.

Its face was filled with an ineluctable sadness. I felt a sense of loss as I stared at it, as if something . . . *necessary* . . . had gone out of the world.

The ringing of the phone inside broke through the fugue. The sun had risen while I had stood transfixed. My feet and hands felt like blocks of wood from standing, in my underwear, in the cold winter morning.

I lurched back inside and picked up the phone in clumsy hands. It was my workplace, calling to find out why I had not arrived or called in sick.

I made some kind of excuse and hung up, only then realizing that I still held the gun in my hand. I remembered that sense of loss I had felt. Carefully, I unloaded the gun and put it into a drawer.

I went back outside and down the ladder into the pool.

The angel blood's luminosity was beginning to dim. I touched one of the streaks running over the angel's face; the streak dimmed completely, taking on the appearance of clear water.

I brought the damp finger-tip to my mouth and tasted the angel's blood. It tasted of salt and honey. For a moment blood roared in my head. I closed my eyes but could still see the angel through my eyelids.

The roaring faded, and I knew that my solitude with the angel had ended. It was time to share his presence.

I climbed back out of the pool one-handed and went back inside. After a moment, I came back to the kitchen and made coffee, then called my wife.

'Hello, Kelly.'

'Carl? Are you calling from work?'

'No. Kelly, can you keep the kids home from school and bring them over here?'

'You'll have them this weekend, Carl.'

'This is something that won't wait.'

'Carl, what's going on?'

'There's an angel in our swimming pool.'

There was a long pause. 'Have you been drinking?'

'No. This is important. They have to come and see while they still can. I want you to come too.'

'You're scaring me, Carl.'

I was silent for a few seconds. Finally: 'Please don't be.'

There was another long pause, then the sound of a receiver being placed back in its cradle, then a dial tone.

I hung up my end, poured a cup of coffee and thought about what to do next. Go to Kelly's parents' house, talk to Kelly face to face?

Take the kids and bring them here?

No, not acceptable.

The coffee tasted weak. As I finished the cup, still unsure what to do, the doorbell rang.

It was Kelly's dad at the door. He looked angry, as usual.

'Hello, Roger.'

'What the hell's going on, Carl? Kelly said you were talking crazy on the phone.'

'Come out back and see.'

I let him look for about five minutes, then shook him until his attention was diverted from the angel. Time was running short. We went back inside. He called Kelly this time.

'It's OK, Kelly. Bring the kids over.' A pause. 'Yes, I'm sure.' Another pause, longer. Roger looked at me, made his hand into a pistol and pointed it towards me.

'It's in the drawer,' I told him. 'It's unloaded. You can take it if you want.'

He took the gun from the drawer, checked the cylinder, then tucked it into his waistband. 'I've got it,' he told Kelly. 'It's safe to come over. Bring your mother too.'

We watched until the angel blood had faded completely. Billy touched one of the angel's wingfeathers. Cynthia took one of the angel's huge hands in her tiny one and held it for a moment. Kelly and I sat on the pool steps, an arm around each other. Her parents were seated on the pool's edge, also holding each other.

Finally, the last trace of luminescence was gone. We went back inside and sat around the dining table, silent for a while. Finally, I stood and went to the phone.

After a while, a reporter showed up. He sounded bored as he asked about my call. I led him out back. He looked, then ran back into the house and grabbed the phone.

A news helicopter came over several minutes later and hovered for aerial shots of the pool. A car screeched to a stop in front of our house a few minutes after that, discharging photographers and other, more senior, reporters.

A few minutes after that the police arrived and began evicting the reporters. They strung yellow tape around the house and yard.

The rest of the day was pretty hectic until the federal agents showed up. They dispersed the crowds that had gathered in the street, barricaded the entire block, evicted the regular police, then brought in a flatbed truck and a crane. They wrapped the angel's body in black plastic and winched it on to the flatbed. Technicians took samples of the pool plaster where the angel had lain. Then the truck, the technicians and the agents drove away. We were allowed back in the house.

We closed the curtains and disconnected the phone. I put a sign on the door that told people not to knock until tomorrow. I made dinner for everyone.

Kelly's parents returned to their own home. The kids went back to their old rooms. Kelly and I went to bed.

It was the first time in months for both of us. It was very good.

The federal government denied seizing the angel's body, and its very existence. A small crowd remained constant outside the house, composed of the hopeful, the frightened and the certain. It was the ones with the absolute certainty that were hardest to tolerate. We coped.

The crowd disappeared a week later, when a second dead angel crashed into a Christmas-tree farm in Washington state.

A few days after that a third angel was reported from Morocco. Then Germany, Brazil, rural Alabama.

An angel crashed into a Los Angeles freeway during rush hour. Three people died in the resulting accidents.

Passengers on a cruise liner reported seeing an angel plunge into the ocean.

More angels fall every day. There have been religious riots, proclamations of the millennium's imminence.

Some have tried to say that the angels are not God's angels. That these falling angels are the Fallen Angels of Lucifer, defeated and destroyed in their final assault on Heaven. That all is right, all is as foreordained and that the righteous need not fear.

I know better.

Hidden between the mattress and the springs of our bed is a sword. I took it from the angel's hand and placed it there that morning. It is long but light and easy to wield; reddish lights dance along its blade.

When I reach beneath the mattress and touch the sword, the angel blood sings in my veins.

I know that there is a war in Heaven. I know that the angels are losing. I know that when the battle above is decided, we will face the consequences on our own.

When the moment comes, I will use the sword to defend my family.

I hope that I will be worthy.

In Gethsemane

STEPHEN GALLAGHER

There was a thick haze in the sky and rain on the stones out in Station Square. Borthwick, the press agent, was waiting for them, stepping out through the crowd with his arm raised. The crowd parted and pushed on around him, heading out into the drizzle.

'I've taxis for the boarding house and a boy with a handcart for Mr Goulston's boxes,' he told the travelling party of five.

'A boy, Mr Borthwick?' Goulston spoke up suspiciously from the back.

'A reliable boy, sir,' the press agent assured him. 'I've used him before. He'll get your trunks to the hall and he'll see them secure. His father's the doorkeeper there. Now if you'll follow me, gentlemen, I've some journalists waiting.'

Two petrol-engined taxicabs awaited the party by the railway station's awning, between the row of charabancs and the stop for the new electric trams. Borthwick rode in the first with Goulston and Frederick Kelly. The others followed behind. Goulston looked back through the cab's tiny rear window, but in all of the activity out in the crowded boulevard there was no boy or handcart to be seen. He settled uncomfortably in his seat and tried to turn his thoughts to other matters.

He hadn't been to Blackburn in ten years. No bookings here, no reason to. He looked out and saw yet another cotton town in the rain, glory and squalor all pushed together. It was a market day, caps and clogs and baskets much in evidence. He was half-listening as Borthwick discussed arrangements with Frederick Kelly, but he played no part in their conversation.

Their lodgings were on one of the streets that inclined steeply toward the moors on the northern side of town. The cab laboured to make the climb, and their driver repeatedly crashed his gears. Goulston winced at the sound. When they'd finally stopped before the genteel but sturdy red-brick villa that was to be their base for the next three days, Borthwick got out first and led them into the house. Walter Ward, Kelly's secretary and keeper of the purse, stayed behind and settled the tariffs. Some bicycles leaned on the fence alongside the path to the front door; the press party had already arrived and were inside. Goulston and Kelly were greeted by the landlady, handed over their wet coats to be hung in the scullery and then were shown through into the stifling warmth of the drawing-room where their first audience waited.

Six chairs had been set out for the journalists and two, facing them, for the key performers of the troupe. They were arranged before the hearth, where a mature fire glowed with the intensity of lava. Not all of the newspapermen's seats had been filled.

'What kind of a show can we expect tonight?' was the opening question and it was fielded, as always, by Frederick Kelly. Kelly was an unlikely-looking captain, with his pale skin and broad forehead and fine moustache; he looked like a young man of delicate health who only ever ventured out of doors after a stern warning from his mother. But his apparent frailty was misleading, Goulston knew. Tireless was not the word to describe him, for Goulston had seen him in a state of complete exhaustion on more than one occasion; but however low his energies might fall, Frederick Kelly always found the strength to rise again and go on.

He said, 'Mr Goulston will begin with a demonstration of spirit effects and fake mediumship. I can tell you now that he's very impressive.'

'And yourself, sir?'

'I will then do what little I can in the face of the scepticism he engenders.'

'Mr Kelly is being extremely modest,' Borthwick, the advance man, put in from where he stood at the side of the room. 'His appearances have caused a sensation in every town on the tour so far.'

'We end the evening with comments from the audience and a debate on the spiritualist issue,' Kelly added. 'Mr Goulston gives me no quarter in this, I can tell you.'

Two of the four journalists present made notes, and the man from the *Northern Telegraph* said, 'Can I ask Mr Goldston why he consents to appear on a bill with a practising medium when he's declared all clairvoyants to be frauds and charlatans?'

'That's very simple,' Goulston said, with a glance at Borthwick to be sure that the error over his name would not go uncorrected. 'I'm here to catch Mr Kelly out.'

'Have you done that yet?'

'Perhaps tonight.'

The man from the *Blackburn Times* said, 'What are we going to see? Do we see physical manifestations?'

'Goulston does all of those,' Kelly told him. 'You want to see a table tip and fly, Goulston does it better than anyone I've ever seen. I practise a form of clairvoyance that is far less spectacular. I handle objects, and I say whatever comes into my mind. Rarely do I do more than that.'

'Do you raise the dead?' the *Telegraph* man said, and there was a tone in his voice and a look in his eye that seemed to urge Kelly to say yes, just so that the *Telegraph* man could go into print and make him regret it.

'I do not raise the dead,' Kelly said. And then he added, with care and certain emphasis, 'Sometimes I believe the dead can speak through me.'

The *Telegraph* man switched his gaze. He looked like a bank clerk, but his manner showed the wiry energy of a whippet. 'Mr Goulston?'

'Let me be diplomatic,' Goulston said. 'I believe that Mr Kelly is an exceptional performer of his type.'

'Do you think he's a fraud?'

'I have no doubt.'

'But no proof.'

'Proof will come.'

Three pencils scratched away in three notebooks, the exception being the cheerful-looking young man at the back of the room who, Goulston had already concluded, was congenitally damaged in some way. He had a notebook like the others, but he'd so far written nothing. Coals settled in the grate, the only other sound to break the patient silence.

The man from the *Blackburn Times* said, 'Mr Kelly, you make much of the fact that Goulston is an independent observer. He freely asserts that he's looking to expose the means he thinks you use. So if we can assume there's no collusion between you, what exactly is the advantage to you of his presence?'

'Publicity,' murmured the cheerful-looking young man from the back, but Frederick Kelly, seeming not to hear him, said, 'I can give you two answers to that. The first I'll state freely. Goulston is a showman. I am not. His performance and our public conflict fills more seats than I could hope to fill alone. I'm raising funds to build a spiritualist temple. Empty halls will raise not a single stone of it, and the law will have me if I use my talents to raise money in any other way. If Goulston doesn't feel that he's made a deal with the devil for his ends, then neither need I.'

'But you travel and lodge together,' the man from the *Times* persisted. 'Do you argue in private?'

It was Borthwick who broke in with a reply. 'Constantly,' he said, and with such a long-suffering air that all were prompted to smile.

The *Telegraph* man said, 'What's the second answer?'

Kelly considered his words before he spoke. His long fingers intertwined before him, almost as if in prayer.

'I am human,' he said, 'and the pressures are many. But Goulston's eyes are always on me.' The medium looked at the stage conjurer then, and the conjurer returned his gaze steadily.

'Goulston is my conscience,' Kelly said. 'And my guarantor.'

Kelly went upstairs to rest, the newspapermen fell upon the tea and cakes that Borthwick had thought ahead to arrange for them, and Goulston made his way through to the back of the house to find his overcoat and to ensure that he had, as he'd thought, left his keys in one of its pockets. His bags had been taken up to his room, but he would unpack them later. Goulston always made a point of unpacking, even for a single night's stay. The party would be here for three days, and then they would move on. They had one night's engagement, in which Goulston would be performing, the remaining time being set aside for Frederick Kelly's private consultations. It was always the same. Goulston would take the stage first and thoroughly discredit every trick and technique that Kelly might use. And yet still they would line up after the public show, begging for the medium's private attentions.

His coat was damp, but he had no other. He said to the landlady, 'I need to find King George's Hall. Is it far from here?'

'Five minutes to walk it, sir, no more,' the landlady told him. 'Shall I send you someone to show you the way?'

'Just point me in the right direction. I can ask as I go.'

King George's Hall stood with its back half-turned against the middle of town, huge and solid and bursting with civic dignity. Goulston's heart sank a little when he saw it. Already he could imagine it inside, a great gilded barn of a place. The main doors were locked, but he found a stage door in a yard around to the side, and he banged on this. A handcart stood in the yard, its wheels braced with iron and its well-worn handles tilted toward the sky. Goulston looked up. The drizzle had cleared, but the sky had not. It was a yellowish-grey, the colours of soot and ochre.

'I'm Goulston,' he told the doorkeeper when the door was finally opened. 'Did my boxes arrive?'

'Ay, they did, sir,' the doorkeeper said, moving back to let him enter.

'I want to check my properties and look at the stage. You have all-electric light here, I assume?'

'We do.'

The doorkeeper moved ahead of him. His frame was that of a powerful man, but it was bent as if by injury or long misuse, and he shuffled. He'd a walrus moustache, and blond stubble on the back of his neck. Goulston had noted that his blue eyes were as pale as water. His hands touched almost everything that he passed; door handles, newel posts, the angles of walls.

Goulston's boxes had been placed in a bare room under the stage. The room was undecorated and had illumination from a single, unshaded bulb. In the middle of the floor stood a wickerwork livestock basket and two big metal-bound trunks, rugged enough for a long safari. He'd bought them at a railway company sale and they now held all of his effects and properties. First he counted his doves, checking their water and grain. All were alive, all seemed alert. Then, taking out his keys, he unlocked the first of the trunks and opened it up to check its contents.

It had not always been so. Goulston's properties and major illusions had once filled a railway car to themselves and required a full-time baggage master on the payroll to get them around the major cities of Europe without loss or damage. He'd employed a staff of eleven and his own small orchestra and with them had presented a full evening show.

How the wheel could turn. Now he opened for another headline performer and had to rely on doorkeepers' boys and push-along wagons for transport.

All was in order. He closed the boxes and relocked them.

He said, 'I'll be here to set the stage at six. Can you put someone to watch my properties between then and the time of performance? It's essential that once I've laid them out they shouldn't be touched.'

'I'll see they're safe,' the doorman said.

They went from the room and along a narrow, black-painted passageway to reach the stage. Some carpenters could be heard working up on the balcony, and the house lights were already on. He walked out on to the stage and looked into the auditorium.

It was more or less as Goulston had expected. An assembly hall, rather than a playhouse. Limited space in the wings, no rake to the seats in the stalls and a distant, shallow balcony that was like the spectators' gallery in a public swimming bath. Space and civic pride but no intimacy. Good for a big temperance meeting with a brass band and all the lights on but not for much else.

'I'll have a list of cues for the house electrician,' Goulston said dispiritedly. 'I'll need to go through them with him before the performance.'

He walked forward and clapped his hands once to gauge the acoustic. Almost immediately one of the carpenters upstairs began to hammer.

The doorkeeper waited with patience, breathing steadily and noisily through his nose.

Goulston turned to him and said, 'Has anybody been asking to see a seating plan?'

'I couldn't tell thee that,' the doorkeeper said. 'I wouldn't know.'

'Could you ask around for me? Not just about the seating. I'd like to know of anything unusual. Anything. Strangers asking questions. New wiring or mirrors fitted in odd places. Someone buying more than one ticket for tonight, but for seats in different parts of the house. I'll pay you a guinea for any information I can use.'

The doorkeeper's face creased, knowingly. 'I know what tha'rt after,' he said. 'But watch who tha asks. There's some round here, they'd take tha guinea and they'd tell thee owt.'

Goulston looked out across a packed and half-illuminated house and said, 'Tales of ghosts and spirits have been with us since early man cowered in his cave and sought some form of expression for his fears of the darkness outside. When daylight entered the cave and the fears departed, the ghosts departed with them. Today, when mediums claim to conjure spirits, what is the first step in what they do?'

He raised his hand and, after a second's delay, the house lights began to lower.

'Are there any spirits with us tonight?'

There came a loud bang, apparently from the very air above the stalls, that electrified the house.

'Have you a message for anyone here?'

Two rapid bangs now, close together, and someone up on the balcony shrieked and giggled and was hushed.

Goulston pressed on, 'Can you spell out a name for us?'

'Ang on, came a sepulchral voice from midair, speaking with a local accent that was as thick as newly dug peat, *I've dropped me 'ammer.*

There was a braying laugh of released tension from the audience, and Goulston lowered his hand and smiled. It was a simple effect using stereophonic speaking tubes and concealed horns, but it always set the mood. He'd refined and adapted his act considerably in the weeks of the tour, ever since that first night when he'd peeped out from behind the tabs and seen, to his dismay, that a good third of the night's audience were in mourning. He'd played some tough houses in his career, but never before had he been obliged to walk out and begin his act before row upon row of stone-faced widows.

He'd made it through, all the same. Empathy was the key. They were wound up like springs, and in order to let the tension go they needed permission. Goulston let them believe that he understood their pain. They ached for the unknown, and the unknown was his business.

When the audience's reaction began to die down, he went on, 'To those who are here to be amused I say, you shall not be disappointed. To those who come in grief and hope – and I know that the Great War has made so many of you – I say this. See what I am about to show you, and be on your guard thereafter. Grief makes us vulnerable, and death is life's greatest mystery. All that you are about to see is achieved by natural means. You will not think it so. But that, ladies and gentlemen, is the very soul of the conjurer's art. I do not show you magic. I show you wonder.'

He performed the white-dove production then, sending it out from his fingertips to fly up to the rafters. During the distraction that it caused, he let his hand move back to load his next effect from the profonde in the tail of his coat.

'I stand before you as an honest deceiver,' he said. 'I stand here and I say, beware of those who are not.'

The act ran a little over forty-five minutes. After a few simple sleights to get them warmed up he brought forward the spirit cabinet and, after having himself bound to a chair by audience volunteers, he ran through much of the old repertoire of the Davenport brothers; then he turned the cabinet around and did it all again with the back open and the interior exposed, with his volunteer observers at the back of the stage being duped in plain view. The house roared. He let them see what he was doing; but as to the exact details of the escapes and rope releases that let him do it, he left them wondering.

Then some billet reading and mentalism, a display of muscle-reading down on the floor of the hall and then, for the finale, a table levitation in which the table flew about the stage under the hands of a dozen volunteers. He revealed no more tricks after the first, and there he revealed little that wasn't either obvious or hackneyed in terms of technique. He had them, he knew. The grievers and the good-timers, all of them were his.

And then he handed them over to Frederick Kelly.

'Thank you,' Kelly said. 'May I ask you all for a moment of silence as I concentrate?'

Despite the way that the medium had presented his act to the pressmen, Kelly was the one they'd really come to see. Goulston might be the showman, but Kelly was the real draw. The advantages that he held over Goulston were those of promise and challenge; for whereas Goulston assured them of the fakery they already suspected, Kelly purported to offer them genuine entry into the unknown. Bogus or not, the invitation was one that could not be resisted.

Goulston did not leave the hall but took a position where he could observe both the audience and the stage. His purpose in this was to use his professional experience to watch for evidence of fraud. Occasionally he'd intervene and request some change or modification, like an opposing counsel.

Kelly's approach was a straightforward one, and Goulston had yet to fathom it. He used no apparatus, none of the usual routines. Walter Ward or one of the other young men of the party would bring from the audience an object, any kind of an object. Sometimes a laundered handkerchief, sometimes a pipe or a snuff-box, often a medal. The medals were of least use, most of them never having been handled by the recipient. Personal items were supposedly the best. Kelly would hold one for a while and then speak about the life and sometimes the afterlife of its owner. Then the person who had brought the object would be invited to stand, and Kelly's story would be checked against the reality.

There would be gasps sometimes. Often tears. Kelly's part of the performance rarely ran for less than three hours, and then Goulston would return to the stage where he and Kelly would stand, alone and on opposing sides of the platform, to rehearse some well-worn arguments for and against a belief in the spirit world.

Tonight it went as it almost always did. Even the audience questions had grown familiar.

'Mr Goulston,' said a man about thirty-five years old, standing half-way down the hall and wearing a long overcoat. 'You've asserted that the spirits only ever bring us knowledge that is already available to us by common means. Does anything you've seen tonight alter that view?'

'No sir,' Goulston said, 'it does not.'

'Mr Kelly was extremely detailed and convincing in a large number of his perceptions.'

Goulston shaded his eyes and peered at the man, and seemed to give a start. 'Sir,' he said, wonderingly. 'What if I were to say that I see the shade of a woman standing beside you? Her hand is on your shoulder and she looks on you with love. I believe she very much resembles your mother.'

'My mother is very much alive, sir,' the man said, with a glance down to his side.

'I did not say she was your mother,' Goulston snapped before the audience could react. 'I said she resembled your mother.'

A mature woman, seated beside the man and partly obscured by the person before her, was heard to exclaim, 'Lillian!'

'Lillian is speaking,' Goulston said, 'but you don't hear her. She says a name. Edward?'

'My name is Albert,' said the man, extremely dark-faced.

'Then, who is Edward?'

'I do not know,' the man said, seeming deliberately to ignore the woman's tugging at his sleeve.

Goulston turned to the rest of the house and said, in a passable imitation of Frederick Kelly's rising agitation, 'I see Edward now. He's a young man. I see him in uniform. He looks weary. He has passed on, and he is lost. Anyone. He's appealing to you. Will anyone acknowledge Edward?'

In various parts of the house, hands began to rise. Goulston nodded, and his manner abruptly changed.

'Who could deny the appeals of the dead?' he said. 'Sit down, sir. And lower your hands, my friends. At least I have the grace to apologize for raising your hopes. The dead sleep on. They tell us nothing.'

A man in uncomfortable-looking Sunday-best clothes stood waving his hand and, when acknowledged, said, 'Are you familiar with the suggestion that spirits are actually the telepathic constructs of the living?'

'I am, sir,' Goulston said. 'I give it no more credence than spirit photographs or flying tambourines.'

'So you're saying, then, that Mr Kelly's character is that of a cheat and a liar?'

Goulston hesitated. He did not look at Kelly, who stood some yards away, content, as always, to let Goulston run the debate. Apart from having been exhausted by what he claimed was the personal toll taken by the use of his powers, he had few arguments to advance. He claimed no great understanding of his gift. It was there, he said, and it functioned, and he could explain it no better than the next man. See what you see, he would say, and judge for yourself.

Goulston could feel the tension of the house. There had to be close to a thousand faces out there, millworkers and shopworkers and professional people, and their will to believe in Kelly was almost palpable. He did, after all, offer them a hope that they could carry away. What could Goulston offer them? A much colder certainty. But it was like prizes at the fair. Even though they might be worthless, who could want to go home without?

He said, 'I have, in these past weeks, spent much time in Mr Kelly's company. As to his character, I believe him to be a sincere man.' He looked across at Kelly then. The medium stood with his gaze directed down, swaying slightly. His shirt was damp with perspiration from the evening's efforts, and his fine hair stuck to his forehead.

Goulston was telling no less than the truth. He had entered into this arrangement without a trace of doubt that here was a fellow practitioner who abused their common craft. Nothing in that belief had changed. But his personal impression of the man had been utterly at odds with that certainty, and he had yet to find a way to reconcile the two. Only one possible explanation had suggested itself.

'Which is to say,' Goulston went on, 'that I must number him among the ranks of the deceived.'

Their landlady being used to the hours kept by theatricals, as she called them, there was a hot supper waiting even though the hour was close to midnight. The lady's husband had been deputed to wait up, and he let them in, locked the front door, showed them where to find the kitchen and then disappeared off to bed.

As ever after a show, nobody was quite ready for sleep. After they'd eaten, the two assistants went off to their shared attic room to play cards (they'd flatly refused to play with Goulston after he'd demonstrated a few simple lifts and steals and flourishes by way of a warm-up on a train out of Harrogate), and Walter Ward took a table in the front parlour to check receipts and to read and sort the various messages that had been delivered to the stage door in the course of the evening. Goulston and Kelly each took a glass of port before the embers of the drawing-room fire. As always, Kelly had the wan but bright-eyed look of a man who'd just shaken off a fever and found a reason to live. After a while Walter Ward brought in the accounts for Kelly to check, along with the letters and messages and a dampened towel on a tray.

The letters went to Goulston first. One of the conditions that he'd set was that all advance correspondence had to be held, unopened, by the theatre's management until after the performance it anticipated. He would check the seals and postmarks before passing them over. Had any been tampered with, he would know. A halfway competent medium would be able to construct an evening's revelations out of the contents of such letters alone.

The night's stage-door messages went straight to Kelly. Two or three would always contain banknotes as a sign of gratitude or support. The rest would mostly be direct appeals or invitations from which something more might follow. Goulston glanced across and said, 'More donations in prospect for you, Kelly?'

'Perhaps,' Kelly said as he first took the books and

looked over Walter Ward's figures. 'I won't deny it. Do I prostitute my gift in your eyes, Goulston?'

'You have no gift in my eyes, as well you know. You have a skill. If you'd only be content to have it recognized and admired for what it is, you and I would have no argument.'

Kelly seemed not to hear or, if he did, to take no offence. 'Look at these,' he said, turning to the first of a number of engraved visiting cards with messages or requests written on their backs. 'Tonight we had the public show for the souls of the infantry. Now even in death, the officer classes expect some privileged consideration.'

Kelly did little more than glance through the notes and cards, leaving Walter Ward to make any necessary appointments and replies. He lay back and placed the dampened towel over his forehead as Goulston opened and read through a few of the notes at random.

He looked for cues, for clues, for recurrences of handwriting or paper. Many were barely literate; some were in educated hands. Private seances and the donations that followed them were almost as profitable as ticket sales, the difference being that Goulston took no share in these. He still attended when invited, as many of the requests were from prominent families and notables in some of the larger houses. Like any professional player or performer, he never passed up an opportunity to move in exalted circles – even though the circles in some towns were rather less exalted than elsewhere. He'd go along and say his piece and then withdraw.

He gave the letters back to Walter Ward, who inclined his head and returned with them to the parlour.

'Ever-vigilant, eh, Will?' Kelly said as he took the linen compress from his brow and refolded it.

'You're good, Frederick, I'll give you that.'

'Does the possibility of authenticity appear nowhere in your considerations?'

'You know it does not,' Goulston said, taking out his pocket watch and checking the time. It was getting late.

'A scientist should exclude nothing.'

'I'm no scientist.'

'But you know what you know.'

'I know what is real,' Goulston said, preparing to rise, 'and what is not.'

'Oh!' said Kelly. 'Then your faith is as blind as any other man's. May I?'

Kelly was holding out his hand for Goulston's watch. Goulston hesitated, then handed it to him and settled once more in his chair. But not so comfortably now, in the knowledge that he'd be moving again in a minute or so.

As Kelly turned the watch case over in his hands, Goulston said, 'From where do you draw your confederates? I don't believe I've seen the same face twice.'

'I have none,' Kelly said with a smile and without looking up from the timepiece. 'Keep trying.'

'Who scouts ahead for you?'

'You watch me all the time. I know you've had me followed. I've found the secret marks you've made on my bedroom windows. When would I ever have a chance to confer?'

'I'll expose you, Frederick,' Goulston said calmly. 'Believe that I will.'

Kelly opened the watch's cover, looked at the face and then held it to his ear as if it was a small animal for whose heartbeat he listened. He smiled when it came.

'I can tell you one thing,' he said. 'If you can ever work out how I do what I do, I'll be the happiest man alive. Because it's God's own truth, Will, I do not know it.' He closed the cover on Goulston's watch and held it out to him.

'Your father's work?' he said. 'I know he was a watchmaker. What better training for the design and construction of a magician's stage effects?'

Goulston took it. The metal felt warm. 'That won't wash, Frederick,' he said, with a warning in his voice. 'Don't attempt to tell me you learned all of that from the handling of a timepiece.'

Kelly laid his head back on the chair again. 'No,' he said. 'I learned all of that from the London *Times* when you were headlining at Maskelyne's.'

Leaving Kelly to finish his port and watch the embers fall, Goulston climbed the stairs to his room. There was a street lamp outside, and it threw a watery shadow of lace curtain across the wallpaper. Headlining at Maskelyne's. That had been two years before. Eight weeks as a featured performer at the end of a European tour that had barely broken even, but no matter; the set-up costs of the show had been immense, but now the sets and properties had almost been paid for and would go on to earn him his fortune. Everything had been run in to perfection and the show was ready, bar a few running repairs and adjustments, for an extensive North American tour. He'd moved everything to his Manchester workshop and gone ahead by liner to New York, only to learn of the fire on his arrival.

Everything had gone. Everything. The timber and canvas and size had burned with utter ferocity and made the place unapproachable. Nothing had been saved. Two people had died, along with all his animals. With every borrowed penny sunk into his show, Goulston was under-insured; he hadn't been able to envisage losing everything, all at once, and had thought instead that it would be better economy to make up any losses or damage himself as he went along.

He'd gone out to New York on a first-class passage. He'd returned, steerage, after only two days and had been forced to leave his hotel bill unpaid to afford even that. Now in essence he worked for Kelly, to clear his debts and to keep his name before the public until his show might be rebuilt.

Whenever that might be.

Goulston drew the curtains in his room, splashed his face at the washstand and tried the bed. It was cold and lumpy and smelled of new laundry, with a weight of covers that would hold him down like six feet of dirt over a tomb.

Perfect. He slept better than he had in a week.

The next morning, Goulston bought all of the northern newspaper editions that he could find and set himself up at a corner table in Booth's Café where he could read through them undisturbed. Frederick Kelly was still up at the boarding house. He would seldom rise before noon, claiming the need to recover from his evening's exertions. Sheer sloth, was Goulston's interpretation. Once awake, Kelly would rarely go out but would spend the afternoon writing letters or reading. He found it difficult to walk abroad without gathering a crowd, some merely curious but most wanting a part of his attention for some pressing and personal need. He couldn't begin to satisfy them all. He'd once spent an hour simply trying to cross the lobby of a large hotel. So instead he stayed in and only ventured out to keep appointments or to make unannounced evening visits to local spiritualist circles.

A strange kind of professional, in Goulston's view. The very inverse of a showman. No mauve limousine, no monkeys, not even a visiting card. Something new in the art of misdirection, perhaps.

Kelly never even troubled to read his notices.

There was a piece in the early edition of the *Northern Telegraph*, something in the *Standard*, one in the *Times*. Only the *Telegraph* man gave a good account of Goulston's involvement. Out of interest, he then turned to the advertising and announcements to see who might be playing at the local halls. There were some names that he knew, but no one whom he cared to look up. Selbit was touring, he noted, but it was advance publicity with no firm dates. Selbit was the magician who had taken up a £500 spirit challenge from the *Sunday Express* and fooled a committee that had included Conan Doyle. When the truth had been revealed, the committee had clung to its belief in the clairvoyant demonstration and expressed doubt over the explanation. Selbit's tour was built around his new sawing-through-a-lady illusion.

And good luck to him, Goulston thought, and made a face which caused the waitress to look twice.

Not for the first time, his thoughts turned to his difficulties over Kelly.

Frederick Kelly was so artless, and from Goulston's point of view that was the problem. He simply did what he did, with no apparent technique. One of Goulston's theories was that Kelly might be a kind of *idiot savant* of the craft, functioning in a way that even he himself didn't fully recognize. This was an explanation that had gained ground in his mind of late. It allowed for Kelly's sincerity without opening a door into realms of patent unreality. Exactly how the man worked was something that Goulston had still to determine. The method had almost certainly been staring him in the face from the beginning and was no doubt elegant and utterly simple. Simplicity was always the hardest to spot.

And when he spotted it, what then? He'd have to sink the raft on which he stood. End of tour, end of contract, end of income. And he'd do it, as well. His pride would allow nothing less. He'd come to realize that until then he'd be like some emasculated courtier, not a true and principled opponent at all. His function here, he'd realized, was to fail; and in his continuing failure, to prove Kelly's authenticity so that the show could go on and the temple could eventually rise.

That evening he put on a clean shirt and his formal wear and accompanied Kelly and Walter Ward to one of the large houses that overlooked the east side of the town's Corporation Park. It was the house of the Graingers, a family whose money came from three generations of rope-making in the town. The pattern was familiar to Goulston. A son had been lost in the war. Bereavement so sudden, so out of time and at such a distance . . . It evaded the normal processes of grief and left people suspended, uncertain, unable to respond. They'd fall gratefully upon someone like Frederick Kelly, as those lost in a strange land might fall upon a guide.

A housemaid showed them through a stained-glass vestibule into a pleasant, panelled hallway, where Mrs Grainger emerged to greet them. She was well spoken and well mannered, graceful but without pretensions. She introduced them to her sister Dora Isabel and her daughter Enid and directed their attention to the wall where hung a picture of her son James in his uniform. The picture's oval frame had been draped with black crêpe ribbon. James had been a smooth and good-looking boy, in the manner of all who had sat for such photographs. Smooth and good-looking boys just like him had gone to their deaths in their thousands.

They moved into the drawing-room, which had been prepared for the seance. Goulston introduced himself and gave the short lecture-demonstration that he always gave on such occasions. He sought to inform rather than to entertain and to encourage a healthy scepticism in Kelly's audience-to-be. He showed them how a glass could move, how a table could be turned and tilted. He demonstrated rappings. Kelly stood there nodding, he realized. Kelly seemed entirely on his side.

'Spirit effects are fashionable tricks,' he concluded. 'They did not exist before they were devised. The skills used are exactly those I have shown you. If all expect the table to turn, it will turn without help.'

Through all of this, Enid Grainger had been watching with great intensity, and Goulston had found himself responding to her attention, to the extent that he'd had to remind himself to favour the others equally. Now she said, 'Will you be staying for the seance, Mr Goulston?'

'No, Miss Grainger,' he told her. 'I've said all that I can say.'

He walked the half-mile or so back to the boarding house. He felt like a drink, but he was over-dressed for any of the public houses or hotels that he passed.

So grave. So serious.

He found himself envying Frederick Kelly for the comfort which he would be bringing to Enid Grainger and which he, Will Goulston, could not. All that

Goulston could offer her was the certainty that her pain had no remedy.

And who, anywhere in this world, could find a shred of comfort in that?

Over breakfast the next morning he managed to quiz Walter Ward about the progress of the seance. It had, from Ward's account, been one of Kelly's finer performances. Mrs Grainger had fainted, and the evening had ended in great consternation all around, with neighbours hearing the cries and summoning the police.

At ten, soberly dressed, Will Goulston presented himself at the house and was again shown inside. Mrs Grainger consented to see him, and he waited in a first-floor library that contained a number of rare-looking coins and documents and illustrated manuscripts under glass. The collection of Mr Grainger, he supposed. According to Walter Ward, Grainger had busied himself in this room after refusing to attend any seance and had appeared amidst the uproar to insist that it ended and to forbid any repetition.

'Mrs Grainger,' Goulston said respectfully as the lady appeared. She was pale and her eyes were reddened, but she held herself with dignity.

'If you are here to debate with me, Mr Goulston,' she said, 'I will have to decline.'

'I am here to inquire after your health. I understand the evening was a harrowing one for you.'

She hesitated and then inclined her head, as if in apology for her misapprehension. She said, 'My son died a terrible death in a terrible place. We relived it in his presence last night. Mr Kelly tells us that we helped to bring his soul to peace by doing so.'

'My warnings meant nothing to you, then.'

'I wish you had stayed. You might now understand more. My health is good. My mind is calm. I have a strength I did not have before. Nothing in your parlour tricks could bring me to this.'

Goulston descended the stairs to find not only the housemaid waiting to hand him his hat and stick but Enid Grainger as well.

She said, 'May I ask you a question, Mr Goulston?'

'Of course.'

'Have you never considered that your participation in these events may validate Mr Kelly's work far more than it can debunk it?'

'I struggle with that thought, madam,' Goulston said. 'Believe that I do.'

She seemed in no hurry to see him go. She said, 'Mr Kelly seemed drained last night. Is that common?'

'It would appear to be. He's an enthusiastic performer.'

'He did none of the things you talked about. He wouldn't even have us turn out the lights.'

'I'm aware of that,' Goulston said.

'I feel the need of air. Would you walk with me through the park?'

Goulston declared himself at her service. She disappeared and returned a few minutes later, dressed for outdoors and carrying a spray of cut flowers from the garden which she laid along her arm.

Once outside, they crossed the street and entered the park by its East Gate. The slope of the land here had been tamed a little by terracing and landscaping, but still the park fell away to a wide and open view across the slate-and-soot vista of the roofs and chimneys of the town. Here a broad promenade passed above formal gardens, while below could be seen a bandstand and a succession of ornamental ponds.

Enid Grainger said, 'My mother is utterly convinced.'

'And you?'

'I have an open mind. I believe it's important to have an open mind on everything. You don't.'

The assertion took Goulston aback slightly. 'How so?' he said.

'You're certain he's a fraud and you've set out to prove it. That doesn't sound like an open mind to me. That's like a scientist who fixes his result and then rejects the experiment that doesn't give it.'

'I'm not a scientist, ma'am,' Goulston said, doing his best to hide his irritation. 'I'm a common man with a common man's sense. The only thing that sets me apart from a common man is the knowledge of how these effects are achieved.'

'That sounds rather like a person trying to make a virtue out of ignorance.'

'Let me try to explain it.' They descended a flight of stone steps that would lead them down from the garden terraces and into the landscaped field at the heart of the park. Miss Grainger seemed to know where she was going, and Goulston was happy to go where she led.

He said, 'When I was a boy, I saw the great Kellar on tour. I sat through the show three times, and I was convinced that his powers were genuine. I left my seat and tried to get backstage to see if it was true, but they were used to boys like me. It was two years before I was able to watch a magician work. That was at the Salford Hippodrome, in 1901. He was old and he drank, but he was a craftsman. And I watched the secrets unfold, one by one, and I saw . . . that they were nothing. Most of them were so simple, just a matter of timing and misdirection . . . and preparation. Preparation was every-thing. I felt then that I had a vocation. To make such wonder out of dust seemed to me like one of the most subtle achievements of man. But the wonder lies in that moment of uncertainty. It's a trick. But how can it be? And what Frederick Kelly and all the other false medi-ums do is to betray that moment. They betray my vocation. They tell you, yes, it is so, when they *know* it is not. They show you false heavens where the dead wander and spout rubbish. And my sense at that betrayal is one of outrage.'

Enid Grainger said drily, 'I take it you give no credence to any part of the spirit world.'

'No.'

'No kernel of truth, obscured by the deceits of the ill-intentioned?'

Again: 'No.'

Now they had crossed the open spaces, a matter of a hundred yards or so, and had picked up the carriage drive that would lead them on down to the lowest point of the park. The drive was scattered with yellow seeds and shaded by overhanging trees that threw pat-terns of gently moving light across the ground.

Here Enid said, 'Did you go to war, Mr Goulston?'

'I was in uniform,' Goulston said.

'But did you go to the front?'

Uncomfortable now, Goulston found some cause to look at the ground and said, 'The army looked at a showman and saw a recruitment officer. I toured the halls with a call to arms. I did not go to the front. But many of the boys who died there were sent to it by the likes of me.'

But Enid was not seeking to embarrass him, or to question his courage. She'd another purpose in mind.

She said earnestly, 'James wrote in his letters of a wondrous happening at the Battle of Mons. He had it direct from a man who'd been there.'

Goulston nodded his head, slowly. 'The Angels of Mons.'

'You know of this?'

'The bowmen of Agincourt appeared in the sky and rescued British troops whose retreat had been blocked. It's a tale.'

'I am telling you it is true. The bodies of Prussian soldiers were found with the wounds of arrows.'

'It was a published fiction, Miss Grainger. It's there in the files of the *Evening News* for anyone to check.'

'So how, then, were these arrow wounds caused?'

Goulston was helpless. 'What would you force me to say?'

'That my brother was a liar?' she said, almost daring him to agree.

'Your brother was misled,' Goulston said. 'The tale was a persuasive one. There is something in us all that aches to believe. A well-chosen tale can sway millions.'

They were almost at the park's ornate lower gateway now. But here, revealed to view as they followed the curve of the driveway, stood a few square yards that had been set aside to create a garden of remembrance.

In the garden was a war memorial. Behind an oval pool fed by twin fountains stood a larger-than-life bronze on a plinth, showing a young woman draped in folds of cloth who appeared to be raising one of the dead or wounded to his feet. Already the bronze was beginning to darken and turn green, as if the entire construction was being absorbed by the nature that surrounded it on all sides. From somewhere behind it came the tumbling sound of a stream running down the hillside and through the trees, waxen-leaved evergreens.

They stood in silence, looking up at it for a while.

Then Enid said, 'And how do you stand on the Resurrection, Mr Goulston? Was that another trick, or another myth distorted in the retelling?'

Such was dangerous ground, and Goulston declined to walk upon it.

'I'm no theologian, Miss Grainger,' he said.

'Suddenly, no,' she observed. 'But don't worry. I shan't embarrass you further.'

She laid the cut flowers with others that had been placed on the stones before the pool. The flowers for the boys that had no tombs, who slept in anonymous communion with their brothers. James had been brought home, as far as Goulston understood, and buried in the family grave in the town cemetery.

As they were walking back, Enid said to him, 'You don't seem like a happy man to me, Mr Goulston. I wonder whether it might have been different for you if the boy had stayed in his seat.'

That evening – his last in the town – Goulston sat quietly behind his whisky and soda in the bar of the White Bull Hotel until someone recognized him, after which he was drawn into performing some table magic for the other patrons. He was hardly in the mood, but he rose to the occasion. But then they started pressing him to repeat some of the effects, which he would not do, and then someone tried to catch him out by snatching away the handkerchief during a coin exchange, after which he contained his anger and made a cool and courteous withdrawal.

Walking back through the night-lit streets, past the

silent market place and across the tramlines before the old Cotton Exchange Hall, he felt as if some force were compressing his temples and weighing heavy on his heart. He felt as if the direction of his life had become a punishment for something that he was not even aware of having done. It was unfair. Kelly fed them guff, and they were happy. Goulston shone the light of truth into their darkness, and they turned from him.

He didn't choose the truth. The truth was there. And it stayed there, whether they chose to acknowledge it or not.

For once, he found, he was starting to envy them. Almost wishing not to know what he knew, almost aching to share the uncomplicated bliss of their ignorance.

To be the little boy, back in his seat, and never to have sneaked backstage at all.

Walter Ward was writing letters in the drawing-room. 'Where's Kelly tonight?' Goulston asked him.

'He went with a Mr Tyrell to give a reading at a local temple. He left you the address, for if you cared to have him followed.'

Goulston went upstairs and sat on his bed for a while and then, unable to settle or rest, he put on his coat and went out again.

The spiritualist meeting was in an unassuming back-street hall with a sign over the door. The sign had been lettered with more love than skill and was misspelled. The door was open to all.

Goulston went through a tiny cloakroom with a stove in it and emerged into a place that was like a raftered, high-ceilinged schoolroom. Union flags and bunting hung across from wall to wall, leftovers of some past celebration. There were dark wooden benches on a plain board floor. The seating was about two-thirds filled. Goulston moved into the shadows beyond the pillars at the side of the room.

Kelly was up at the front, speaking. A working woman of about fifty years old stood beside him and he held her by the hand, his other on her shoulder. Goulston glanced at the rest of the crowd. They were ordinary people. Just ordinary people.

'I see green,' Kelly was saying. 'The colour green.'

'His favourite coat was green,' the woman said.

'Don't help me! This is a field. It's on the side of a hill but it's so smooth. It doesn't look real. The sky's a deep blue. Deep, like . . . like iron, when you cut it.'

The place was freezing. Why was it so cold? All this stone, and only the heat of the gaslights. But no one seemed to mind. Kelly would be working this crowd for no reward. He did this everywhere. The idly curious could pay into the cause, but to the genuinely dedicated he gave and asked nothing.

The door opened again, and Goulston glanced toward it. Everyone else kept their attention on Frederick Kelly. Two young women entered and quickly made for the nearest available seats; there was a moment's lapse in time and then Goulston recognized them. Enid Grainger and the maidservant from the big house.

He felt shocked. He couldn't have explained why, but he did. Enid hadn't seen him. Her eyes were on Kelly, and she was pulling off her gloves, settling in.

Goulston knew that look. It was the look of the lost. The look of those who, instead of seeing the world as it really was, preferred to gaze out into the vaguest of mists where they could imagine a sunlit landscape of ghosts and unicorns.

Staying out in that part of the hall beyond the pillars,

he moved to the door in order to leave. He was halfway through it when he heard Frederick Kelly calling his name.

No. This was the last thing that he wanted.

But he turned.

'You don't have to leave us, Will,' Kelly said. 'There may be something here for you.'

'I don't believe so, Frederick,' Goulston said, uncomfortably aware that every face in the hall was now turning toward him. He wouldn't look down and meet Enid Grainger's eyes, but he knew that she'd turned and was gazing on him too.

'You walked the streets to get here,' Kelly called to him, 'but you don't walk alone. You think you do, but you don't.'

'Please,' Goulston said with a pained expression and threw open the door to the cloakroom.

Kelly's raised voice pursued him.

'I can't give you what you need,' Kelly called after him. 'No one can. You create wonders for others, but you've lost the faculty of wonder in yourself. It doesn't matter what shape your faith takes, Will. What matters is that you have some capacity for it in any form.'

These last words followed him almost out on to the pavement. And then Kelly was in the doorway, in his waistcoat and shirtsleeves, and he was holding on to the sides and calling out after him.

'He cries tears for you, Will,' Kelly shouted down the street. 'They're not of pain or of joy. I don't understand them. But his tears run black. Does that mean anything to you, Will? His tears run black!'

Goulston made a sound that he meant to be defiant, but which came out like a growl of pain.

Goulston ran. He turned a corner, saw the lights of a

public house, and slowed. He smoothed down his clothes, got a grip on himself, tried to control his breathing. He drank in moderation, but never had he felt the need for a drink as he felt it now.

He pushed open the doors and went inside. The warmth of the place stung his eyes. He pushed through to the bar and ordered himself a glass of whisky.

Of course the tears ran black. It was the black of soot and mucus.

For the coroner had told him that when his father had died it was the smoke from the burning paints and canvases, not the heat or the flames, that had first choked and then killed him.

He swallowed the whisky, let it burn its way through him. And then he looked around.

He remembered this place. Ten years before. The Theatre Royal stood next door, and this was where the artistes came to drink. He searched for any face he might know.

Then he spied one.

And as recognition dawned, something else – akin to elation, not far from disbelief – began to rise in him and swell.

The nervous-looking man in the shabby clothes stood before a hastily convened gathering in the offices of the *Northern Telegraph* and, turning his hat in his hands, said his piece.

'I have been a confederate of Mr Kelly's,' he told his audience. 'I would go in advance to the towns where he planned to appear. I would intercept letters that people sent to him. I would read them and then place them in new envelopes and send them through the post a second time so that they would appear not to have been tampered with. I'd get other names from newspaper files and from recent headstones, and sometimes I would pass out free tickets in public houses to be sure that the right people came.'

The *Telegraph* man said, 'Why are you making this confession?'

The man glanced towards the figure by the door.

'Mr Goulston recognized me last night,' he said. 'I have done similar work in the past for mind-reading acts and mentalists. I specialized in being a plant or a confederate for a number of magicians. I had the look, and I could carry it off. Ours is a small world. Goulston knew me of old. He bought me a drink and we talked. I was on my guard, but he tricked me into confessing.'

'Does Kelly have any psychic powers at all, to your knowledge?'

'Ask Goulston,' the man said.

Well, that was it. It was over. The man went on to respond to some detailed questions with dates and case histories, but as far as Goulston was concerned the job was at an end. He left the offices and spent an hour at King George's Hall securing his properties and exercising his doves before arranging the dispatch of everything to the station, and then he gave two interviews over lunch in the Adelphi Hotel alongside the *Telegraph*'s offices on Station Square. By the time he returned to the boarding house to pick up his luggage, the late editions were out and the word was all around. There was a crowd in front of the boarding house, and an ugly crowd at that. He pushed his way through and learned that Frederick Kelly had left some time before, making a hasty exit through the back yards behind the buildings to avoid attention.

When Goulston brought his bags downstairs to the

hallway, he found Enid Grainger there, hearing much the same story from the landlady.

She looked at Goulston as if dazed.

'I am dismayed,' she said.

'I'm sorry.'

Enid made an effort to gather herself. She held up an envelope, unsealed. She said, 'I had this draft to give to Mr Kelly. How will I get it to him now?'

'Mr Kelly is exposed,' Goulston said gently. 'The charade is over.'

'Then he will need his friends more than ever,' Enid said, offering the envelope and leaving him with no choice but to receive it. 'Please see this safely into his hands.'

Goulston began to attempt to protest, but already she was turning away. 'Miss Grainger,' he began, but she was walking out of the door without a backward glance.

He took a look inside the envelope. She could hardly have intended it to be a secret, or she'd have sealed the flap before handing it to him.

It was a banker's order, left open, for the sum of £800.

Goulston's mind reeled. What moved these people to the extent that, despite discredit and disgrace, they persisted in their sympathy and support? No truth, no logic could touch them. Now Enid had made him responsible for a sum that could have bought out the very house in which he was standing. His impulse was to chase her down the street and hand it back.

But he could not bring himself to do it.

He'd heard that Frederick Kelly had travelled to Preston in the hope of avoiding notice at the railway station there, but when Goulston arrived by taxi it was to find that another mob had tracked him down and, by one means or another, had managed to get on to the platforms and had gathered outside the waiting-room where Kelly and his party now hid. The police had been brought in to keep order, and their uniformed presence was considerable. They presented an intimidating wall of blue to the crowd and refused Goulston entry until one of them recognized him from his photograph in the newspaper. The wall parted, the crowd yelled, and Goulston squeezed through with his collar split and his hat gone missing. He stumbled as he fell in through the door, and a hand caught and helped him.

The hand was Frederick Kelly's.

'They're like dogs,' he told Goulston as he raised him to his feet. 'Right now they'll tear at anything that moves.'

The windows of the waiting-room were of obscured glass, like those of a saloon-bar. They admitted light and a sense of the turmoil outside, but none of the details. Goulston did his best to straighten himself as Kelly stepped back and looked on. He didn't know what to say.

He said, 'Do you have adequate protection?'

Kelly gave a slight shrug. 'I'll change trains,' he said.

Goulston made a helpless gesture, and said, 'I'm sorry, Frederick. This is not as I'd expected.'

'I had far to fall. Why did you come?'

Goulston glanced across the waiting-room. Walter Ward sat there, head down, lost in his own concerns. Of the two paid assistants there was no sign.

Goulston pulled out the envelope and said, 'I was placed under an obligation. Miss Grainger asked me to give you this.'

Kelly took it and briefly checked the contents, but

beyond that he seemed to give it little attention. 'I thought you might have more to say.'

'It's over. Nothing to be said.'

But Kelly obviously thought differently.

He said, 'Why?'

He was looking at Goulston with intensity, and Goulston had to look away.

Kelly said, 'If you were so sure of your case, why didn't you put some trust in it? Why resort to this?'

Goulston gave him no answer. Kelly moved closer to him and put his face only inches from Goulston's own.

'Who was he, Will? One of your old employees? One of your own confederates, or just someone you could trust to perform the lines that you gave him?'

'I had to end this farce,' Goulston said, his voice almost a whisper. 'Conscience demanded it. I'd have exposed you in the end. All I did was make it sooner and cut down on the mountain of lies.'

'But don't you see? You've robbed only yourself. Now you can never know for certain.'

Somebody blew a whistle outside. A dark-uniformed arm came up against the glass, as if out of a fog, and rapped against it hard. Kelly's train was about to depart, and it was time to get him on to it. Walter Ward was getting to his feet. He seemed slow, broken.

'Tell me, then,' Goulston said with urgency. 'Now that you have nothing to lose. Tell me how it was done.'

Kelly drew himself up straight. In the midst of everything, he seemed almost composed. He said, 'You're sincere in your way, Will. How can I blame you for doing wrong when you don't know how wrong you are?' He looked at the banker's draft, still in his hand.

'There'll be no temple now,' he said, and then he leaned forward and stuffed it into Goulston's handkerchief pocket.

'Tour's cancelled,' Kelly said. 'I can't meet your contract any more. But you can rebuild your act with this. I know it's important to you.'

'Are you mocking me?' Goulston said. He'd meant it to sound indignant, but somehow he failed.

'No,' Frederick Kelly said. 'I'm forgiving you.'

The waiting-room door slammed inward then, and a corridor of uniformed bodies showed the way across the platform to the waiting train. Beyond the corridor was a sea of snarling faces and waving fists. Kelly went out without hesitating, and the uniforms immediately closed around him and carried him forward; the mob went after and Kelly was almost lost to Goulston's sight, buffeted and borne along until he reached the carriage door. Kelly was hauled up and pushed inside, the door was slammed, and the policemen formed a line to hold the crowd back from the carriage as the train made ready to depart. Other doors could be heard slamming all the way down the platform, and then the guard's whistle sounded. Goulston could see Kelly through the window now.

The train began to move, and the angry crowd broke through and tried to keep pace with Kelly's compartment. Their rage seemed to be formless, reasonless, something abstract that opportunity had made personal. They beat on the windows. Kelly was looking down, and he didn't react.

Goulston watched him go. He didn't see Kelly raise his eyes or look back.

Five minutes later, the platform was clear. Walter Ward had scuttled out and boarded the train somewhere